NICK HORNBY

CORNELSEN SENIOR ENGLISH LIBRARY

Abou

Cornelsen

Nick Hornby

About a Boy

Herausgegeben von
Peter Bruck

Verlagsredaktion
Neil Porter

Technische Umsetzung
Peter Richter

Umschlaggestaltung
Cornelsen Schulverlage Design;
Bildrecherche: Josephine Wolff

Umschlagfoto
© Matt Carr/Getty Images

Herausgeber der *Cornelsen Senior English Library*
Prof. Dr. Albert-Reiner Glaap

www.cornelsen.de

1. Auflage, 18. Druck 2013

Alle Drucke dieser Auflage sind inhaltlich unverändert und können im Unterricht nebeneinander verwendet werden.

Druckerei: Offizin Andersen Nexö Leipzig

ISBN 978-3-464-37164-0

Inhalt gedruckt auf säurefreiem Papier aus nachhaltiger Forstwirtschaft.

CONTENTS

Love and thanks to David Evans, Adrienne Maguire,
Caroline Dawnay, Virginia Bovell, Abigail Morris,
Wendy Carlton, Harry Ritchie and Amanda Posey.
Music provided by Wood in Upper Street, London N1.

In memory of Liz Knights

Abbreviations

adj	adjective	n	noun
e.g.	exempli gratia; for example	pl	plural
esp.	especially	prep	preposition
etc.	et cetera; and so on	sb.	somebody
fml	formal	sl	slang
i.e.	id est; in other words	sth.	something
infml	informal	usu.	usually
jdm./jdn.	jemandem/en	v	verb

One

'Have you split up now?'

'Are you being funny?'

People quite often thought Marcus was being funny when he wasn't. He couldn't understand it. Asking his mum whether she'd split up with Roger was a perfectly sensible question, he thought: they'd had a big row, then they'd gone off into the kitchen to talk quietly, and after a little while they'd come out looking serious, and Roger had come over to him, shaken his hand and wished him luck at his new school, and then he'd gone.

'Why would I want to be funny?'

'Well, what does it look like to you?'

'It looks to me like you've split up. But I just wanted to make sure.'

'We've split up.'

'So he's gone?'

'Yes, Marcus, he's gone.'

He didn't think he'd ever get used to this business. He had quite liked Roger, and the three of them had been out a few times; now, apparently, he'd never see him again. He didn't mind, but it was weird if you thought about it. He'd once shared a toilet with Roger, when they were both busting for a pee after a car journey. You'd think that if you'd peed with someone you ought to keep in touch with them somehow.

▷ **6** *row* (n) [raʊ]: serious argument **18** *weird* [wɪəd]: unusual, strange **20** *bust* (usu. *burst*) *for a pee:* have to go to the toilet to urinate immediately

'What about his pizza?' They'd just ordered three pizzas when the argument started, and they hadn't arrived yet.

'We'll share it. If we're hungry.'

'They're big, though. And didn't he order one with pepperoni on it?' Marcus and his mother were vegetarians. Roger wasn't.

'We'll throw it away, then,' she said.

'Or we could pick the pepperoni off. I don't think they give you much of it anyway. It's mostly cheese and tomato.'

'Marcus, I'm not really thinking about the pizzas right now.'

'OK. Sorry. Why did you split up?'

'Oh ... this and that. I don't really know how to explain it.'

Marcus wasn't surprised that she couldn't explain what had happened. He'd heard more or less the whole argument, and he hadn't understood a word of it; there seemed to be a piece missing somewhere. When Marcus and his mum argued, you could hear the important bits: too much, too expensive, too late, too young, bad for your teeth, the other channel, homework, fruit. But when his mum and her boyfriends argued, you could listen for hours and still miss the point, the thing, the fruit and homework part of it. It was like they'd been told to argue and just came out with anything they could think of.

'Did he have another girlfriend?'

'I don't think so.'

'Have you got another boyfriend?'

She laughed. 'Who would that be? The guy who took the pizza orders? No, Marcus, I haven't got another boyfriend. That's not how it works. Not when you're a thirty-eight-year-old working mother. There's a time problem. Ha! There's an everything problem. Why? Does it bother you?'

'I dunno.'

And he didn't know. His mum was sad, he knew that – she cried a lot now, more than she did before they moved to London – but he had no idea whether that was anything to do with boyfriends. He kind of hoped it was, because then it would all get sorted out. She would meet someone, and he would make her happy. Why not? His mum was pretty, he thought, and nice, and funny sometimes, and he reckoned there must be loads of blokes like Roger around. If it wasn't boyfriends, though, he didn't know what it could be, apart from something bad.

'Do you mind me having boyfriends?'

'No. Only Andrew.'

'Well, yes, I know you didn't like Andrew. But generally? You don't mind the idea of it?'

'No. Course not.'

'You've been really good about everything. Considering you've had two different sorts of life.'

He understood what she meant. The first sort of life had ended four years ago, when he was eight and his mum and dad had split up; that was the normal, boring kind, with school and holidays and homework and weekend visits to grandparents. The second sort was messier, and there were more people and places in it: his mother's boyfriends and his dad's girlfriends; flats and houses; Cambridge and London. You wouldn't believe that so much could change just because a relationship ended, but he wasn't bothered. Sometimes he even thought he preferred the second sort of life to the first sort. More happened, and that had to be a good thing.

Apart from Roger, not much had happened in London yet. They'd only been here for a few weeks – they'd moved on the first day of the summer holidays – and so far it had been pretty boring. He had been to see two films with his mum, *Home Alone 2*, which wasn't as good as *Home Alone 1*, and *Honey, I Blew Up the Kid*, which wasn't as good as *Honey, I Shrunk the Kids*, and his mum had said that modern films were too commercial, and that when she was his age … something, he couldn't remember what. And they'd been to have a look at his school, which was big and horrible, and wandered around their new neighbourhood, which was called Holloway, and had nice bits and ugly bits, and they'd had lots of talks about London, and the changes that were happening to them, and how they were all for the best, probably. But really they were sitting around waiting for their London lives to begin.

The pizzas arrived and they ate them straight out of the boxes.

'They're better than the ones we had in Cambridge, aren't they?' Marcus said cheerfully. It wasn't true: it was the same pizza company,

▷ **4** *pepperoni:* type of spicy Italian salami **30** *dunno* (infml): don't know **36** *reckon* (infml): suppose, think **37** *loads* (pl): a large number · *bloke* (infml): man **51** *messy:* unpleasant and confusing **54** *bothered* ['bɒðərd]: worried **66** *Holloway:* area in north London but in Cambridge the pizzas hadn't had to travel so far, so they weren't quite as soggy. It was just that he thought he ought to say something optimistic. 'Shall we watch TV?'

'If you want.'

He found the remote control down the back of the sofa and zapped through the channels. He didn't want to watch any of the soaps, because soaps were full of trouble, and he was worried that the trouble in the soaps would remind his mum of the trouble she had in her own life. So they watched a nature programme about this sort of fish thing that lived right down the bottom of caves and couldn't see anything, a fish that nobody could see the point of; he didn't think that would remind his mum of anything much.

Two

How cool was Will Freeman? This cool: he had slept with a woman he didn't know very well in the last three months (five points). He had spent more than three hundred pounds on a jacket (five points). He had spent more than twenty pounds on a haircut (five points) (How was it possible to spend less than twenty pounds on a haircut in 1993?). He owned more than five hip-hop albums (five points). He had taken Ecstasy (five points), but in a club and not merely at home as a sociological exercise (five bonus points). He intended to vote Labour at the next general election (five points). He earned more than forty thousand pounds a year (five points), and he didn't have to work very hard for it (five points, and he awarded himself an extra five points for not having to work *at all* for it). He had eaten in a restaurant that served polenta and shaved parmesan (five points). He had never used a flavoured condom (five points), he had sold his Bruce Springsteen albums (five points), and he had both grown a goatee (five points) *and* shaved it off again (five points). The bad news was that he hadn't ever had sex with someone whose photo had appeared on the style page of a newspaper or magazine (minus two), and he did still think, if he was honest (and if Will had anything approaching an ethical belief, it was that lying about yourself in questionnaires was utterly wrong), that owning a fast car was likely to impress women (minus two). Even so, that gave him ... sixty-six!

▷ **2** *soggy:* wet and no longer crispy **5** *remote control:* Fernbedienung **23** *award sb. sth.:* give sb. sth. special **25** *polenta:* Italian dish made of cornmeal · *shave sth.:* cut very thin slices from sth. **28** *goatee:* small beard around the mouth and chin **30** *style page:* page about celebrities

He was, according to the questionnaire, sub-zero! He was dry ice! He was Frosty the Snowman! He would die of hypothermia!

Will didn't know how seriously you were supposed to take these questionnaire things, but he couldn't afford to think about it; being men's-magazine cool was as close as he had ever come to an achievement, and moments like this were to be treasured. Sub-zero! You couldn't get much cooler than sub-zero! He closed the magazine and put it on to a pile of similar magazines that he kept in the bathroom. He didn't save them all, because he bought too many for that, but he wouldn't be throwing this one out in a hurry.

Will wondered sometimes – not very often, because historical speculation wasn't something he indulged in very often – how people like him would have survived sixty years ago. ('People like him' was, he knew, something of a specialized grouping; in fact, there couldn't have been anyone like him sixty years ago, because sixty years ago no adult could have had a father who had made his money in quite the same way. So when he thought about people like him, he didn't mean people *exactly* like him, he just meant people who didn't really do anything all day, and didn't want to do anything much, either.) Sixty years ago, all the things Will relied on to get him through the day simply didn't exist: there was no daytime TV, there were no videos, there were no glossy magazines and therefore no questionnaires and, though there were probably record shops, the kind of music he listened to hadn't even been invented yet. (Right now he was listening to Nirvana and Snoop Doggy Dogg, and you couldn't have found too much that sounded like them in 1933.) Which would have left books. Books! He would have had to get a job, almost definitely, because he would have gone round the twist otherwise.

Now, though, it was easy. There was almost too much to do. You didn't have to have a life of your own any more; you could just peek over the fence at other people's lives, as lived in newspapers and *East-Enders* and films and exquisitely sad jazz or tough rap songs. The twenty-year-old Will would have been surprised and perhaps disappointed to learn that he would reach the age of thirty-six without finding a life for himself, but the thirty-six-year-old Will wasn't particularly unhappy about it; there was less clutter this way.

Clutter! Will's friend John's house was full of it. John and Christine had two children – the second had been born the previous week, and

Will had been summoned to look at it – and their place was, Will couldn't help thinking, a disgrace. Pieces of brightly coloured plastic were strewn all over the floor, videotapes lay out of their cases near the TV set, the white throw over the sofa looked as if it had been used as a piece of gigantic toilet paper, although Will preferred to think that the stains were chocolate ... How could people live like this?

Christine came in holding the new baby while John was in the kitchen making him a cup of tea. 'This is Imogen,' she said.

'Oh,' said Will. 'Right.' What was he supposed to say next? He knew there was something, but he couldn't for the life of him remember what it was. 'She's ...' No. It had gone. He concentrated his conversational efforts on Christine. 'How are you, anyway, Chris?'

'Oh, you know. A bit washed out.'

'Been burning the candle at both ends?'

'No. Just had a baby.'

'Oh. Right.' Everything came back to the sodding baby. 'That would make you pretty tired, I guess.' He'd deliberately waited a week so that he wouldn't have to talk about this sort of thing, but it hadn't done him any good. They were talking about it anyway.

John came in with a tray and three mugs of tea.

'Barney's gone to his grandma's today,' he said, for no reason at all that Will could see.

'How is Barney?' Barney was two, that was how Barney was, and therefore of no interest to anyone apart from his parents, but, again, for reasons he would never fathom, some comment seemed to be required of him.

'He's fine, thanks,' said John. 'He's a right little devil at the moment, mind you, and he's not too sure what to make of Imogen, but ... he's lovely.'

▷ **2** *Frosty the Snowman:* character from a children's story · *hypothermia* [ˌhaɪpəˈθɜːmiə]: very low body temperature **12** *indulge in sth.:* allow yourself to do sth. that you like **22** *glossy:* shiny **28** *go round the twist* (infml): go crazy **31–32** *EastEnders:* one of Britain's most popular TV soaps **36** *clutter:* disorder, untidiness **39** *summon sb.* (fml): ask sb. to come to you **40** *disgrace:* thing that one should be ashamed of **41** *strew sth. over sth. else:* cover sth. with sth. else **42** *throw* (n): cover that can be put over a sofa or chairs **51** *washed out* (infml): very tired, exhausted **52** *burn the candle at both ends:* do too many things so you have to go to bed late and get up early **54** *sodding* (adj): used as a swear word to refer to sth. you dislike **63** *fathom sth.:* understand sth., work sth. out

Will had met Barney before, and knew for a fact he wasn't lovely, so he chose to ignore the *non sequitur*.

'What about you, anyway, Will?'

'I'm fine, thanks.'

'Any desire for a family of your own yet?'

I would rather eat one of Barney's dirty nappies, he thought.

'Not yet,' he said.

'You are a worry to us,' said Christine.

'I'm OK as I am, thanks.'

'Maybe,' said Christine smugly. These two were beginning to make him feel physically ill. It was bad enough that they had children in the first place; why did they wish to compound the original error by encouraging their friends to do the same? For some years now Will had been convinced that it was possible to get through life without having to make yourself unhappy in the way that John and Christine were making themselves unhappy (and he was sure they were unhappy, even if they had achieved some peculiar, brain-washed state that prevented them from recognizing their own unhappiness). You needed money, sure – the only reason for having children, as far as Will could see, was so they could look after you when you were old and useless and skint – but he had money, which meant that he could avoid the clutter and the toilet-paper throws and the pathetic need to convince friends that they should be as miserable as you are.

John and Christine used to be OK, really. When Will had been going out with Jessica, the four of them used to go clubbing a couple of times a week. Jessica and Will split up when Jessica wanted to exchange the froth and frivolity for something more solid; Will had missed her, temporarily, but he would have missed the clubbing more. (He still saw her, sometimes, for a lunchtime pizza, and she would show him pictures of her children, and tell him he was wasting his life, and he didn't know what it was like, and he would tell her how lucky he was he didn't know what it was like, and she would tell him he couldn't handle it anyway, and he would tell her he had no intention of finding out one way or the other; then they would sit in silence and glare at each other.) Now John and Christine had taken the Jessica route to oblivion, he had no use for them whatsoever. He didn't want to meet Imogen, or know how Barney was, and he didn't want to hear about Christine's tiredness, and there wasn't anything else to them any more. He wouldn't be bothering with them again.

'We were wondering,' said John, 'whether you'd like to be Imogen's godfather?' The two of them sat there with an expectant smile on their faces, as if he were about to leap to his feet, burst into tears and wrestle them to the carpet in a euphoric embrace. Will laughed nervously.

'Godfather? Church and things? Birthday presents? Adoption if you're killed in an air crash?'

'Yeah.'

'You're kidding.'

'We've always thought you have hidden depths,' said John.

'Ah, but you see I haven't. I really am this shallow.'

They were still smiling. They weren't getting it.

'Listen. I'm touched that you asked. But I can't think of anything worse. Seriously. It's just not my sort of thing.'

He didn't stay much longer.

A couple of weeks later Will met Angie and became a temporary stepfather for the first time. Maybe if he had swallowed his pride and his hatred of children and the family and domesticity and monogamy and early nights, he could have saved himself an awful lot of trouble.

▷ **2** *non sequitur* (fml): illogical statement **6** *nappy:* Windel **10** *smug:* pleased with yourself **12** *compound sth.:* make sth. which is bad even worse **21** *skint* (infml): without money **22** *pathetic:* pitiful, stupid **25** *go clubbing:* go to nightclubs **27** *froth and frivolity:* amusing activities that have no real value **35** *glare at sb./sth.:* stare at sb./sth. intently **36** *oblivion:* state in which sb./sth. has become umimportant or has been forgotten **41** *godfather:* Taufpate **50** *shallow:* lacking depth **52** *touched* (infml): emotionally moved **57** *domesticity:* state of living at home with a family

Three

During the night after his first day Marcus woke up every half-hour or so. He could tell from the luminous hands of his dinosaur clock: 10.41, 11.19, 11.55, 12.35, 12.55, 1.31 ... He couldn't believe he was going to have to go back there the next morning, and the morning after that, and the morning after that, and ... well, then it would be the weekend, but more or less every morning for the rest of his life, just about. Every time he woke up his first thought was that there must be some kind of way past, or round, or even through, this horrible feeling; whenever he had been upset about anything before, there had usually turned out to be some kind of answer – one that mostly involved telling his mum what was bothering him. But there wasn't anything she could do this time. She wasn't going to move him to another school, and even if she did it wouldn't make a whole lot of difference. He'd still be who he was, and that, it seemed to him, was the basic problem.

He just wasn't right for schools. Not secondary schools, anyway. That was it. And how could you explain that to anyone? It was OK not to be right for some things (he already knew he wasn't right for parties, because he was too shy, or for baggy trousers, because his legs were too short), but not being right for school was a big problem. Everyone went to school. There was no way round it. Some kids, he knew, got taught by their parents at home, but his mum couldn't do that because she went out to work. Unless he paid her to teach him – but she'd told him not long ago that she got three hundred and fifty pounds a week from her job. Three hundred and fifty pounds a week! Where was he going to get that kind of money from? Not from a paper round, he knew that much. The only other kind of person he could think of who didn't go to school was the Macaulay Culkin kind. They'd had something about him on Saturday-morning TV once, and they said he got taught in a caravan sort of thing by a private tutor. That would be OK, he supposed. Better than OK, because Macaulay Culkin probably got three hundred and fifty pounds a week, maybe even more, which meant that if he were Macaulay Culkin he could pay his mum to teach him. But if being Macaulay Culkin meant being good at drama, then forget it: he was crap at drama, because he hated standing up in front of people. Which was why he hated school. Which was why he wanted to be Macaulay Culkin. Which was why he was never going to be Macaulay Culkin in a thousand years, let alone in the next few days. He was going to have to go to school tomorrow.

All that night he thought like boomerangs fly: an idea would shoot way off into the distance, all the way to a caravan in Hollywood and, for a moment, when he had got as far away from school and reality as it was possible to go, he was reasonably happy; then it would begin the return journey, thump him on the head, and leave him in exactly the place he had started from. And all the time it got nearer and nearer to the morning.

He was quiet at breakfast. 'You'll get used to it,' his mum said as he was eating his cereal, probably because he was looking miserable. He just nodded, and smiled at her; it was an OK thing to say. There had been times when he knew, somewhere in him, that he would get used to it, whatever it was, because he had learnt that some hard things became softer after a very little while. The day after his dad left, his mum had taken him to Glastonbury with her friend Corinne and they'd had a brilliant time in a tent. But this was only going to get worse. That first terrible, horrible, frightening day was going to be as good as it got.

He got to school early, went to the form room, sat down at his desk. He was safe enough there. The kids who had given him a hard time yesterday were probably not the sort to arrive at school first thing;

▷ **11** *bother sb.:* worry, upset sb. **19** *baggy:* fitting loosely **26–27** *paper round:* job of delivering newspapers to houses **28** *Macaulay Culkin:* child star of the *Home Alone* films **35** *crap* (sl): very bad **45** *thump sb.:* hit sb. hard **53** *Glastonbury:* town in south-west England that hosts a music festival each year they'd be off somewhere smoking and taking drugs and raping people. He thought darkly. There were a couple of girls in the room, but they ignored him, unless the snort of laughter he heard while he was getting his reading book out had anything to do with him.

What was there to laugh at? Not much, really, unless you were the kind of person who was on permanent lookout for something to laugh at. Unfortunately, that was exactly the kind of person most kids were, in his experience. They patrolled up and down school corridors like sharks, except that what they were on the lookout for wasn't flesh but the wrong trousers, or the wrong haircut, or the wrong shoes, any or all of which sent them wild with excitement. As he was usually wearing the wrong shoes or the wrong trousers, and his haircut was wrong all the time, every day of the week, he didn't have to do very much to send them all demented.

Marcus knew he was weird, and he knew that part of the reason he was weird was because his mum was weird. She just didn't get this, any of it. She was always telling him that only shallow people made judgements on the basis of clothes or hair; she didn't want him to watch rubbish television, or listen to rubbish music, or play rubbish computer games (she thought they were all rubbish), which meant that if he wanted to do anything that any of the other kids spent their time doing he had to argue with her for hours. He usually lost, and she was so good at arguing that he felt good about losing. She could explain why listening to Joni Mitchell and Bob Marley (who happened to be her two favourite singers) was much better for him than listening to Snoop Doggy Dogg, and why it was more important to read books than to play on the Gameboy his dad had given him. But he couldn't pass any of this on to the kids at school. If he tried to tell Lee Hartley – the biggest and loudest and nastiest of the kids he'd met yesterday – that he didn't approve of Snoop Doggy Dogg because Snoop Doggy Dogg had a bad attitude to women, Lee Hartley would thump him, or call him something that he didn't want to be called. It wasn't so bad in Cambridge, because there were loads of kids who weren't right for school, and loads of mums who had made them that way, but in London it was different. The kids were harder and meaner and less understanding, and it seemed to him that if his mum had made him change schools just because she had found a better job, then she should at least have the decency to stop all that let's-talk-about-this stuff.

He was quite happy at home, listening to Joni Mitchell and reading books, but it didn't do him any good at school. It was funny, because most people would probably think the opposite – that reading books at home was bound to help, but it didn't: it made him different, and because he was different he felt uncomfortable, and because he felt uncomfortable he could feel himself floating away from everyone and everything, kids and teachers and lessons.

It wasn't all his mum's fault. Sometimes he was weird just because of who he was, rather than what she did. Like the singing ... When was he going to learn about the singing? He always had a tune in his head, but every now and again, when he was nervous, the tune just sort of slipped out. For some reason he couldn't spot the difference between inside and outside, because there didn't seem to be a difference. It was like when you went swimming in a heated pool on a warm day, and you could get out of the water without noticing that you were getting out, because the temperatures were the same; that seemed to be what happened with the singing. Anyway, a song had slipped out yesterday during English, while the teacher was reading; if you wanted to make people laugh at you, really, really laugh, then the best way, he had discovered, better even than to have a bad haircut, was to sing out loud when everybody else in the room was quiet and bored.

This morning he was OK until the first period after break. He was quiet during registration, he avoided people in the corridors, and then it was double maths, which he enjoyed, and which he was good at, although they were doing stuff that he'd already done before. At breaktime he went to tell Mr Brooks, one of the other maths teachers, that he wanted to join his computer club. He was pleased he did that, because his instinct was to stay in the form room and read, but he toughed it out; he even had to cross the playground.

But then in English things went bad again. They were using one of those books that had a bit of everything in them; the bit they were looking at was taken from *One Flew Over the Cuckoo's Nest*. He

▷ **3** *snort* (n): loud sound made through the nose **9** *shark:* Hai **14** *demented:* mad **19** *rubbish* (adj) (infml): stupid; of poor quality **28** *pass on sth. to sb.* (infml): (here) talk about sth., let sb. know sth. **38** *decency:* politeness, respect **43** *bound to do sth.:* likely or certain to do sth. **45** *float away from sb.:* move lightly away from sb. **49** *tune:* melody **51** *spot sth.:* see, notice sth. **69** *tough sth. out:* stay firm in a difficult situation knew the story, because he'd seen the film with his mum, and so he could see really clearly, so clearly that he wanted to run from the room, what was going to happen.

When it happened it was even worse than he thought it was going to be. Ms Maguire got one of the girls who she knew was a good reader to read out the passage, and then she tried to get a discussion going.

'Now, one of the things this book is about is … How do we know who's mad and who isn't? Because, you know, in a way we're all a bit mad, and if someone decides that we're a bit mad, how do we … how do we show them we're sane?'

Silence. A couple of the kids sighed and rolled their eyes at each other. One thing Marcus had noticed was that when you came into a school late you could tell straight away how well the teachers got on with a class. Ms Maguire was young and nervous and she was struggling, he reckoned. This class could go either way.

'OK, let's put it another way. How can we tell if people are mad?'

Here it comes, he thought. Here it comes. This is it.

'If they sing for no reason in class, miss.'

Laughter. But then it all got worse than he'd expected. Everyone turned round and looked at him; he looked at Ms Maguire, but she had this big forced grin on and she wouldn't catch his eye.

'OK, that's one way of telling, yes. You'd think that someone who does that would be a little potty. But leaving Marcus out of it for a moment …'

More laughter. He knew what she was doing and why, and he hated her.

Four

Will first saw Angie – or, as it turned out, he didn't see her – in Championship Vinyl, a little record shop off the Holloway Road. He was browsing, filling up the time, vaguely trying to hunt down an old R & B anthology he used to own when he was younger, one of those he had loved and lost; he heard her tell the surly and depressive assistant that she was looking for a Pinky and Perky record for her niece. He was trawling through the racks while she was being served, so he never caught a glimpse of her face, but he saw a lot of honey-blond hair, and he heard the kind of vaguely husky voice that he and everyone else thought of as sexy, so he listened while she explained that her niece didn't even know who Pinky and Perky were. 'Don't you think that's terrible? Fancy being five and not knowing who Pinky and Perky are! What are they teaching these kids!'

She was trying to be jolly, but Will had learnt to his cost that jollity was frowned upon in Championship Vinyl. She was, as he knew she would be, met with a withering look of contempt and a mumble which indicated that she was wasting the assistant's valuable time.

▷ **12** *sigh* (v): let out a deep breath to show that you are bored **24** *potty* (adj): crazy or foolish **30** *browse* [braʊz]: look at things (in a shop) in a casual way **31** *R & B:* Rhythm and Blues **32** *surly:* rude and ill-mannered **33** *Pinky and Perky:* pig puppets in a TV show that lasted from 1957 until 1973 **34** *trawl through sth.:* search through sth. · *rack:* equipment used for holding or storing things **35** *catch a glimpse of sb./sth.:* see sb./sth. only partially or for a very short time **36** *husky:* sounding rough or deep **41** *jolly:* cheerful and silly **42** *frown upon sth.:* disapprove of sth. **43** *meet sb. with sth.:* make sb. experience sth. (esp. unpleasant) · *withering:* intended to make sb. feel foolish · *contempt:* feeling that sb. deserves no respect

Two days later, he found himself sitting next to the same woman in a café on Upper Street. He recognized her voice (they both ordered a cappuccino and croissant), the blond hair and her denim jacket. They both got up to get one of the café's newspapers – she took the *Guardian*, so he was left with the *Mail* – and he smiled, but she clearly didn't remember him, and he would have left it at that if she hadn't been so pretty.

'I like Pinky and Perky,' he said in what he hoped was a gentle, friendly and humorously patronizing tone, but he could see immediately that he had made a terrible mistake, that this was not the same woman, that she didn't have the faintest idea what he was talking about. He wanted to tear out his tongue and grind it into the wooden floor with his foot.

She looked at him, smiled nervously and glanced across at the waiter, probably calculating how long it would take for the waiter to hurl himself across the room and wrestle Will to the floor. Will both understood and sympathized. If a complete stranger were to sit down next to you in a coffee shop and tell you quietly that he liked Pinky and Perky as an opening conversational gambit, you could only presume that you were about to be decapitated and hidden under the floorboards.

'I'm sorry,' he said. 'I thought you were someone else.' He blushed, and the blush seemed to relax her: his embarrassment was some kind of indication of sanity, at least. They returned to their newspapers, but the woman kept breaking into a smile and looking across at him.

'I know this sounds nosy,' she said eventually, 'but I've got to ask you. Who did you think I was? I've been trying to come up with some kind of story, and I can't.'

So he explained, and she laughed again, and then finally he was given a chance to start over and converse normally. They talked about not working in the morning (he didn't own up to not working in the afternoon either), and the record shop, and Pinky and Perky, of course, and several other children's television characters. He had never before attempted to start a relationship cold in this way, but by the time they had finished their second cappuccino he had a phone number and a date for dinner.

When they met again she told him about her kids straight away; he wanted to throw his napkin on the floor, push the table over and run.

'So?' he said. It was, of course, the right thing to say.

'I just thought you ought to know. It makes a difference to some people.'

'In what way?'

'Guys, I mean.'

'Well, yes, I worked that out.'

'I'm sorry, I'm not making this very easy, am I?'

'You're doing fine.'

'It's just that ... if this is a date date, and it feels like one to me, then I thought I ought to tell you.'

'Thank you. But really, it's no problem. I would have been disappointed if you didn't have children.'

She laughed. 'Disappointed? Why?'

This was a good question. Why? Obviously he had said it because he thought it sounded smooth and winning, but he couldn't tell her that.

'Because I've never been out with someone who was a mum before, and I've always wanted to. I think I'd be good at it.'

'Good at what?'

Right. Good at what? What was he good at? This was the million-dollar question, the one he had never been able to answer about anything. Maybe he would be good at children, even though he hated them and everyone responsible for bringing them into the world. Maybe he had written John and Christine and baby Imogen off too hastily. Maybe this was it! Uncle Will!

'I don't know. Good at kids' things. Messing about things.'

He must be, surely. Everyone was, weren't they? Maybe he should have been working with kids all this time. Maybe this was a turning point in his life!

▷ **3** *denim:* strong cotton cloth used for making jeans, etc. **9** *patronizing*: herablassend **12** *grind sth.* [graɪnd]: crush sth. into very small pieces **16** *hurl yourself across sth.:* rush across sth. **19** *opening gambit:* the first thing you say **20** *decapitate sb.:* cut sb.'s head off **22** *blush:* become red in the face **26** *nosy* (infml): curious about things that do not concern you **31** *own up to sth.:* confess, admit sth. **34** *cold:* unprepared **47** *date date:* (here) meeting between two people who do not know each other well but have romantic intentions **53** *smooth:* charming, but often in an insincere way · *winning* (adj): making sb. feel friendly towards you **62** *write sb. off:* decide sb. is no longer worth paying attention to **63** *hasty:* quick, without taking time to think properly **64** *mess about:* do silly things for pleasure

It had to be said that Angie's beauty was not irrelevant to his decision to reassess his affinity with children. The long blond hair, he now knew, was accompanied by a calm, open face, big blue eyes and extraordinarily sexy crow's feet – she was beautiful in a very winning, wholesome, Julie Christie-type way. And that was the point. When had he ever been out with a woman who looked like Julie Christie? People who looked like Julie Christie didn't go out with people like him. They went out with other film stars, or peers of the realm, or Formula One drivers. What was happening here? He decided that children were what was happening here; that children served as a symbolic blemish, like a birthmark or obesity, which gave him a chance where previously there would have been none. Maybe children *democratized* beautiful single women.

'I'll tell you,' Angie was saying, although he had missed much of the cogitation that had brought her to this point, 'when you're a single mother, you're far more likely to end up thinking in feminist clichés. You know, all men are bastards, a woman without a man is like a ... a ... something without a something that doesn't have any relation to the first something; all that stuff.'

'I'm sure,' said Will, sympathetically. He was getting excited now. If single mothers really thought that all men were bastards, then he could clean up. He could go out with women who looked like Julie Christie forever. He nodded and frowned and pursed his lips while Angie ranted, and while he plotted his new, life-changing strategy.

For the next few weeks he was Will the Good Guy, Will the Redeemer, and he loved it. It was effortless, too. He never managed to strike up much of a rapport with Maisy, Angie's mysteriously sombre five-year-old, who seemed to regard him as frivolous to his core. But Joe, the three-year-old, took to him almost at once, mostly because during their first meeting Will held him upside-down by his ankles. That was it. That was all it took. He wished that relationships with proper human beings were that easy.

They went to McDonald's. They went to the Science Museum and the Natural History Museum. They went on a boat down the river. On the very few occasions when he had thought about the possibility of children (always when he was drunk, always in the first throes of a new relationship), he had convinced himself that fatherhood would be a sort of sentimental photo-opportunity, and fatherhood Angie-style was exactly like that: he could walk hand-in-hand with a beautiful woman, children gambolling happily in front of him, and everyone could see him doing it, and when he had done it for an afternoon he could go home again if he wanted to.

And then there was the sex. Sex with a single mother, Will decided after his first night with Angie, beat the sort of sex he was used to hands down. If you picked the right woman, someone who'd been messed around and eventually abandoned by the father of her children, and who hadn't met anyone since (because the kids stopped you going out and anyway a lot of men didn't like kids that didn't belong to them, and they didn't like the kind of mess that frequently coiled around these kids like a whirlwind) ... if you picked one of these, then she loved you for it. All of a sudden you became better-looking, a better lover, a better person.

As far as he could see, it was an entirely happy arrangement. All those so-so couplings going on out in the world of the childless singles, to whom a night in a foreign bed was just another fuck ... they didn't know what they were missing. Sure, there were right-on people, men and women, who would be repelled and appalled by his logic, but that was fine by him. It reduced the competition.

In the end, the thing that swung it for him in his affair with Angie was that he was not Someone Else. That meant in this case he wasn't Simon, her ex, who had problems with drink and work, and who, with a cavalier disregard for cliché, turned out to be screwing his secretary. Will found it easy not to be Simon; he had a positive flair for

▷ **2** *reassess sth.:* think again about sth. to see if you should change your opinion **4** *crow's feet:* Krähenfüße **5** *Julie Christie* (born 1941): attractive British actress **8** *peer of the realm* [relm]: aristocrat **11** *blemish:* mark on your skin that makes you less attractive · *birthmark:* Muttermal · *obesity* [əʊ'bi:səti]: quality of being too fat **15** *cogitation:* process of thinking **22** *clean up:* have a lot of success **23** *frown* [fraʊn]: draw your eyebrows together · *purse your lips:* draw your lips into a small round shape to show disapproval **24** *rant* (v): speak or complain in an excited way for a long time · *plot sth.:* plan sth. secretively **25** *redeemer:* saviour (like Jesus Christ) **26–27** *strike up sth. with sb.:* start sth. with sb. **27** *rapport* [ræ'pɔ:]: pleasant relationship · *sombre:* sad and serious **28** *core:* centre of sth. **29** *take to sb.:* like sb. **36** *in the throes of sth.:* in the middle of sth. (esp. an activity) **40** *gambol:* run about **45** *hands down* (infml): completely **46** *mess sb. around:* treat sb. badly **50** *coil around sb.:* surround sb. **54** *so-so* (infml): average **56** *right-on* (infml): politically correct **57** *repel sb.:* disgust sb. · *appal sb.:* shock sb. **59** *swing it for sb.:* make it work out for sb. **62** *cavalier:* not caring about sb./sth. · *screw sb.* (sl): have sex with sb.

not being Simon, he was brilliant at it. It seemed unfair, in fact, that something he found so effortless should bring him any kind of reward at all, but it did: he was loved for not being Simon more than he had ever been loved simply for being himself.

Even the end, when it came, had an enormous amount to recommend it. Will found endings difficult: he had never quite managed to grasp the bull by the horns, and as a consequence there had hitherto always been some kind of messy overlap. But with Angie it was easy – indeed, it was so easy that he felt there had to be some kind of catch.

They had been going out for six weeks, and there were certain things that he was beginning to find unsatisfactory. Angie wasn't very flexible, for a start, and the whole kid thing really got in the way sometimes – the week before he had bought tickets for the new Mike Leigh film on the opening night, but she didn't make it to the cinema until thirty minutes after it had started because the babysitter hadn't turned up. That really pissed him off, although he felt he managed to disguise his annoyance pretty well, and they had a reasonable evening out anyway. And she could never stay over at his place, so he always had to go round there, and she didn't have many CDs, and there was no VCR or satellite or cable, so on a Saturday night they always ended up watching *Casualty* and a crap made-for-TV movie about some kid with a disease. He was just beginning to wonder whether Angie was exactly what he was looking for when she decided to finish it.

They were in an Indian restaurant on Holloway Road when she told him.

'Will, I'm so sorry, but I'm not sure this is working out.'

He didn't say anything. In the past, any conversation that began in this way usually meant that she had found something out, or that he had done something mean, or stupid, or grotesquely insensitive, but he really thought that he had kept a clean sheet in this relationship. His silence bought him time while he scanned through the memory bank for any indiscretions he might have forgotten about, but there was nothing. He would have been extremely disappointed if he had found something, an overlooked infidelity, say, or a casual, unmemorable cruelty. As the whole point of this relationship was his niceness, any blemish would have meant that his untrustworthiness was so deeply ingrained as to be ungovernable.

'It's not you. You've been great. It's me. Well, my situation, anyway.'

'There's nothing wrong with your situation. Not as far as I'm concerned.' He was so relieved that he felt like being generous.

'There are things you don't know. Things about Simon.'

'Is he giving you a hard time? Because if he is …' You'll what? he wanted to ask himself contemptuously. You'll roll yourself a joint when you get home and forget them? You'll go out with someone a lot easier?

'No, not really. Well, I suppose it would look like that from the outside. He's not very happy about me seeing somebody else. And I know how that sounds, but I know him, and he just hasn't come to terms with us splitting up. And I'm not sure I have either, more to the point. I'm not ready to launch into a relationship with anybody new yet.'

'You've been doing pretty well.'

'The tragedy is that I've met someone just right for me at precisely the wrong time. I should have started with a meaningless fling, not a … not with someone who …'

This, he couldn't help feeling, was kind of ironic. If she but knew it, he was exactly right; if there was a man better equipped for the meaningless fling, he wouldn't like to meet him. I've been putting this on! He wanted to tell her. I'm horrible! I'm much shallower than this, honest! But it was too late.

'I did wonder whether I was rushing you. I've really cocked this up, haven't I?'

'No, Will, not at all. You've been brilliant. I'm so sorry that …'

She was starting to get a little tearful, and he loved her for it. He had never before watched a woman cry without feeling responsible, and he was rather enjoying the experience.

▷ **7** *grasp the bull by the horns:* face a difficult situation with courage **8** *overlap* (n): period of time in which two things happen together **10** *catch* (n): hidden problem **14–15** *Mike Leigh:* British film director **17** *piss sb. off* (sl): annoy sb. **21** *VCR:* video cassette recorder **22** *Casualty*: TV soap about a hospital **28** *work out:* develop successfully **32** *keep a clean sheet:* not do anything incorrect **36** *infidelity:* act of not being sexually faithful to your partner **36–37** *unmemorable:* not worth being remembered **39** *ingrained:* deeply fixed **46** *contemptuous:* scornful **51–52** *come to terms with sth.:* accept sth. **57** *fling:* short romantic relationship **61–62** *put sth. on:* pretend to be or feel sth. **64** *cock sth. up* (sl): completely ruin sth.

‘You don’t have to be sorry for anything. Really.’ Really, really, really.

‘Oh, I do.’

‘You don’t.’

When was the last time he had been in a position to bestow forgiveness? Certainly not since school, and possibly not even then. Of all the evenings he had spent with Angie, he loved the last one the best.

This, for Will, was the clincher. He knew then that there would be other women like Angie – women who would start off by thinking that they wanted a regular fuck, and end up deciding that a quiet life was worth any number of noisy orgasms. As he felt something not dissimilar, although for very different reasons, he knew he had a lot to offer. Great sex, a lot of ego massage, temporary parenthood without tears and a guilt-free parting – what more could a man want? Single mothers – bright, attractive, available women, thousands of them, all over London – were the best invention Will had ever heard of. His career as a serial nice guy had begun.

Five

One Monday morning his mother started crying before breakfast, and it frightened him. Morning crying was something new, and it was a bad, bad sign. It meant that it could now happen at any hour of the day without warning; there was no safe time. Up until today the mornings had been OK; she seemed to wake up with the hope that whatever was making her unhappy would somehow have vanished overnight, in her sleep, the way colds and upset stomachs sometimes did. And she had sounded OK this morning – not angry, not unhappy, not mad, just kind of normal and mum-like – when she shouted for him to get a move on. But here she was, already at it, slumped over the kitchen table in her dressing-gown, a half-eaten piece of toast on her plate, her face all puffed-up, snot pouring out of her nose.

Marcus never said anything when she cried. He didn't know what to say. He didn't understand why she did it, and because he didn't understand he couldn't help, and because he couldn't help, he just ended up standing there and staring at her with his mouth open, and she'd just carry on as if nothing was happening.

'Do you want some tea?'

He had to guess at what she was saying, because she was so snuffled up.

▷ **5** *bestow sth.:* give sth. in a generous way **9** *clincher:* fact, remark or event that settles a decision or affirms an opinion **15** *parting:* act of separating **18** *serial* (adj): Serien- **28** *slumped over sth.* (adj): sitting and leaning over sth. **30** *puffed-up:* swollen · *snot* (infml): liquid that comes out of a nose **38** *snuffled up:* breathing noisily because you have been crying

'Yeah. Please.' He took a clean bowl from the draining board and went to the larder to choose his cereal. That cheered him up. He'd forgotten that she'd let him put a variety pack in the supermarket trolley on Saturday morning. He went through all the usual agonies of indecision: he knew he should get through the boring stuff, the cornflakes and the one with fruit in it, first of all, because if he didn't eat them now he'd never eat them, and they'd just sit on the shelf until they got stale, and Mum would get cross with him, and for the next few months he'd have to stick to an economy-sized packet of something horrible. He understood all that, yet still he went for the Coco Pops, as he always did. His mother didn't notice – the first advantage of her terrible depression that he'd found so far. It wasn't a big advantage, though; on the whole he'd rather she was cheerful enough to send him back to the larder. He'd quite happily give up Coco Pops if she'd give up crying all the time.

He ate his cereal, drank his tea, picked up his bag and gave his mother a kiss, just a normal one, not a soppy, understanding one, and went out. Neither of them said a word. What else was he supposed to do?

On the way to school he tried to work out what was wrong with her. What could be wrong with her that he wouldn't know about? She was in work, so they weren't poor, although they weren't rich either – she was a music therapist, which meant that she was a sort of teacher of handicapped children, and she was always saying that the money was pitiful, pathetic, lousy, a crime. But they had enough for the flat, and for food, and for holidays once a year, and even for computer games, once in a while. What else made you cry, apart from money? Death? But he'd know if anybody important had died; she would only cry that much about Grandma, Grandpa, his uncle Tom and Tom's family, and they'd seen them all the previous weekend, at his cousin Ella's fourth birthday party. Something to do with men? He knew she wanted a boyfriend; but he knew because she joked about it sometimes, and he couldn't see that it was possible to go from joking about something now and again to crying about it all the time. Anyway, she was the one who had got rid of Roger, and if she was desperate she would have kept it going. So what else was there? He tried to remember what people cried about in *EastEnders*, apart from money, death and boyfriends, but it wasn't very helpful: prison sentences, unwanted pregnancies, Aids, stuff that didn't seem to apply to his mum.

He'd forgotten about it all by the time he was inside the school gates. It wasn't like he'd *decided* to forget about it. It was simply that an instinct for self-preservation took over. When you were having trouble with Lee Hartley and his mates, it hardly mattered whether your mum was going round the bend or not. But it was OK, this morning. He could see them all leaning against the wall of the gym, huddled around some item of treasure, safe in the distance, so he reached the form room without any difficulty.

His friends Nicky and Mark were already there, playing Tetris on Mark's Gameboy. He went over to them.

'All right?'

Nicky said hello, but Mark was too absorbed to notice him. He tried to position himself so he could see how Mark was getting on, but Nicky was standing in the only place that offered a glimpse of the Gameboy's tiny screen, so he sat on a desk waiting for them to finish. They didn't finish. Or rather, they did, but then they just started again; they didn't offer him a game or put it away because he had arrived. Marcus felt he was being left out deliberately, and he didn't know what he was supposed to have done wrong.

'Are you going to the computer room at lunchtime?' That was how he knew Nicky and Mark – through the computer club. It was a stupid question, because they always went. If they didn't go, then like him they would be tiptoeing timidly around the edges of lunchtime, trying not to get noticed by anybody with a big mouth and a sharp haircut.

'Dunno. Maybe.What do you reckon, Mark?'

'Dunno. Probably.'

'Right. See you there, then, maybe.'

He'd see them before then. He was seeing them now, for example – it wasn't like he was going anywhere. But it was something to say.

*

▷ **1** *draining board:* place next to a kitchen sink where you put wet dishes to dry **2** *larder:* small room next to a kitchen for keeping food **3** *variety pack:* packet which contains various small packs of cereals (= Frühstücks-Cerealien) **8** *stale:* no longer fresh **11** *Coco Pops:* type of chocolate-flavoured cereal **17** *soppy* (infml): sentimental, silly **25** *pitiful:* so little that you deserve pity · *pathetic:* (here) worthless · *lousy:* terrible **45** *go round the bend:* become crazy **47** *huddle:* gather closely together **49** *Tetris:* type of computer game **63** *tiptoe* (v): walk very carefully and quietly **64** *sharp:* (here) trendy

Breaktime was the same: Nicky and Mark on the Gameboy, Marcus hovering around on the outside. OK, they weren't real friends – not like the friends he'd had in Cambridge – but they got on OK, usually, if only because they weren't like the other kids in their class. Marcus had even been to Nicky's house once, after school one day. They knew they were nerdy and geeky and all the other things some of the girls called them (all three of them wore specs, none of them was bothered about clothes, Mark had ginger hair and freckles, and Nicky looked a good three years younger than everyone else in year seven), but it didn't worry them much. The important thing was that they had each other, that they weren't hugging the corridors trying desperately not to get noticed.

'Oi! Fuzzy! Give us a song.' A couple of year eights were standing in the doorway. Marcus didn't know them, so his fame was obviously spreading. He tried to look more purposeful: he craned his neck to make it look as though he was concentrating on the Gameboy, but he still couldn't see anything, and anyway Mark and Nicky started to back away, leaving him on his own.

'Hey, Ginger! Chris Evans! Speccy!' Mark started to redden.

'They're all speccy.'

'Yeah, I forgot. Oi, Ginger speccy! Is that a love bite on your neck?'

They thought this was hilarious. They always made jokes about girls and sex; he didn't know why. Probably because they were sex-mad.

Mark gave up the struggle and turned the Gameboy off. This had been happening a lot recently, and there wasn't much you could do about it. You just had to stand there and take it until they got bored. It was finding something to do in the meantime, some way to be and to look, that made it difficult. Marcus had recently taken to making lists in his head; his mum had a game where you had cards with categories on them, like, say, 'Puddings', and the other team had to guess what twelve examples were on the card, and then you swapped round and had to guess what twelve examples were on the other team's card, like 'Football teams'. He couldn't play it here because he didn't have the cards and there wasn't another team, but he played a variation of this: he thought of something that had lots of examples, like, say, 'Fruit', and tried to think of as many different fruits as he could before whoever it was who was giving them a hard time went away again.

Chocolate bars. Mars, of course. Snickers. Bounty. Were there any more ice-cream ones? He couldn't remember. Topic. Picnic.

'Hey, Marcus, who's your favourite rapper? Tupac? Warren G?' Marcus knew these names, but he didn't know what they meant, or any of their songs, and anyway he knew he wasn't meant to give an answer. If he gave an answer he'd be sunk.

His mind had gone blank, but then this was part of the point of the game. It would be easy to think of the names of chocolate bars at home, but here, with these kids giving him a hard time, it was almost impossible.

Milky Way.

'Oi, Midget, do you know what a blow job is?' Nicky was pretending to stare out of the window, but Marcus could tell he wasn't seeing anything at all.

Picnic. No, he'd already had that one.

'Come on, this is boring.'

And they were gone. Only six. Pathetic.

The three of them didn't say anything for a while. Then Nicky looked at Mark, and Mark looked at Nicky, and finally Mark spoke.

'Marcus, we don't want you hanging around with us any more.'

He didn't know how to react, so he said, 'Oh,' and then, 'Why not?'

'Because of them.'

'They're nothing to do with me.'

'Yes they are. We never got in any trouble with anyone before we knew you, and now we get this every day.'

Marcus could see that. He could imagine that if they had never met him, Nicky and Mark would have had as much contact with Lee Hartley and the rest of them as koala bears have with piranha fish. But now, because of him, the koala bears had fallen into the sea and

▷ **2** *hover around:* move nervously around **6** *nerdy, geeky* (sl): unfashionable, hard-working, good at computers **7** *specs* (pl) (infml): glasses **8** *ginger:* kupferrot · *freckle:* Sommersprosse **11** *hug sth.:* move along very close to sth., e.g. a wall **13** *fuzzy:* having curly hair **15** *crane sth.:* stretch sth. (esp. your neck) to see better **19** *Chris Evans:* popular TV presenter who has ginger hair · *speccy* (derog): person who wears glasses **21** *love bite:* Knutschfleck **22** *hilarious:* very funny **29** *take to sth.:* begin to do sth. as a habit **31** *say:* for example · *pudding:* Nachtisch **38** *give sb. a hard time:* be mean to sb. on purpose **45** *be sunk* (infml): (here) fail, have more problems **51** *midget:* small person · *blow job* (sl): oral sex the piranhas were taking an interest in them. Nobody had hurt them, not yet, and Marcus knew all the stuff about sticks and stones and names. But insults were hurled in just the same way as missiles, if you thought about it, and if other people happened to be standing in the line of fire they got hit too. That's what had happened with Nicky and Mark: he had made them visible, he had turned them into targets, and if he was any kind of a friend at all he'd take himself well away from them. It's just that he had nowhere else to go.

Six

I'm a single father. I have a two-year old boy. I'm a single father. I have a two-year-old boy. I'm a single father. I have a two-year-old boy. However many times Will told himself this, he could always find some reason that prevented him from believing it; in his own head – not the place that counted the most, but important nevertheless – he didn't feel like a parent. He was too young, too old, too stupid, too smart, too groovy, too impatient, too selfish, too careless, too careful (whatever the contraceptive circumstances of the woman he was seeing, he always, always used a Durex, even in the days before you had to), he didn't know enough about kids, he went out too often, he drank too much, he took too many drugs. When he looked in the mirror, he didn't, couldn't, see a dad, especially a single dad.

He was trying to see a single dad in the mirror because he had run out of single mums to sleep with; in fact, Angie had so far proved to be both the beginning and the end of his supply. It was all very well deciding that single mums were the future, that there were millions of sad, Julie Christie-like waifs just dying for his call, but the frustrating truth was that he didn't have any of their phone numbers. Where did they hang out?

▷ **2–3** *sticks and stones and names:* reference to a children's rhyme which goes 'sticks and stones may break my bones, but names can never hurt me' **3** *name:* insult · *hurl sth.:* throw sth. · *missile* ['mɪsaɪl]: rocket **15** *groovy:* trendy **16** *contraceptive:* Verhütungsmittel **17** *Durex:* (brand name) condom **26** *waif* [weɪf]: person who is very thin and pale

It took him longer than it should have done to realize that, by definition, single mothers had children, and children, famously, prevented one from hanging out anywhere. He had made a few gentle, half-hearted enquiries of friends and acquaintances, but had so far failed to make any real headway; the people he knew either didn't know any single mothers, or were unwilling to effect the necessary introductions due to Will's legendarily poor romantic track record. But now he had found the ideal solution to this unexpected dearth of prey. He had invented a two-year-old son called Ned and had joined a single parents' group.

Most people would not have bothered to go to these lengths to indulge a whim, but Will quite often bothered to do things that most people wouldn't bother to do, simply because he had the time to bother. Doing nothing all day gave him endless opportunities to dream and scheme and pretend to be something he wasn't. He had, after a fit of remorse following a weekend of extreme self-indulgence, volunteered to work in a soup kitchen, and even though he never actually reported for duty, the phone call had allowed him to pretend, for a couple of days, that he was the kind of guy who might. And he had thought about VSO and filled in the forms, and he had cut out an advert in the local paper about teaching slow learners to read, and he had contacted estate agents about opening a restaurant and then a bookshop …

The point was that if you had a history of pretending, then joining a single parent group when you were not a single parent was neither problematic nor particularly scary. If it didn't work out, then he'd just have to try something else. It was no big deal.

SPAT (Single Parents – Alone Together) met on the first Thursday of the month in a local adult education centre, and tonight was Will's first time. He was almost sure that tonight would be his last time, too: he'd get something wrong, like the name of Postman Pat's cat, or the colour of Noddy's car (or, more crucially, the name of his own child – for some reason he couldn't stop thinking of him as Ted, and he had only christened him Ned this morning), and he'd be exposed as a fraud and frogmarched off the premises. If there was a chance of meeting someone like Angie, however, it had to be worth a try.

The car park at the centre contained just one other vehicle, a beaten-up B-reg 2CV which had, according to the stickers in its window, been to Chessington World of Adventure and Alton Towers; Will's car, a new GTi, hadn't been anywhere like that at all. Why not? He couldn't think of any reason why not, apart from the glaringly obvious one, that he was a childless single man aged thirty-six and therefore had never had the desire to drive miles and miles to plunge down a plastic fairy mountain on a tea-tray.

The centre depressed him. He hadn't set foot inside a place with classrooms and corridors and home-made posters for nearly twenty years, and he had forgotten that British education smelt of disinfectant. It hadn't occurred to him that he wouldn't be able to find the SPAT party. He thought he'd be led straight to it by the happy buzz of people forgetting their troubles and getting roaring drunk, but there was no happy buzz, just the distant, mournful clank of a bucket. Finally he spotted a piece of file paper pinned to a classroom door with the word SPAT! scrawled on it in felt-tip pen. The exclamation mark put him off. It was trying too hard.

There was only one woman in the room. She was taking bottles – of white wine, beer, mineral water and supermarket-brand cola – out of a cardboard box and putting them on to a table in the centre of the room. The rest of the tables had been pushed to the back; the chairs were stacked in rows behind them. It was the most desolate party venue Will had ever seen.

▷ **5** *make headway:* make progress **7–8** *track record:* past achievements or history **9** *dearth* [dɜːθ]: lack of sth. · *prey:* (here) person who can easily be influenced or deceived **11** *go to these lengths:* use these methods to achieve sth. **12** *indulge a whim:* let yourself have sth. unimportant that you really want **16** *fit:* strong feeling · *remorse:* feeling of being sorry because you did sth. bad **18** *report for duty:* go somewhere and say you are ready to work **20** *VSO = Voluntary Service Overseas:* organization that sends volunteers overseas to teach skills **22** *estate agent:* person who buys or sells houses for people **31–32** *Postman Pat, Noddy:* characters from children's TV **34** *expose sb.:* reveal sb. **35** *fraud:* person who deceives others · *frogmarch sb.:* force sb. to walk somewhere by having two people at his/her side holding his/her arms · *premises* (pl): building, property **38** *B-reg:* having the letter B on the number plate (i.e. being first registered in 1984–85) · *2CV:* Citroen Ente **39** *Chessington World of Adventure, Alton Towers:* amusement parks **40** *GTi:* type of Volkswagen car **41–42** *glaringly obvious:* clear for all to see **43–44** *plunge down sth.:* move down sth. quickly **49** *buzz:* background noise, esp. of voices **51** *mournful:* very sad · *clank:* dull sound **60** *venue:* place where people meet for an organized event

‘Have I come to the right place?’ he asked the woman. She had pointy features and red cheeks; she looked like Worzel Gummidge’s friend Aunt Sally.

‘SPAT? Come in. Are you Will? I’m Frances.’

He smiled and shook her hand. He had spoken to Frances on the phone earlier in the day.

‘I’m sorry there’s nobody else here yet. We quite often get off to a slow start. Babysitters.’

‘Of course.’ So he was wrong to be prompt. He had more or less given himself away already. And, of course, he should never have said ‘of course’, which implied that she had clarified something he was finding puzzling. He should have rolled his eyes and said, ‘Tell me about it’, or, ‘Don’t talk to me about babysitters’, something weary and conspiratorial.

Maybe it wasn’t too late. He rolled his eyes. ‘Don’t talk to me about babysitters,’ he said. He laughed bitterly and shook his head, just for good measure. Frances ignored the eccentric conversational timing and took the cue.

‘Did you have trouble tonight, then?’

‘No. My mother’s looking after him.’ He was proud of the use of the pronoun. It implied familiarity. On the debit side, though, there had been an awful lot of head-shaking, eye-rolling and bitter laughter for a man with no apparent babysitting difficulties.

‘I’ve had trouble before, though,’ he added hastily. The conversation was less than two minutes old and already he was a nervous wreck.

‘Haven’t we all?’ said Frances.

Will laughed heartily. ‘Yes,’ he said. ‘I know I have.’

It was now perfectly clear, he felt, that he was either a liar or a lunatic, but before he could dig himself any deeper into a hole which was already shipping water other SPAT members – all of them women, all but one of them in their thirties – started to arrive. Frances introduced him to each of them: Sally and Moira, who looked tough, ignored him completely, helped themselves to a paper cupful of white wine and disappeared off to the further corner of the room (Moira, Will noted with interest, was wearing a Lorena Bobbitt T-shirt); Lizzie, who was small, sweet and scatty; Helen and Susannah, who obviously regarded SPAT as beneath their dignity, and made rude comments about the wine and the location; Saskia, who was ten years younger than anybody else in the room, and looked more like somebody's daughter than somebody's mother; and Suzie, who was tall, blond, pale, nervy-looking and beautiful. She would do, he thought, and stopped looking at anyone else who came in. Blond and beautiful were two of the qualities he was looking for; pale and nervy-looking were two of the qualities that gave him the right to do so.

'Hello,' he said. 'I'm Will, I'm new, and I don't know anybody.'

'Hello, Will. I'm Suzie. I'm old, and I know everybody.' He laughed. She laughed. He spent as much of the evening as courtesy allowed in her company.

His conversation with Frances had sharpened him up, so he did better on the Ned front. In any case Suzie wanted to talk, and in these circumstances he was extremely happy to listen. There was a lot to listen to. Suzie had been married to a man called Dan, who had started an affair when she was six months pregnant and had left her the day before she went into labour. Dan had only seen his daughter Megan once, accidentally, in the Body Shop in Islington. He hadn't seemed to want to see her again. Suzie was now poor (she was trying to retrain as a nutritionist) and bitter, and Will could understand why.

Suzie looked around the room.

'One of the reasons I like coming here is that you can be angry and no one thinks any the less of you,' she said. 'Just about everyone's got something they're angry about.'

'Really?' They didn't look that angry to Will.

'Let's see who's here ... The woman in the denim shirt over there? Her husband went because he thought their little boy wasn't his. Ummm ... Helen ... boring ... he went off with someone from work ... Moira ... he came out ... Susannah Curtis ... I think he was running two families ...'

▷ **2** *Worzel Gummidge:* children's TV series about a scarecrow (= Vogelscheuche) **9** *prompt:* on time **10** *give yourself away:* show who you really are **13** *weary* ['wɪəri]: very tired **14** *conspiratorial:* sharing a secret **18** *cue* [kjuː]: word or phrase that signals it is sb.'s turn to speak **21** *on the debit side:* (here) negatively **31** *ship water:* (here) take in water **36** *Lorena Bobbit:* woman who in 1993 cut off her husband's penis **37** *scatty* (infml): tending to be forgetful and behave in a silly way **42** *nervy* (infml): nervous **48** *courtesy:* politeness **51** *front:* (here) topic of discussion **55** *go into labour:* start to deliver a baby **58** *nutritionist:* person who is an expert on the relationship between food and health **67** *come out:* say that you are homosexual

There were endless ingenious variations on the same theme. Men who took one look at their new child and went, men who took one look at their new colleague and went, men who went for the hell of it. Immediately Will understood Moira's sanctification of Lorena Bobbitt completely; by the time Suzie had finished her litany of treachery and deceit, he wanted to cut off his own penis with a kitchen knife.

'Aren't there any other men who come to SPAT?' he asked Suzie.

'Just one. Jeremy. He's on holiday.'

'So women do leave sometimes?'

'Jeremy's wife was killed in a car crash.'

'Oh. Oh well.'

Will was becoming so depressed about his sex that he decided to redress the balance.

'So. I'm on my own,' he said, in what he hoped was a mysteriously wistful tone.

'I'm sorry,' said Suzie. 'I haven't asked you anything about yourself.'

'Oh … It doesn't matter.'

'Did you get dumped then?'

'Well, I suppose I did, yes.' He gave her a sad, stoical smile.

'And does your ex see Ned?'

'Sometimes. She's not really that bothered.' He was beginning to feel better; it was good to be the bearer of bad news about women. True, this bad news was entirely fictitious, but there was, he thought, an emotional truth here somewhere, and he could see now that his role-playing had a previously unsuspected artistic element to it. He was acting, yes, but in the noblest, most profound sense of the word. He wasn't a fraud. He was Robert De Niro.

'How does he cope with that?'

'Oh … he's a good little boy. Very brave.'

'They have amazing resources, kids, don't they?'

To his astonishment he found himself blinking back a tear, and Suzie put a reassuring hand on his arm. He was in here, no doubt about it.

Seven

Some things carried on as normal. He went to his dad's in Cambridge for the weekend and watched a load of telly. On the Sunday he and his dad and Lindsey, his dad's girlfriend, went to Lindsey's mum's house in Norfolk, and they went for a walk on the beach and Lindsey's mum gave him a fiver for no reason. He liked Lindsey's mum. He liked Lindsey, too. Even his mum liked Lindsey, although she said nasty things about her every now and again. (He never stuck up for her. In fact, he stored up stupid things that Lindsey said or did and told his mum about them when he got home; it was easier that way.) Everyone was OK, really. It was just that there were so many of them now. But he got on with them all OK, and they didn't think he was weird, or at least they didn't seem to. He went back to school wondering whether he'd been making a fuss about nothing.

On the way home, though, it all started again, in the newsagent's round the corner. They were nice in there, and they didn't mind him looking at the computer magazines. He could stand browsing for ten minutes or so before they said anything, and even then they were gentle and jokey about it, not mean and anti-kid, like in so many of the shops. 'Only three children allowed in at the same time.' He hated

▷ **3** *for the hell of it* (infml): for no real reason **4** *sanctification:* act of making sb. holy **5** *litany:* long list **6** *treachery:* disloyalty · *deceit:* dishonesty **14** *redress the balance:* make a situation fair **16** *wistful:* sad **20** *dump sb.:* get rid of sb. **21** *stoical:* showing that you can deal with a painful matter **29** *Robert De Niro:* American actor **30** *cope with sth.:* manage with sth. **33** *blink:* shut and open your eyes quickly **34** *be in here* (infml): (here) have a good chance of success **42** *nasty:* unkind, unpleasant **43** *stick up for sb.:* support or defend sb. **48** *fuss* (n): unnecessary worry all that. You were a thief just because of how old you were ... He wouldn't go in shops that had that sign in the window. He wouldn't give them his money.

'How's your lovely mum, Marcus?' the man behind the counter asked when he walked in. They liked his mother here, because she talked to them about the place where they came from; she had been there once, a long time ago, when she was a real hippy.

'She's OK.' He wasn't going to tell them anything.

He found the magazine he'd got halfway through last week, and forgot about everything else. The next thing he knew they were all in there, crowded in really close, and they were laughing at him again. He was sick of that sound. If no one laughed again in the whole world for the rest of his life, he wouldn't care.

'What you singing, Fuzzy?'

He'd done it again. He'd been thinking of one of his mum's songs, a Joni Mitchell one about a taxi, but it had obviously slipped out again. They all started humming tunelessly, throwing in nonsense words every now and again, prodding him to get him to turn round. He ignored them, and tried to concentrate on what he was reading. He didn't need to think of stuff like chocolate bars when he had a computer article to lose himself in. He started off just pretending, but within seconds he was properly lost, and he forgot all about them, and the next thing he knew they were on their way out of the shop.

'Oi, Mohammed,' one of them shouted. That wasn't Mr Patel's name. 'You ought to check his pockets. He's been thieving.' And then they were gone. He checked his own pockets. They were full of chocolate bars and packets of chewing gum. He hadn't even noticed. He felt sick. He started trying to explain, but Mr Patel interrupted him.

'I was watching them, Marcus. It's OK.'

He walked over to the counter and piled the stuff on top of the newspapers.

'Are they at your school?'

Marcus nodded.

'You'd better keep out of their way.'

Yeah, right. Bloody hell. Keep out of their way.

When he got home his mother was lying on the floor with a coat draped over her, watching children's cartoons. She didn't look up.

'Didn't you go to work today?'

'This morning. I took the afternoon off sick.'

'What kind of sick?'

No answer.

This wasn't right. He was only a kid. He'd been thinking that more and more recently, as he got older and older. He didn't know why. Maybe it was because, when he really was only a kid, he wasn't capable of recognizing it – you had to be a certain age before you realized that you were actually quite young. Or maybe when he was little there was nothing to worry about – five or six years ago his mum never spent half the day shivering under a coat watching stupid cartoons, and even if she had he might not have thought it was anything out of the ordinary.

But something was going to have to give. He was having a shit time at school and a shit time at home, and as home and school was all there was to it, just about, that meant he was having a shit time all the time, apart from when he was asleep. Someone was going to have to do something about it, because he couldn't do anything about it himself, and he couldn't see who else there was, apart from the woman under the coat.

She was funny, his mum. She was all for talking. She was always on at him to talk and tell her things, but he was sure she didn't really mean it. She was fine on the little things, but he knew that if he went for the big stuff then there'd be trouble, especially now, when she cried and cried about nothing. But at the moment he couldn't see any way of avoiding it. He was only a kid, and she was his mum, and if he felt bad it was her job to stop him feeling bad, simple as that. Even if she didn't want to, even if it meant that she'd end up feeling worse. Tough. Too bad. He was angry enough to talk to her now.

'What are you watching this for? It's rubbish. You're always telling me.'

'I thought you liked cartoons.'

'I do. I just don't like this one. It's terrible.'

They both stared at the screen without speaking. This weird dog-type thing was trying to get at a boy who could turn himself into a kind of flying saucer.

▷ **7** *hippy* (n): person who rejects traditional ways of life and wears unusual, brightly coloured clothes **18** *prod sb.:* give sb. a push with your finger **51** *give:* (here) change due to pressure **58–59** *be on at sb. to do sth.:* constantly ask sb. to do sth. **61** *big stuff:* (here) important things which trouble sb.

'What sort of sick?' He asked the question roughly, the way a teacher would ask someone like Paul Cox whether he'd done his homework.

No answer again.

'Mum, what sort of sick?'

'Oh, Marcus, it's not the sort of sick that – '

'Don't treat me like an idiot, Mum.'

She started crying again, long, low sobs that terrified him.

'You've got to stop this.'

'I can't.'

'You've got to. If you can't look after me properly then you'll have to find someone who can.'

She rolled over on to her stomach and looked at him.

'How can you say I don't look after you?'

'Because you don't. All you do is make my meals and I could do that. The rest of the time you just cry. That's … that's no good. That's no good to me.'

She cried even harder then, and he let her. He went upstairs to his room and played NBA Basketball with the earphones on, even though he wasn't supposed to on school nights. But when he came downstairs she was up and the duvet had been put away. She was spooning pasta and sauce on to plates, and she seemed OK. He knew she wasn't OK – he may have been just a kid, but he was old enough to know that people didn't stop being nuts (and that, he was beginning to realize, was what sort of sick it was) just because you told them to stop – but he didn't care, as long as she was OK in front of him.

'You're going to a picnic on Saturday,' she said out of the blue.

'A picnic?'

'Yes. In Regent's Park.'

'Who with?'

'Suzie.'

'Not that SPAT lot.'

'Yes, that SPAT lot.'

'I hate them.' Fiona had taken Marcus to a SPAT summer party in someone's garden when they first moved to London, but she hadn't been back since; Marcus had been to more meetings than she had, because Suzie had taken him on one of their outings.

'*Tant pis*.'

What did she have to say things like that for? He knew it was French for 'tough shit', but why couldn't she just say 'tough shit'? No wonder he was a weirdo. If you had a mum who spoke French for no reason, you were more or less bound to end up singing out loud in newsagents' without meaning to. He put loads and loads of cheese on his pasta and stirred it around.

'Are you going?'

'No.'

'So why do I have to?'

'Because I'm having a rest.'

'I can keep out of your way.'

'I'm doing what you said. I'm getting someone else to look after you. Suzie's much more capable than I am.'

Suzie was her best friend; they'd known each other since school-days. She was nice; Marcus liked her a lot. But he still didn't want to go on a picnic with her and all those horrible little kids from SPAT. He was ten years older than most of them, and every time he'd done anything with them before, he'd hated it. The last time, when they all went to the zoo, he'd come home and told his mum he wanted a vasectomy. That made her laugh a lot, but he'd meant it. He knew for a fact that he was never going to have children, so why not get it over and done with now?

'I could do anything. I could sit in my room all day playing games. You wouldn't even know I was in the house.'

'I want you to get out. Do something normal. It's too intense here.'

'What do you mean?'

'I mean ... Oh, I don't know what I mean. I just know that we're not doing each other any good.'

Hold on a moment. They didn't do *each other* any good? For the first time since his mother had started crying, he wanted to cry too. He knew she wasn't doing him any good, but he had no idea that it worked both ways. What had he done to her? He couldn't think of a single thing. One day he'd ask her what she was on about, but not today, not now. He wasn't sure he'd like the answer.

▷ **19** *NBA Basketball:* (here) computer game about basketball **21** *duvet* ['du:veɪ]: Bettdecke **24** *nuts* (adj) (infml): crazy **28** *out of the blue:* suddenly and unexpectedly **42** *weirdo* ['wɪədəʊ] (infml): person who behaves strangely **59** *vasectomy:* operation that leads to sterilization **72** *be on about sth.:* mean by sth., talk about sth. constantly

Eight

'What a *bitch*.'

Will looked at his feet and made noises intended to convey to Suzie that his ex-wife wasn't that bad, not really.

'Will, it's just not on. You can't ring up five minutes in advance and change plans like that. You should've told her to ...' – she looked around to see whether Marcus, the strange kid they were apparently stuck with for the day, was still listening – '... eff off.'

His ex (who, according to Suzie, was called Paula, a name he must have mentioned the other night) was always going to get the blame for Ned's non-appearance at the picnic, but he felt obscurely loyal to her in the face of Suzie's empathetic anger. Had he pushed it too far?

'Oh, well,' he kept saying, while Suzie raged on, 'you know.'

'You can't afford to be soft. You'll just get messed around all the time.'

'She's never done it before.'

'No, but she'll do it again. You watch. You're too nice. This is a nasty business. You'll have to toughen up.'

'I suppose so.' Being told that he was too nice, that he needed to be meaner, was an unusual experience for Will, but he was feeling so weedy that it was easy to see how Paula had walked all over him.

'And the car! I can't believe she took the car.'

He had forgotten about the car. Paula had also taken that, first thing this morning, for reasons too complicated to explain, thus obliging Will to phone up Suzie and ask for a lift to Regent's Park.

'I know, I know. She's ...' Words failed him. If you looked at the whole picture, the Ned thing and the car thing, Paula had behaved outrageously, he could see that, but it was still hard for him to summon up the requisite anger. He was going to have to, though, if only to show Suzie that he wasn't a hopeless, spineless wimp. 'She's a cow.'

'That's more like it.'

It was much more confusing than he had imagined, making people up, and he was beginning to realize that he hadn't thought it through properly at all. He already had a cast of three – Paula, Ned and his mother (who wasn't imaginary in quite the same way, having at least been alive once, although not, admittedly, recently) – and he could see that if he was going to carry this through, then there would soon be a cast of thousands. But how could he carry it through? How many times could Ned reasonably be whisked away by his mother, or maternal grandmother, or international terrorists? What reasons could he give for not inviting Suzie round to his flat, where there were no toys or cots or nappies or bowls, where there was no second bedroom even? Could he kill Ned off with some awful disease, or a car crash – tragic, tragic, life goes on? Maybe not. Parents got pretty cut up about kids dying, and he'd find the requisite years of grief a real drain on his thespian resources. What about Paula? Couldn't he just pack Ned off to her, even though she didn't want to see him much? Except ... except then he wouldn't be a single father any more. He'd lose the point of himself, somehow.

No, disaster was approaching, and there was nothing he could do about it. Best pull out now, walk away, leave them all with the impression that he was an inadequate eccentric, nothing more – certainly not a pervert, or a fantasist, or any of the bad things he was about to turn into. But walking away wasn't Will's style. He always

▷ **1** *bitch* (derog): nasty woman **4** *be not on* (infml): be unacceptable · *in advance:* before sth. happens **6–7** *be stuck with sb.:* not able to get rid of sb. **7** *eff off* (derog): get lost **11** *empathetic:* understanding, feeling the same way as sb. else **17** *toughen up* ['tʌfn]: become stronger **20** *weedy* (infml): weak · *walk all over sb.:* treat sb. badly **24** *oblige sb. to do sth.:* make it necessary for sb. to do sth. **27** *outrageous:* extremely unfair **28** *summon up sth.:* experience sth. (esp. a particular feeling) · *requisite:* needed for a particular purpose **29** *spineless:* weak, without courage · *wimp* (infml): weak, useless person **34** *cast:* group of actors in a film or play **37** *carry sth. through:* finish sth. successfully **39** *whisk sb. away:* take sb. quickly away **42** *cot:* bed for a baby **45** *cut up:* very unhappy · *grief:* sorrow **46** *drain:* thing that uses a lot of energy, time, etc. · *thespian:* of an actor felt something would turn up, even though nothing ever did, or even could, most of the time. Once, years ago, when he was a kid, he told a schoolfriend (having first ascertained that this friend was not a C.S. Lewis fan) that it was possible to walk through the back of his wardrobe into a different world, and invited him round to explore. He could have cancelled, he could have told him anything, but he was not prepared to suffer a moment's mild embarrassment if there was no immediate need to do so, and the two of them scrabbled around among the coathangers for several minutes until Will mumbled something about the world being closed on Saturday afternoons. The thing was, he could still remember feeling genuinely hopeful, right up until the last minute: maybe there will be something there, he had thought, maybe I won't lose face. There wasn't and he did, loads of it, a whole headful of face, but he hadn't learnt a thing from the experience: if anything, it seemed to have left him with the feeling that he was bound to be lucky next time. So here he was, in his mid-thirties, knowing in all the places there were to know that he didn't have a two-year-old son, but still working on the presumption that, when it came to the crunch, one would pop up from somewhere.

'I'll bet you could do with a coffee,' said Suzie.

'I could murder one. What a morning!' He shook his head in amazement, and Suzie blew her cheeks out sympathetically. It occurred to him that he was really enjoying himself.

'I don't even know what you do,' Suzie said, when they were settled into the car. Megan was in the baby seat beside her; Will was in the back with Marcus, the weird kid, who was humming tunelessly.

'Nothing.'

'Oh.'

He usually made something up, but he had made too much up already over the last few days … if he added a fictitious job to the list, not only would he begin to lose track, he'd be offering Suzie nothing real at all.

'Well, what did you do before?'

'Nothing.'

'You've never worked?'

'I've done the odd day here and there, but –'

'Oh. Well, that's …'

She trailed off, and Will knew why. Not having a job ever, that's … nothing. There was nothing to say about it at all, not immediately, anyway.

'My dad wrote a song. In nineteen thirty-eight. It's a famous song, and I live off the royalties.'

'You know Michael Jackson, right? He makes a million pounds a minute,' said the weird kid.

'I'm not sure it's a million pounds a minute,' said Suzie doubtfully. 'That's an awful lot.'

'A million pounds a minute!' Marcus repeated. 'Sixty million pounds an hour!'

'Well I don't make sixty million pounds an hour,' said Will. 'Nothing like.'

'How much, then?'

'Marcus,' said Suzie. 'So what's this song, Will? If you can live off it, we must have heard of it.'

'Umm … "Santa's Super Sleigh",' said Will. He said it neutrally, but it was useless, because there was no way of saying it that didn't make it sound silly. He wished his father had written any other song, in the world, with the possible exception of 'Itsy Bitsy Teeny Weeny Yellow Polka Dot Bikini', or 'How Much Is That Doggie In The Window?'

'Really? "Santa's Super Sleigh"?' Suzie and Marcus both started singing the same part of the song:

"So just leave out the mince pies, and a glass of sherry,
And Santa will visit you, and leave you feeling merry,
Oh, Santa's super sleigh,
Santa's super sleigh …"

▷ **3** *ascertain* [ˌæsəˈteɪn]: make sure **4** *C.S. Lewis* (1898–1963): English writer of fantasy novels for children, whose novel *The Lion, the Witch and the Wardrobe* tells of a magic wardrobe which allows the characters to pass into another world **6** *cancel sth.:* arrange that sth. (esp. a planned activity) will not happen **8** *scrabble around:* move around searching for sth. **19** *come to the crunch:* when it comes to the final moment **21** *murder sth.* (infml): very much want sth. to eat or drink **22** *blow your cheeks out* (infml): sigh **31** *lose track:* forget what you have said or done **36** *odd:* occasional **38** *trail off:* stop talking **42** *live off sth.:* get your income from sth. · *royalties* (pl): payments made to the writer of a book, song, etc. **54** *sleigh* [sleɪ]: Schlitten **61** *mince pie:* Weihnachtsgebäck mit Dörrobst und Sirup

People always did this. They always sang, and they always sang the same part. Will had friends who began every single phone call with a quick burst of 'Santa's Super Sleigh', and when he didn't laugh they accused him of a sense of humour failure. But where was the joke? And even if there was one, how was he supposed to make himself laugh at it every time, year after year after year?

'I expect people always do that, don't they?'

'You two are the first, actually.'

Suzie glanced at him in the rear-view mirror. 'Sorry.'

'No, it's OK. I ask for it, really.'

'But I don't understand. How does that make money? Do carol singers have to pay you ten per cent?'

'They should do. But you can't always catch them. No, it's on every Christmas album ever made. Elvis did it, you know. And the Muppets.' And Des O'Connor. And the Crankies. And Bing Crosby. And David Bowie, in a duet with Zsa Zsa Gabor. And Val Doonican, and Cilla Black, and Rod Hull and Emu. And an American punk band called the Cunts, and, at the last count, at least a hundred other recording artists. He knew the names from the royalty statements, and he didn't like any of them. Will prided himself on his cool; he hated making his living from Val Doonican.

'But haven't you ever wanted to work?'

'Oh, yes. Sometimes. It's just ... I don't know. I never seem to get round to it.' And that was the long and the short of it. He never seemed to get round to it. Every day for the last eighteen years he had got up in the morning with the intention of sorting out his career problem once and for all; as the day wore on, however, his burning desire to seek a place for himself in the outside world somehow got extinguished.

Suzie parked the car in the Outer Circle and unfolded Megan's buggy, while Will stood awkwardly on the pavement with Marcus. Marcus had shown no interest in him whatsoever, although he could hardly claim to have made a vigorous effort to get to know the boy. It did occur to Will, however, that there were few adult males better equipped than him to deal with a teenager (if that is what Marcus was – it was hard to tell. He had a strange frizzy bush of hair, and he dressed like a twenty-five-year-old chartered accountant on his day off: he was wearing brand-new jeans and a Microsoft T-shirt). After all, Will was a sports fan and a pop music fan, and he of all people knew how heavy time could hang on one's hands; to all intents and purposes he *was* a teenager. And it wouldn't do him any harm with Suzie if he were to strike up a sparky, mutually curious relationship with her friend's son. He'd work on Megan later. A quick tickle would probably do the trick.

'So, Marcus. Who's your favourite footballer?'

'I hate football.'

'Right. What a shame.'

'Why?'

Will ignored him.

'Who are your favourite singers then?'

Marcus snorted. 'Are you getting these questions out of a book?'

Suzie laughed. Will blushed.

'No, I was just interested.'

'OK. My favourite singer is Joni Mitchell.'

'Joni Mitchell? Don't you like MC Hammer? Or Snoop Doggy Dogg? Or Paul Weller?'

'No, don't like any of them.' Marcus looked Will up and down, taking in the trainers, the haircut and the sunglasses, and added cruelly, 'Nobody does. Only old people.'

'What, everyone in your school listens to Joni Mitchell?'

'Most people.'

Will knew about hip-hop and acid house and grunge and Madchester and indie; he read *Time Out* and *iD* and the *Face* and

▷ **3** *burst:* sudden and loud singing **15** *Des O'Connor, Val Doonican, Cilla Black:* popular entertainers, singers and TV show presenters in the 1970s, 80s and 90s · *the Crankies:* children's Scottish comic duo **17** *Rod Hull and Emu:* comedy act which featured a puppet emu, held by Rod Hull, which would attack people **20** *pride yourself on sth.:* be particularly proud of sth. **24** *the long and short of sth.:* the essential facts of sth. **29** *extinguish sth.:* put sth. out **31** *awkwardly:* uncomfortably **33** *claim* (v): say that sth. is true · *vigorous:* strong **36** *frizzy:* curly **37** *chartered accountant* (BE): geprüfter Bilanzbuchhalter **40** *how heavy time could hang on one's hands:* wie lang einem die Zeit werden konnte **40–41** *to all intents and purposes:* if not in reality, at least in the effect you have **42** *strike up sth.:* start sth. · *sparky:* lively **62** *acid house:* dance music especially popular in the late 1980s · *grunge:* music style popular in the early 1990s **63** *Madchester:* term used to refer to the club and music scene in Manchester in the late 1980s and early 1990s · *indie:* independent (esp. rave and acid house) music · *Time Out:* London magazine listing all the events in the city · *iD, the Face:* magazines or papers concentrating on fashion or music

Arena and the *NME*, still. But nobody had ever mentioned anything about a Joni Mitchell revival. He felt dispirited.

Marcus went on ahead, and Will made no move to keep up with him. At least his failure gave him a chance to talk to Suzie.

'Do you have to look after him often?'

'Not as often as I'd like, eh, Marcus?'

'What?' Marcus stopped and waited for them to catch up.

'I said, I don't look after you as often as I'd like.'

'Oh.'

He walked on ahead again, but not as far as before, so Will was unsure about how much he could hear.

'What's up with his mum?' Will asked Suzie quietly.

'She's just a bit ... I don't know. Under the weather.'

'She's going nuts,' said Marcus matter-of-factly. 'Cries all the time. Doesn't go to work.'

'Oh, come on, Marcus. She's just had a couple of afternoons off. We all do that when we're, you know, off colour.'

'Off colour? Is that what you call it?' said Marcus. 'I call it nuts.' Will had only previously heard that note of amused belligerence in the voices of old people who were trying to tell you things were much worse than you wanted to pretend: his father had been like that in the last few years of his life.

'Well, she doesn't seem nuts to me.'

'That's because you don't see her very often.'

'I see her as often as I can.'

Will noted the tetchy defensiveness in her voice. What was it with this kid? Once he had seen where you were vulnerable, he was merciless.

'Maybe.'

'Maybe? What does "maybe" mean?'

Marcus shrugged. 'Anyway, she's not nuts with you. She's only nuts at home, when it's the two of us.'

'She'll be fine,' said Suzie. 'She just needs a weekend taking it easy. We'll have a nice picnic, and when you get back tonight she'll be rested up and ready to go.'

Marcus snorted and ran on. They were in the park now, and they could see the SPAT crowd over by the lake in front of them, filling juice containers and unwrapping silver-foil packages.

'I see her at least once a week,' said Suzie. 'And I phone as well. Does he really expect more than that? It's not as if I'm messing around all day. I study. I've got Megan. Jesus.'

'I don't believe all these kids are listening to Joni Mitchell,' said Will. 'I would have read about it. I'm not that out of touch.'

'I suppose I'm going to have to ring every day,' said Suzie.

'I'm giving up those magazines. They're useless,' said Will.

They trudged towards the picnic, feeling old and beaten and found out.

Will felt that his apologies and explanations for Ned's absence were taken at face value by the SPAT picnickers, although there was, he knew, absolutely no reason why they should not have been. Nobody was so desperate for an egg-and-cress sandwich and a game of rounders that they would go to all the trouble of inventing a child. But he still felt a little uncomfortable, and as a consequence threw himself into the afternoon with an enthusiasm that he was only usually able to muster with chemical or alcoholic assistance. He played ball, he blew bubbles, he burst crisp packets (a mistake – many tears, lots of irritated glances), he hid, he sought, he tickled, he dangled ... He did more or less anything that would keep him away from the knot of adults sitting on blankets under a tree, and away from Marcus, who was wandering around the boating lake throwing pieces of leftover sandwich at the ducks.

He didn't mind. He was better at hiding and seeking than he was at talking, and there were worse ways to spend an afternoon than making small children happy. After a while Suzie and Megan, asleep in her buggy, came over to join him.

'You miss him, don't you?'

'Who?'

▷ **1** *Arena, NME:* magazines or papers concentrating on fashion or music **2** *dispirited:* discouraged, hopeless **13** *under the weather* (infml): slightly ill **17** *off colour:* not in good health **19** *belligerence:* unfriendliness, aggression **26** *tetchy:* bad-tempered, easily angry **28** *merciless:* cruel **35** *ready to go:* full of energy, back to normal **43** *be out of touch:* no longer be up-to-date on news, fashion, etc. **46** *trudge:* walk slowly **46–47** *found out:* ertappt **49** *take sth. at face value:* believe that sth. is what it appears to be without questioning it **51** *cress:* Brunnenkresse **52** *rounders* (pl): children's game like baseball **55** *muster sth.:* find as much of sth. (esp. a feeling) as you can **57** *seek sb. – sought – sought:* search for sb. who is hiding · *tickle sb.:* jdn. kitzeln **58** *dangle sb.:* hang or swing sb. loosely **59** *knot:* group

He meant it; he had no idea what she was talking about. But Suzie smiled knowingly, and so Will, on the case again, smiled back.

'I'll see him later. It's no big deal. He would have enjoyed it here, though.'

'What's he like?'

'Oh … Nice. He's a really nice boy.'

'I can imagine. Who does he look like?'

'Ummm … Me, I guess. He drew the short straw.'

'Oh, he could have done worse. Anyway, Megan looks just like Dan, and I hate it.'

Will looked at the sleeping child. 'She's beautiful.'

'Yeah. That's why I hate it. When I see her like this, I think, what a gorgeous baby, and then I think, you bastard, and then I think … I don't know what I think. I get into a mess. You know, she's a bastard, he's gorgeous … You end up hating your own child and loving the man who dumped her.'

'Oh, well,' said Will. He was beginning to feel cheap and churned up. If the conversation was taking a mournful turn, it was time to make a move. 'You'll meet someone else.'

'D'you reckon?'

'Well. There'll be lots of men … I mean, you know, you're a very … You know. I mean, you've met me, and I know I don't count, but … You know, there are plenty …' He trailed off hopefully. If she didn't bite, forget it.

'Why don't you count?'

Bingo.

'Because … I don't know …'

Suddenly Marcus was in front of them, hopping from foot to foot as if he were about to wet himself.

'I think I've killed a duck,' he said.

Nine

Marcus couldn't believe it. Dead. A dead duck. OK, he'd been *trying* to hit it on the head with a piece of sandwich, but he *tried* to do all sorts of things, and none of them had ever happened before. He'd *tried* to get the highest score on the Stargazer machine in the kebab shop on Hornsey Road – nothing. He'd *tried* to read Nicky's thoughts by staring at the back of his head every maths lesson for a week – nothing. It really annoyed him that the only thing he'd ever achieved through trying was something he hadn't really wanted to do that much in the first place. And anyway, since when did hitting a bird with a sandwich ever kill it? Kids must spend half their lives throwing things at the ducks in Regent's Park. How come he managed to pick a duck that pathetic? There must have been something wrong with it. It was probably just about to die from a heart attack or something; it was just a coincidence. But if it was, nobody would believe him. If there were any witnesses, they'd only have seen the bread hit the duck right on the back of the head, and then seen it keel over. They'd put two and two together and make five, and he'd be imprisoned for a crime he never committed.

Will, Suzie, Megan and Marcus stood on the path at the edge of the lake, staring at the dead body floating in the water.

▷ **2** *on the case again:* (here) realizing what was being talked about **8** *draw the short straw:* (here) be unlucky **13** *gorgeous:* lovely **17–18** *churned up* (infml): emotionally upset **26** *bingo:* used to express pleasant surprise **47** *keel over:* fall over sideways

'There's nothing we can do about it now,' said Will, the trendy bloke who was trying to get off with Suzie. 'Just leave it. What's the problem?'

'Well ... Supposing someone saw me?'

'D'you think anyone did?'

'I don't know. Maybe. Maybe they said they were going to tell the park-keeper.'

'Maybe someone saw you, or definitely? Maybe they said they were going to get the park-keeper, or definitely?' Marcus didn't like this bloke, so he didn't answer him.

'What's that floating next to it?' Will asked. 'Is that the bread you threw at it?'

Marcus nodded unhappily.

'That's not a sandwich, that's a bloody french loaf. No wonder it keeled over. That would have killed me.'

'Oh, Marcus,' Suzie sighed. 'What were you playing at?'

'Nothing.'

'No, it looks like it,' said Will. Marcus hated him even more. Who did this Will think he was?

'I'm not sure it was me.' He was going to test out his theory. If Suzie didn't believe him, there was no chance the police and judges would.

'How do you mean?'

'I think it must have been ill. I think it was going to die anyway.' Nobody said anything; Will shook his head angrily. Marcus decided this line of defence was a waste of time, even though it was true.

They were staring so hard at the scene of the crime that they didn't notice the park-keeper until he was standing right next to them. Marcus felt his insides turn to mush. This was it.

'One of your ducks has died,' said Will. He made it sound as if it were the saddest thing he'd ever seen. Marcus looked up at him; maybe he didn't hate him after all.

'I was told that you had something to do with it,' said the park-keeper. 'You know that's a criminal offence, don't you?'

'You were told that I had something to do with it?' said Will. 'Me?'

'Maybe not you, but your lad here.'

'You're suggesting that Marcus killed this duck? Marcus *loves* ducks, don't you, Marcus?'

'Yeah. They're my favourite animal. Well, second favourite. After dolphins. They're definitely my favourite bird, though.' This was rubbish, because he hated all animals, but he thought it helped.

'I was told he was throwing bloody great french loaves at it.'

'He was, but I've stopped him now. Boys will be boys,' said Will. Marcus hated him again. He might have known he'd grass him up.

'So he killed it?'

'Oh, God no. Sorry, I see what you mean. No, he was throwing bread at the body. I think he was trying to sink it, because Megan here was getting upset.'

The park-keeper looked at the sleeping form in the buggy.

'She doesn't look very upset now.'

'No. She cried herself to sleep, poor love.'

There was a silence. Marcus could see that this was the crucial time; the attendant could either accuse them all of lying, and call the police or something, or forget all about it.

'I'll have to wade in and get it,' he said. They were in the clear. Marcus wasn't going to jail for a crime he probably – OK, possibly – didn't commit.

'I hope there's not some sort of epidemic,' said Will sympathetically, as they started to walk back towards the others.

It was then that Marcus saw – or thought he saw – his mum. She was standing in front of them, blocking the path, and she was smiling. He waved and turned around to tell Suzie that she'd turned up, but when he looked back his mum wasn't there. He felt stupid and didn't say anything about it to anyone, ever.

Marcus was never able to work out why Suzie had insisted on coming back to the flat with him. He'd been out with her before, and she'd just dropped him off outside, waited until he'd let himself in and then driven off. But that day she parked the car, lifted Megan out in her car seat, and came in with him. She was never able to explain why she had done it.

Will wasn't invited, but he followed them in, and Marcus didn't tell him not to. Everything about that two minutes was mysteriously

▷ **2** *get off with sb.:* start a sexual relationship with sb. **14** *french loaf:* Baguette **27** *mush* (infml): soft, thick mass **42** *grass sb. up:* betray sb. **53** *wade in:* go into shallow water · *in the clear:* free from suspicion **63** *work sth. out:* find the reason for sth.

memorable, even at the time, somehow: climbing the stairs, the cooking smells that got trapped in the hall, the way he noticed the pattern on the carpet for the first time ever. Afterwards he thought he could recall being nervous, too, but he must have made that up, because there wasn't anything to be nervous about. Then he put the key in the door and opened it, and a new part of his life began, bang, without any warning at all.

His mum was half on and half off the sofa: her head was lolling towards the floor. She was white, and there was a pool of sick on the carpet, but there wasn't much on her – either she'd had the sense to puke away from herself, or she'd just been lucky. In the hospital they told him it was a miracle she hadn't choked on her own vomit and killed herself. The sick was grey and lumpy, and the room stank.

He couldn't speak. He didn't know what to say. He didn't cry either. It was much too serious for that. So he just stood there. But Suzie dropped the car seat and ran over to her and started screaming at her and slapping her. Suzie must have seen the empty pill bottle as soon as she walked in, but Marcus didn't spot it until later, when the ambulancemen came, so at first he was just confused; he couldn't understand why Suzie was so mad at someone who was not very well.

Suzie yelled at Will to call for an ambulance and told Marcus to make some black coffee; his mum was moving now and making a terrible moaning noise that he had never heard before and never wanted to hear again. Suzie was crying, and then Megan started up too, so in seconds the room had gone from a terrifying silence and stillness to noisy, terrifying panic.

'Fiona! How could you do this?' Suzie screamed. 'You've got a kid. How could you do this?'

It was only then it occurred to Marcus that all this reflected badly on him.

Marcus had seen some things, mostly on video at other people's houses. He had seen a bloke put another bloke's eye out with a kebab skewer in *Hellhound 3*. He had seen a man's brains come out of his nostrils in *Boilerhead – The Return*. He had seen arms taken off with a single swing of a machete, he had seen babies with swords where their willies should be, he had seen eels coming out of a woman's belly-button. None of it had ever stopped him sleeping or given him nightmares. OK, he hadn't seen many things in real life, but up until now he hadn't thought it mattered: shocks are shocks, wherever you find them. What got him about this was that there wasn't even anything very shocking, just some puke and some shouting, and he could see his mum wasn't dead or anything. But this was the scariest thing he'd ever seen, by a million miles, and he knew the moment he walked in that it was something he'd have to think about forever.

▷ **8** *loll:* hang down **9** *sick* (n) (infml): food that you have thrown up through your mouth **11** *puke* (v): throw up **12** *choke on sth.:* be unable to breathe because sth. is stuck in your throat · *vomit* (n): things you throw up **13** *lumpy:* full of hard pieces **23** *moan:* make a long deep sound expressing pain or pleasure **29–30** *reflect badly on sb.:* make sb. appear in a bad light **33** *skewer* ['skju:ə]: Spieß **34** *nostril:* one of the two openings at the end of your nose **36** *willy* (infml): penis · *eel:* Aal **40** *get sb.* (infml): confuse, upset sb.

Ten

When the ambulance came there was a long, complicated discussion about who would go to the hospital and how. Will was hoping he'd be packed off home, but it didn't work out like that. The ambulancemen didn't want to take Suzie and Marcus and the baby, so in the end he had to drive Megan and Marcus there in Suzie's car, while she went with Marcus's mother in the ambulance. He tried to stay tucked in behind them, but he lost them the moment they got out on to the main road. He would have liked nothing better than to pretend he had a flashing blue light on the top of the car, drive on the wrong side of the road and crash through as many red lights as he wanted, but he doubted whether either of the mothers ahead of him would thank him for it.

In the back seat Megan was still crying hard; Marcus was staring grimly through the windscreen.

'See if you can do anything with her,' said Will.

'Like what?'

'I don't know. Think of something.'

'You think of something.'

Fair enough, Will thought. Asking a kid to do anything at all in these circumstances was probably unreasonable.

'How do you feel?'

'I don't know.'

'She'll be OK.'

'Yeah, I suppose so. But ... that's not the point, is it?'

Will knew it wasn't the point, but he was surprised that Marcus had worked it out quite so quickly. For the first time it occurred to him that the boy was probably pretty bright.

'What do you mean?'

'Work it out for yourself.'

'Are you worried she'll try it again?'

'Just shut up, all right?'

So he did, and they travelled to the hospital in as much silence as a screaming baby would allow.

When they arrived Fiona had already been carted off somewhere, and Suzie was sitting in the waiting room clutching a styrofoam cup. Marcus dumped the car seat and its apoplectic load down next to her.

'So what's happening?' Will only just managed to restrain himself from rubbing his hands together. He was completely absorbed in all of this – absorbed almost to the point of enjoyment.

'I don't know. They're pumping her stomach or something. She was talking a little in the ambulance. She was asking after you, Marcus.'

'That's nice of her.'

'This isn't anything to do with you, Marcus. You know that, don't you? I mean, you're not the reason she … You're not the reason she's here.'

'How do you know?'

'I just do.' She said it with warmth and humour, shaking her head and ruffling Marcus's hair, but everything about the intonation and her gestures was wrong: they belonged to other, quieter, more domestic circumstances, and though they might have been appropriate for a twelve-year-old, they were not appropriate for the oldest twelve-year-old in the world, which Marcus had suddenly become. Marcus pushed her hand away.

'Has anyone got any change? I want to get something from the machine.'

Will gave him a handful of silver, and he wandered off.

'Fucking hell,' said Will. 'What are you supposed to tell a kid whose mum has just tried to top herself?' He was merely curious, but

▷ **7** *tucked in behind sb./sth.:* (of a car) right behind sb./sth. **34** *cart sb. off* (infml): take sb. somewhere **35** *clutch sth.:* hold sth. tightly **36** *apoplectic:* (here) screaming **37–38** *restrain sb. from sth.:* stop sb. from sth. **49** *ruffle sb.'s hair:* move your hand through sb.'s hair **59** *top yourself* (infml): deliberately kill yourself luckily the question came out as if it were rhetorical, and therefore sympathetic. He didn't want to sound like someone watching a really good disease-of-the-week film

'I don't know,' said Suzie. She had Megan on her lap, and she was trying to get her to chew on a breadstick. 'But we'll have to try and think of something.'

Will didn't know if he was a part of the 'we' or not, but it didn't matter one way or the other. However absorbing he was finding the evening's entertainment, he certainly didn't intend repeating it: this lot were just too weird.

The evening dragged on. Megan cried, then whined, then fell asleep; Marcus made repeated visits to the vending machine and came back with cans of Coke and Kit-Kats and bags of crisps. None of them talked much, although occasionally Marcus grumbled about the people waiting for treatment.

'I hate this lot. They're drunk, most of them. Look at them. They've all been fighting.'

It was true. More or less everyone in the waiting room was some kind of deadbeat – a vagrant, or a drunk, or a junkie, or just mad. The few people who were there through sheer bad luck (there was a woman who had been bitten by a dog and was waiting for a shot, and a mother with a little girl who looked as though she might have broken her ankle in a fall) looked anxious, pale, drained; tonight was really something out of the ordinary for them. But the rest had simply transferred the chaos of their daily life from one place to another. It made no difference to them if they were roaring at passers-by in the street or abusing nurses in a hospital casualty department – it was all just business.

'My mum's not like these people.'

'No one said she was,' said Suzie.

'Supposing they think she is, though?'

'They won't.'

'They might. She took drugs, didn't she? She came in with sick all over her, didn't she? How would they know the difference?'

'Of course they'll know the difference. And if they don't, we'll tell them.'

Marcus nodded, and Will could see that Suzie had said the right thing: who could believe that Fiona was any kind of derelict with friends like these? For once, Will thought, Marcus was asking the wrong question. The right question was: what the hell difference did it make? Because if the only things that separated Fiona from the rest of them were Suzie's reassuring car keys and Will's expensive casual clothes, then she was in trouble anyway. You had to live in your own bubble. You couldn't force your way into someone else's, because then it wouldn't be a bubble any more. Will bought his clothes and his CDs and his cars and his Heal's furniture and his drugs for himself, and himself alone; if Fiona couldn't afford these things, and didn't have an equivalent bubble of her own, then that was her lookout.

Right on cue, a woman came over to see them – not a doctor or a nurse, but somebody official.

'Hello. Did you come in with Fiona Brewer?'

'Yes. I'm her friend Suzie, and this is Will, and this is Fiona's son Marcus.'

'Right. We're going to be keeping Fiona in overnight, and obviously we don't want you to have to stay. Is there somewhere Marcus could go? Is there anyone else at home, Marcus?'

Marcus shook his head.

'He'll be staying with me tonight,' said Suzie.

'OK, but I'll have to get his mother's permission for that,' said the woman.

'Sure.'

'That's where I want to go,' Marcus said to the woman's retreating back. She turned round and smiled. 'Not that anyone cares.'

'Of course they do,' said Suzie.

'You reckon?'

The woman came back a couple of minutes later, smiling and nodding as if Fiona had given birth to a baby, rather than given permission for an overnight stay.

'That's fine. She says thank you.'

▷ **5** *chew on sth.:* bite sth. continuously **11** *whine* (v): make a series of high and unpleasant sounds **12** *vending machine:* machine you get cigarettes, drinks, etc. from **19** *deadbeat* (n) (infml): drop-out · *vagrant* ['veɪgrənt] (n): homeless person **20** *sheer:* total **21** *shot:* injection **23** *drained:* worn out **27** *abuse sb.:* insult sb. · *casualty department:* part of a hospital where people hurt in accidents are treated **38** *derelict* (n): homeless person **44** *bubble:* (here) isolated world **46** *Heal's:* name of an expensive furniture shop **48** *equivalent:* similar · *lookout:* (here) problem **49** *right on cue:* just at the right moment

'Great. Come on, then, Marcus. You can help me open the sofa bed.'

Suzie put Megan back into the car seat and they made their way out to the car park.

'I'll see you,' said Will. 'I'll call you.'

'I hope you get things sorted out with Ned and Paula.'

Again the momentary blankness: Ned and Paula, Ned and Paula ... Ah, yes, his ex-wife and his son.

'Oh, it'll be fine. Thanks.' He kissed Suzie on the cheek, punched Marcus on the arm, waved to Megan and went off to hail a cab. It had all been very interesting, but he wouldn't want to do it every night.

Eleven

It was there, on the kitchen table. He was just putting the flowers in the vase, like Suzie had told him to do, when he spotted it. Everyone had been in such a hurry and a mess last night that they hadn't noticed. He picked it up and sat down.

Dear Marcus,

I think that whatever I say in this letter, you'll end up hating me. Or maybe end up is a bit too final: perhaps when you're older, you'll feel something else other than hate. But there's certainly going to be a long period of time when you'll think I did a wrong, stupid, selfish, unkind thing. So I wanted to give myself a chance to explain, even if it doesn't do any good.

Listen. A big part of me knows that I'm doing a wrong, stupid, selfish, unkind thing. Most of me, in fact. The trouble is that it's not the part that controls me any more. That's what's so horrible about the sort of illness I've had for the last few months – it just doesn't listen to anything or anybody else. It just wants to do its own thing. I hope you never get to find out what that's like.

None of this is anything to do with you. I've loved being your mum, always, even though it's been hard for me and I've found it difficult sometimes. And I don't know why being your mum isn't enough for me, but it isn't. And it isn't that I'm so unhappy I don't want to live any more. That's not what it feels like. It feels more like

▷ **7** *blankness:* state of having nothing in your head **10** *hail sth.:* signal sth. (esp. a taxi) to stop

I'm tired and bored and the party's gone on too long and I want to go home. I feel flat and there doesn't seem to be anything to look forward to, so I'd rather call it a day. How can I feel like that when I've got you? I don't know. I do know that if I kept it all going just for your sake, you wouldn't thank me, and I reckon that once you've got over this things will be better for you than they were before. Really. You can go to your dad's, or Suzie has always said she'll look after you if anything happened to me.

I'll watch out for you if I am able to. I think I will be. I think that when something happens to a mother, she's allowed to do that, even if it's her fault. I don't want to stop writing this, but I can't think of any reason to keep it going.

Love you,
Mum.

He was still sitting at the kitchen table when she came back from the hospital with Suzie and Megan. She could see straight away what he had found.

'Shit, Marcus. I'd forgotten about it.'

'You forgot? You forgot a suicide letter?'

'Well, I didn't think I'd ever have to remember it, did I?'

She laughed at that. She actually laughed. That was his mother. When she wasn't crying over the breakfast cereal, she was laughing about killing herself.

'Jesus,' said Suzie. 'Is that what it was? I shouldn't have left him here before I went to get you. I thought it would be nice if he tidied the place up.'

'Suzie, I don't honestly think you're to blame for anything.'

'I should have thought.'

'Maybe Marcus and I ought to have a little talk on our own.'

'Of course.'

Suzie and his mum hugged, and Suzie came over to give him a kiss.

'She's fine,' Suzie whispered, loud enough for his mum to hear. 'Don't worry about her.'

When Suzie had gone, Fiona put the kettle on and sat down at the table with him.

'Are you angry with me?'

'What do you think?'

'Because of the letter?'

‘Because of the letter, because of what you did, everything.’

‘I can understand that. I don’t feel the same as I did on Saturday, if that’s any help.’

‘What, it’s all just gone away, all that?’

‘No, but ... at the moment I feel better.’

‘At the moment’s no good to me. I can see that you’re better at the moment. You’ve just put the kettle on. But what happens when you’ve finished your tea? What happens when I go back to school? I can’t be here to watch you all the time.’

‘No, I know. But we’ve got to look after each other. It shouldn’t all be one way.’

Marcus nodded, but he was in a place where words didn’t matter. He had read her letter, and he was no longer very interested in what she said; it was what she did, and what she was going to do, that counted. She wasn’t going to do anything today. She’d drink her tea, and tonight they’d get a takeaway and watch TV, and they would feel as though it were the beginning of a different, better time. But that time would run out, and then there would be something else. He had always trusted his mother – or rather, he had never *not* trusted her. But for him, things would never be the same again.

Two wasn’t enough, that was the trouble. He’d always thought that two was a good number, and that he’d hate to live in a family of three or four or five. But he could see the point of that now: if someone dropped off the edge, you weren’t left on your own. How could you make a family grow if there was no one around to, you know, help it along? He was going to have to find a way.

‘I’ll make the tea,’ he said brightly. At least now he had something to work on.

They decided to have a quiet, normal evening. They ordered a delivery curry, and Marcus went to the newsagent’s to get a video, but it took him ages: everything he looked at seemed to have something about death in it, and he didn’t want to watch anything about death. He didn’t want his mum to watch anything about death, come to that, although he wasn’t sure why. What did he think would happen if his

▷ **3** *call it a day* (infml): give up **31** *hug sb.:* hold sb. in your arms **54** *takeaway:* meal bought at a restaurant to eat at home **62** *drop off the edge* (infml): (here) die mum saw Steven Seagal blast some guys in the head with a gun? That wasn't the kind of death they were trying not to think about tonight. The kind of death they were trying not to think about was the quiet, sad, real kind, not the noisy, who-cares kind. (People thought that kids couldn't tell the difference, but they could, of course.) In the end he got *Groundhog Day*, which he was pleased with, because it was new on video and it said it was funny on the back of the box.

They didn't start watching it until the food arrived. Fiona served it up, and Marcus wound the tape on past the trailers and adverts so that they would be ready to go the moment they took their first bite of poppadum. The back of the box was right: it was a funny film. This guy was stuck in the same day, over and over again, although they didn't really explain how that happened, which Marcus thought was weak – he liked to know how things worked. Maybe it was based on a true story, and there had been this guy who was stuck in the same day over and over again, and he didn't know himself how it had happened. This alarmed Marcus. Supposing he woke up tomorrow and it was yesterday again, with the duck and the hospital and everything? Best not to think about it.

But then the film changed, and became all about suicide. This guy was so fed up with being stuck in the same day over and over for hundreds of years that he tried to kill himself. It was no good, though. Whatever he did, he still woke up the next morning (except it wasn't the next morning. It was this morning, the morning he always woke up on).

Marcus was really angry. They hadn't said anything about suicide on the video box, and yet this film had a bloke trying to kill himself about three thousand times. OK, he didn't succeed, but that didn't make it funny. His mum hadn't succeeded either, and nobody felt like making a comedy film about it. Why wasn't there any warning? There must be loads of people who wanted to watch a good comedy just after they'd tried to kill themselves. Supposing they all chose this one?

At first Marcus was quiet, so quiet that he almost stopped breathing. He didn't want his mum to hear his breaths, in case she thought they were noisier than usual because he was upset. But then he couldn't stand it any more, and he turned the film off with the remote.

'What's up?'

'I just wanted to watch this.' He gestured at the TV screen where a man with a French accent and a chef's hat was trying to teach one of the Gladiators how to cut open a fish and take its guts out. It didn't look like the sort of programme Marcus usually watched, especially as he hated cooking. And fish. And he wasn't very keen on *Gladiators*, either.

'This? What do you want to watch this for?'

'We're doing cooking at school, and they said we had to watch this for homework.'

'*Au revoir*,' said the man in the chef's hat. 'See you,' said the Gladiator. They waved and the programme ended.

'So you'll be in trouble tomorrow,' said his mum. 'Why didn't you tell me you had to watch this tonight?'

'I forgot.'

'Anyway, we can watch the rest of the film now.'

'Do you really want to?'

'Yes. It's funny. Don't you think it's funny?'

'It's not very realistic, is it?'

She laughed. 'Oh, Marcus! You make me watch things where people jump from exploding helicopters on to the tops of trains, and you complain about realism.'

'Yeah, but you can see them doing it. You can actually see them doing those things. You don't know for sure he's waking up on the same day over and over again, because they can just pretend that, can't they?'

'You do talk some rot.'

This was great. He was trying to save his mum from watching a man committing suicide for hours on end, and she was calling him an idiot.

'Mum, you must know why I turned it off really?'

'No.'

▷ **1** *Steven Seagal:* American actor famous for action films **9** *wind sth. – wound – wound*: move sth. (e.g. a video or tape) forwards or backwards **11** *poppadum:* thin, crispy Indian bread **12** *be stuck in sth.:* be unable to get out of sth. **21** *fed up with sth.:* tired of sth. **38** *remote* (usu. *remote control*): Fernbedienung **41** *chef:* cook **42** *Gladiator:* member of the TV show *Gladiators*, in which members of the public compete with each other and fight against the 'Gladiators' in a series of sporting games · *guts* (pl): inner organs **65** *rot* (n) (sl): nonsense

He couldn't believe it. Surely she must be thinking about it all the time, like he was?

'Because of what he was trying to do.'

She looked at him.

'I'm sorry, Marcus. I'm still not with you.'

'The ... thing.'

'Marcus, you're an articulate boy. You can do better than this.'

She was driving him mad. 'He's spent the last five minutes trying to kill himself. Like you did. I didn't want to watch it, and I didn't want you to watch it.'

'Ah.' She reached for the remote control and turned the TV off. 'I'm sorry. I was being pretty thick, wasn't I?'

'Yes.'

'I just never made the connection at all. Incredible. God.' She shook her head. 'I'm going to have to get my act together.'

Marcus was starting to lose track of his mother. Right up until recently he had always thought she was ... not *perfect*, because they had arguments, and she didn't let him do things that he wanted to do, and so on, but he had never spent any time thinking she was stupid, or mad, or wrong. Even when they had arguments, he could see what she was on about: she was just saying the things that mothers were supposed to say. But at the moment, he wasn't getting her at all. He hadn't understood the crying, and now, when he had been expecting her to be twice as miserable as she had been before, she was completely normal. He was beginning to doubt himself. Wasn't trying to kill yourself a really big deal? Didn't you have long talks about it afterwards, and tears, and hugs? Apparently not. You just sat on the sofa and watched videos and acted as though nothing had happened.

'Shall I put the film back on?' he asked her. This was like a test. The old mum would know he didn't mean that.

'Do you mind?' she said. 'I'd like to see how it turns out.'

Twelve

Filling days had never really been a problem for Will. He might not have been proud of his lifelong lack of achievement, but he was proud of his ability to stay afloat in the enormous ocean of time he had at his disposal; a less resourceful man, he felt, might have gone under and drowned.

The evenings were fine; he knew people. He didn't know how he knew them, because he'd never had colleagues, and he never spoke to girlfriends when they became ex-girlfriends. But he had managed to pick people up along the way – guys who once worked in record shops that he frequented, guys he played football or squash with, guys from a pub quiz team he once belonged to, that kind of thing – and they sort of did the job. They wouldn't be much use in the unlikely event of some kind of suicidal depression, or the even more unlikely event of a broken heart, but they were pretty good for a game of pool, or a drink and a curry.

No, the evenings were OK; it was the days that tested his patience and ingenuity, because all of these people were at work – unless they were on paternity leave, like John, father of Barney and Imogen, and Will didn't want to see them anyway. His way of coping with the days was to think of activities as units of time, each unit consisting of about

▷ **7** *articulate* (adj): able to talk clearly and intelligently **12** *thick* (sl): stupid, foolish **15** *get your act together* (infml): sort your life out **22** *get sb.* (infml): understand sb. **35** *resourceful:* good at doing things and solving problems **43** *do the job:* be alright for a particular purpose **48** *ingenuity:* cleverness **49** *paternity leave:* period of time a father is allowed to stay at home because of a newborn baby thirty minutes. Whole hours, he found, were more intimidating, and most things one could do in a day took half an hour. Reading the paper, having a bath, tidying the flat, watching *Home and Away* and *Countdown*, doing a quick crossword on the toilet, eating breakfast and lunch, going to the local shops ... that was nine units of a twenty-unit day (the evenings didn't count) filled by just the basic necessities. In fact, he had reached a stage where he wondered how his friends could juggle life and a job. Life took up so much time, so how could one work *and* say, take a bath on the same day? He suspected that one or two people he knew were making some pretty unsavoury short cuts.

Occasionally, when the mood took him, he applied for jobs advertised in the media pages of the *Guardian*. He liked the media pages, because he felt he was qualified to fill most of the vacancies on offer. How hard could it be to edit the building industry's in-house journal, or run a small arts workshop, or write copy for holiday brochures? Not very hard at all, he imagined, so he doggedly wrote letters explaining to potential employers why he was the man they were looking for. He even enclosed a CV, although it only just ran on to a second page. Rather brilliantly, he thought, he had numbered these two pages 'one' and 'three', thus implying that page two, the page containing the details of his brilliant career, had got lost somewhere. The idea was that people would be so impressed by the letter, so dazzled by his extensive range of interests, that they would invite him in for an interview, where sheer force of personality would carry him through. Actually, he had never heard from anybody, although occasionally he received a standard rejection letter.

The truth was he didn't mind. He applied for these jobs in the same spirit that he had volunteered to work in the soup kitchen, and in the same spirit that he had become the father of Ned: it was all a dreamy alternative reality that didn't touch his real life, whatever that was, at all. He didn't need a job. He was OK as he was. He read quite a lot; he saw films in the afternoon; he went jogging; he cooked nice meals for himself and his friends; he went to Rome and New York and Barcelona every now and again, when boredom became particularly acute ... He couldn't say that the need for change burned within him terribly fiercely.

In any case, this morning he was somewhat distracted by the curious events of the weekend. For some reason – possibly because he encountered real drama very rarely in the course of an average twenty-time-unit quick-crossword-on-the-toilet day – he kept being drawn back to thinking about Marcus and Fiona, and wondering how they were. He had also, in the absence of a *Media Guardian* advertisement that had really grabbed him, begun to entertain strange and probably unhealthy notions of entering their lives in some way. Maybe Fiona and Marcus needed him more than Suzie did. Maybe he could really ... *do* something with those two. He could take an avuncular interest in them, give their lives a bit of shape and gaiety. He would bond with Marcus, take him somewhere every now and again – to Arsenal, possibly. And perhaps Fiona would like a nice dinner somewhere, or a night out at the theatre.

Mid-morning he phoned Suzie. Megan was having a nap, and she was just sitting down to a cup of coffee.

'I was wondering how things are up the road,' he said.

'Not too bad, I think. She hasn't gone back to work, but Marcus went to school today. How about you?'

'Fine, thanks.'

'You sound pretty cheerful. Did things get sorted out?'

If he sounded cheerful, then obviously they must have done. 'Oh, yes. It's all blown over now.'

'And Ned's OK?'

'Yes, he's fine. Aren't you, Ned?' Why had he done that? It was a completely unnecessary embellishment. Why couldn't he just leave well alone?

'Good.'

'Listen, do you think there's any way I could help with Marcus and Fiona? Take Marcus out or something?'

'Would you like to?'

▷ **1** *intimidating:* frightening **3** *Home and Away:* Australian TV soap **4** *Countdown:* TV game show **8** *juggle sth. and sth. else:* deal with sth. at the same time as sth. else **10** *unsavoury:* unpleasant **13** *Guardian:* left-of-centre newspaper **14** *vacancy:* job that is available **15** *edit sth.:* prepare sth. for publication **17** *doggedly:* in a way that shows you are not discouraged **19** *CV* (abbr) = *curriculum vitae:* Lebenslauf **21** *imply sth.:* suggest sth. **24** *dazzle sb.:* make sb. feel admiration for you **37** *fiercely:* strongly **43** *Media Guardian:* special Monday supplement of the *Guardian* dealing with media affairs **44** *grab sb.:* catch sb.'s attention **48** *avuncular:* like a friendly uncle **50** *Arsenal:* London football team **60** *blow over:* be no longer important **63** *embellishment:* added invention

'Of course. He seemed ...' What? What did Marcus seem, other than slightly batty and vaguely malevolent? 'He seemed nice. We got on OK. Maybe I could, you know, build on the other day.'

'Why don't I ask Fiona?'

'Thanks. And it'd be nice to see you and Megan again soon.'

'I'm still dying to meet Ned.'

'We'll fix something up.'

So, there it was then: an enormous, happy, extended family. True, this happy family included an invisible two-year-old, a barmy twelve-year-old and his suicidal mother; but sod's law dictated that this was just the sort of family you were bound to end up with when you didn't like families in the first place.

Will bought a *Time Out* and read it from cover to cover in an attempt to find something that a twelve-year-old boy might want to do on a Saturday afternoon – or rather, something that might make it clear to Marcus that he was not dealing with your average, desperately unhip thirty-six-year-old here. He started with the children's section, but soon realized that Marcus was not a brass-rubbing sort of a child, or a puppet theatre sort of a child, or even a child at all; at twelve, his childhood was over. Will tried to remember what he liked doing at that age, but could come up with nothing, although he could remember what he hated doing. What he hated doing were things that adults made him do, however well-intentioned those adults were. Maybe the coolest thing he could do for Marcus was let him run wild on Saturday – give him some money, take him to Soho and leave him there. He had to admit, though, that while this might score points on the coolometer, it didn't do quite so well on the responsible *in loco parentis* scale: if Marcus were to embark on a career as a rent-boy and his mother never saw him again, Will would end up feeling responsible and possibly even regretful.

Films? Video arcades? Ice-skating? Museums? Art galleries? Brent Cross? McDonald's? Jesus, how did anyone get through childhood without falling into a slumber lasting several years? If he were forced to relive his childhood, he would go to bed when *Blue Peter* had ceased to exert its allure and ask to be woken up when it was time to sign on. It was no wonder young people were turning to crime and drugs and prostitution. They were turning to crime and drugs and prostitution simply because they were on the menu now, an exciting, colourful and tasty new range of options that he had been denied. The real question was why his generation had been quite so apathetically, unenterprisingly law-abiding – especially given the lack of even the token sops to teens, the Australian soaps and the chicken dippers, that passed for youthful entertainment in contemporary society.

He was in the process of wondering whether the British Gas wildlife Photographer of the Year Exhibition could possibly be any duller than it sounded, when the telephone rang.

'Hi, Will, it's Marcus.'

'Hi. Funnily enough. I was just wondering –'

'Suzie said you want to take me out for the day somewhere.'

'Yeah, well, that's just –'

'I'll come if my mum can come.'

'I'm sorry?'

'I'll come if you can take my mum too. And she hasn't got any money, so either we'll have to go somewhere cheap or you'll have to treat us.'

'Right. Hey, say what you mean, Marcus. Don't beat around the bush.'

'I don't know how else to say it. We're broke. You're not. You pay.'

'It's OK. I was joking.'

'Oh. I didn't get it.'

▷ **2** *batty* (infml): slightly crazy · *malevolent* [mə'levələnt]: wanting to harm other people **9** *barmy* (infml): slightly crazy **10** *sod's law:* tendency for things to go wrong **16** *unhip* (sl): unfashionable, not cool **18** *brass-rubbing:* popular children's activity which involves rubbing a soft pencil over a piece of paper, which has been put on a flat piece of brass ornament (= Grabplatte aus Messing) in a church, and tracing the figure **27** *coolometer:* (here) measure that indicates how cool you are **27–28** *in loco parentis* (Latin): taking on the position of the parents **28** *embark on sth.:* start sth. · *rent-boy:* young male prostitute **32** *Brent Cross:* very large shopping centre **33** *slumber* (n): sleep **34–35** *Blue Peter:* children's TV show **35** *exert your allure:* be influential and attractive **36** *sign on:* register yourself as being unemployed **38** *on the menu:* (here) on offer **41** *apathetic:* (here) showing no interest in anything · *unenterprising:* not having the ability to do new things · *law-abiding:* respecting and obeying the law **42** *token:* (here) symbolic, pretended · *sop:* small and unimportant thing offered to sb. to keep them happy **43** *chicken dipper:* chicken that is covered in batter and intended for dipping into sauces **56** *treat sb.:* pay for sb. **57–58** *beat around the bush:* not say sth. directly **59** *broke* (infml): having no money

'No. Listen, I'm quite safe, you know. I thought it might be better just you and me.'

'Why?'

'Give your mum a break?'

'Yeah, well.'

Suddenly, belatedly, he got it. Giving Marcus's mum a break was what they had been doing last weekend; she had spent the leisure time tipping a bottle of pills down her throat and having her stomach pumped.

'I'm sorry, Marcus. I was being dim.'

'Yeah.'

'Of course your mum can come. That would be great.'

'We haven't got a car either. You'll have to bring yours.'

'Fine.'

'You can bring your little boy if you like.'

He laughed. 'Thanks.'

'That's OK,' Marcus said generously. 'It's only fair.' Sarcasm, Will was beginning to see, was a language that Marcus found peculiarly baffling, which as far as Will was concerned meant it was absolutely irresistible.

'He'll be with his mum again on Saturday.'

'Fine. Come round about half-past twelve or something. You remember where we live? Flat 2, 31 Craysfield Road, Islington, London N1 2SF.'

'England, the world, the universe.'

'Yeah,' Marcus said blankly – simple confirmation for a simpleton.

'Right. See you then.'

In the afternoon Will went out to buy a car seat in Mothercare. He had no intention of filling his whole flat with cots and potties and high chairs, but if he was going to start ferrying people around at weekends, he felt he should at least make some concession to Ned's reality.

'That's sexist, you know,' he said to the assistant smugly.

'Sorry?'

'Mothercare. What about the fathers?'

She smiled politely.

'Fathercare,' he added, just in case she was missing his point.

'You're the first person ever to say that.'

'Really?'

'No.' She laughed. He felt like Marcus.

'Anyway. How can I help you?'

'I'm looking for a car seat.'

'Yes.' They were in the car-seat section. 'What make are you looking for?'

'Dunno. Anything. The cheapest.' He laughed matily. 'What do most people get?'

'Well. Not the cheapest. They're usually worried about safety.'

'Ah. Yes.' He stopped laughing. Safety was a serious business. 'Not much point in saving a few quid if he ends up through the windscreen, is there?'

In the end – possibly to over-compensate for his previous callousness – he bought the most expensive car seat in the store, an enormous padded bright blue contraption that looked as though it might last Ned until he was a father himself.

'He'll love it,' he said to the assistant as he handed over his credit card.

'It looks nice now, but he'll mess it up soon enough with his biscuits and crisps and what have you.'

Will hadn't thought about his biscuits and crisps and what have you, so on the way home he stopped off for some chocolate chip cookies and a couple of bags of cheese and onion, squashed everything up, and sprinkled the crumbs generously over his new purchase.

▷ **1** *safe:* not dangerous **4** *give sb. a break:* give sb. a period of rest **6** *belatedly:* happening a little too late **10** *dim* (infml): stupid **19** *baffling:* hard to understand **26** *blankly:* not showing any reaction · *simpleton:* person with not much intelligence **28** *Mothercare:* chain of shops selling things for babies **29** *potty* (n): young child's toilet **30** *ferry sb. around:* drive sb. to various places **43** *make* (n): brand **45** *matily* (infml): behaving as if you are sb.'s friend **49** *quid* (infml): pound **51–52** *callousness:* uncaring behaviour **53** *padded:* filled with soft material · *contraption:* piece of equipment **57** *mess sth. up:* make sth. dirty **58** *and what have you:* and so on **61** *cheese and onion:* type of crisp **61–62** *squash sth. up:* press sth. together so it breaks

Thirteen

Contrary to what he told Will, Marcus wasn't really bothered about leaving his mum on her own. He knew that if she did try anything again it wouldn't be for a while, because right now she was still in this weird, calm mood. But telling Will that he wanted his mum to come with them was a way of getting her and Will together, and after that, he reckoned, it should be easy. His mum was pretty, and Will seemed quite well off, they could go and live with Will and his kid, and then there'd be four of them, and four was twice as good as two. And maybe, if they wanted to, they could have a baby. His mum wasn't too old. She was thirty-eight. You could have a baby when you were thirty-eight. So then there would be five of them, and it wouldn't matter quite so much if one of them died. Well, it would matter, of course it would matter, but at least it wouldn't leave somebody, him or his mum or Will or his little boy, completely on their own. Marcus didn't even know whether he liked Will or not, but that didn't come into it any more; he could see he wasn't bad, or a drunk, or violent, so he would have to do.

It wasn't as if he didn't know anything about Will, because he did: Marcus had checked him out. On his way back from school one afternoon he had seen Will out shopping, and he had followed him home like a private detective. He hadn't really found out much about him, apart from where he lived and what shops he went in. But he seemed to be on his own – no girlfriend, no wife, no little boy, even. Unless the little boy was with his girlfriend at home. But if he had a girlfriend, why was he trying to chat up Suzie?

'What time is this guy coming?' his mum asked. They were tidying the house and listening to *Exodus* by Bob Marley.

'In about ten minutes. You're going to get changed, aren't you?'

'Why?'

'Because you look a wreck, and he's going to take us to Planet Hollywood for lunch.' Will didn't know that last bit yet, because Marcus hadn't told him, but he wouldn't mind.

She looked at him. 'Why does it bother you what I wear?'

'Planet Hollywood.'

'What about it?'

'You don't want to look like an old bag there. In case one of them sees you.'

'In case one of who sees me?'

'Bruce Willis or one of them.'

'Marcus, they won't be there, you know.'

'They're there all the time. Unless they're working. And even then they try to make films in London so they can go for lunch.'

Fiona laughed and laughed. 'Who told you that?'

A kid at his old school called Sam Lovell had told him that. Now Marcus thought about it, Sam had told him some other things that turned out not to be true: that Michael Jackson and Janet Jackson were the same person, and that Mr Harrison the French teacher had been in the Beatles.

'It's just well known.'

'Do you still want to go there if you're not going to see any stars?'

He didn't really, but he wasn't going to let her know that.

'Yeah. Course.'

His mum shrugged and went off to get changed.

Will came into the flat before they went out. He introduced himself, which Marcus thought was pretty stupid as everyone knew who everyone else was anyway.

▷ **25** *chat sb. up:* talk to sb. in a friendly way because you find him/her attractive **27** *Bob Marley* (1945–1981): Jamaican reggae singer **30** *wreck:* person who looks tired and unhealthy **30–31** *Planet Hollywood:* fast-food chain owned by film stars such as Bruce Willis **36** *old bag* (derog): unattractive woman **46** *Michael Jackson, Janet Jackson:* singers who are brother and sister

'Hi. I'm Will,' he said. 'We've ... Well, I ...' But he obviously couldn't think of a polite way of saying that he'd seen her conked out on the sofa by a pool of her own sick the week before, so he stopped and just smiled.

'I'm Fiona.' His mum looked good, Marcus thought. She was wearing her best leggings and a baggy, hairy jumper, and she was wearing make-up for the first time since the hospital, and a pair of nice dangly earrings someone had sent her from Zimbabwe. 'Thanks for all you did last weekend. I really appreciate it.'

'Pleasure, I hope you're feeling ... I hope you've – '

'My stomach's fine. I suppose I must still be a bit barmy, though. That sort of thing doesn't clear up so quickly, does it?'

Will looked shocked, but she just laughed. Marcus hated it when she made jokes to people who didn't know her very well.

'Have you decided where you want to go, then, young Marcus?'

'Planet Hollywood.'

'Oh, God. Really?'

'Yeah. Supposed to be brilliant.'

'Is it? We obviously don't read the same restaurant reviews.'

'It wasn't a restaurant reviewer. It was Sam Lovell from my old school.'

'Oh, well, in that case ... Shall we go?'

Will opened the door and waved at Fiona to go through. Marcus wasn't sure what to look for, but he had a feeling that this was going to work.

They didn't take the car, because Will said Planet Hollywood was in Leicester Square and they wouldn't be able to park, so they caught the bus. On the way to the bus stop Will showed them his car.

'This is mine. The one with the car seat in the back. Look at it. What a mess.'

'Gosh,' said Fiona.

'Right,' said Marcus.

They couldn't think of much else to say about it, so they walked on.

There were loads of people outside Planet Hollywood waiting to get in, and it was raining. They were the only people that spoke English in the whole queue.

'Are you sure this is where you want to go, Marcus?' his mum asked him.

'Yeah. Where else is there anyway?' If someone came up with an even half-decent suggestion, he'd take it. He didn't want to stand around with a load of French and Italian people. It wasn't right.

'There's a Pizza Express round the corner,' said Will.

'No thanks.'

'You're always on about wanting to go out for a pizza,' said his mum.

'No, I'm not.' He was, but pizza was too cheap, he reckoned.

They went back to queuing in silence. Nobody was going to get married to anybody at this rate. It was too wet and too horrible.

'Tell me why you want to go to Planet Hollywood and I'll see if I can think of anywhere like it,' said Will.

'I don't know. Because it's famous. And it's got the sort of food I like. Fries and things.'

'So if I can think of somewhere famous that serves fries, we can go there?'

'Yeah. But it's got to be my sort of famous, not your sort of famous.'

'What does that mean?'

'It's got to be the sort of famous that kids know about. You can't just tell me it's famous, because if I've never heard of it then it's not.'

'So if I said to you, how about Twenty-Eight, you wouldn't want to go.'

'No. Not famous. Never heard of it.'

'But famous people go there.'

'Like who?'

'Actors and so on.'

'Which actors?'

'I should think they've all been there at some time or another. But they don't tell you in advance. I'll be straight with you, Marcus. We could go there now and we might bump into Tom Cruise and Nicole Kidman. Or we might see nobody at all. But they do good fries. The thing is, we'll be standing here for an hour, and then when we get in there'll be nobody there worth seeing anyway.'

'OK then.'

▷ **2** *conked out:* unconscious **6** *baggy:* (of clothes) hanging loosely · *jumper:* type of sweater **8** *dangly:* (of earrings) hanging loosely **8** *Zimbabwe:* country in southern Africa **31** *gosh:* expression of surprise **53** *fries:* chips **68** *bump into sb.* (infml): meet sb. by accident **68–69** *Tom Cruise, Nicole Kidman:* film stars who used to be married to each other

'Seriously?'

'Yeah.'

'Good man.'

No famous people ever went to this Twenty-Eight place. You could tell. It was nice, and the fries were good, but it was just normal; it didn't have anything on the walls, like Clint Eastwood's jacket, or the mask Michael Keaton wore in *Batman*. It didn't even have any signed photos. The Indian restaurant near their flat that delivered their takeaways wasn't famous at all, but even that had a signed picture of someone who used to play for Arsenal ages ago. He didn't mind though. The main thing was that they were sat down and dry, and Will and his mother could begin to talk.

They needed some help at first; nobody said anything until the waiter came to take their order.

'Mushroom omelette and fries, please. And a Coke,' said Marcus.

'I'll have the swordfish steak,' said Will. 'No vegetables, just a side salad.'

Fiona was having difficulty deciding.

'Why don't you have the swordfish steak?' said Marcus.

'Ummm ...'

He tried to get his mother's attention across the table without Will noticing. He nodded hard, once, and then he coughed.

'Are you all right, sweetie?'

He just felt it would help if his mum ordered the same food as Will. He didn't know why. It wasn't like you could talk for ages about swordfish steak or anything, but maybe it would show them that they had something in common, that sometimes they thought the same way about things. Even if they didn't.

'We're vegetarian,' said Marcus. 'But we eat fish.'

'So we're not really vegetarian.'

'We don't eat fish very often though. Fish and chips sometimes. We never cook fish at home, do we?'

'Not often, no.'

'Never.'

'Oh, don't show me up.'

He didn't know how saying she never cooked fish was showing her up – did men like women who cooked fish? Why? – but that was the last thing he wanted to do.

'All right,' he said. 'Not never. Sometimes.'

‘Shall I come back in a couple of minutes?’ said the waiter. Marcus had forgotten he was still there.

‘Ummm …’

‘Have the swordfish,’ said Marcus.

‘I’ll have the penne pesto,’ said his mother. ‘With a mixed salad.’

Will ordered a beer, and his mum ordered a glass of white wine. Nobody said anything again.

Marcus didn’t have a girlfriend, nor had he ever come close to having one, unless you counted Holly Garrett, which he didn’t. But he knew this: if a girl and a boy met, and they didn’t have a boyfriend or a girlfriend, and they both looked all right, and they didn’t mind each other, then they might as well go out together. What was the point in not? Will didn’t have a girlfriend, unless you counted Suzie, which he didn’t, and his mum didn’t have a boyfriend, so … It would be good for all of them. The more he thought about it, the more obvious it seemed.

It wasn’t that he needed someone to replace his dad. He’d talked about that with his mum ages ago. They’d been watching a programme on TV about the family, and some silly fat Tory woman said that everyone should have a mother and a father, and his mum got angry and later depressed. Then, before the hospital thing, he’d thought the Tory woman was stupid, and he’d told his mum as much, but at the time he hadn’t worked out that two was a dangerous number. Now he had worked that out, he wasn’t sure it made much difference to what he thought about the fat Tory woman’s idea; he didn’t care whether the family he wanted were all men, or all women, or all children. He simply wanted people.

‘Don’t just sit there,’ he said suddenly.

Will and his mother looked at him.

‘You heard me. Don’t just sit there. Talk to each other.’

‘I’m sure we will in a moment,’ said his mother.

‘Lunch will be over before you two’ve thought of anything to say,’ Marcus grumbled.

‘What do you want us to talk about?’ Will asked.

‘Anything. Politics. Films. Murders. I don’t care.’

▷ **6, 7** *Clint Eastwood, Michael Keaton:* American film stars **35** *show sb. up* (infml): make sb. feel awkward or ashamed **58** *Tory:* member of the Conservative Party

'I'm not sure that's how conversation happens,' said his mother.

'Maybe you should have worked it out by now. You're old enough.'

'Marcus!'

Will was laughing, though.

'He's right. We have, I don't know how old you are, Fiona, but we have at least sixty years of conversational experience between us here, and maybe we ought to be able to get something going.'

'OK then.'

'So.'

'After you.'

They both laughed, but neither of them said anything.

'Will,' said Marcus.

'Yes, Marcus,' said Will.

'What do you think of John Major?'

'Not much.'

'What about you, Mum?'

'You know what I think of him.'

'Tell Will.'

'Not much.'

This was useless.

'Why?'

'Oh, Marcus, leave us alone. You're making it more difficult, not easier. You're making us self-conscious. We'll start talking soon.'

'When?'

'Stop it.'

'Have you ever been married, Will?'

'Marcus, I'm going to get cross with you in a minute.'

'It's OK. Fiona. No, I haven't. Have you?'

'No, course not. I'm not old enough.'

'Oh.'

'Now ask Mum.'

'Fiona, have you ever been married?'

'No.'

For a moment, Marcus was confused; when he was a real kid, a little kid, he used to think that you had to be married to be a father or mother, in the same way that you had to have a driving licence to drive. He knew now that this wasn't true, and he knew too that his parents had never been married, but somehow the ideas you grew up with were hard to shake off.

'Did you want to get married, Mum?'

'Not really. It didn't seem important.'

'So why do other people bother?'

'Oh, all sorts of reasons. Security. Pressure from family. Misguided notions of romance.'

Will laughed at this. 'Cynic,' he said.

Marcus didn't understand this, but that was good: his mum and Will now had something that he hadn't started.

'Do you still see Marcus's dad?'

'Sometimes. Not very often. Marcus sees him quite a lot. How about you? Do you still see your ex?'

'Ummm ... Well, yes. All the time. She picked Ned up this morning.' He said this in a funny way, Marcus thought. Almost like he'd forgotten and then remembered.

'And is that all right?'

'Oh, it's OK. We have our moments.'

'How come you ended up looking after Ned? I mean, I'm sure you're a brilliant dad and everything, but that's not usually how it works, is it?'

'No. She was going through a *Kramer vs Kramer* kind of thing at the time. You know, a sort of I-want-to-find-out-who-I-am malarkey.'

'And did she find out who she was?'

'Not really. I don't know if anyone really does, do they?'

The food arrived, but the two adults hardly noticed; Marcus dug happily into his omelette and fries. Would they move into Will's place, he wondered, or buy somewhere new?

▷ **14** *John Major:* British Conservative prime minister (1990–1997) **23** *self-conscious:* very aware of yourself, awkward and embarrassed **43** *security:* safety, protection · *misguided:* wrong **44** *notion:* idea **45** *cynic:* person who believes in the worst in human nature **55** *have your moments:* have good and interesting periods of time **59** *Kramer vs Kramer:* film in which a mother leaves her family but then returns to claim custody of the child **60** *malarkey* (infml): nonsense

Fourteen

Will knew that Fiona was not his type. For a start, she didn't look the way he wanted women to look – in fact, he doubted whether looks were important to her at all. He couldn't be doing with that. People, women and men, had a duty to care, he felt, even if they didn't have the requisite raw material – unless they weren't interested in the sexual side of life at all, in which case, fair enough. You could do what you wanted then. Einstein, for example ... Will didn't know the first thing about Einstein's private life, but in his photos he looked like a guy with other things on his mind. But Fiona wasn't Einstein. She might have been as brainy as Einstein, for all he knew, but she was clearly interested in relationships, judging from the conversation they had had over lunch, so why didn't she make more of an effort? Why didn't she have a decent hair cut, instead of all that frizz, and why didn't she wear clothes which looked like they mattered to her? He didn't get that at all.

And she was just too hippy. He could see now why Marcus was so weird. She believed in alternative things, like aromatherapy and vegetarianism and the environment, stuff he didn't give much of a shit about, really. If they went out they'd fight terribly, he knew, and that would upset her, and the last thing he wanted to do at the moment was upset her.

He had to say that the thing he found most attractive about her was that she had tried to kill herself. Now that was interesting – sexy, almost, in a morbid kind of way. But how can you contemplate dating a woman who might top herself at any moment? Before, he thought that going out with a mother was a heavy number; how much heavier would it be going out with a suicidal mother? But he didn't want to let it drop. He still had this sense that Fiona and Marcus could replace soup kitchens and *Media Guardian* jobs, possibly forever. He wouldn't have to do that much, after all – the occasional swordfish steak, the odd visit to a crappy film that he might have gone to anyway. How hard could that be? It was a damn sight easier than trying to force-feed vagrants. Good works! Helping people! That was the way forward for him now. The way he saw it, he'd helped Angie by sleeping with her (although admittedly there had been a little speck of self-interest there) and now he was going to find out whether it was possible to help someone without sleeping with them. It had to be, surely? Other people had managed, Mother Teresa and Florence Nightingale and so on, although he suspected that when he entered the good-works fray his style would be somewhat different.

They had made no further arrangement after the lunch. They left the restaurant, wandered around Covent Garden, caught the tube back to north London, and he was back home in time for *Sports Report*. But he knew they'd all started something that wasn't finished.

Within a few days he'd changed his mind completely. He had no interest in good works. He had no interest in Marcus and Fiona. He would, he felt sure, break out into a cold sweat of embarrassment every time he thought of them. He would never see them again; he doubted, in fact, whether he would ever be able to go to Holloway again, just in case he bumped into them. He knew he was overreacting, but not by much. Singing! How could you have anything to do with someone who makes you sing! He knew they were both a little flaky, but …

▷ **7** *Albert Einstein* (1879–1955): German-American physicist **16** *hippy* (adj): unconventional, eccentric, alternative **20** *upset sb.:* make sb.worried or unhappy **24** *morbid:* unhealthy **26** *heavy number:* something that is very difficult and demanding **31** *crappy* (sl): bad, worthless, stupid **32** *a damn sight:* a lot **33** *force-feed sb.:* force sb. to eat by putting food down their throat **38** Mother Teresa (1894–1995): nun who worked for the poor in India **38–39** *Florence Nightingale* (1820–1910): British nurse, famous for her service in military hospitals, esp. during the Crimean War (1853–1856) **40** *fray* (n): challenging activity **54** *flaky* (infml): slightly crazy and useless

It began ordinarily enough, with an invitation to supper, and though he didn't like what they had to eat – something vegetarian with chickpeas and rice and tinned tomatoes – he quite enjoyed the conversation. Fiona told him about her job as a music therapist, and Marcus told Fiona that Will earned millions of pounds a minute because his dad had written a song. Will helped with the washing up, and Fiona made them a cup of tea, and then she sat down at the piano and started to play.

She wasn't bad. The piano playing was better than her voice, but her voice wasn't awful, simply adequate, if a little thin, and she could certainly carry a tune. No, it wasn't the quality that embarrassed him, it was the sincerity. He'd been with people who had picked up guitars and sat down at pianos before (although not for a very long time), but they had always sent themselves up in some way: they had chosen stupid songs to play, or sung them in a stupid way, or camped them up or done anything to show they didn't mean it.

Fiona meant it. She meant 'Knocking On Heaven's Door', and then she meant 'Fire And Rain', and then she meant 'Both Sides Now'. There was nothing between her and the songs; she was inside them. She even closed her eyes when she was singing.

'Do you want to come over here so you can see the words?' she asked him after 'Both Sides Now'. He'd been sitting at the dining table staring hard at Marcus, until Marcus started singing too, at which point he turned his attention to the wall.

'Ummm ... what's next?'

'Any requests?'

He wanted her to play something that she couldn't close her eyes to, 'Roll Out The Barrel,' say, or 'Knees Up, Mother Brown', but the mood had already been set.

'Anything.'

She chose 'Killing Me Softly With His Song'. There was nothing he could do but stand next to her and let the odd half-syllable of lyric crawl choking out of his mouth. 'Smile ... While ... Boy ... Ling ...' He knew, of course he knew, that the song couldn't last forever, that the evening couldn't last forever, that he would soon be home tucked up in bed, that singing round the piano with a depressive hippy and her weirdo son wouldn't kill him. He knew all that, but he didn't *feel* it. He couldn't do anything with these people after all, he could see that now. He'd been stupid to think there was anything here for him.

When he got home he put a Pet Shop Boys CD on, and watched *Prisoner: Cell Block H* with the sound down. He wanted to hear people who didn't mean it, and he wanted to watch people he could laugh at. He got drunk, too; he filled a glass with ice and poured himself scotch after scotch. And as the drink began to take hold, he realized that people who meant it were much more likely to kill themselves than people who didn't: he couldn't recall having even the faintest urge to take his own life, and he found it hard to imagine that he ever would. When it came down to it, he just wasn't that engaged. You had to be engaged to be a vegetarian; you had to be engaged to sing 'Both Sides Now' with your eyes closed; when it came down to it, you had to be engaged to be a mother. He wasn't much bothered either way about anything, and that, he knew, would guarantee him a long and depression-free life. He'd made a big mistake thinking that good works were a way forward for him. They weren't. They drove you mad. Fiona did good works and they had driven her mad: she was vulnerable, messed-up, inadequate. Will had a system going here that was going to whizz him effortlessly to the grave. He didn't want to fuck it up now.

Fiona called him once more, soon after the excruciating supper; she left a message on the machine, and he didn't answer it. Suzie called him too, and though he wanted to see her, he suspected she was ringing on Fiona's behalf, so he was vague and non-committal. It looked to him like he'd taken the single mum thing as far as it would go, and he was preparing for a return to the life he had been living before he met Angie. Maybe it was for the best.

He went record shopping, he went clothes shopping, he played a bit of tennis, he went to the pub, he watched telly, he went to see films and bands with friends. Time units were filled effortlessly. He had even gone back to reading books in the afternoon; he was halfway through

▷ **3** *chickpea:* Kichererbse **11** *carry a tune:* sing correctly **14** *send sb. up:* make fun of sb. **15** *camp sth. up* (infml): behave in a funny and silly way **29** *mood:* way you feel **33** *crawl* (v): move very slowly **44** *take hold:* have an effect **49** *engaged:* involved in sth., committed to sth. **56** *vulnerable:* easily hurt · *inadequate:* (here) not able to deal with life **57** *whizz sb.* (infml): move sb. quickly **58** *fuck sth. up* (sl): ruin sth. **59** *excruciating:* extremely awful or embarrassing **62** *non-committal:* not saying anything specific a James Ellroy thriller one Thursday, in that horrible dead dark time between *Countdown* and the news, when the doorbell went.

He was expecting to see someone selling J-cloths and brushes, so he found himself looking at nothing when he opened the door, because his visitor was a good foot shorter than the average hawker.

'I've come to see you,' said Marcus.

'Oh. Right. Come in.' He said it warmly enough, as far as he could tell, but for some reason he felt a rising tide of panic.

Marcus marched into the sitting room, sat down on the sofa and stared intently at everything.

'You haven't got a kid, have you?'

That was certainly one explanation for the panic.

'Well,' said Will, as if he were about to launch into a very long and involved story, the details of which were currently eluding him.

Marcus got up and walked around the flat.

'Where's your loo? I'm dying for a pee.'

'Just down the hall there.'

While Marcus was gone, Will tried to think of a story that would account for the complete absence of anything Ned-related, but there was nothing. He could either tell Marcus that *of course* he had a child, and that the lack of both child and child-related paraphernalia was simply … simply something he would think of later; or he could dissolve into tears and own up to being a pathetic fantasist. He decided against the latter version.

'You've only got one bedroom,' said Marcus when he got back.

'Have you been nosing around?'

'Yeah. You've got one bedroom, you've got no children's toys in the bathroom, there are no toys in here … You haven't even got any photos of him.'

'What business is it of yours?'

'None. Apart from you've been lying to me and my mum and my mum's friend.'

'Who told you where I lived?'

'I followed you home once.'

'Where from?'

'I saw you out wandering around and I followed you.'

This was plausible. He was often out wandering around and, in any case, he hadn't told Suzie or Fiona or the SPAT woman where he lived, so there was no other explanation.

'Why?'

'Dunno. Something to do.'

'Why don't you just go home, Marcus?'

'All right. But I'm going to tell my mum.'

'Ooooh. I'm scared.'

Will could feel himself tumbling down a hill towards the kind of panicky guilt he hadn't felt since schooldays, and it seemed natural to resort to the kind of phrases he used then. There was no explanation he could give Marcus, other than the truth – that he had invented a child so he could meet women – and the truth sounded much seedier than it was ever intended to be.

'Go on then, off you go.'

'I'll do you a deal. I won't say anything to my mum if you go out with her.'

'Why do you want your mum to go out with someone like me?'

'I don't think you're too bad. I mean, you told lies, but apart from that you seem OK. And she's sad, and I think she'd like a boyfriend.'

'Marcus, I can't go out with someone just because you want me to. I'd have to like the person as well.'

'What's wrong with her?'

'Nothing's wrong with her, but – '

'You want to go out with Suzie, don't you?'

'I don't want to talk about this with you.'

'I thought so.'

'I didn't say anything. All I said was … Listen, I really don't want to talk about this with you. Go home.'

'OK. But I'll be back.' And off he went.

When Will had conceived this fantasy and joined SPAT, he had imagined sweet little children, not children who would be able to track him down and come to his house. He had imagined entering their world, but he hadn't foreseen that they might be able to penetrate his. He was one of life's visitors; he didn't want to be visited.

▷ **3** *J-cloth:* cloth for cleaning surfaces in a kitchen, etc. **5** *hawker:* person who goes from place to place to sell things **13** *launch into sth:* start sth. enthusiastically **14** *involved:* complex · *elude sb.:* not be remembered by sb. **16** *loo* (infml): toilet **21** *paraphernalia:* objects **23** *dissolve into tears:* begin to cry a lot **26** *nose around* (infml): look around a place that belongs to another person **45** *tumble down:* fall down **49** *seedy:* unpleasant; immoral **67** *conceive sth.:* invent sth.

Fifteen

Marcus wasn't daft. Well, OK, he was daft sometimes, like with the singing, but he wasn't stupid-daft, just brush-daft. He could see instantly that the things he knew about Will, the stuff about him not having a kid and not having an ex, were too good to give up all at once; they were worth something. If he'd gone straight home after his first visit to Will's flat and told his mum and Suzie everything immediately, then that would have been the end of it. They would have stopped him from talking to Will, and he didn't want that.

He wasn't sure why he didn't want that. He just knew that he didn't want to spend this information straight away, in the same way that he didn't want to spend birthday money straight away: he wanted to leave it in his pocket while he looked around, to work out what it was worth. He knew he couldn't make Will go out with his mum if he wasn't bothered, but he could make him do something else, maybe, something he hadn't even thought of yet, so he started going round to Will's house more or less every day after school to get some ideas.

The first time he went back, Will wasn't too pleased to see him. He just stood in the doorway with his hand on the latch.

'What?' said Will.

'Nothing. Thought I'd pop round.' That made Will smile, although Marcus couldn't see why. 'What are you doing?'

'What am I doing?'

'Yeah.'

'Watching TV.'

'What are you watching?'

'*Countdown.*'

'What's that? Marcus knew what it was. Every kid who had ever come home from school knew what it was: it was the most boring programme in the history of television.

'A quiz show. Words and numbers.'

'Oh. Would I like it?' Of course he wouldn't like it. Nobody liked it, apart from his dad's girlfriend's mum.

'I'm not sure I care.'

'I could watch it with you, if you want.'

'That's very nice of you, Marcus, but I usually manage on my own.'

'I'm good at anagrams. And maths. I'd be really helpful, if you were serious about doing well.'

'So you do know what *Countdown* is.'

'Yes. I remember now. I really like it. I'll go when it's finished.'

Will looked at him and shook his head. 'Oh, hell. Come in.'

Marcus was almost in anyway. He sat down on Will's long cream sofa, kicked his shoes off and stretched himself out. It was as useless as he remembered, *Countdown*, but he didn't complain or ask to watch another channel. (Will had cable, Marcus noted for future reference.) He just sat there patiently. Will didn't do anything while the programme was on: he didn't shout the answers at the screen, or tut when somebody got something wrong. He just smoked.

'You need a pen and paper to do it properly,' Marcus observed at the end.

'Yeah, well.'

'Do you ever do that?'

'Sometimes.'

'Why didn't you today?'

'I don't know. Jesus.'

'You could have done. I wouldn't have minded.'

'That's very big of you.'

He turned the TV off with the remote and they sat in silence.

'What do you want, Marcus? Haven't you got any homework to do?'

'Yeah. Do you want to help me?'

▷ **1** *daft* (infml): foolish **2** *brush-daft* (infml): silly in an unusual way **18** *latch:* fastening on a door **20** *pop round:* visit sb. without informing them beforehand **36** *anagram:* word formed by changing the order of letters in another word **47** *tut* (v): make a sound that shows you are annoyed or disapprove of sth. **56** *be big of sb.* (infml): (always used ironically) be kind or generous

'That wasn't what I meant. I meant, why don't you go home and do it?'

'I'll do it after supper. You shouldn't smoke, you know.'

'No, I know. Thank you for telling me. What time does your mum get home?'

'About now.'

'So?'

Marcus ignored him and started poking around the flat. Last time he'd only noticed that there was no Ned, and he'd missed a lot of things: the flash hi-fi, the hundreds of CDs and thousands of records and tapes, the black and white photos of people playing saxophones and the film posters on the wall, the wooden floors, the rug. It was small, which surprised Marcus. If Will earned what Marcus thought he earned, then he could afford something a lot bigger than this. It was cool, though. If Marcus had a flat of his own, he'd make it look just like this, although he'd probably choose different film posters. Will had posters of old films he'd never heard of – *Double Indemnity*, *The Big Sleep*. Marcus would have *Honey, I Shrunk the Kids*, definitely, and *Free Willy* and ... he wouldn't have *Hellhound 3* or *Boilerhead*, though. Not now. The Dead Duck Day had really put him off things like that.

'Nice flat.'

'Thank you.'

'Quite small, though.'

'It's big enough for me.'

'But you could get something bigger if you wanted to.'

'I'm happy with this one.'

'You've got a lot of CDs. More than anyone I've met.' Marcus went over to look at them, but he didn't really know what he was looking for. 'Iggy Pop,' he said, and laughed at the funny name, but Will just looked at him.

'Who are those people on the wall? The ones with the saxophones and the trumpets?'

'Saxophonists and trumpeters.'

'But who are they? And why are they on your wall?

'That's Charlie Parker, and that's Chet Baker. And they're on my wall because I like their music and they're cool.'

'Why are they cool?'

Will sighed. 'I don't know. Because they took drugs and died, probably.'

Marcus looked at him to see if he was joking, but he didn't seem to be. Marcus wouldn't want pictures on his walls of people who took drugs and died. He'd want to forget all about that kind of thing, not look at it every day of his life.

'Do you want anything? A cup of tea or a Coke or something?'

'Yeah, OK.'

Marcus followed him into the kitchen. It wasn't like their kitchen at home. It was much smaller and whiter, and it had loads more gadgets, all of which looked as though they had never been used. At home, they had a liquidizer and a microwave, both of which were covered in stains that had gradually become black.

'What's this?'

'Espresso machine.'

'And this?'

'Ice-cream maker. What do you want?

'I'll have some ice-cream, if you're making it.'

'I'm not. It takes hours.'

'Might as well buy it from the shop, then.'

'Coke?'

'Yeah.'

Will handed him a can and he snapped it open.

'Do you watch telly all day then?'

'No, of course not.'

'So what else do you do?'

'Read. Shop. See friends.'

'Nice life. Did you go to school when you were a kid?'

'Yeah, course.'

'Why? I mean, you didn't really need to, did you?'

'How d'you work that out? What do you think school's for?'

'Getting a job.'

'What about reading and writing?'

'I could do that years ago, and I'm still going to school. Because I've got to get a job. You could have left school when you were about

▷ **10** *flash* (adj) (infml): impressive and expensive **30** *Iggy Pop:* pop singer **49** *gadget:* machine **50** *liquidizer:* machine that turns solid foods (e.g. fruit) into a liquid **51** *stain:* dirty mark six or seven. Saved yourself all the hassle. You don't really need to do history to go shopping or read, do you?'

'Depends if you want to read about history.'

'Is that what you read about?'

'Not often, no.'

'OK, so why did you go to school?'

'Shut up, Marcus.'

'If I knew I wasn't going to get a job, I wouldn't bother.'

'Don't you like it?' Will was making himself a cup of tea. When he'd put the milk in they went back into the living room and sat down on the sofa.

'No. I hate it.'

'Why?'

'It doesn't suit me. I'm not a school sort of person. I'm the wrong personality type.' His mum had told him about personality types a while ago, just after they had moved. They were both introverts, she said, which made a lot of things – making new friends, starting at new schools and new places of work – more difficult for them. She'd said it as if it would make him feel better, but of course it hadn't helped at all, and he couldn't understand how on earth she thought it might: as far as he could see, being an introvert just meant that it wasn't even worth trying.

'Do people give you a hard time?'

Marcus looked at him. How did he know that? Things must be worse than he thought, if people knew even before he had said anything.

'Not really. Just a couple of kids.'

'What do they give you a hard time about?'

'Nothing really. Just, you know, my hair and glasses. And singing and stuff.'

'What about singing?

'Oh, just … sometimes I sing without noticing.'

Will laughed.

'It's not funny.'

'I'm sorry.'

'I can't help it.'

'You could do something about the hair.'

'Like what?'

'Get it cut.'

'Like how?'

'Like how! Like how you want it.'

'This is how I want it.'

'You'll have to put up with the other kids, then. Why do you want your hair like that?'

''Cos that's how it grows, and I hate going to the hairdresser.'

'I can see that. How often do you go?'

'Never. My mum cuts it.'

'Your mum? Jesus. How old are you? Twelve? I would have thought you're old enough to get your own hair cut.'

Marcus was interested in that 'old enough'. It wasn't something he was told very often. 'D'you think?'

'Course. Twelve? You could get married in four years' time. Are you going to get your mum to cut your hair then?'

Marcus didn't think he'd be getting married in four years' time, but he could see what Will was telling him.

'She wouldn't like it, would she?' he said.

'Who?'

'My wife. If I had a wife, but I don't think I will. Not in four years.'

'I wasn't really thinking of that. I was thinking that you might feel a bit of a wally if your mum had to come round and do everything like that. Cut your hair and cut your toenails and scrub your back –'

'Oh, right. Yeah, I see what you mean.'

And yes, he saw what Will meant, and yes, Will was right. In those circumstances he would feel like a wally. But there was another way of looking at it: if his mum was coming round in four years' time to cut his hair, then that would mean nothing terrible had happened in the meantime. The way he was feeling at the moment, he'd settle for looking like a bit of a wally once every couple of months.

Marcus visited Will a lot that autumn, and by about the third or fourth time he felt that Will was getting used to him. They had a bit of an argument the second time – Will didn't want to let him in again, and Marcus had to insist, but eventually they reached a stage where Marcus would ring the bell and Will would open the door without even bothering to check who it was; he'd just wander back in to the

▷ **1** *save sb. sth:* help sb. avoid sth. · *hassle* (n) (infml): trouble **45** *'cos:* because **60** *wally* (infml): stupid person **72** *insist:* firmly demand sth.

living room and expect Marcus to follow him. A couple of times he was out, but Marcus didn't know whether he went out deliberately, and he didn't want to know, either, so he didn't ask him.

They didn't talk about much at first, but eventually, when the visits became routine, Will seemed to think they should have proper conversations. He wasn't very good at them, though. The first time it happened they were talking about this fat bloke who kept winning on *Countdown*, when Will said, 'How's it going at home?', for no reason at all that Marcus could see.

'You mean my mum?'

'I suppose.'

It was so obvious that Will would rather talk about the fat bloke on *Countdown* than about what had happened before that for a moment Marcus felt a little stab of temper because he didn't have the same kind of choice. If it was up to him he'd spend all his time thinking about the fat bloke on *Countdown*, but he couldn't because there were too many other things to think about. He wasn't annoyed for long, though. It wasn't Will's fault and at least he was trying, even though it was difficult for him.

'She's all right, thanks,' Marcus said, in a way that suggested she was always all right.

'No, you know –'

'Yeah, I know. No, nothing like that.'

'Does it still bother you?'

He'd never talked about it since the night it happened, and even then he'd never said what he felt. What he felt, all the time, every single day, was a horrible fear. In fact, the main reason he came round to Will's after school was that he was able to put off going back to the flat; he could no longer climb the stairs at home without looking at his feet and remembering the Dead Duck Day. By the time he got to the bit where he had to put his key in the lock, his heart was thumping in his chest and his arms and his legs, and when he saw his mum watching the news or cooking or preparing work on the dining table, it was all he could do not to cry, or be sick, or something.

'A bit. When I think about it.'

'How often do you think about it?'

'I dunno.' All the time, all the time, all the time. Could he say that to Will? He didn't know. He couldn't say it to his mum, he couldn't say it to his dad, he couldn't say it to Suzie; they'd all make too much of a fuss. His mum would get upset, Suzie would want to talk about it, his dad would want him to move back to Cambridge ... he didn't need that. So why tell anyone anything? What was the point? All he wanted was a promise from someone, anyone, that it wouldn't happen again, ever, and no one could do that.

'Fucking hell,' said Will. 'Sorry, I shouldn't say that in front of you, should I?'

'It's OK. People say it at school all the time.'

And that was it. That was all Will said. 'Fucking hell.' Marcus didn't know why Will had sworn like that, but Marcus liked it; it made him feel better. It was serious, it wasn't too much and it made him see that he wasn't being pathetic to get so scared.

'You might as well stay for *Neighbours* now,' Will said. 'Otherwise you'll miss the beginning.' Marcus never watched *Neighbours*, and didn't know how Will had got the idea that he did, but he stayed anyway. He felt he should. They watched in silence, and when the theme music started up, Marcus said thank you politely and went home.

▷ **2** *deliberately:* intentionally **5** *proper:* real, correct

Sixteen

Will found himself working Marcus's visits into the fabric of his day. This wasn't difficult to do, since the fabric of his day was tatty, and filled with any number of large and accommodating holes, but even so, he could have filled them with other, easier things, like more shopping, or more afternoon cinema visits; nobody could argue that Marcus was the equivalent of a crap Steve Martin film and a sackful of liquorice allsorts. It wasn't that he behaved badly when he came round, because he didn't, and it wasn't that he was hard to talk to, because he wasn't. Marcus was difficult simply because he frequently gave the impression that he was merely stopping off on this planet on his way to somewhere else, somewhere he might fit in better. Periods of blankness, when he seemed to disappear into his own head completely, were followed by periods when he seemed to be trying to compensate for these absences, and would ask question after question.

Once or twice Will decided he couldn't face it and went shopping or to the cinema; but most of the time he was in at four-fifteen, waiting for the buzzer – sometimes because he couldn't be bothered to go out, sometimes because he felt he owed Marcus something. What and why he owed him he didn't know, but he could see he was serving some purpose in the kid's life at the moment, and as he served no purpose in anybody else's he was hardly going to die of compassion fatigue. It was still a bit of a drag, though, having some kid inflict himself on you every afternoon. Will would be relieved when Marcus found a purpose to life somewhere else.

On the third or fourth visit he asked Marcus about Fiona, and ended up wishing he hadn't, because it was quite clear that the boy was messed up about it. Will couldn't blame him, but couldn't think of anything to say that would be of even the smallest consolation or value, so he ended up simply swearing sympathetically and, given Marcus's age, inappropriately. Will wouldn't make that mistake again. If Marcus wanted to talk about his suicidal mother, he could do it with Suzie, or a counsellor, or someone like that, someone capable of something more than an obscenity.

The thing was, Will had spent his whole life avoiding real stuff. He was, after all, the son and heir of the man who wrote 'Santa's Super Sleigh', Santa Claus, whose existence most adults had real cause to doubt, bought him everything he wore and ate and drank and sat on and lived in; it could reasonably be argued that reality was not in his genes. He liked watching real stuff on *EastEnders* and *The Bill*, and he liked listening to Joe Strummer and Curtis Mayfield and Kurt Cobain singing about real stuff, but he'd never had real stuff sitting on his sofa before. No wonder, then, that once he'd made it a cup of tea and offered it a biscuit he didn't really know what to do with it.

Sometimes they managed conversations about Marcus's life that skirted round the twin disasters of school and home.

'My dad's stopped drinking coffee,' Marcus suddenly said one evening after Will had complained of caffeine poisoning (an occupational hazard, he supposed, of those with no occupation).

Will had never really thought about Marcus's father. Marcus seemed so much a product of his mother that the idea of a father seemed almost incongruous.

'What does he do, your dad?'

▷ **1** *fabric:* structure; material **3** *tatty:* (esp. of clothes) in a bad condition, e.g. with holes · *accomodating:* (here) helpful **6** *Steve Martin:* American director and actor **7** *liquorice allsorts* ['lɪkərɪs]: Süßigkeiten aus Lakritz **18** *buzzer:* door bell **22–23** *compassion fatigue:* feeling that you can no longer have sympathy for the sufferings of others (e.g. poor people in the Third World) **23** *drag* (infml): boring nuisance **23–24** *inflict yourself on sb.:* force sb. to spend time with you **29** *consolation:* comfort **31** *inappropriate:* improper, not suitable for the occasion **33** *counsellor:* person whose job it is to help and advise people **34** *obscenity:* rude and offensive word or phrase **35** *real stuff:* (here) reality **40** *The Bill:* TV series about the police ('the bill' is slang for 'the police') **46** *skirt round sth.:* avoid talking about sth. **49** *occupational hazard:* danger or risk associated with a person in a particular job **52** *incongruous:* strange and not suitable in a particular situation

'He works for Cambridge Social Services.'

That figured, Will thought. All of these people came from another country, a country full of things that Will knew nothing about and had no use for, like music therapists and housing officers and health-food shops with noticeboards and aromatherapy oils and brightly coloured sweaters and difficult European novels and feelings. Marcus was the fruit of their loins.

'What does he do for them?'

'I dunno. He doesn't get much money, though.'

'Do you see him often?'

'Quite often. Some weekends. Half-terms. He's got a girlfriend called Lindsey. She's nice.'

'Oh.'

'Do you want me to say more about him?' Marcus asked helpfully. 'I will if you want.'

'Do you want to say more about him?'

'Yeah. We don't talk about him at home much.'

'What do you want to say?'

'I dunno. I could tell you what car he's got, and whether he smokes.'

'OK, does he smoke?' Will was no longer thrown by Marcus's somewhat eccentric conversational patterns.

'No. Given up,' Marcus said triumphantly, as if he had lured Will into a trap.

'Ah.'

'It was hard, though.'

'I'll bet. Do you miss your dad?'

'How do you mean?'

'Well, you know. Do you … I don't know … do you miss him? You understand what that means.'

'I see him. How can I miss him?'

'Do you wish you saw him more than you do?'

'No.'

'Oh. That's all right, then.'

'Can I have another Coke?'

Will didn't understand at first why Marcus had introduced the subject of his father, but clearly there was a value in talking about something that didn't remind Marcus of the awful messes that surrounded him. The triumph over nicotine addiction wasn't

Marcus's triumph, exactly, but in a life that was at the moment decidedly triumph-free it was the closest he had come for a while.

Will could see how sad this was, but he could also see that it wasn't his problem. No problem was his problem. Very few people were in a position to say they had no problems, but then, that wasn't his problem either. Will didn't see this as a source of shame, but as a cause for wild and raucous celebration; to reach the age he had without encountering any serious difficulties seemed to him a record worth preserving, and though he didn't mind giving Marcus the odd can of Coke, he wasn't about to embroil himself in the sorry dog's dinner that was Marcus's life. Why would he want to do that?

The following week Will's date with *Countdown* was interrupted by a hail of what sounded like gravel against his sitting-room window, followed quickly by a continuous, urgent-sounding and annoying ring on the doorbell. Will knew it was trouble – you didn't get gravel smashing into your windows and frantic doorbell-ringing without trouble, he imagined – and his first instinct was to turn the volume on the TV up and ignore it all. But in the end some sense of self-respect drove the cowardice away, and he propelled himself off the sofa towards the front door.

Marcus was standing on the step being bombarded with some kind of confectionery, rock-shaped and rock-hard lumps that could easily do as much damage as rocks. Will knew this because he took several direct hits himself. He ushered Marcus in and managed to locate the bombardiers, two mean-looking french-cropped teenage boys.

'What do you think you're doing?'

'Who are you?'

▷ **7** *fruit of sb.'s loins:* sb.'s child **11** *half-term:* short holiday in the middle of a school term **21** *thrown* (adj): confused **23** *lure sb. into sth.:* persuade sb. to go into sth. **39** *addiction:* strong need to have sth. (e.g. cigarettes, drugs) **41** *decidedly:* definitely **46** *raucous* ['rɔːkəs]: unpleasantly loud **49** *embroil sb. in sth.:* involve sb. in sth. (esp. a difficult situation) · *sorry* (adj): sad · *dog's dinner* (infml): mess **52** *hail* (n): large number of things thrown · *gravel:* small stones **58** *cowardice:* fear, lack of courage · *propel sb.:* move sb. forwards **61** *confectionery:* sweets **63** *usher sb. in:* hurry sb. inside **64** *mean* (adj): bad, nasty · *french-cropped:* having very short hair round the sides but slightly longer and flat on top

'Never mind who I am. Who the fuck are you?' Will couldn't remember the last time he felt like thumping someone, but he felt like thumping these two. 'Fuck off.'

'Ooo-er,' said one of them obscurely. Will presumed it was intended to indicate their lack of fear, but their bravado was somewhat undercut by their immediate and rapid disappearance. This was a surprise and a relief. Will would never have run away from Will in a million years (or rather, in the admittedly unlikely event that Will should meet himself down a dark alley, both Wills would have run away at equal and very fast speeds in opposite directions). But he was an adult now, and though it was of course true that teenagers had lost all respect, bring back National Service and so on and so forth, only the very bad or very armed were likely to risk a confrontation with someone bigger and older than them. Will went back into the flat feeling bigger and older, and not altogether displeased with himself.

Marcus had helped himself to a biscuit, and was sat on the sofa watching TV. He looked just as he normally looked, absorbed in the programme, the biscuit poised halfway to the mouth; there was no visible sign of distress at all. If this boy, the one on the sofa watching *Countdown*, had ever been bullied, it was ages ago, and he had long since forgotten all about it.

'Who were they, then?'

'Who?'

'Who? Those kids who were just trying to embed sweets into your skull.'

'Oh, them,' said Marcus, his eyes still on the screen. 'I don't know their names. They're in year nine.'

'And you don't know their names?'

'No. They just started following me home after school. So I thought I'd better not go home, so they wouldn't find out where I lived. I thought I'd come round here.'

'Thanks a lot.'

'They won't chuck sweets at you. They were after me.'

'And does this happen often?'

'They've never chucked sweets before. They thought of that today. Just now.'

'I'm not talking about the sweets. I'm talking about ... older kids trying to kill you.'

Marcus looked at him.

'Yeah. I told you before.'

'You didn't make it sound so dramatic before.'

'What do you mean?'

'You said a couple of kids gave you a hard time. You didn't say that people you don't even know follow you around and chuck things at you.'

'They hadn't done it then,' said Marcus patiently. 'They've only just invented it.'

Will was beginning to lose his temper; if he'd had any sweets to hand he would have started flinging them at Marcus himself. 'Marcus, for Christ's sake, I'm not talking about the bloody sweets. Are you always this bloody literal-minded? I understand that they've never done that before. But they've been giving you a hard time for ages.'

'Oh yeah. Not those two ...'

'No, OK, OK, not those two. But others like them.'

'Yeah. Loads.'

'Right. That's all I've been trying to find out.'

'You could have just asked.'

Will walked into the kitchen and put the kettle on, if only to give himself something to do which wouldn't result in a prison sentence, but he couldn't let it drop.

'So what are you going to do about it?'

'How do you mean?'

'Are you going to let it go on like this for the next however many years?'

'You're like the teachers at school.'

'What do they say?'

'Oh, you know. "Keep out of their way." I mean, I don't try to get in their way.'

'But it must make you unhappy.'

▷ **4** *obscure:* difficult to understand **5** *bravado:* bold behaviour **12** *bring back … and so on and so forth:* (here) reference to statements made by older people · *National Service:* period of compulsory service in the armed forces **18** *poised:* held carefully in a particular position **19** *distress* (n): great worry **20** *bully sb.:* give sb. younger or weaker than you a difficult time **24** *embed sth. into sth. else:* fix sth. in sth. else **30** *chuck sth.* (infml): throw sth. **48** *lose your temper:* become angry and start shouting **51** *literal-minded:* following or understanding only the exact meaning of sth.

'I s'pose so. I just don't think about it. Like when I broke my wrist falling off that climbing-frame thing.'

'You've lost me.'

'I tried not to think about that. It happened and I wished it hadn't, but it's just life, isn't it?'

Sometimes Marcus sounded as though he were a hundred years old, and it broke Will's heart.

'It doesn't have to be life, though, does it?'

'I dunno. You tell me. I haven't done anything. I just started at a new school and then I got all this. I don't know why.'

'What about your old school?'

'It was different there. Not every kid was the same. There were clever ones and thick ones and trendy ones and weird ones. I didn't feel different there. Here I feel different.'

'They can't be different sorts of kids here. Kids are kids.'

'So where are all the weird ones, then?'

'Maybe they start off weird, and then they get their act together. They're still weird but you just can't see them. The trouble is, these kids can see you. You make yourself obvious.'

'So I've got to make myself invisible?' Marcus snorted at the magnitude of the task. 'How do I do that? Is one of the machines in your kitchen an invisible machine?'

'You don't have to make yourself invisible. You just have to go in disguise.'

'What, with a moustache and stuff?

'Yeah, right, with a moustache. Nobody would notice a twelve-year-old boy with a moustache, would they?'

Marcus looked at him. 'You're joking. Everyone would notice. I'd be the only one in the whole school.'

Will had forgotten about the sarcasm thing. 'OK, no moustache, then. Bad idea. But how about if you wore the same clothes and haircut and glasses as everyone else? You can be as weird as you want on the inside. Just do something about the outside.'

They started with his feet. Marcus wore the kind of shoes that Will didn't think they made any more, plain black slip-ons whose only discernible ambition was to get their owner up and down school corridors without attracting the attention of the deputy head.

'Do you like those shoes?' Will asked him. They were walking up Holloway Road to look at trainers. Marcus peered down at his feet through the early-evening gloom and promptly collided with a large woman carrying several over-stuffed Lo-Cost bags.

'How do you mean?'

'I mean, do you like them?'

'They're my school shoes. I'm not supposed to like them.'

'You can like everything you wear, if you can be bothered.'

'Do you like everything you wear?'

'I don't wear anything I hate.'

'What do you do with the stuff you hate, then?'

'I don't buy it, do I?'

'Yeah, because you haven't got a mum. Sorry to say it like that, but you haven't.'

'It's OK. I've got used to the idea.'

The trainer shop was huge and crowded, and the lighting made all the customers look ill; everyone had a green tinge, regardless of their original colour. Will caught sight of the pair of them in a mirror, and was shocked to see that they could easily pass for father and son; he had somehow imagined himself as Marcus's elder brother, but the reflection threw age and youth into sharp relief – Will's stubble and crow's feet versus Marcus's smooth cheeks and gleaming white teeth. And the hair ... Will prided himself on having avoided even the tiniest of bald patches, but he still had less on top than Marcus, almost as if life had worn some of it away.

'What do you fancy?'

'I don't know.'

'It's got to be Adidas, I think.'

'Why?'

'Because that's what everyone wears.'

▷ **1** *wrist* [rɪst]: Handgelenk **2** *climbing-frame:* Klettergerüst **21** *magnitude:* largeness **23–24** *in disguise:* not recognizeable **35** *slip-ons* (pl): shoes without laces or a fastening **36** *discernible:* noticeable **40** *gloom:* darkness **41** *Lo-Cost:* brand name of a chain of bargain stores **54** *tinge* (n): small amount of a particular colour **58** *throw sth. into relief:* make sth. more noticeable because it is next to its opposite · *stubble:* the short hairs on a man's face when he has not shaved **59** *versus:* against · *gleam:* shine **61** *bald* [bɔːld]: having no hair · *patch:* spot, area

The shoes were displayed according to manufacturer, and the Adidas section of the shop was attracting more than its fair share of shoppers.

'Sheep,' said Marcus as they were approaching. 'Baaaa.'

'Where did you get that from?'

'That's what my mum says when she thinks people haven't got a mind of their own.'

Will suddenly remembered that a boy at his old school had had a mum like Fiona – not exactly like her, because it seemed to Will that Fiona was a peculiarly contemporary creation, with her seventies albums, her eighties politics and her nineties foot lotion, but certainly a sixties equivalent of Fiona. Stephen Fullick's mother had a thing about TV, that it turned people into androids, so they didn't have a set in the house. 'Did you see *Thund* ...' Will would say every Monday morning and then remember and blush, as if the TV were a parent who had just died. And what good had that done Stephen Fullick? He was not, as far as Will was aware, a visionary poet, or a primitive painter; he was probably stuck in some provincial solicitor's office, like everyone else from school. He had endured years of pity for no discernible purpose.

'The whole idea of this expedition, Marcus, is that you learn to become a sheep.'

'Is it?'

'Of course. You don't want anyone to notice you. You don't want to look different. Baaaa.'

Will picked out a pair of Adidas basketball boots that looked cool but relatively unshowy.

'What do you think of them?'

'They're sixty pounds.'

'Never mind how much they cost. What do you think of them?'

'Yeah, good.'

Will grabbed an assistant and asked him to bring the right size, and Marcus stomped up and down for a while. He looked at himself in the mirror and tried to repress a smile.

'You think you look cool, don't you?' said Will.

'Yeah. Except ... except now the rest of me looks all wrong.'

'So next time we'll make the rest of you look OK.'

Marcus went straight home afterwards, his boots stuffed into his school bag; Will walked back beaming at his own munificence. So this was what people meant by a natural high! He couldn't recall having felt like this before, so at peace with himself, so convinced of his own self-worth. And, unbelievably, it had only cost him sixty quid! How much would he have had to pay for an equivalent unnatural high? (Probably about twenty-five quid, thinking about it, but unnatural highs were indisputably inferior.) He had made an unhappy boy temporarily happy, and there hadn't been anything in it for him at all. He didn't even want to sleep with the boy's mother.

The following day Marcus turned up at Will's door, tearful, a pair of soggy black socks where his Adidas basketball boots should have been; they'd stolen them, of course.

▷ **12–13** *have a thing about sth.* (infml): (here) have a dislike of sth. **13** *android* ['ændrɔɪd]: robot that looks like a human **18** *solicitor:* lawyer **27** *unshowy:* not attracting much attention **39** *munificence* [mjuː'nɪfɪsəns]: generosity

Seventeen

Marcus would have told his mum where the trainers had come from, if she'd asked, but she didn't because she didn't even notice he was wearing them. OK, his mum wasn't the most observant person in the world, but the trainers seemed so big and white and peculiar and attention-seeking that Marcus felt as though he wasn't wearing shoes at all, but something alive – a pair of rabbits, maybe.

But she noticed they had gone. Typical. She didn't notice the rabbits, which you never see on feet, but she spotted the socks, which were only where they should be.

'Where are your shoes?' she shrieked when he came home. (Will had given him a lift, but it was November, and wet, and during the short walk across the pavement and up the stairs to the front door of the flats he had soaked his socks through again.) He looked at his feet, and for a moment he didn't say anything: he toyed with the idea of acting all surprised and telling her he didn't know, but he quickly realized she wouldn't believe him.

'Stolen,' he said eventually.

'Stolen? Why would anyone steal your shoes?'

'Because ...' He was going to have to tell the truth, but the problem was that the truth would lead to a whole lot more questions. 'Because they were nice ones.'

'They were just ordinary black slip-on shoes.'

'No, they weren't. They were new Adidas trainers.'

'Where did you get new Adidas trainers from?'

'Will bought them for me.'

'Will who? Will the guy who took us out to lunch?'

'Yeah, Will. The bloke from SPAT. He's sort of become my friend.'

'He's sort of become your friend?'

Marcus was right. She had loads more questions, except the way she asked them was a bit boring: she just repeated the last thing he said, stuck a question mark on the end of it and shouted.

'I go round his flat after school.'

'YOU GO ROUND HIS FLAT AFTER SCHOOL?'

Or:

'Well, you see, he doesn't really have a kid.'

'HE DOESN'T REALLY HAVE A KID?'

And so on. Anyway, at the end of the question session he was in a lot of trouble, although probably not as much trouble as Will.

Marcus put his old shoes back on, and then he and his mother went straight back to Will's flat. Fiona started raging at Will the moment they had been invited in and, at the beginning, when she was having a go at him about SPAT and his imaginary son he looked embarrassed and apologetic – he had no answers to any of her questions, so he stood there staring at the floor. But as it went on he started to get angry too.

'OK,' Fiona was saying. 'Now what the hell are these little after-school tea parties about?'

'I'm sorry?'

'Why would a grown man want to hang out with a twelve-year-old boy day after day?'

Will looked at her. 'Are you suggesting what I think you're suggesting?'

'I'm not suggesting anything.'

'I don't think that's true, is it? You're suggesting that I've been … fiddling with your son.'

Marcus looked at Fiona. Was that really what she was on about? Fiddling?

'I'm simply asking why you entertain twelve-year-olds in your flat.'

Will lost his temper. He went red in the face and started shouting very loud. 'I don't have any fucking choice, do I? Your son comes round fucking uninvited every night. Sometimes he's pursued by

▷ **10** *shriek* [ʃriːk] (v): scream in a high-pitched voice **13** *soak sth. through:* make sth. completely wet **14** *toy with sth.:* consider sth. (esp. an idea) but not seriously or for a long time **37** *session*: period **43** *apologetic:* sorry **55** *fiddle with sb.:* (here) touch sb. sexually gangs of savages. I could leave him outside to take his chances, but I've been letting him in for his own safety. I won't fucking bother next time. Sod the pair of you. Now, if you've finished, you can piss off.'

'I haven't finished yet, actually. Why did you buy him a pair of expensive trainers?'

'Because ... because look at him.' They looked at him. Marcus even looked at himself.

'What's wrong with him?'

Will looked at her. 'You haven't got a clue, have you? You really haven't got a clue.'

'About what?'

'Marcus is being eaten alive at school, you know. They take him to pieces every single fucking day of the week, and you're worried about where his trainers come from and whether I'm molesting him.'

Marcus suddenly felt exhausted. He hadn't properly realized how bad things were until Will started shouting, but it was true, he really was being taken to pieces every single fucking day of the week. Up until now he hadn't linked the days of the week in that way: each day was a bad day, but he survived by kidding himself that each day was somehow unconnected to the day before. Now he could see how stupid that was, and how shit everything was, and he wanted to go to bed and not get up until the weekend.

'Marcus is doing fine,' his mother said. At first he didn't believe she'd said it, and then, when he'd had a chance to listen to the words ringing in his ears, he tried to find a different meaning for them. Maybe there was another Marcus? Maybe there was something else he was doing fine at, something he'd forgotten about? But of course there was no other Marcus, and he wasn't doing fine at anything; his mum was just being blind and stupid and nuts.

'You're kidding,' said Will.

'I know he's taking some time to settle at his new school, but – '

Will laughed. 'Yeah. Give him a couple of weeks and he'll be OK, eh? Once they've stopped stealing his shoes and following him home from school everything'll be great.'

That was wrong. They were all mad. 'I don't think so,' said Marcus. 'It's going to take longer than a couple of weeks.'

'It's OK, I know,' said Will. 'I was joking.'

Marcus didn't think it was the sort of conversation that jokes fitted into, but at least it meant that someone understood what was going on. How come it was Will, though, whom he'd known for two minutes, and not his mum, whom he'd known for, well, all his life?

'I think you're being a bit melodramatic,' said Fiona. 'Maybe you haven't had very much contact with kids before.'

Marcus didn't know what the 'melo' bit of 'melodramatic' meant, but it made Will even angrier.

'I used to be a fucking kid,' said Will. He was swearing a lot now. 'And I used to go to a fucking school. I know the difference between kids who can't settle down and kids who are just plain miserable, so don't give me any shit about being melodramatic. I'm supposed to take this from someone who – '

'Ow!' Marcus shouted. 'Cowabunga!'

They both stared at him and he stared back. He had no way of explaining his outburst; he had made the first two noises he could think of, because he could see that Will was going to bring up the subject of the hospital, and he didn't want that. It wasn't fair. Just because his mum was being dim, it didn't mean that Will had the right to have a go at her about that. The way he saw it the hospital stuff was more serious than the sweets and trainers stuff, and no one should mix them in together.

'What's wrong with you?' asked Will.

Marcus shrugged. 'Nothing. Just … I don't know. Wanted to have a shout.'

Will shook his head. 'Jesus,' he said. 'What a family.'

Marcus hadn't enjoyed the afternoon's rows, but when they had finished he could see the point of them. His mum knew about Will not having a kid, which was probably a good thing, and she knew that he visited Will after school most days, which was also a good thing, probably, because he'd had to tell her a lot of fibs recently, and he'd been feeling bad about it. And, most importantly, she knew about what went on at school, because Will had spelt it out. Marcus hadn't been able to spell it out, because he'd never been able to see the whole word before, but it didn't really matter who'd done it; the point was that Fiona understood.

▷ **3** *sod sb.* (vulg): used when you are annoyed about sb. **9** *have a clue:* know what is going on **12–13** *take sb. to pieces:* jdm. fertig machen **14** *molest sb.:* attack sb. sexually **42** *melodramatic:* overreacting in an emotional way **68** *fib* (n): lie about sth. unimportant **71** *spell sth. out:* explain sth. clearly

'You're not going round there again,' she said on the way home.

Marcus knew she'd say it, and he also knew that he'd take no notice, but he argued anyway.

'Why not?'

'If you've got anything to say, you say it to me. If you want new clothes, I'll get them.'

'But you don't know what I need.'

'So tell me.'

'I don't know what I need. Only Will knows what I need.'

'Don't be ridiculous.'

'It's true. He knows what things kids wear.'

'Kids wear what they put on in the mornings.'

'You know what I mean.'

'You mean that he thinks he's trendy, and that even though he's God knows how old he knows which trainers are fashionable, even though he doesn't know the first thing about anything else.'

That was exactly what he meant. That was what Will was good at, and Marcus thought he was lucky to have found him.

'We don't need that kind of person. We're doing all right our way.'

Marcus looked out of the bus window and thought about whether this was true, and decided it wasn't, that neither of them were doing all right, whichever way you looked at it.

'If you are having trouble it's nothing to do with what shoes you wear, I can tell you that for nothing.'

'No, I know, but – '

'Marcus, trust me, OK? I've been your mother for twelve years. I haven't made too bad a job of it. I do think about it. I know what I'm doing.'

Marcus had never thought of his mother in that way before, as someone who knew what she was doing. He had never thought that she didn't have a clue either; it was just that what she did with him (for him? to him?) didn't appear to be anything like that. He had always looked on being a mother as straightforward, something like, say, driving: most people could do it, and you could mess it up by doing something really obvious, by driving your car into a bus, or not telling your kid to say please and thank you and sorry (there were loads of kids at school, he reckoned, kids who stole and swore too much and bullied other kids, whose mums and dads had a lot to answer for). If you looked at it that way, there wasn't an awful lot to think about. But his mum seemed to be saying that there was more to it than that. She was telling him she had a plan.

If she had a plan, then he had a choice. He could trust her, believe her when she said she knew what she was doing; that meant putting up with things at school because they'd turn out all right in the end and she could see things he couldn't. Or he could decide that, actually, she was off her head, someone who took drug overdoses and then apparently forgot all about them afterwards. Either way it was scary. He didn't want to put up with things as they were, but the other choice meant that he'd have to be his own mother, and how could you be your own mother when you were only twelve? He could tell himself to say sorry and please and thank you, that was easy, but he didn't know where to start with the rest of it. He didn't even know what the rest of it was. He hadn't even known until today that there was a rest of it.

Every time he thought about this, it came back to the same problem: there were only two of them, and at least – *at least* – one of them was nuts.

In the next few days he began to notice more things about the way Fiona talked to him. Everything she said about what he could and should watch or listen to or read or eat made him curious: was this part of the plan, or was she just making it up as she went along? It never occurred to him to ask her until she told him to go to the shops to get some eggs for their dinner: it struck him that he was a vegetarian only because she was too.

'Did you always know I was going to be a vegetarian?'

She laughed. 'Of course I did. I didn't decide on the spur of the moment because we'd run out of sausages.'

'And do you think that's fair?'

'How do you mean?'

'Shouldn't I have been allowed to make up my own mind?'

'You can when you're older.'

'Why aren't I old enough now?'

'Because you don't do your own cooking. I don't want to cook meat, so you have to eat what I eat.'

▷ **46** *be off your head* (infml): be crazy **63** *strike sb.:* come into sb.'s mind suddenly **66–67** *on the spur of the moment:* suddenly, without planning in advance

'But you don't let me go to McDonald's either.'

'Is this premature teenage rebellion? I can't stop you going to McDonald's.'

'Really?'

'How can I? I'd just be disappointed if you did.'

Disappointed. Disappointment. That was how she did it. That was how she did a lot of things.

'Why?'

'I thought you were vegetarian because you believed in it.'

'I do.'

'Well, you can't go to McDonald's then, can you?'

She'd done him again. She always told him he could do what he wanted, and then argued with him until what he wanted was what she wanted anyway. It was beginning to make him angry.

'That's not fair.'

She laughed. 'That's what life is, Marcus. You have to work out what you believe in, and then you have to stick to it. It's hard, but it's not unfair. And at least it's easy to understand.'

There was something wrong with this, but he didn't know what. All he knew was that not everyone thought like this. When they talked in class about things like smoking, everyone agreed it was bad, but then loads of kids smoked; when they talked about violent films, everyone said they disapproved of them, but they still watched them. They thought one thing and did another. In Marcus's house it was different. They decided what was bad and then they never touched it or did it again. He could see how that made sense: he thought stealing was wrong and killing was wrong, and he didn't steal things or kill people. So was that all there was to it? He wasn't sure.

But of all the things that made him different, he could see this was the most important. It was why he wore clothes that other kids laughed at – because they'd had this talk about fashion, and they'd agreed that fashion was stupid – and why he listened to music that was old-fashioned, or that no one else had ever heard of – because they'd had this talk about modern pop music, and they'd agreed it was just a way for record companies to make a lot of money. It was why he wasn't allowed to play violent computer games, or eat hamburgers, or do this or that or the other. And he'd agreed with her about all of it, except he hadn't agreed really; he'd just lost the arguments.

'Why don't you just tell me what to do? Why do we always have to talk about it?'

'Because I want to teach you to think for yourself.'

'Was that your plan?'

'What plan?'

'When you said the other day that you knew what you were doing.'

'About what?'

'About being a mum.'

'Did I say that?'

'Yeah.'

'Oh. OK. Well, of course I want you to think for yourself. All parents want that.'

'But all that happens is we have an argument and I lose, and I do what you want me to do. We might as well save time. Just tell me what I'm not allowed, and leave it at that.'

'So what's brought all this on?'

'I've been thinking for myself.'

'Good for you.'

'I've been thinking for myself, and I want to go round to Will's house after school.'

'You've already lost that argument.'

'I need to see someone else who's not you.'

'What about Suzie?'

'She's like you. Will's not like you.'

'No. He's a liar, and he doesn't do anything, and – '

'He bought me those trainers.'

'Yes. He's a rich liar who doesn't do anything.'

'He understands about school and that. He knows things.'

'He knows things! Marcus, he doesn't even know he's born.'

'You see what I mean?' He was getting really frustrated now. 'I'm thinking for myself and you just ... it just doesn't work. You win anyway.'

'Because you're not backing it up. It's not enough to tell me that you're thinking for yourself. You've got to show me, too.'

'How do I show you?'

'Give me a good reason.'

▷ **2** *premature:* earlier than expected

He could give her a reason. It wouldn't be the right reason, and he'd feel bad saying it, and he was pretty sure it would make her cry. But it was a good reason, a reason that would shut her up, and if that was how you had to win arguments, then he'd use it.

'Because I need a father.'

It shut her up, and it made her cry. It did the job.

Eighteen

November the nineteenth. November the fucking nineteenth. That was definitely a new record, Will noted darkly. Last year it had been November the fucking twenty-sixth. He hadn't made it through into December for years now; he could see that when he was fifty or sixty he'd be hearing his first rendition of 'Santa's Super Sleigh' in July or August. This year it was a busker at the bottom of the escalator at the Angel station, a cheerful, attractive young woman with a violin who was obviously trying to supplement her music scholarship. Will scowled at her with all the hatred he could muster, a look intended to convey not only that he wouldn't be giving her any money, but that he would like to smash up her instrument and then staple her head to the escalator steps.

Will hated Christmas, for the obvious reason: people knocked on his door, singing the song he hated more than any song in the world and expected him to give them money. It had been worse when he was a kid, because his dad hated Christmas too, for the obvious reason (although Will hadn't realized it was the obvious reason until he was much older – back then, he just thought that his dad was as sick of the song as everybody else): it was a terrible reminder of how badly he had failed in his life. Quite often people wanted to interview his father about 'Santa's Super Sleigh', and they always used to ask what else he

▷ **9–10** *make it through into sth.:* successfully reach sth. **11** *rendition:* performance **12** *busker:* street musician **13** *Angel station:* Underground station in north London **14** *supplement sth.:* add extra money to sth. **15** *scowl at sb.* [skaʊl]: show your dislike for sb. by your facial expression **18** *staple sth. to sth.:* fasten sth. to sth. with a stapler (= Tacker) had written, and he would tell them, sometimes even play them things, or show them records which featured another of his songs. They would look embarrassed, cluck sympathetically and tell him how hard it was for everyone who was famous for only one thing, a long time ago, and ask him whether the song had ruined his life, or made him wish he'd never written it. He would get angry, and tell them not to be so stupid and patronizing and insensitive, and when they had gone, he would complain bitterly that the song had ruined his life, and say he wished he'd never written it. One radio journalist even went away and made a series called *One-Hit Wonders* inspired completely by his interview with Charles Freeman, all about people who'd written one great book, or appeared in one film, or written one famous song; the journalist had had the cheek to ask him for another interview and, perhaps understandably, Will's father had refused.

So Christmas was the season of anger and bitterness and regret and recrimination, of drinking binges, of frantic and laughably inadequate industry (one Christmas day his father wrote an entire, and entirely useless, musical, in a doomed attempt to prove that his talent was durable). It was a season of presents by the chimney too, but even when he was nine Will would gladly have swapped his Spirographs and his Batmobiles for a little peace and goodwill.

But things changed. His father died, and then his mother, and he lost touch with his stepbrother and stepsister, who were old and dull anyway, and Christmas was usually spent with friends, or girlfriends' families, and all that was left was 'Santa's Super Sleigh' and the cheques it carried to him through the snow. But that was more than enough. Will had often wondered whether there was any other stupid song which contained, somewhere deep within it, as much pain and despair and regret. He doubted it. Bob Dylan's ex-wife probably didn't listen to *Blood On The Tracks* too often, but *Blood On The Tracks* was different – it was about misery and damage. 'Santa's Super Sleigh' wasn't supposed to be like that at all, but he still felt he needed a stiff drink, or counselling, or a good cry, when he heard it in a department-store lift or through a supermarket tannoy in the weeks leading up to 25 December. Maybe there were others like him somewhere; maybe he should form a Successful Novelty Song support group, where rich, bitter men and women would sit around in expensive restaurants and talk about doggies and birdies and bikinis and milkmen and horrible dances.

He had no plans for this Christmas whatsoever. There was no girlfriend, and so there were no girlfriend's parents, and though he had friends on whom he could inflict himself, he didn't feel like it. He would sit at home and watch millions of films and get drunk and stoned. Why not? He was as entitled to a break as anyone else, even if there was nothing to break from.

If the first thing he had thought of when he heard the busker at the tube station was his father, the unexorcizable ghost of Christmas past, the second was Marcus. He didn't know why. He hadn't thought about him much since the trainers' incident, and he'd had no contact with him since Fiona dragged him out of the flat the previous week. Maybe it was because Marcus was the only child he really knew, although Will doubted whether he was soppy enough to swallow the repulsive notion that Christmas was a time for children; the more likely explanation was that he had made some kind of link between Marcus's childhood and his own. It wasn't as if Will had been a nerdy kid with the wrong trainers; on the contrary, he had worn the right shoes and the right socks and the right trousers and the right shirts, and he had gone to the right hairdresser for the right haircut. That was the point of fashion, as far as Will was concerned; it meant that you were with the cool and the powerful, and against the alienated and the weak, just where Will wanted to be, and he'd successfully avoided being bullied by bullying furiously and enthusiastically.

But there was more than a whiff of the Freeman household in Fiona's flat: you got that same sense of hopelessness and defeat and bewilderment and straightforward lunacy. Of course, Will had grown

▷ **3** *cluck* (v): express understanding by making a noise with youir tongue **13** *have the cheek to do sth.:* do sth. that is lacking respect **16** *recrimination:* accusations · *binge* (infml): period spent doing sth. in excess · *laughable:* ridiculous **17** *industry:* hard work **18** *doomed:* certain to fail **19** *durable:* lasting **21** *Spirograph:* toy instrument that allows you to draw things by using circles · *Batmobile:* car used by the comic and film figure Batman **33** *stiff:* containing a lot of alcohol **34** *tannoy:* system of loud speakers in a shop, etc. **36** *Novelty Song:* song that becomes famous for one particular unusual line or aspect **44** *stoned* (infml): high on drugs, esp. marijuana · *be entitled to sth.:* have the right to sth. **47** *unexorcizable* [ˌʌn'eksɔːsaɪzəbl]: (esp. of a ghost) that cannot be removed from a place · *ghost of Christmas past:* reference to Charles Dickens's *Christmas Carol* (1843), in which the ghost of Christmas past shows Ebenezer Scrooge visions of his youth **53** *repulsive:* horrible and disgusting **62** *whiff:* sign, hint; faint smell **64** *bewilderment* [bɪ'wɪldəmənt]: total confusion up with money and Marcus had none, but you didn't need dosh to be dysfunctional. So what if Charles Freeman had killed himself with expensive malt whisky, and Fiona had tried to kill herself with National Health tranquillizers? The two of them would still have found plenty to talk about at parties.

Will didn't like the connection he had made very much, because it meant that if he had any decency in him at all he would have to take Marcus under his wing, use his own experience of growing up with a batty parent to guide the boy through to a place of safety. He didn't want to do that, though. It was too much work, and involved too much contact with people he didn't understand and didn't like, and he preferred watching *Countdown* on his own anyway.

But he had forgotten that he seemed to have no control over his relationship with Marcus and Fiona. On November the fucking twentieth, the day after November the fucking nineteenth, when he had more or less decided that Marcus would have to get by without his help, Fiona rang and started saying mad things down the phone.

'Marcus doesn't need a father, and he certainly doesn't need a father like you,' she said. Will was lost even before they'd started. At this point in the conversation he had contributed an admittedly guarded but otherwise entirely unprovocative, 'Hello, how are you?'

'I'm sorry?'

'Marcus seems to think he needs adult male company. A father figure. And somehow your name came up.'

'Well, I can tell you, Fiona, I didn't put him up to it. I don't need junior male company, and I definitely don't need a son figure. So, fine. You and I are in complete agreement.'

'So you won't see him even if he wants to see you?'

'Why doesn't he use his father as a father figure? Isn't that the easiest solution, or am I being dim?'

'His father lives in Cambridge.'

'What, Cambridge, Australia? Cambridge, California? Presumably we're not talking about the Cambridge just up the M11?'

'Marcus can't drive up the M11. He's twelve.'

'Hold on, hold on. You phoned up to tell me to keep out of Marcus's way. I told you that I had no intention of getting in Marcus's way. And now you're telling me ... What? I missed a bit somewhere.'

'You just seem very keen to be shot of him.'

'So you're *not* telling me to leave him alone. You're telling me to apply for custody.'

'Are you incapable of conducting a conversation without resorting to sarcasm?'

'Just explain to me clearly and simply, without changing your mind halfway through, what you want me to do.'

She sighed. 'Some things are a little more complicated than that, Will.'

'Is that what you phoned me up to tell me? Because I got the wrong end of the stick early on, I think, during the bit about how I was the most unsuitable man in the world.'

'You're really not very easy to deal with.'

'So don't deal with me!' He was nearly shouting now. He was certainly angry. They had been talking for less than three minutes, yet he was beginning to feel as though this telephone conversation was going to be his life's work; that once every few hours he would put the receiver down to eat and sleep and go to the toilet, and the rest of the time Fiona would be telling him one thing and then its opposite over and over again. 'Just put the phone down! Hang up on me! I really won't be offended!'

'I think we need to talk about this properly, don't you?'

'What? What do we need to talk about properly?'

'This whole thing.'

'There isn't a whole thing. There isn't even a half thing!'

'Are you free for a drink tomorrow night? Maybe it would be better to talk face to face. We're not getting anywhere here.'

There was no point in fighting her. There wasn't even any point in not fighting her. They made arrangements to meet for a drink, and it was a mark of Will's frustration and confusion that he was able to look on the agreement of a time and a place as a resounding triumph.

▷ **1** *dosh* (sl): money **2** *dysfunctional:* (of a relationship) not working normally **4** *National Health (System):* British medical system which provides free or cheap medical care to everybody · *tranquillizer:* medical drug that calms you **7–8** *take sb. under your wing:* protect sb., take care of sb. **33** *M11:* the motorway between London and Cambridge **38** *be shot of sb.* (infml): get rid of sb. **40** *custody:* legal right to take care of sb. **41–42** *resort to sth.:* end up making use of sth. **47–48** *get the wrong end of the stick:* completely misunderstand a situation **68** *resounding:* great

Will had never been alone with Fiona; up until now Marcus had always been there, telling them when to talk, and what to talk about – apart from the trainers day, when he was kind of telling them what to talk about, even though he wasn't saying anything. But when Will had got the drinks in – they went to a quiet pub off the Liverpool Road where they knew they would get a seat and be able to talk without competing against a juke-box, or a grunge band, or an alternative comedian – and sat down opposite Fiona, and ascertained, once again, without even meaning to, that he did not find her in the least attractive, he realized something else: he had been drinking in pubs for nearly twenty years and not once had he been to a pub with a woman in whom he had no sexual interest whatsoever. He thought again. Could that be right? OK, he'd carried on seeing Jessica, the ex, who always insisted he was missing out, after they had split up. But there had been sexual interest once upon a time, and he knew that if Jessica were ever to announce that she was looking for a discreet extra-marital affair, he would certainly apply for the job, put his name forward for consideration.

No, this was certainly a first for him, and he had no idea whether different rules applied in these situations. Obviously it would be neither appropriate nor sensible to take her by the hand and look into her eyes, or move the subject gently on to sex so that he could introduce a more flirtatious note into the proceedings. If he had no desire to sleep with Fiona, then of course there was no necessity to pretend that every single thing she said was interesting. But a strange thing happened: he was interested, mostly. Not in a well-I-never-knew-that kind of way, because even though Fiona probably knew a lot of things that Will didn't, he was almost sure that all of them would be very dull ... It was just that he was absorbed in the conversation. He listened to what she said, he thought about it, he answered. He couldn't remember the last time that had happened, so why was it happening now? Was it just sod's law – you don't fancy someone, so they're bound to be endlessly fascinating – or was something happening here that he should think about?

She was different today. She didn't want to tell him what a useless human being he was, and she didn't want to accuse him of molesting her son; it was almost as if she had decided that this was a relationship she was stuck with. Will didn't like the implications of that.

'I'm sorry about yesterday,' she said.

'That's OK.'

Will lit a cigarette, and Fiona made a face and wafted the smoke away. Will hated people who did that in places where they had no right to do so. He wasn't going to apologize for smoking in a pub; in fact, what he was going to do was single-handedly create a fug so thick that they would be unable to see each other.

'I was very upset when I called. When Marcus said he felt he needed some male input, I felt as though I'd been slapped round the face.'

'I can imagine.'

He didn't have a clue what she was talking about. Why would anyone take the blindest bit of notice of anything Marcus said?

'You know, it's the first thing you think of when you split up with the father of your son, that he's going to need a man around and so on. And then good feminist common sense takes over. But ever since Marcus has been old enough to understand we've talked about it, and every time he's assured me that it doesn't matter. And then yesterday it came right out of the blue ... He's always known how worried I am about that.'

Will didn't want to get involved in any of this. He didn't care whether Marcus needed a man in his life or not. Why should he? It wasn't his business, even though he seemed to be the man in question. He hadn't asked to be and, anyway, he was pretty sure that if Marcus did need a man, it wasn't his sort. But listening to Fiona now, he realized that in some respects at least he understood Marcus better than she did – possibly, he conceded reluctantly, because he was a man and Fiona wasn't, and possibly because Marcus was, in his own junior and eccentric way, a devious man. Will understood devious men.

'Well there you are then,' he said flatly.

'Where am I?'

'That's why he said it. Because he knew it would do the job.'

'What job?'

▷ **14** *miss out:* not have sth. that would be good for you **23** *proceedings* (pl): events that are taking place **41** *waft sth.:* move sth. gently through the air **44** *single-handedly:* without any help · *fug* (infml): bad air because of too much smoke **51** *blindest bit of notice:* any notice at all **65** *concede sth.:* admit sth. **67** *devious* ['diːviəs]: not straightforward, dishonest in order to get sth.

'Whatever job he wanted it to do at the time. I expect he's been saving it. That was his nuclear option. What were you arguing about?'

'I'd just reiterated my opposition to his relationship with you.'

'Oh.' That was very bad news. If Marcus was willing to go nuclear on his account, then he was in even deeper than he'd feared.

'Are you saying what I think you're saying? That he was attacking me in my most vulnerable spot just so he could win an argument?'

'Yeah. Course he was.'

'Marcus isn't capable of that.'

Will snorted. 'Whatever.'

'Do you really think so?'

'He's not daft.'

'It's not his intelligence I'm worried about. It's his ... emotional honesty.'

Will snorted again. He had intended to keep his thoughts to himself throughout this conversation, but they kept escaping through his nose. What planet did this woman live on? She was so unworldly that she seemed to him to be an unlikely suicidal depressive, even though she sang with her eyes closed: surely anyone who floated that high above everything was protected in some way? But of course that was part of the problem. They were sitting here because a twelve-year-old's craftiness had brought her crashing down to earth, and if Marcus could do it, any boyfriend or boss or landlord – any adult who didn't love her – could do it. There was no protection in that. Why did these people want to make things so hard for themselves? It was *easy*, life, easy-peasy, a matter of simple arithmetic: loving people, and allowing yourself to be loved, was only worth the risk if the odds were in your favour, but they quite clearly weren't. There were about seventy-nine squillion people in the world, and if you were very lucky, you would end up being loved by fifteen or twenty of them. So how smart did you have to be to work out that it just wasn't worth the risk? OK, Fiona had made the mistake of having a child, but it wasn't the end of the world. In her position, Will wouldn't let the little sod drag him under.

Fiona was looking at him. 'Why does everything I say make you do that?'

'What?'

'Make that snorting noise?'

‘I’m sorry. It’s just that ... I don’t know anything about, you know, stages of development and what kids should do when and all that. But I do know that it’s around now you shouldn’t trust anything a human male says about what he feels.’

Fiona looked bleakly at her Guinness.

‘And when does that stop, in your expert opinion?’ The last two words had a rusty serrated edge on them, but Will ignored it.

‘When he’s around seventy or eighty, and then he can use the truth at highly inappropriate moments to shock people.’

‘I’ll be dead then.’

‘Yup.’

She went to the bar to get him a drink, and then sat back down heavily in her seat. ‘But why you?’

‘I just told you. He doesn’t really need a male influence. He just said it to get his own way.’

‘I know, I know. I understand that. But why does he want to see you so much he’d do that to me?’

‘I don’t know.’

‘Do you really not know?’

‘Really.’

‘Maybe it is best if he doesn’t see you.’

Will said nothing. He had learnt something from the previous day’s conversation, anyway.

‘What do you think?’

‘I don’t.’

‘What?’

‘I don’t think. I don’t think anything. You’re his mother. You make the decisions.’

‘But you’re involved now. He keeps coming round to your house. You take him out to buy shoes. He’s living this whole life I can’t control, which means you have to.’

‘I’m not going to control anything.’

‘In which case, it’s best that he doesn’t see you.’

▷ **2** *nuclear:* (here) strongest **3** *reiterate sth.* [ri'ɪtəreɪt]: say sth. again **22** *craftiness:* cleverness, skill **26** *easy-peasy* (infml): very easy **27–28** *the odds are in your favour:* you are likely to win **29** *squillion:* (here) very large number **33** *sod* (sl): unpleasant person **33–34** *drag sb. under:* make sb. depressed **43** *bleakly* (adv): depressed **45** *serrated:* formed like the sharp edge of a saw

'We've been here before. What do you want me to do if he rings on the bell?'

'Don't let him in.'

'Fine.'

'I mean, if you're not prepared to think about how to help me, then keep out.'

'Right.'

'God, you're a selfish bastard.'

'But I'm on my own. There's just me. I'm not putting myself first, because there isn't anybody else.'

'Well, he's there too now. You can't just shut life out, you know.'

She was wrong, he was almost positive. You could shut life out. If you didn't answer the door to it, how was it going to get in?

Nineteen

Marcus didn't like the idea of his mum talking to Will. A while ago he would have got excited about it, but he no longer thought that he and his mum and Will and Ned and another baby perhaps were going to live together in Will's flat. For a start, Ned didn't exist, and for another start, if you could have two starts, Fiona and Will didn't like each other very much, and anyway Will's flat was nowhere near big enough for them all, even though there weren't as many of them as he had originally thought.

But now everyone knew too much, and there were too many things that he didn't want the two of them to talk about without him. He didn't want Will to talk to his mum about the hospital, in case it made her go funny again; and he didn't want Will to tell her about how he'd tried to blackmail Will into going out with her; and he didn't want his mum to talk about how much telly he was allowed to watch, in case Will started turning it off when he went round ... As far as he could tell, every possible topic of conversation meant trouble of some sort.

She was only gone for a couple of hours after tea time, so they didn't have to find a baby-sitter; he put the chain on the door, did his homework, watched a bit of TV, played on the computer and waited. At five past nine she buzzed the special buzz on the doorbell. He let her in, and stared at her face to try to work out just how angry or depressed she was, but she seemed OK.

'Did you have a good time?'

'It was OK.'

'What does that mean?'

'He's not a very nice man, is he?'

'I think he is. He bought me those trainers.'

'Well, you're not to go round any more.'

'You can't stop me.'

'No, but he's not going to answer the door, so it's a waste of time.'

'How do you know he's not going to answer the door?'

'Because he told me he wouldn't.'

Marcus could just hear Will saying that, but it didn't worry him. He knew how loud the buzzer was inside the flat, and he had the time to ring it and ring it and ring it.

Marcus had to go and see the headmistress about his trainers. His mum had made a complaint to the school, even though Marcus had told her, *begged* her, not to. They'd spent so long arguing about it that he ended up having to go days after the event. So now he had a choice: he could lie to the headmistress, tell her that he had no idea who had stolen his shoes, and make himself look stupid; or he could tell her and lose his shoes, jacket, shirt, trousers, underpants and probably an eye or a piece of ear on the way home. He couldn't see that he'd lose much sleep worrying about what to do.

He went at the beginning of lunch break, the time his form teacher had told him to go, but Mrs Morrison wasn't ready for him; he could hear her through the door, shouting at someone. He was on his own at first, but then Ellie McCrae, this sulky, scruffy girl from year ten who hacked off her own hair and wore black lipstick, sat down on the far end of the row of chairs outside the office. Ellie was famous. She was always in trouble for something or other, usually something quite bad.

They sat in silence for a bit, and then Marcus thought he'd try to talk to her; his mum was always on at him to talk to people at school.

'Hello, Ellie,' he said. She looked at him and laughed once under her breath, shook her head bitterly and then turned her face away. Marcus didn't mind. In fact, he almost laughed. He wished he had a video camera. He'd love to show his mum what happened when you tried to talk to another kid at school, especially an older kid, especially a girl. He wouldn't bother trying again.

'How come every squitty little shitty snotty bastard knows my name?'

Marcus couldn't believe she was talking to him, and when he looked at her it seemed as though he was right to be doubtful, because she was still looking the other way. He decided to ignore her.

'Oi, I'm talking to you. Don't be so fucking rude.'

'Sorry. I didn't think you were talking to me.'

'I don't see any other squitty little shitty bastards here, do you?'

'No,' Marcus admitted.

'So. How come you know my name? I haven't got a bloody clue who you are.'

'You're famous.' He knew that was a mistake as soon as he had said it.

'What am I famous for?'

'Dunno.'

'Yes you do. I'm famous because I'm always in trouble.'

'Yes.'

'Fucking hell.'

They sat there for a while longer. Marcus didn't feel like breaking the silence; if saying 'Hello, Ellie' caused that much trouble, then he wasn't about to ask her whether she'd had a nice weekend.

'I'm always in trouble, and I've never done anything wrong,' she said eventually.

'No.'

'How do you know?'

'Because you just said so.' Marcus thought that was a good answer. If Ellie McCrae said she hadn't done anything wrong, then she hadn't.

'If you're being cheeky, you'll get a slap.'

Marcus wished Mrs Morrison would hurry up. Even though he was prepared to believe that Ellie had never done anything wrong, ever, he could see why some people might think she had.

'Do you know what I've done wrong this time?'

'Nothing,' Marcus said firmly.

'OK, do you know what I'm supposed to have done wrong?'

'Nothing.' This was his line, and he was sticking to it.

'Well, they must think I've done something wrong, or I wouldn't be sitting here, would I?'

▷ **23** *sulky:* (here) bad-tempered · *scruffy:* untidy **24** *hack sth. off:* cut sth. off in a rough way **36** *squitty:* (here) insignificant · *snotty* (infml): (here) unpleasant **63** *cheeky:* rude · *slap* (n): act of hitting with the side of the hand

'No.'

'It's this sweatshirt. They don't want me to wear it, and I'm not going to take it off. So there's going to be a row.'

He looked at it. They were all supposed to wear sweatshirts with the school logo on them, but Ellie's showed a bloke with scraggy hair and half a beard. He had big eyes and looked a little bit like Jesus, except more modern and with bleached hair.

'Who's that?' he asked politely.

'You must know.'

'Ummm ... Oh, yes.'

'So who is it?'

'Ummm ... Forgotten.'

'You never knew it.'

'No.'

'That's incredible. That's like not knowing the name of the prime minister or something.'

'Yeah.' Marcus gave a little laugh, to show her that at least he knew how stupid he was, even if he didn't know anything else. 'Who is it, then?'

'Kirk O'Bane.'

'Oh, yes.'

He'd never heard of Kirk O'Bane, but he'd never heard of anybody.

'What does he do?'

'He plays for Manchester United.'

Marcus looked at the picture on the sweatshirt again, even though that meant sort of looking at Ellie's tits. He hoped she understood that he wasn't interested in her tits, only in the picture.

'Does he?' He looked much more like a singer than a footballer. Footballers weren't sad, usually, and this man looked sad. He wouldn't have thought that Ellie would be the sort of person who liked football, anyway.

'Yeah. He scored five goals for them last Saturday.'

'Wow,' said Marcus.

Mrs Morrison's door opened and two white-faced year sevens came out. 'Come in, Marcus,' said Mrs Morrison.

'Bye, Ellie,' said Marcus. Ellie went through her head-shaking routine again, still apparently bitter that her reputation had gone before her. Marcus wasn't looking forward to seeing Mrs Morrison, but if the alternative was sitting out in the corridor with Ellie, then he'd take the head's office any day of the week.

He lost his temper with Mrs Morrison. Bad idea, he could see afterwards, losing your temper with the headmistress of your new school, but he couldn't help it. She was being so thick that in the end he just had to shout. They started off OK: no, he'd never had any trouble from the shoe-stealers before, no, he didn't know who they were and no, he wasn't very happy at school (only one lie there). But then she started talking about what she called 'survival strategies', and that was when he got cross.

'I mean, I'm sure you've thought of this, but couldn't you just try keeping out of their way?'

Did they all think he was thick? Did they reckon that he woke up every morning thinking, I must find the people who call me names and give me shit and want to steal my trainers, so that they can do more things to me?

'I have tried.' That was all he could say for the moment. He was too frustrated to say any more.

'Maybe you haven't tried hard enough.'

That did it. She had said this not because she wanted to be helpful, but because she didn't like him. Nobody at this school liked him and he didn't understand why. He'd had enough, and he stood up to go.

'Sit down, Marcus. I haven't finished with you yet.'

'I've finished with you.'

He didn't know he was going to say that, and he was amazed when he had. He had never been cheeky to a teacher before, mostly because there hadn't been a need for it. Now he could see that he hadn't started in a great place. If you were going to get yourself into trouble, maybe it was best to work up to it slowly, get some practice in first. He had started right at the top, which was probably a mistake.

'SIT down.'

But he didn't. He just walked out the way he had come in, and kept on walking.

As soon as he left Mrs Morrison's office he felt different, better, as if he'd let go and he was now falling through space. It was an exciting

▷ **5** *scraggy:* messy **7** *bleached:* dyed blond **26** *tit* (sl): woman's breast **37** *reputation:* opinion other people have of you **47** *survival strategies:* (here) ways to keep yourself out of trouble **52** *call sb. names:* use rude words about sb.

feeling, really, and it was much better than the feeling of hanging on that he'd had before. He wouldn't have been able to describe it as 'hanging on' until just now, but that was definitely what it was. He'd been pretending that everything was normal – difficult, yes, but normal – but now he'd let go he could see it had been everything but normal. You don't get your shoes stolen *normally*. Your English teacher doesn't make out you're a nutter *normally*. You don't get boiled sweets thrown at your head *normally*. And that was just the school stuff.

And now he was a truant. He was walking down Holloway Road while everyone else at school was … actually, they were eating their lunch, but he wasn't going back. Soon he'd be walking down Holloway Road (well, not Holloway Road, probably, because he was almost at the end of it already, and lunch would go on for another thirty minutes yet) during history, and then he'd be a proper truant. He wondered whether all truants started like that, whether there was always a Mrs Morrison moment which made them blow their top and leave. He supposed there had to be. He'd always presumed that truants were different sort of people entirely, not like him at all, that they'd been born truants, sort of thing, but he was obviously wrong. In May, before they moved to London, when he was in his last term at his old school, he wasn't a truant kind of person in any way whatsoever. He turned up at school, listened to what people said, did his homework, took part. But six months later that had all changed, bit by bit.

It was probably like that for tramps, too, he realized. They walked out of their house one evening and thought, I'll sleep in this shop doorway tonight, and when you'd done it once, something changed in you, and you became a tramp, rather than someone who didn't have anywhere to sleep for one night. And the same with criminals! And drug addicts! And … He decided to stop thinking about it all then. If he carried on, walking out of Mrs Morrison's office might begin to look like the moment his whole life changed, and he wasn't sure he was ready for that. He wasn't someone who wanted to become a truant or a tramp or a murderer or a drug addict. He was just someone who was fed up with Mrs Morrison. There had to be a difference.

Twenty

Will loved driving around London. He loved the traffic, which allowed him to believe he was a man in a hurry and offered him rare opportunities for frustration and anger (other people did things to let off steam, but Will had to do things to build it up); he loved knowing his way around; he loved being swallowed up in the flow of the city's life. You didn't need a job or a family to drive around London; you only needed a car, and Will had a car. Sometimes he just drove for the hell of it, and sometimes he drove because he liked to hear music played at a volume that would not be possible in the flat without a furious knock on the door or the wall or the ceiling.

Today he had convinced himself that he had to drive to Waitrose, but if he was honest the real reason for the trip was that he wanted to sing along to 'Nevermind' at the top of his voice, and he couldn't do that at home. He loved Nirvana, but at his age they were kind of a guilty pleasure. All that rage and pain and self-hatred! Will got a bit … *fed up* sometimes, but he couldn't pretend it was anything stronger than that. So now he used loud angry rock music as a replacement for real feelings, rather than as an expression of them, and he didn't even mind very much. What good were real feelings anyway?

The cassette had just turned itself over when he saw Marcus ambling down Upper Street. He hadn't seen him since the day of the

▷ **7** *make sth. out* (infml): imply sth. · *nutter* (infml): mad person **10** *truant:* pupil who stays away from school **17** *blow your top* (sl): lose your temper **26** *tramp:* homeless person **48** *Waitrose:* British chain of supermarkets **58** *amble:* walk slowly and in a relaxed way trainers, nor had he wanted to see him particularly, but he suddenly felt a little surge of affection for him. Marcus was so locked into himself, so oblivious to everyone and everything, that affection seemed to be the only possible response: the boy somehow seemed to be asking for absolutely nothing and absolutely everything all at the same time.

The affection that Will felt was not acute enough to make him want to stop the car, or even toot: he had discovered that it was much easier to sustain one's fondness for Marcus if one just kept one's foot down, literally and metaphorically. But it was funny, seeing him out in the street in broad daylight, wandering aimlessly ... Something nagged at him. Why was it funny? Because Will had never really seen Marcus in broad daylight before. He had only previously seen him in the gloom of a winter afternoon. And why had he only seen him in the gloom of a winter afternoon? Because Marcus only came round after school. But it was just after two o'clock. Marcus should be in school now. Bollocks.

Will wrestled with his conscience, grappled it to the ground and sat on it until he couldn't hear a squeak out of it. Why should he care if Marcus went to school or not? OK, wrong question. He knew very well why he should care whether Marcus went to school. Try a different question: *how much* did he care whether Marcus went to school or not? Answer: not a lot. That was better. He drove home.

At exactly 4.15, right in the middle of *Countdown*, the buzzer went. If Will hadn't seen Marcus bunking off this afternoon, the precision of the timing would have escaped his notice, but now it just seemed transparently obvious: Marcus had clearly decided that arriving at the flat before 4.15 would arouse suspicion, so he'd timed it to the second. It didn't matter, however; he wasn't going to answer the door.

Marcus buzzed again; Will ignored him again. On the third buzz he turned *Countdown* off and put *In Utero* on, in the hope that Nirvana might block out the sound more effectively than Carol Vorderman. By the time he got to 'Pennyroyal Tea', the eighth or ninth track, he'd had enough of listening to Kurt Cobain and Marcus: Marcus could obviously hear the music through the door, and was providing his own accompaniment by buzzing in time. Will gave up.

'You're not supposed to be here.'

'I came to ask you a favour.' Nothing in Marcus's face or voice suggested that he had been the least bit inconvenienced or bored during his thirty-odd minutes of buzzing.

They had a brief bout of leg-wrestling: Will was standing in Marcus's way, but Marcus managed to force his way into the flat regardless.

'Oh no, *Countdown*'s finished. Did that fat bloke get knocked out?'

'What favour do you want to ask me?'

'I want you to take me and a friend to football.'

'Your mum can take you.'

'She doesn't like football.'

'Neither do you.'

'I do now. I like Manchester United.'

'Why?'

'I like O'Bane.'

'Who the hell's O'Bane?'

'He scored five goals for them last Saturday.'

'They drew nil-nil at Leeds.'

'It was probably the Saturday before, then.'

'Marcus, there isn't a player called O'Bane.'

'I might have got it wrong. Something that sounds like that. He's got bleached hair and a beard and he looks like Jesus. Can I have a Coke?'

'No. There's nobody who plays for Man United with bleached hair and a beard who looks like Jesus.'

'Tell me some of their names.'

'Hughes? Cantona? Giggs? Sharpe? Robson?'

'No. O'Bane.'

'O'Kane?'

Marcus's face lit up. 'That must be it!'

▷ **3** *oblivious to sb./sth.:* not noticing sb./sth. **8** *toot:* make a sound with a car's horn **9** *sustain sth.:* continue doing or feeling sth. **11** *nag at sb.* (infml): make sb. feel worried or uneasy **17** *bollocks* (sl): expression of anger or annoyance **19** *squeak* (n): short high cry or noise **25** *bunk off* (infml): stay away from school **32–33** *Carol Vorderman:* presenter of *Countdown* **39** *inconvenienced:* troubled **41** *bout* [baʊt]: wrestling match **56** *draw – drew – drawn:* finish a match without a either team winning · *nil:* zero

'Used to play for Nottingham Forest about twenty-five years ago. Didn't look like Jesus. Didn't bleach his hair. Never scored five goals. How was school today?'

'OK.'

'How was the afternoon?'

Marcus looked at him, trying to work out why he might have asked the question.

'OK'

'What did you have?'

'History, and then … ummm …'

Will had intended to store the skiving up, just as Marcus had stored the Ned thing up, but now he had him wriggling on the hook he couldn't resist taking him off and making him swim round and round in the bucket.

'It's Wednesday today, isn't it?'

'Er … Yes.'

'Don't you have double walking up and down Upper Street on Wednesday afternoons?'

He could see Marcus beginning the slow descent towards panic.

'What do you mean?'

'I saw you this afternoon.'

'What, in school?'

'Well, I couldn't have seen you in school, Marcus, could I? Because you weren't there.'

'This afternoon?'

'Yes, this afternoon.'

'Oh, right. I had to nip out and get something.'

'You had to nip out? And they're all right about nipping out, are they?'

'Where did you see me?'

'I drove past you on Upper Street. I have to say, it didn't look as though you were nipping. It looked like you were skiving.'

'It was Mrs Morrison's fault.'

'Her fault that you had to nip out? Or her fault that you had to skive?'

'She told me to keep out of their way again.'

'You're losing me, Marcus. Who is Mrs Morrison?'

'The head. You know they always say when I get in trouble that I should keep out of their way? She said that about the training shoe kids.' His voice rose an octave, and he started to speak more quickly. 'They followed me! How can I keep out of their way if they follow me?'

'OK, OK, keep your hair on. Did you tell her that?'

'Course I did. She just didn't take any notice.'

'Right. So you go home and tell your mum this. It's no good telling me. And you've got to tell her that you bunked off as well.'

'I'm not telling her that. She's got enough problems without me.'

'Marcus, you're already a problem.'

'Why can't you go and see her? Mrs Morrison?'

'You're joking. Why should she take any notice of me?'

'She would. She – '

'Marcus, listen, I'm not your father, or your uncle, or your stepfather, or anybody at all. I'm nothing to do with you. No headmistress is going to take any notice of what I say, and nor should she, either. You've got to stop thinking I know the answer to anything, because I don't.'

'You know about things. You knew about the trainers.'

'Yeah, and what a triumph they were. I mean, they were a source of endless happiness, weren't they? You'd have been in school this afternoon if I hadn't bought you the trainers.'

'And you knew about Kirk O'Bane.'

'Who?'

'Kirk O'Bane.'

'The footballer?'

'Except I don't think he can be a footballer. Ellie was making one of those jokes that you make.'

'But his first name's Kirk?'

'I think so.'

'Kurt Cobain, you jerk.'

'Who's Kurt Cobain?'

'The singer with Nirvana.'

'I thought he must be a singer. Bleached hair? Looks a bit like Jesus?'

▷ **11** *skive* (infml): stay away from school without permission **11–12** *store sth. up:* put sth. away until you need it **12** *wriggle* ['rɪgl]: twist and turn with short movements · *hook:* curved piece of metal for catching fish **17** *double:* consisting of two lessons of the same subject **27** *nip out* (infml): go somewhere quickly **43** *keep your hair on* (infml): stay calm **69** *jerk* (sl): idiot

'I suppose so.'

'There you are, then,' said Marcus triumphantly. 'You knew about him, too.'

'Everyone knows about him.'

'I didn't.'

'No, you didn't. But you're different, Marcus.'

'And my mum wouldn't.'

'No, she wouldn't either.'

'You see, you know things. You can help.'

It was then, for the first time, that Will saw the kind of help Marcus needed. Fiona had given him the idea that Marcus was after a father figure, someone to guide him gently towards male adulthood, but that wasn't it at all: Marcus needed help to be a kid, not an adult. And, unhappily for Will, that was exactly the kind of assistance he was qualified to provide. He wasn't able to tell Marcus how to grow up, or how to cope with a suicidal mother, or anything like that, but he could certainly tell him that Kurt Cobain didn't play for Manchester United, and for a twelve-year-old boy attending a comprehensive school at the end of 1993, that was maybe the most important information of all.

Twenty-one

Marcus went back to school the following morning. Nobody seemed to have noticed that he hadn't been around the previous afternoon: his form teacher knew he'd had to go to see Mrs Morrison during afternoon registration, and Mr Sandford the history teacher never noticed him even when he was there. The other kids in the class might have worked out that he was bunking off, but as they never spoke to him anyway, how would he ever know?

He bumped into Ellie at breaktime at the vending machine. She was wearing her Kurt Cobain sweatshirt and standing with a friend from her class.

'Kurt Cobain doesn't play for Manchester United,' he told her. The girl from her class burst into hysterical laughter.

'Oh, no!' said Ellie, mock-horrified. 'Have they got rid of him?'

Marcus was confused for a moment – maybe Ellie really did think he was a footballer? But then he realized she was making one of those jokes he never got.

'Ha, ha,' he said, without laughing at all. That was what you were supposed to do, and he felt the thrill of having done something right for a change. 'No, he plays ... he sings for Nirvana.'

'Thanks for telling me.'

'That's OK. A friend of mine has got one of their records. *Nevermind.*'

'Everybody's got that one. I'll bet he hasn't got the new one.'

'He might have. He's got lots of stuff.'

▷ **33** *mock:* not real

'What year's he in? I didn't think anyone in this school like Nirvana.'

'He's left school. He's quite old. It's grunge, isn't it, Nirvana? I don't know what I think of grunge.' He didn't, either. Will had played him some Nirvana the previous evening, and he'd never heard anything quite like it. At first he hadn't been able to hear anything apart from noise and shouting, but there were some quiet bits, too, and in the end he had been able to make out a tune. He didn't think he'd ever like it as much as he liked Joni or Bob or Mozart, but he could sort of see why someone like Ellie might like it.

The two girls looked at each other and laughed louder than they had done the first time.

'And what do you think you might think of it?' asked Ellie's friend.

'Well,' said Marcus. 'It's a bit of a racket, but it's got a good beat, and the picture on the cover is very interesting.' It was a picture of a baby underwater, swimming after a dollar bill. Will had said something about the picture, but he couldn't remember what it was. 'I think the cover has a meaning. Something about society.'

The girls looked at him, looked at each other and laughed.

'You're very funny,' said Ellie's friend. 'Who are you?'

'Marcus.'

'Marcus. Cool name.'

'Do you think so?' Marcus hadn't thought about his name that much, but he'd never thought it was cool.

'No,' said Ellie's friend, and they laughed again. 'See you around, Marcus.'

'See you.'

It was the longest conversation he'd had with anyone at school for weeks.

'So we've scored,' said Will when Marcus told him about Ellie and her friend. 'I don't fancy yours much, though.'

Sometimes he didn't understand one word Will said, and when that happened Marcus just ignored him completely.

'They said I was funny.'

'You are funny. You're hilarious. But I don't know if it's much to build a whole relationship on.'

'Can I invite Ellie round?'

'I'm not sure she'd come, Marcus.'

'Why not?'

'Well ... I'm not sure that ... How old is she?'

'I dunno. Fifteen?'

'I'm not sure that fifteen-year-olds hang out with twelve-year-olds. I'll bet you her boyfriend is twenty-five, drives a Harley Davidson and works as a roadie for some band. He'd beat you up. He'd squash you like a bug, man.'

Marcus hadn't thought of that.

'I don't want to go out with her. I know she'd never go for someone like me. But we can come round here and listen to your Nirvana records, can't we?

'She's probably heard them already.'

Marcus was getting frustrated with Will. Why didn't he want him to make friends?

'OK, forget it, then.'

'I'm sorry. Marcus. I'm glad you spoke to Ellie today, I really am. But a two-minute conversation with someone who's taking the piss out of you ... I can't see that working out long-term, you know?'

Marcus wasn't really listening. Ellie and her friend had said he was funny, and if he could be funny once, he could be funny again.

He saw them by the vending machine the next day. They were leaning against it and saying things about anyone who had the nerve to come up and put money in. Marcus watched them for a little while before he went up to them.

'Hello, Ellie.'

'Marcus! My man!'

Marcus didn't want to think about what that might mean, so he didn't take any notice.

'Ellie, how old is your boyfriend?'

He'd only asked one question, and already he had made the girls laugh. He knew he could do it.

'A hundred and two.'

'Ha, ha.' He'd done it right again.

'Nine.'

▷ **30** *score* (infml): have success with a girl **43** *Harley Davidson:* brand name of a motorbike **44** *roadie:* person who works with pop bands when on tour · *squash sb.:* step on sb. so that they become flat **45** *bug* (AE): small insect **55–56** *take the piss out of sb.:* make fun of sb.

'Ha, ha.'

'Why do you want to know? How do you even know I've got a boyfriend?'

'My friend Will said he was probably about twenty-five and drove a Harley Davidson and he'd squash me like a bug.'

'Aaaah, Marcus.' Ellie grabbed him round the neck and ruffled his hair. 'I wouldn't let him.'

'Good. Thank you. I have to admit I was a bit worried when he said that.'

More laughter. Ellie's friend was staring at him as if he was the most interesting person she'd ever met.

'How old is your girlfriend, anyway? She probably wants to kill me, doesn't she?' They were laughing all the time now. You couldn't tell where one laugh ended and the next one began.

'No, because I haven't got one.'

'I don't believe that. A good-looking boy like you? We'll have to fix you up.'

'It's OK, thanks. I don't really want one at the moment. I don't feel ready yet.'

'Very sensible.'

Mrs Morrison suddenly appeared beside them.

'In my office now, Ellie.'

'I'm not changing the sweatshirt.'

'We'll talk about it in my office.'

'There's nothing to talk about.'

'Do you want to argue in front of everyone?'

Ellie shrugged. 'I don't mind if you don't.'

Ellie genuinely didn't care. Marcus could see that. Loads of kids acted as if they weren't scared, but dropped the act the moment a teacher said anything to them. Ellie could keep going forever, though, and there was nothing Mrs Morrison could do. There was a load of stuff she could do to him, though, and Ellie's friend didn't look like she wanted to pick a fight with Mrs Morrison either. Ellie had something that they didn't have – or they had something Ellie didn't have, he didn't know which.

'Zoe, Marcus, I want to talk to Ellie in private. And Marcus, you and I have some unfinished business to attend to, don't we?'

'Yes, Mrs Morrison.' Ellie caught his eye and smiled, and for a moment he really felt as if the three of them were a trio. Or maybe a triangle, with Ellie at the top and him and Zoe at the bottom.

'Off you go.'

And off they went.

Ellie and Zoe came looking for him at lunchtime. He was sitting at his desk eating his sandwiches, listening to Frankie Ball and Juliet Lawrence talk about some bloke in year nine, when they just turned up.

'Here he is, look!'

'Oooeee! Marcus!'

Just about every kid in the room stopped what they were doing and turned round. You could see what they were thinking: Ellie and *Marcus????????* Even Nicky and Mark, who hadn't spoken to him for weeks and liked to pretend that they had never known him, looked up from their Gameboy; Marcus hoped that one of them had lost a life. He felt great. If Kurt Cobain himself had walked through the form-room door looking for him, the mouths of his classmates couldn't have opened any wider.

'What are you lot staring at? Marcus is our friend, aren't you, Marcus?'

'Yes,' said Marcus. Whatever his relationship with Ellie and Zoe was, 'yes' was definitely the right answer here.

'Come on, then, let's go. You don't want to hang around here all lunchtime, do you? Come to our form room. It's a waste of time hanging out with this lot. Boring fuckers.'

Marcus could see some of them start to blush but nobody said anything. They couldn't, unless they were prepared to argue with Ellie, which clearly none of them were. What would be the point? Even Mrs Morrison couldn't argue with Ellie, so what chance did Frankie Ball and the rest of them have?

'OK,' said Marcus. 'Hang on a minute.' He wanted them to wait simply because he wanted the moment to last longer: he didn't know whether Ellie and Zoe would come looking for him ever again and, even if they did, he doubted whether they'd announce to the world,

▷ **16–17** *fix sb. up:* find sb. a girl- or boyfriend **37** *attend to sth.:* deal with sth. **69** *hang on:* wait or the part of the world eating sandwiches in his classroom, that he was their friend and that everyone else was a boring fucker. That would be too much to ask. But now he'd asked them to hang on, he had no idea what they might be hanging on for.

'Shall I ... Do you want me to bring anything?'

'Like what?' said Zoe. 'A bottle?'

'No, but, like ...'

'Or condoms?' said Ellie. 'Is that what you mean? We can't have sex in our room, Marcus, even though I'd like to, of course. There are too many people in there.' Zoe was laughing so hard that Marcus thought she might be sick. Her eyes were closed and she was sort of choking.

'No, I know, O ...' Maybe asking them to hang on had been a mistake. He was turning his moment of triumph into what seemed like a year of horrible awfulness.

'Just bring your sweet self, Marcus. But get a move on, eh?'

He knew he was red in the face, and the condom bit had been bad. But he still got to walk from his desk to where Ellie and Zoe were standing while everyone else watched, and when he got there Ellie gave him a kiss. OK, she was making fun of him, but it didn't matter, there weren't many people in his class that Ellie would bother to spit on, let alone kiss. 'There's no such thing as bad publicity,' his dad had said once, ages ago, when Marcus had asked him why some actor was letting Noel Edmonds pour stuff over his head, and now he could see what he meant. Ellie had kind of poured stuff over his head, but it was really, really worth it.

Ellie's form room was upstairs and the walk made the good bit, the fucking-hell-Marcus-and-Ellie bit, last longer. One of the teachers even stopped him to ask if he was OK, as if anyone hanging around with Ellie must have been kidnapped or brainwashed.

'We're adopting him, sir,' said Ellie.

'I wasn't asking you, Ellie. I was asking him.'

'They're adopting me, sir,' said Marcus. He didn't mean it as a joke – he just thought that saying what Ellie said was sensible – but they all laughed anyway.

'And you couldn't hope for more responsible parents,' said the teacher.

'Ha, ha,' said Marcus, although he wasn't sure he should have done this time.

'We'll take that as a compliment,' said Ellie. 'Thank you. We'll look after him. Have him home by midnight and all that.'

'Make sure you do,' said the teacher. 'In one piece.'

Ellie made him wait outside her form room while she announced him. He could hear her shouting.

'OK, listen everybody, I want you to meet Marcus. The only other Kurt Cobain fan in the whole fucking school. Come in, Marcus.'

He walked into he room. There weren't many people in there, but those that were all laughed when they saw him.

'I didn't say I was a fan as such,' he said. 'I just think they have a good beat and their cover means something.'

Everyone laughed again. Ellie and Zoe stood beside him proudly, as if he had just done a magic trick that they had told everyone he could do even though nobody believed them. They were right; he did feel he'd been adopted.

▷ **21–22** *spit on sb.:* jdn. anspucken **24** *Noel Edmonds:* TV presenter of game shows

Twenty-two

Will had been trying not to think about Christmas, but as it got nearer he was beginning to go off the idea of watching a few hundred videos and smoking a few thousand joints. It didn't seem very festive, somehow, and even though festivities invariably entailed The Song somewhere along the line, he didn't want to ignore them completely. It struck him that how you spent Christmas was a message to the world about where you were at in life, some indication of how deep a hole you had managed to burrow for yourself, and therefore spending three days bombed out of your head on your own said things about you that you might not want saying.

So he would spend Christmas in the bosom of a family – not his family, because he didn't have one, but a family. There was one family he wanted to avoid at all costs: no way did he want to spend Christmas eating nut fucking roast, not watching TV, and singing carols with his eyes closed. He had to be careful, though, because if he just let himself drift along he'd be carried right over the weir; he had to start swimming in the opposite direction fast.

Having decided with such unshakeable firmness that he would absolutely definitely not be celebrating 25 December with Fiona and Marcus, it came as something of a surprise to him to find himself accepting an invitation from Marcus the following afternoon to do exactly that.

'Do you want to spend Christmas round ours?' Marcus asked even before he had stepped into the flat.

'Ummm,' said Will. 'That's, ah, very kind of you.'

'Good,' said Marcus.

'I only said that's very kind of you,' said Will.

'But you're coming.'

I don't know.

'Why not?'

'Because – '

'Don't you want to come?'

'Yes, of course I do, but ... What about your mum?'

'She'll be there too.'

'Yes, I'd sort of presumed that. But she wouldn't want me there.'

'I've already spoken to her about it. I said I wanted to invite a friend, and she said OK.'

'So you didn't tell her it was me?'

'No, but I think she guessed.'

'How?'

'I haven't got any other friends, have I?'

'Does she know you still come round here?'

'Sort of. She's stopped asking me, so I think she's given up worrying about it.'

'And there really isn't anyone else you'd rather ask?'

'No, course not. And if there was, they wouldn't be allowed to come to my house for Christmas lunch. They'd be going to their own houses. Except they live in their own houses, so they wouldn't be going anywhere, would they?'

Will was finding the conversation depressing. What Marcus was saying, in his artful, skewed way, was that he didn't want Will to be alone on Christmas day.

'I'm not sure what I'm doing yet.'

'Where might you be going instead?'

'Nowhere, but ...'

Any conversational holes that needed filling were usually filled by Marcus. His concentration was such that any ums and ers and buts he looked on as cues to change the subject entirely. For some reason, though, he suddenly abandoned his usual technique and stared at Will intently.

'What are you staring at?' Will said eventually.

▷ **4** *festive:* full of joy · *invariably:* always **5** *somewhere along the line:* at some particular time or place **8** *burrow sth.:* dig sth. **11** *in the bosom of sth.:* (here) in the centre of sth. **14** *nut roast:* type of vegetarian food **16** *weir* [wɪə]: Wehr **51** *skewed* [skjuːd]: not straight, indirect

'I wasn't staring. I was waiting for you to answer the question.'

'I answered it. "Nowhere," I said.'

'You said "Nowhere, but …". I was waiting for what came after the but.'

'Well, nothing. I'm not going anywhere for Christmas.'

'So you can come to us.'

'Yes, but – '

'But what?'

'Stop asking me "But what?" all the time.'

'Why?'

'Because … it's not polite.'

'Why not?'

'Because … I clearly have reservations, Marcus. That's why I keep saying "But". I'm obviously not one hundred per cent convinced that I want to come to your house for Christmas.'

'Why not?'

'Are you being funny?'

'No.'

It was true, of course, Marcus was never deliberately funny. One look at Marcus's face was enough to convince Will that the boy was merely curious, and that his curiosity showed no signs of abating. The conversation had already been extended way beyond Will's comfort point, and now he was beginning to worry that he would eventually be forced to articulate the cruellest of truths: that Marcus's mother was, like her son, a lunatic; that even disregarding the sanity aspect of things they were both a pair of losers anyway; that he couldn't imagine a gloomier Christmas; that he would much, much rather revert to his original plan for oblivion and the entire output of the Marx Brothers than pull wishbones with either of them; that any sane person would feel the same way. If the kid couldn't take a hint, what option did he have? Unless …

'I'm sorry, Marcus, I was being rude. I'd love to spend Christmas with you.'

That was the other option. It wasn't his chosen option, but it was the other option.

As it turned out it wasn't just the three of them, which helped him no end when he showed up. He was expecting one of Fiona's logic-free lectures, but all he got was a look; she clearly didn't want to resume hostilities in front of her other guests. There was Marcus's dad Clive, and his girlfriend Lindsey, and his girlfriend's mum, six of them altogether, all squashed round the fold-out dining table in the flat. Will didn't know that the world was like this. As the product of a 1960s' second marriage, he was labouring under the misapprehension that when families broke up some of the constituent parts stopped speaking to each other, but the set-up here was different: Fiona and her ex seemed to look back on their relationship as the thing that had brought them together in the first place, rather than something that had gone horribly wrong and driven them apart. It was as if sharing a home and a bed and having a child together was like staying in adjacent rooms in the same hotel, or being in the same class at school – a happy coincidence that had given them the opportunity for an occasional friendship.

This couldn't happen all the time, Will thought otherwise SPAT would have been full of happy but estranged couples, all introducing their exes and their nexts and their kids from here, there and everywhere; but it hadn't been like that at all – it had been full of justified and righteous anger, and a very great deal of unhappiness. From what he had seen that evening he didn't think too many SPAT families would be reconvening for a game of Twister and a sing-song round the tree today.

But even if it didn't happen very often, it was happening here, today, which at first Will found rather sickening; if people couldn't live together, he reckoned, they should at least have the decency to loathe each other. But actually, as the day wore on and he had a little more to drink, Will could dimly see that to strive for pleasantness and harmony once a year wasn't an entirely contemptible ambition. A room full of people trying to get on made Marcus happy, for a start,

▷ **13** *reservation:* feeling of doubt about sth. **21** *abate* (fml): become less strong **24** *articulate sth.:* say sth. **28** *revert to sth.:* go back so sth. · *oblivion:* state of being unnoticed · *output:* work **29** *Marx Brothers:* American comedians of the 1930s and 40s **29** *wishbone:* bone of a chicken or turkey which two people pull apart to decide who will make a wish **36–37** *no end:* a lot, enormously **41** *fold-out table:* table you can enlarge **43** *labour under sth.:* believe sth. that is not true **43–44** *misapprehension* (fml): wrong idea about sth. **44** *constituent* (adj): forming together a whole of sth. **50** *adjacent* [ə'dʒeɪsnt]: next door **54** *estranged:* no longer living together **57** *righteous* ['raɪtʃəs]: believing you are morally right **59** *reconvene:* get together again · *Twister:* game in which participants have to twist over each other **64** *loathe sb.:* hate sb. very much **66** *contemptible:* not deserving respect and even Will was not cynical enough to wish Marcus anything but happiness on Christmas Day. On New Year's Eve he would make a resolution to recover some of his previous scepticism, but until then he would do as the Romans do, and smile at people even if he disapproved of them. Smiling at people didn't mean that you had to be friends with them forever, surely? Much later in the day, when common sense prevailed and everyone started squabbling, he learnt that smiling at people didn't even mean that you had to be friends for a day, but for a few hours he was happy to believe in an inverted universe.

He had bought presents for Fiona and Marcus. He gave Marcus a vinyl copy of *Nevermind*, because they didn't own a CD player, and a Kurt Cobain T-shirt, so he could keep in with Ellie; he gave Fiona a pretty groovy and pretty expensive plain glass vase, because she'd complained after the hospital business that she didn't know what to do with the flowers. Marcus gave him a crossword-solver's book to help him with *Countdown*, and Fiona gave him *The Single Parent's Handbook* as a joke.

'What's the joke?' Lindsey asked him.

'Nothing,' said Will quickly and, he could see as soon as he'd said it, feebly.

'Will pretended to have a kid so's he could join this single parents' group,' said Marcus.

'Oh,' said Lindsey. The strangers in the room, Lindsey and her mum and Clive, looked at him with some interest, but he declined to elucidate. He just smiled at them, as if it were something anyone would do in the circumstances. He wouldn't like to have to explain what those circumstances were, however.

The present-giving part of the day didn't take that long, and for the most part it was the usual stuff – alarmingly so, given the complicated web of relationships in the room. Penis-shaped chocolate was all very well, Will thought (actually he didn't think that at all, but never mind – he was trying to live and let live) but was penis-shaped chocolate an appropriate gift for your boyfriend's currently boyfriendless and celibate ex-lover? He really didn't know, but it seemed a little tasteless, somehow – surely the whole subject of penises was best left alone on occasions like this? – and anyway Fiona had never struck Will as a penis-shaped-chocolate kind of woman, but she laughed anyway.

As the pile of discarded wrapping paper grew bigger, it struck Will that just about any present given in these circumstances could be deemed inappropriate or darkly meaningful. Fiona gave Lindsey some silk underwear, as if to say, 'Hey, it doesn't matter to me what you two get up to at nights,' and she gave Clive a new book called *The Secret History*, as if to say something rather different. Clive gave Fiona a Nick Drake cassette, and though Clive did not know about the hospital business, as far as Will was aware, there still seemed to be something weird about him forcing a possibly suicidal depressive's music on a possibly suicidal depressive.

Clive's presents for Marcus were in themselves uncontroversial, computer games and sweatshirts and a baseball cap and the Mr Blobby record and so on, but what made them seem pointed was their contrast with the joyless little pile that Fiona had given Marcus earlier in the day: a jumper that wouldn't do him any favours at school (it was baggy and hairy and arty), a couple of books and some piano music – a gentle and very dull material reminder, it transpired, that Marcus had given up on his lessons some time ago. Marcus showed him this miserable haul with a pride and enthusiasm that almost broke Will's heart ... 'And a really nice jumper, and these books look really interesting, and this music because one day when I ... when I get a bit more time I'm going to really give it a go ...' Will had never properly given Marcus credit for being a good kid – up until now he'd only noticed his eccentric, troublesome side, probably because there hadn't been much else to notice. But he was good, Will could see that now. Not good as in obedient and uncomplaining; it was more of a mindset kind of good, where you looked at something like a pile of crap presents and recognized that they were given with love and chosen with care, and that was enough. It wasn't even that he was choosing to see the glass as half-full, either – Marcus's glass was full

▷ **4** *do as the Romans do:* (here) behave like the people whose house you are in **7** *prevail:* come into existence, win through · *squabble* (v): quarrel **9** *inverted:* being the opposite of what is normally the case **12** *vinyl copy:* (here) record **21** *feeble:* weak **25** *decline to do sth.:* refuse to do sth. **26** *elucidate sth.:* explain sth. **35** *celibate:* not having sex **40** *discard sth.:* throw sth. away **42** *deem:* consider · *darkly:* mysteriously **46** *Nick Drake* (1948–1976): English singer who died from taking too many tranquillisers **51–52** *Mr Blobby:* character in a children's TV show **52** *pointed:* noticeable **55** *arty*: (here) exaggerated in style **56** *transpire:* become known **58** *haul* [hɔːl] (n): number of things **66** *mindset:* set of attitudes that sb. has to overflowing, and he would have been amazed and mystified if anyone had attempted to tell him there were kids who would have hurled the hairy jumper and the sheet music back in the parental face and demanded a Nintendo.

Will knew he would never be good in that way. He would never look at a hairy jumper and work out why it was precisely right for him, and why he should wear it at all hours of the day and night. He would look at it and conclude that the person who bought it for him was a pillock. He did that all the time: he'd look at some twenty-five-year-old guy on roller-skates, sashaying his way down Upper Street with his wraparound shades on, and he'd think one of three things: 1) What a prat; or 2) Who the fuck do you think you are?, or 3) How old are you? Fourteen?

Everyone in England was like that, he reckoned. Nobody looked at a roller-skating bloke with wraparound shades on and thought, hey, he looks cool, or, wow, that looks like a fun way of getting some exercise. They just thought: wanker. But Marcus wouldn't. Marcus would either fail to notice the guy at all, or he would stand there with his mouth open, lost in admiration and wonder. This wasn't simply a function of being a child, because, as Marcus knew to his cost, all his classmates belonged to the what-a-prat school of thought; it was simply a function of being Marcus, son of Fiona. In twenty years' time he'd be singing with his eyes closed and swallowing bottles of pills, probably, but at least he was gracious about his Christmas presents. It wasn't much of a compensation for the long years ahead.

Twenty-three

It was good having a mum and dad who didn't decide things together, Marcus thought; that way you got the best of both worlds at Christmas. You got things like jumpers and sheet music, which you had to have, but then you got things like computer games and fun stuff as well. And if his mum and dad had still been together, what would Christmas have been like now, with just the three of them? Pretty boring, probably. This way it was more like a party, what with Will and Lindsey and, well, he wasn't really bothered about Lindsey's mum, if he were honest, but she sort of helped to fill the room up.

After presents they had lunch, which was a big ring doughnut-type thing made of pastry rather than doughnut, with a lovely cream and mushroom sauce in the hole in the middle, and then they had Christmas pudding with five-pence pieces hidden in it (Marcus had two in his portion), and then they pulled crackers and put the hats on, except Will wouldn't wear his for very long. He said it made his head itch.

After they'd watched the queen on TV (nobody wanted to, apart from Lindsey's mum, but whatever old people wanted they got, in

▷ **1** *mystified:* confused **3** *sheet music:* music notes printed on sheets of paper **4** *Nintendo:* computer game **9** *pillock* (sl): idiot **10** *sashay* ['sæʃeɪ] (infml): move in a confident way, in order to be noticed **11** *wraparound shades* (pl): sunglasses that bend around your face **12** *prat* (infml): stupid person **17** *wanker* (sl): stupid, unpleasant person **20** *know to your cost:* know due to an unpleasant experience **24** *gracious:* polite **32** *what with:* used to list sth. to explain why sth. is good or bad **39** *cracker:* Knallbonbon, die Papierhüte und kleine Spielzeuge enthalten **41** *itch* (v): jucken

Marcus's experience), Clive rolled a joint, and there was a bit of a row. Lindsey was angry with Clive because of her mum, who had no idea what he was doing until people started shouting about it, and Fiona was angry with Clive because of Marcus, who had seen him roll a joint about one thousand million times before.

'He's seen me do it hundreds of times before,' said Clive. It was the wrong thing to say, as it turned out, so Marcus was glad he hadn't said it.

'I wish you hadn't told me,' said Fiona. 'I really didn't want to know.'

'What, you thought I'd given up dope the day we separated? Why would I do that?'

'Marcus was younger then. He was always in bed before you started rolling up.'

'I never smoke any, Mum. Dad won't let me.'

'Oh, well that's all right then. As long as you're not smoking any, I have no objection to your father indulging his drug habit in front of you.'

'Ha, ha,' said Marcus. Everyone in the room looked at him, and then they continued the argument.

'I'd hardly describe the occasional spliff as a drug habit, would you?'

'Well obviously I would, because I just have.'

'Can we talk about this another time?' Lindsey asked. Her mother hadn't said anything so far, but she certainly seemed interested in what was going on.

'Why? Because your mother is here?' Marcus had never seen Fiona get cross with Lindsey before, but she was getting cross with her now. 'Unfortunately I can never have a conversation with Marcus's father without your mother being present, for reasons I have yet to fathom. So you'll just have to bloody well put up with it.'

'Look, I'll put the dope away, OK? Then we'll all calm down and watch *International Velvet* and forget about it.'

'*International Velvet* isn't on,' said Marcus. 'It's *Indiana Jones and the Temple of Doom*.'

'That wasn't the point I was making, Marcus.'

Marcus didn't say anything, but inwardly he disagreed: it hadn't been the only point, but it had certainly been one of them.

'I know he takes drugs,' said Lindsey's mum suddenly. 'I'm not daft.'

'I don't ... take drugs, said Clive.

'Well, what do you call it then?' said Lindsey's mum.

'It's not drug-taking. It's ... just normal. Drug-taking is something different.'

'Do you think he takes them on his own? Fiona said to Lindsey's mum. 'Do you think your daughter just sits there watching him?'

'What do you mean?'

'She doesn't mean anything, Mum. I think Clive's idea is an excellent one. Let's put it all away and play charades or something.'

'I didn't say anything about charades. I suggested watching *International Velvet*.'

'It's not *International* –' Marcus begun.

'Shut up, Marcus,' said everybody, and then they all laughed.

The row changed the atmosphere, though. Clive and Fiona agreed to have a proper conversation about the dope thing some other time, Fiona and Lindsey snapped at each other a couple of times, and even Will seemed different, although none of it had had anything to do with him. Marcus reckoned Will had been having a good time up until then, but afterwards he seemed apart from it all, whereas before he'd been one of the family. It was almost like he was laughing at them for rowing, for reasons Marcus couldn't understand. And then, after they'd had supper (there were cold meats for the meat-eaters, and Marcus had some, just to see the look on his mum's face), Suzie came round with her little girl and it was their turn to laugh at Will.

Marcus didn't know that Will hadn't seen Suzie since his mum had told her about Ned and SPAT and all that. Nobody had said anything, but that didn't mean much – Marcus had always presumed that after he had gone to school or to bed adults did all sorts of things they didn't tell him about, but now he was beginning to suspect this wasn't true, and that the adults he knew didn't have any sort of a secret life at all. It was obvious when Suzie walked into the room that this was an awkward moment, especially for Will: he stood up, and then he sat

▷ **11** *dope* (infml): marijuana **17** *indulge sth.:* allow oneself to have sth. **21** *spliff* (sl): cigarette containing cannabis **49** *charades* [ʃə'rɑ:dz]: game in which one person acts the title of a film, book, etc. and the others have to guess the title down, and then he stood up again, and then he went red, and then he said he ought to be going, and then Fiona told him not to be pathetic, so he sat down again. The only spare chair was in Will's corner, so Suzie had to sit next to him.

'Have you had a nice day, Suze?' Fiona asked her.

'OK, yeah. We're just on the way home from Grandma's.'

'And how's Grandma?' asked Will. Suzie turned to look at him, opened her mouth to reply, but changed her mind and ignored him completely. It was one of the most exciting things Marcus had ever seen in real life, and easily the most exciting thing he had ever seen in his own living room. (His mum and the sick on the Dead Duck Day didn't count. That wasn't exciting. It was just horrible.) Suzie was snubbing, he reckoned. He'd heard a lot about snubbing, but he had never watched anyone do it. It was great, if a bit frightening.

Will stood up and sat down again. If he really wanted to leave, Marcus thought, nobody could stop him. Or rather, they could stop him – if everyone in the room grabbed him and sat on him he wouldn't get very far. (Marcus smiled to himself at the thought of Lindsey's mum sitting on Will's head.) But they wouldn't stop him. So why didn't he just stand up, stay stood up and start walking? Why did he keep on bobbing up and down? Maybe there was something about snubbing that Marcus didn't know. Maybe there were snubbing rules, and you just had to sit there and be snubbed, even if you didn't feel like it.

Megan wriggled out of her mother's lap and went over to the Christmas tree.

'There might be a present for you under there, Megan,' said Fiona.

'Oooh, Megan, presents,' said Suzie. Fiona went over to the tree, picked up one of the last two or three parcels and gave it to her. Megan stood there clutching it and looked around the room.

'She's wondering who to give it to,' said Suzie. 'She's had as much fun giving them out as opening them today.'

'How sweet,' said Lindsey's mum. Everyone watched and waited while Megan made her decision; it was almost as if the little girl had understood the snubbing business and wanted to make mischief, because she toddled over to Will and thrust the present at him.

Will didn't move. 'Well, take it from her then, you fool,' said Suzie.

'It's not my bloody present,' said Will. Good for you, Marcus thought. Do some snubbing of your own. The only trouble was that as things stood Will was snubbing Megan, not Suzie, and Marcus didn't think you should snub anyone under the age of three. What was the point? Megan didn't seem to mind, though, because she continued to hold the present out to him until he reached for it.

'Now what?' said Will crossly.

'Open it with her,' said Suzie. She was more patient this time; Will's anger seemed to have calmed her down a little. If she wanted a row with Will, she clearly didn't want it here, in front of all these people.

Will and Megan tore off the paper to reveal some sort of plastic toy that played tunes. Megan looked at it and waved it at Will.

'What now?' said Will.

'Play with her,' said Suzie. 'God, spot the childless person here.'

'Tell you what,' said Will. 'You play with her.' He tossed Suzie the toy. 'As I'm so bloody clueless.'

'Maybe you could learn to be less clueless,' said Suzie.

'What for?'

'I would have thought that in your line of work it might be handy to know how to play with kids.'

'What's your line of work?' Lindsey asked politely, as if this were a normal conversation amongst a normal group of people.

'He doesn't do anything,' Marcus said. 'His dad wrote "Santa's Super Sleigh" and he earns a million pounds a minute.'

'He pretends he has a child so he can join single parent groups and chat up single mothers' said Suzie.

'Yeah, but he doesn't get paid for that,' said Marcus.

Will stood up again, but this time he didn't sit down.

'Thanks for the lunch and everything,' he said. 'I'm off.'

'Suzie has a right to express her anger, Will,' said Fiona.

'Yes, and she's expressed it, and now I have a right to go home.' He started to weave his way through the presents and glasses and people towards the door.

'He's my friend,' Marcus said suddenly. 'I invited him. I should be able to tell him when he goes home.'

'I'm not sure that's how the whole hospitality thing works,' said Will.

▷ **13** *snub sb.:* insult sb. by ignoring them **21** *bob* (infml): go up and down **24** *wriggle out of sth.:* get out of sth. by moving oneself back and forth **34** *mischief:* trouble **35** *toddle:* walk unsteadily **52** *clueless:* stupid, having no idea how to do sth. **68** *weave your way through sth.:* move and change your direction around sth. **72** *hospitality:* friendliness towards guests

'But I don't want him to go yet,' said Marcus. 'It's not fair. How come Lindsey's mum's still here, and no one invited her, and the one person I invited is leaving because everyone's being horrible to him?'

'First of all,' said Fiona, 'I invited Lindsey's mum, and it's my house too. And we haven't been horrible to Will. Suzie's angry with Will, as she has every right to be, and she's telling him so.'

Marcus felt as though he were in a play. He was standing up, and Will was standing up, and then Fiona stood up; but Lindsey and her mum and Clive were sat on the sofa watching, in a line, with their mouths open.

'All he did was make up a kid for a couple of weeks. God. That's nothing. So what? Who cares? Kids at school do worse than that every day.'

'The point is, Marcus, that Will left school a long time ago. He should have grown out of making people up by now.'

'Yeah, but he's behaved better since, hasn't he?'

'Can I go yet?' said Will, but nobody took any notice.

'Why? What's he done?' asked Suzie.

'He never wanted me round his flat every day. I just went. And he bought me those shoes, and at least he listens when I say I'm having a hard time at school. You just tell me to get used to it. And he knew who Kirk O'Bane was.'

'Kurt Cobain,' said Will.

'And it's not like you lot never do anything wrong ever, is it?' said Marcus. 'I mean …' He had to be careful here. He knew he couldn't say too much, or even anything at all, about the hospital stuff. 'I mean, how come I got to know Will in the first place?'

'Because you threw a bloody great baguette at a duck's head and killed it, basically,' said Will.

Marcus couldn't believe Will was bringing that up now. It was supposed to be all about how everyone else did things wrong, not about how he had killed the duck. But then Suzie and Fiona started laughing, and Marcus could see that Will knew what he was doing.

'Is that true, Marcus?' said his father.

'There was something wrong with it,' said Marcus. 'I think it was going to die anyway.'

Suzie and Fiona laughed even harder. The audience on the sofa looked appalled. Will sat down again.

Twenty-four

Will fell in love on New Year's Eve, and the experience took him completely by surprise. She was called Rachel, she illustrated children's books, and she looked a little bit like Laura Nyro on the cover of *Gonna Take A Miracle* – nervy, glamorous, Bohemian, clever, lots of long, unruly dark hair.

Will had never wanted to fall in love. When it had happened to friends it had always struck him as a peculiarly unpleasant-seeming experience, what with all the loss of sleep and weight, and the unhappiness when it was unreciprocated, and the suspect, dippy happiness when it was working out. These were people who could not control themselves, or protect themselves, people who, if only temporarily, were no longer content to occupy their own space, people who could no longer rely on a new jacket, a bag of grass and an afternoon rerun of *The Rockford Files* to make them complete.

Lots of people, of course, would be thrilled to take their seats next to their computer-generated ideal life-partner, but Will was a realist, and he could see immediately that there was only cause for panic. He was almost sure that Rachel was about to make him very miserable indeed, mostly because he couldn't see anything he might have which could possibly interest her.

▷ **38** *appalled* [ə'pɔːld]: horrified, shocked **41** *Laura Nyro:* singer and songwriter **42** *Bohemian:* nonconformist person who does not follow accepted rules of behaviour **43** *unruly:* (of hair) difficult to keep tidy **47** *unreciprocated:* not returned · *dippy* (infml): silly **52** *The Rockford Files:* American TV series about a private detective

If there was a disadvantage to the life he had chosen for himself, a life without work and care and difficulty and detail, a life without context and texture, then he had finally found it: when he met an intelligent, cultured, ambitious, beautiful, witty and single woman at a New Year's Eve party, he felt like a blank twit, a cypher, someone who had done nothing with his whole life apart from watch *Countdown* and drive around listening to Nirvana records. That had to be a bad thing, he reckoned. If you were falling in love with someone beautiful and intelligent and all the rest of it, then feeling like a blank twit put you at something of a disadvantage.

One of his problems, he reflected as he was trying to dredge his memory for a single tiny scrap of experience that this woman might regard as worth her momentary contemplation, was that he was reasonably good-looking and reasonably articulate. It gave people the wrong impression. It gave him admission to a party from which he should be barred by ferocious bouncers with thick necks and tattoos. He may have been good-looking and articulate, but that was just a quirk of genetics, environment and education; at his core he was ugly and monosyllabic. Maybe he should undergo some sort of reverse plastic surgery – something that would rearrange his features so that they were less even, and push his eyes closer together or further apart. Or maybe he should put on an enormous amount of weight, sprout a few extra chins, grow so fat that he sweated profusely all the time. And, of course, he should start grunting like an ape.

Because the thing was that when this Rachel woman sat down next to him at dinner she was interested, for the first five minutes, before she'd worked him out, and in that five minutes he got a glimpse of what life could be like if he were in any way interesting. On balance, he thought, he'd prefer not to have that glimpse. What good did it do him, after all? He wasn't going to get to sleep with Rachel. He wasn't going to go to a restaurant with her, or see what her sitting room looked like, or get to understand how her father's affair with her mother's best friend had affected her views on having children. He hated the five-minute window of opportunity. In the end, he thought, he would be far happier if she turned round to look at him, just about managed not to vomit, and turned her back on him for the rest of the evening.

He missed Ned. Ned had given him an extra something, a little *il ne sait quoi*, that would have come in handy on an evening like this.

He wasn't going to bring him back to life, though, poor little sod. Let him rest in peace.

'How do you know Robert?' Rachel was asking him.

'Oh, just ...' Robert produced television programmes. He hung out with actors and writers and directors. People who knew Robert were arty movers and shakers, and were almost obliged to be glamorous. Will wanted to say that he had written the music for Robert's last film or given him his big break, or that they met for lunch to talk about the godawful mess that was this government's arts policy. He wanted to say that, but he couldn't.

'Just ... I used to buy my dope off him years ago.' That, unhappily, was the truth. Before Robert became a television producer, he was a dope dealer. Not a dope dealer with a baseball bat and a pit-bull, just someone who bought a bit extra to sell on to his mates, who at the time included Will, because Will was going out with a friend of Robert's ... Anyway, it didn't matter why he was knocking around with Robert in the mid-eighties. The point was that he was the only person in the room who neither moved nor shook, and now Rachel knew it.

'Oh, right,' she said. 'But you've kept in touch.'

Maybe he could make up some story about why he still saw Robert, a story that might cast him in a more flattering light, make him seem a little more complicated.

'Yeah. Dunno why, really.' No story, then, obviously. Oh well. The truth was that he didn't know why they'd kept in touch. They got on reasonably well, but Robert had got on reasonably well with most of that crowd, and Will had never been entirely sure why he had been the one who survived the inevitable career-change cull. Maybe – and this sounded paranoid, but he was sure there was a grain of truth in

▷ **3** *texture:* character, form **5** *twit* (infml): silly person · *cypher* ['saɪfə]: person of no importance **11** *dredge sth.:* search or go through sth. with difficulty **16** *bar sb.:* ban sb. · *ferocious:* violent · *bouncer:* doorman who is also responsible for security **18** *quirk:* strange thing that happens by accident · *at sb.'s core:* in sb.'s essence **19** *monosyllabic:* unable to say much **23** *sprout sth.:* begin to grow sth. · *profusely:* greatly **34** *window of opportunity:* time when there is an opportunity for sth. **38–39** *il ne sait quoi* (French): something special **43–44** *hang out with sb.* (infml): spend a lot of time with sb. **45** *arty* (infml): involved in the world of the arts · *movers and shakers:* people with power **55** *knock around with sb.* (infml): spend a lot of time with sb. **67** *cull:* (here) change of friends **68** *grain:* tiny bit here somewhere – he was enough of a deadbeat to demonstrate to the people here that Robert had pre-media roots, while at the same time he was presentable enough not to scare them all away.

He'd lost Rachel, for now at least. She was talking to the person sitting on her other side. What could he reel her back with? He must have had some talent or other which he could exaggerate and dramatize somehow. Cooking? He could cook a bit, but who couldn't. Maybe he was writing a novel and had forgotten about it. What had he been good at when he was at school? Spelling. 'Hey, Rachel, how many c's in necessary?' She probably knew anyway. It was hopeless. The most interesting thing about his life, he realized, was Marcus. That was something which set him apart. 'Sorry to butt in, Rachel, but I have this weird relationship with a twelve-year-old boy. Is that any good to you?' OK, the material needed some work, but it was there, definitely. It just needed shaping. He vowed to bring up Marcus at the first available opportunity.

Rachel had noticed he wasn't talking to anyone, and wheeled round so that he could be included in a conversation about whether there was anything new under the sun, with particular reference to contemporary popular music. Rachel said that to her Nirvana sounded just like Led Zeppelin.

'I know a twelve-year-old who'd kill you for saying that.' Said Will. It wasn't true, of course. A couple of weeks ago, Marcus had thought that the lead singer of Nirvana played for Manchester United, so he was probably not yet at the stage where he wanted to annihilate people who accused the band of being derivative.

'So do I, come to that,' said Rachel. 'Maybe they should meet. What's yours called?'

He's not mine, exactly, he thought. 'Marcus,' he said.

'Mine's Ali. Alistair.'

'Right.'

'And is Marcus into skateboards and rap and *The Simpsons* and so on?'

Will raised his eyes skywards and chuckled fondly, and the misapprehension was cast in concrete. It wasn't his fault, this conversation. He hadn't lied once in the entire minute and a half. OK, he had been speaking more figuratively than the expression usually implied when he had said that Marcus would kill her. And OK, the rolling eyes and the fond chuckle did suggest a certain amount of parental indulgence. But he hadn't actually said that Marcus was his son. That was one hundred per cent her interpretation. Certainly over fifty per cent, anyway. But it definitely wasn't the SPAT thing, when he'd lied through his teeth for the entire duration of the evening.

'And is Marcus's mother here tonight?'

'Ummm ...' Will looked up and down the dinner table as if to remind himself one way or the other. 'No.' Not a lie! Not a lie! Marcus's mother was not there!

'You're not spending New Year's Eve with her?' Rachel was narrowing her eyes and looking down her nose to indicate that she knew this was a leading question.

'No. We, er, we don't live together.' He'd really got the hang of this truth-telling business now, he felt. If anything, he'd moved right away from lying and towards understatement, because not only was he not living with Fiona at the moment, but he had never lived with her, and never intended to live with her in the future.

'I'm sorry.'

'It's OK. How about Ali's dad?'

'Not at this table. Not in this city. Not in this country. He gives me his phone number when he moves.'

'Right.'

Will had at least managed to introduce some friction into the conversation. Until he'd played the Marcus card he'd kept slipping off before he'd even started. Now he felt as though he were climbing a mountain, rather than a glacier. He imagined himself right at the bottom of the cliff-face, looking up and around for footholds.

'Which country is he in, then?'

'The states. California. I'd prefer Australia, but there you are. At least it's the west coast.'

Will reckoned he'd now heard fifty-seven varieties of this conversation, but this gave him an advantage: he knew how it went, and go it did. He might not have done anything in the last decade and

▷ **1** *deadbeat* (infml): outsider, cool person **5** *reel sb. back:* win back sb.'s interest **12–13** *butt in* (infml): interrupt a conversation **15** *vow* [vaʊ]: make a strong promise **26** *derivative* [dɪˈrɪvətɪv]: not original **34** *chuckle* (v): laugh quietly **35** *be cast in concrete:* be fixed permanently **43** *duration:* length of time **50** *leading question:* question you ask to get a particular answer **51** *get the hang of sth.* (infml): learn and understand (how to do) sth. **61** *friction:* conflict a half, but he could cluck sympathetically when a woman told him how badly her ex-husband had behaved. Clucking was something he had got really good at. But it worked, as clucking often did – no one, he decided, ever did themselves any harm by listening attentively to other people's woes. Rachel's story was, by SPAT standards, run-of-the-mill, and it turned out that she hated her ex because of who he was, rather than what he had done to her.

'So why the fuck did you have a child with him?' He was drunk. It was New Year's Eve. He was feeling cheeky.

She laughed. 'Good question. No answer. You change your mind about people. What's Marcus's mother's name?'

'Fiona.' Which of course, it was.

'Did you change your mind about her?'

'Not really.'

'So what happened?'

'I dunno.' He shrugged, and somehow managed to give a rather convincing impression of a man who was still baffled, shell-shocked even. The words and the gesture were born of desperation; it was ironic, then, that they somehow managed to make a connection.

Rachel smiled, and picked up the knife she hadn't used, and examined it. 'In the end, "I dunno" is the only honest answer anyone can give, isn't it? Because I dunno either, and I'd be kidding myself, and you, if I pretended any different.'

At midnight they sought each other out and kissed, a kiss that was somewhere between cheek and lip, the embarrassed ambiguity hopefully significant. And at half-past midnight, just before Rachel left, they arranged to get their lads together to compare skateboards and baseball caps and the Christmas edition of *The Simpsons*.

Twenty-five

Ellie was at Suzie's New Year's Eve party. For a moment, Marcus thought it was just someone who looked like Ellie, and wore the same Kurt Cobain sweatshirt as Ellie, but then the Ellie lookalike saw him and shouted 'Marcus!' and came over and hugged him and kissed him on the head, which kind of cleared up the confusion.

'What are you doing here?' he asked her.

'We always come here on New Year's Eve,' she said. 'My mum's really good friends with Suzie.'

'I've never seen you here.'

'You've never been here on New Year's Eve, you twit.'

It was true. He'd been to Suzie's flat loads of times, but he'd never come to the parties. This was the first year he'd been allowed to go. Why was it that even in the simplest, most straightforward conversations with Ellie he found something stupid to say?

'Which one's your mum?'

'Don't ask,' said Ellie. 'Not now.'

'Why not?'

'Because she's dancing.'

Marcus looked over at the very small group dancing in the corner where the TV usually was. There were four people, three women and a man, and only one of them seemed to be having a good time: she was sort of punching the air with her fists and shaking her hair. Marcus guessed that this had to be Ellie's mum – not because she looked like her (no adult looked like Ellie, because no adult would chop her hair

▷ **5** *woe* [wəʊ]: sorrow **5–6** *run-of-the-mill:* ordinary **31** *lookalike* (n): double up with kitchen scissors and wear black lipstick, and that was all you saw), but because Ellie was clearly embarrassed, and this was the only dancer who would embarrass anyone. The other dancers were embarrassed themselves, which meant that they weren't actually embarrassing; they weren't doing much more than tapping their feet, and the only way you could tell they were dancing at all was that they were facing each other but not looking at each other and not talking.

'I wish I could dance like that,' said Marcus.

Ellie made a face. 'Anyone can dance like that. All you need is no brain and crap music.'

'I think she looks great. She's enjoying herself.'

'Who cares whether she's enjoying herself? The point is she looks like a total cretin.'

'Don't you like your mum, then?'

'She's all right.'

'What about your dad?'

'He's all right. They don't live together.'

'Do you mind?'

'No. Sometimes. Don't want to talk about it. So, Marcus, have you had a good nineteen ninety-three?'

Marcus thought for a moment about 1993, and a moment was all it took to decide that 1993 hadn't been a very good year at all. He only had ten or eleven others to compare it with, and three or four of them he couldn't remember much about, but as far as he could see nobody would have enjoyed the twelve months he'd had. Moving schools, the hospital stuff, the other kids at school ... It had been totally useless.

'No.'

'You need a drink,' said Ellie. 'What do you want? I'll get you a drink and you can tell me all about it. I might get bored and wander off, though. I do that.'

'OK.'

'So, what are you drinking?'

'Coke.'

'You've got to have a proper drink.'

'I'm not allowed.'

'You're allowed by me. In fact, if you're going to be my date for the evening, I insist that you have a proper drink. I'll put something in the Coke, OK?'

'OK'

Ellie disappeared, and Marcus looked round for his mum: she was talking to a man he didn't know and laughing a lot. He was pleased, because he had been worried about tonight. Will had told him to watch out for his mum on New Year's Eve, and though he didn't explain why, Marcus could guess: a lot of people who weren't happy killed themselves then. He had seen it somewhere, *Casualty*, maybe, and as a consequence the night had been hanging over him. He thought he'd be watching her all evening, looking for something in her eyes or her voice or her words that would tell him she was thinking about trying it again, but it wasn't like that: she was getting drunk and laughing, like everyone else. Had anyone ever killed themselves a couple of hours after laughing a lot? Probably not, he reckoned. You were miles away, if you were laughing, and he did now think of it all in terms of distance. Ever since the Dead Duck Day he had imagined his mother's suicide to be something like the edge of a cliff: sometimes, on days when she seemed sad or distracted, he felt as though they were a little too close for comfort, and other days, like Christmas Day or today, they seemed to be a long way away, in the middle lane of a motorway and cruising. On the Dead Duck Day it had been way too close, two wheels over the edge and lots of terrible skidding noises.

Ellie came back with a plastic beaker containing something which looked like Coke but smelt like trifle.

'What's in it?'

'Sherry.'

'Is that what people drink? Coke and sherry?' He took a cautious sip. It was nice, sweet and thick and warming.

'So why has it been such a shit year?' Ellie asked. 'You can tell me. Auntie Ellie will understand.'

'Just … I dunno. Horrible things happened.' He didn't really want to tell Ellie what they were, because he didn't know whether they were friends or not. It could go either way with her: he might go into her form room one morning and she'd shout it all out to anyone who would listen, or she might be really nice. It wasn't worth taking the risk.

▷ **13** *cretin* ['kretɪn]: idiot **47** *hang over sb.:* make sb. feel depressed or worried **61** *skid:* (of a car) slide sideways while moving **62** *beaker:* cup **63** *trifle:* cold pudding made with sherry

'Your mum tried to kill herself, didn't she?'

Marcus looked at her, took a big gulp of Coke and trifle, and was nearly sick all over her feet.

'No,' he said quickly, when he had finished coughing and swallowed the sick back down.

'Are you sure?'

'Well,' he said. 'Not positive.' He knew how stupid that sounded and he started to blush, but then Ellie burst into peals of laughter. He had forgotten that he made Ellie laugh so much and he was grateful.

'I'm sorry, Marcus. I know it's serious, but you are funny.'

He started to laugh too, then, little uncontrollable giggles that tasted of puke and sherry.

Marcus had never had a proper talk with someone of his own age before. He had had proper talks with his mum, of course, and his dad, and Will, kind of, but you expected to have proper talks with people like that and, anyway, you still had to watch what you said. It was different, much easier, with Ellie, even though she was a) a girl, b) older than him, and c) scary.

It turned out she'd known for ages: she'd overheard a conversation between her mum and Suzie just after it happened, but didn't make the connection until much later.

'And do you know what I thought? I feel terrible about it now, but I was like, why shouldn't she kill herself if she wants to?'

'But she's got me.'

'I didn't know you then.'

'No, but I mean, how would you like it if your mum killed herself?'

Ellie smiled. 'How would I like it? I wouldn't like it. Because I like my mum. But, you know. It's her life.'

Marcus thought about that. He didn't know whether it was his mum's life or not.

'What about if you have kids? Then it's not your life any more, is it?'

'Your dad's around, isn't he? He would've looked after you.'

'Yeah, but …' Something wasn't right with what Ellie was saying. She was talking as if his mum might go down with flu, so his dad would have to take him swimming.

'See, if your dad killed himself, nobody would say, you know, oh, he's got a son to look after. But when women do it, people get all upset. It's not fair.'

'That's because I'm living with my mum. If I was living with my dad, I'd think it wasn't his life either.'

'But you aren't living with your dad, are you? How many of us are? At our school, there's about a million kids whose parents have split. And none of them are living with their dads.'

'Stephen Wood is.'

'Yeah, right, Stephen Wood. You win.'

Even though what they were talking about was miserable, Marcus was enjoying the conversation. It seemed big, as though you could walk round it and see different things, and that never happened when you talked to kids normally. 'Did you see *Top of the Pops* last night?' There wasn't much to think about in that, was there? You said yes or no and it was over. He could see now why his mum chose friends, instead of just putting up with anyone she happened to bump into, or sticking with people who supported the same football team, or wore the same clothes, which was pretty much what happened at school; his mum must have conversations like this with Suzie, conversations which moved, conversations where each thing the other person said seemed to lead you on somewhere.

He wanted to keep it going but he didn't know how, because Ellie was the one who said the things that got them started. He was OK at coming up with the answers, he reckoned, but he doubted if he'd ever be clever enough to make Ellie think in the way she made him think, and that panicked him a little: he wished they were equally clever, but they weren't, and they probably never would be, because Ellie would always be older than him. Maybe when he was thirty-two and she was thirty-five it wouldn't matter so much, but it felt to him that unless he said something really smart in the next few minutes, then she wouldn't hang around for the rest of the evening, let alone for the next twenty years. Suddenly he remembered the thing boys were supposed to ask girls at parties. He didn't want to ask, because he knew he was hopeless at it, but the alternative – to let Ellie wander away and talk to somebody else – was just too horrible.

'Would you like to dance, Ellie?'

Ellie stared at him, her eyes wide with surprise.

▷ **8** *peal:* loud series of sounds **35** *go down with sth.* (infml): catch sth. (esp. an illness) **50** *Top of the Pops:* TV show which shows the best-selling music singles

'Marcus!' She started laughing again, really hard. 'You're so funny. Of course I wouldn't like to dance! I couldn't think of anything worse!'

He knew then that he should have thought of another proper question, something about Kurt Cobain or politics, because Ellie disappeared off somewhere for a smoke, and he had to go and find his mum. But Ellie came looking for him at midnight and gave him a hug, so he knew that even though he'd been stupid, he hadn't been unforgivably stupid.

'Happy New Year, darling,' she said, and he blushed.

'Thank you. Happy New Year to you.'

'And I hope nineteen ninety-four is better for all of us than nineteen ninety-three was. Hey, do you want to see something really disgusting?'

Marcus wasn't at all sure that he did, but he was given no choice in the matter. Ellie grabbed his arm and took him through the back door to the garden. He tried to ask her where they were going, but she shushed him.

'Look,' she whispered. Marcus peered into the darkness. He could just make out two human shapes kissing with frantic energy; the man was pressing the woman against the garden shed and his hands were all over her.

'Who is it?' Marcus asked Ellie.

'My mum. My mum and a guy called Tim Porter. She's drunk. They do this every year, and I don't know why they bother. Every New Year's Day she wakes up and says, "My God, I think I went outside with Tim Porter last night." Pathetic. PATHETIC!' She shouted out the last word so that she'd be heard, and Marcus saw Ellie's mum push the man away and look in their direction.

'Ellie? Is that you?'

'You said you weren't going to do that this year.'

'It's none of your business what I do. Go back inside.'

'No.'

'Do as you're told.'

'No. You're disgusting. Forty-three years old and you're snogging against a garden shed.'

'One night of the year I get to behave nearly as badly as you do on the other three hundred and sixty-four, and you stand there giving me a hard time. Go away.'

'Come on, Marcus. Let's leave the SAD OLD TART to get on with it.'

Marcus followed Ellie back into the house. He hadn't seen his mum do anything like that, and he couldn't imagine that she ever would, but he could see how it might happen to other people's mums.

'Doesn't that bother you?' he asked Ellie when they were inside.

'Nah. It doesn't mean anything, does it? It's just her having some fun. She doesn't get much, really.'

Even though it didn't seem to bother Ellie, it bothered Marcus. It was just too odd for words. It wouldn't have happened in Cambridge, he didn't think, but what he couldn't work out was whether Cambridge was different because it wasn't London, or because it was where his parents had lived together, and where, therefore, life was simpler – no snogging with strange people in front of your kid, and no yelling rude words at your mum. There were no rules here, and he was old enough to know that when you went to a place, or a time, with no rules then things were bound to be more complicated.

▷ **18** *shush sb.:* indicate to sb. to be quiet **35** *snog* (v) (infml): kiss sb. passionately **40** *tart* (infml): whore

Twenty-six

'I don't get it,' said Marcus. He and Will had walked down to an amusement arcade at the Angel to play on the video machines, and the Angel Funhouse, with its epileptic lights and sirens and explosions and tramps, turned out to be a suitably nightmarish setting for the difficult conversation Will knew they were going to have. It was, in a way, a grotesque version of popping the question. He had chosen the setting, somewhere that would soften Marcus up and make him more likely to say yes, and all he had to do was spit it out.

'There's nothing to get,' said Will blithely. It wasn't true, of course. There was a lot to get, from Marcus's point of view, and Will could quite see why he wasn't getting it.

'But why did you tell her you were my dad?'

'I didn't tell her. She just sort of got the wrong end of the stick.'

'So why didn't you just say, you know, "Sorry, you've got the wrong end of the stick"? She probably wouldn't have minded. Why would she care whether you were my dad or not?'

'Don't you ever have conversations where someone took a wrong turn at some point, and then it goes on and on and it becomes too late to put things right? Say someone thought your name was Mark, not Marcus, and every time they saw you they said, "Hello, Mark", and you're going to yourself, Oh, no, I can't tell him now, 'cos he'll be really embarrassed that he's been calling me Mark for the last six months.'

'Six months!'

'Or however long it is.'

'I'd just tell him the first time he got it wrong.'

'It's not always possible to do that.'

'How can it not be possible to tell someone they've got your name wrong?'

'Because …' Will knew that sometimes it was not possible through personal experience. One of his neighbours opposite, a nice old guy with a stoop and a horrible little Yorkshire terrier, called him Bill – always had done and presumably always would, right up till the day he died. It actually irritated Will, who was not, he felt, by any stretch of the imagination, a Bill. Bill wouldn't smoke spliffs and listen to Nirvana. So why had he allowed this misapprehension to continue? Why hadn't he just said, four years ago, 'Actually my name's Will'? Marcus was right, of course, but being right was no use if the rest of the world was wrong.

'Anyway,' he continued, in a brisk let's-cut-the-crap tone. 'The point is, this woman thinks you're my son.'

'So tell her I'm not.'

'No.'

'Why not?'

'We're going round and round in circles here, Marcus. Why can't you just accept the facts?'

'I'll tell her, if you like. I don't mind.'

'That's very kind of you, Marcus, but that wouldn't help.'

'Why not?'

'Oh, for Christ's sake! Because she has this rare disease, and if she believes something that's not right and you tell her the truth, her brain will boil in her head and she'll die.'

'How old do you think I am? Shit. You've made me lose a life now.'

Will was beginning to come to the conclusion that he was not, as he had always previously thought, a good liar. He was an enthusiastic liar, certainly, but enthusiasm was not the same thing as efficacy, and he was now constantly finding himself in a situation whereby, having lied through his teeth for minutes or days or weeks, he was obliged to articulate the humiliating truth. Good liars would never do that. Good liars would have persuaded Marcus ages ago that there were

▷ **2** *amusement arcade:* hall with machines operated by coins for playing games **3** *epileptic:* (here) flashing on and off **6** *pop the question* (infml): ask sb. to marry you **9** *blithely* ['blaɪðli]: cheerfully **21** *go to yourself* (infml): say to yourself **32** *stoop* (n): round shoulders bending forward **39** *brisk:* brief and energetic **49** *disease:* illness **55** *efficacy* ['efɪkəsi]: ability to produce the intended result hundreds of good reasons why he should pretend to be Will's son, but Will could only think of one.

'Marcus, listen. I'm really interested in this woman, and the only thing I could think of that might make her interested in me was to let her believe you were my son. So I did. I'm sorry. And I'm sorry I didn't tell you straight out.'

Marcus stared at the video screen – he'd just been exploded by a cross between Robocop and Godzilla – and took a long pull on his can of Coke.

'I don't get it,' he said, and burped ostentatiously.

'Oh, come on, Marcus. We've been here before.'

'What do you mean, you're really interested in her? Why is she so interesting?'

'I mean ...' He groaned with despair. 'Leave me with just one scrap of dignity, Marcus. That's all I'm asking. Just a little tiny, tatty piece.'

Marcus looked at him as if he had suddenly started speaking in Urdu.

'What's dignity got to do with her being interesting?'

'OK. Forget dignity. I don't deserve any. I fancy this woman, Marcus. I want to go out with her. I'd like her to be my girlfriend.'

Finally, Marcus swivelled his eyes away from the TV screen, and Will could see they were shining with fascination and pleasure. 'Really?'

'Yes, really.' Really, really. He had thought of almost nothing else since New Year's Eve (not that he had much to think about, apart from the word Rachel, a vague recollection of lots of long dark hair and a lot of foolish fantasies involving picnics and babies and tearfully devoted mothers-in-law and huge hotel beds) and it was a relief to be able to bring Rachel out into the light, even though it was only Marcus who was up there to inspect her, and even though the words he had had to use did not, he felt, do her justice. He wanted Rachel to be his wife, his lover, the centre of his whole world; a girlfriend implied that he would see her from time to time, that she would have some kind of independent existence away from him, and he didn't want that at all.

'How do you know?'

'How do I know?'

'Yeah. How do you know you want her to be your girlfriend?'

'I don't know. I just feel it in my guts.' That was exactly where he felt it. He wasn't feeling it in his heart, or his head, or even his groin;

it was his guts, which had immediately tensed up and allowed for the ingestion of nothing more calorific than cigarette smoke. If he went on ingesting only cigarette smoke he might lose some weight.

'You just met her the once? On New Year's Eve?'

'Yeah.'

'And that was enough? You knew you wanted her to be your girlfriend straight away? Can I have another fifty pence?'

Will gave him a pound coin abstractedly. It was true that something had happened in him immediately, but what had pushed him over the edge into the land of permanent daydream was a remark Robert had made a couple of days later, when Will had phoned to thank him for the party. 'Rachel liked you,' he said, and though it wasn't much to build a whole future on, it was all Will had needed. Reciprocation was a pretty powerful stimulant to the imagination.

'What is this? How long should I have known her for, according to you?'

'Well, I wouldn't really describe myself as an expert.' Will laughed at Marcus's turn of phrase, and the furrowed brow which both accompanied it and seemed to contradict it: anyone who could look that professional while talking about the minutiae of dating was clearly a twelve-year-old Doctor Love. 'But I didn't know when I met Ellie the first time that I wanted her to be my girlfriend. It took a while to develop.'

'Well, that's a sign of maturity, I guess.' The Ellie business was news to Will, and suddenly he could see this was where they had been heading right from the beginning. 'You want Ellie to be your girlfriend?'

'Yeah. Course.'

'Not just your friend?'

'Well.' He inserted the pound coin into the slot and pressed the one-player button. 'I was going to ask you about that. What would you say are the main differences?'

▷ **10** *burp* (v): rülpsen · *ostentatiously:* in an exaggerated way **14** *groan:* make a deep sound of unhappiness · *scrap:* small bit of sth. **15** *dignity:* self-respect **17** *Urdu:* language spoken in Pakistan **21** *swivel sth.* ['swɪvl]: turn sth. with a circular motion **28** *relief* [rɪ'li:f]: pleasant change **39** *groin:* genital area **40** *guts* (pl) (infml): insides of a person **41** *calorific:* having calories **53** *reciprocation:* act of giving sth. in return for sth. else **57** *furrowed brow:* (here) worried look **59** *minutiae* [maɪ'nju:ʃii:] (pl): small details

'You're funny, Marcus.'

'I know. People keep telling me. I don't care. I just want you to answer the question.'

'OK. Do you want to touch her? That's got to be the first thing.'

Marcus carried on blasting away at the monster on the screen apparently oblivious to Will's profundities.

'Well?'

'I don't know. I'm thinking about it. Go on.'

'That's it.'

'That's it? There's only one difference?'

'Yeah. Marcus. You have heard of sex, haven't you? It's kind of a big deal.'

'I know, I'm not stupid. But I can't believe there's nothing more to it. Oh, piss.' Marcus had lost another life. ''Cos I'm not sure if I want to touch Ellie or not. But I still know that I want her to be my girlfriend.'

'OK, so what things do you want to be different?'

'I want to be with her more. I want to be with her all the time, instead of just when I bump into her. And I want to get rid of Zoe, even though I like Zoe, because I want Ellie to myself. And I want to tell her things first, before I tell anyone, even you or mum. And I don't want her to have another boyfriend. If I could have all those things, I wouldn't mind if I touched her or not.'

Will shook his head, a gesture that Marcus missed because his eyes were still glued to the video screen. 'I tell you, Marcus, you'll learn. You won't feel like that forever.'

But later that night, when he was home on his own and listening to the sort of music he needed to listen to when he felt like this, music that seemed to find the sore spot in him and press up hard against it, he remembered the deal Marcus was prepared to strike. And yes, he wanted to touch Rachel (the fantasies which involved enormous hotel beds definitely involved touching as well), but right now, he thought, if he had the choice, he'd settle for the less and the more that Marcus wanted.

The conversation in the video games arcade at least had the virtue of creating a mutuality between them: they had both confessed to something they wanted, and those somethings were, when all was said and done, not entirely dissimilar, even though the someones connected with the somethings evidently were. Will couldn't get a very clear sense of Ellie from Marcus's descriptions – he always ended up with the impression of an angry ball of black-lipsticked motion, an unimaginable cross between Siouxsie of the Banshees and the Roadrunner – but he could picture her well enough to see that Ellie and Rachel would not pass as twins. This mutuality, however, seemed more than enough to persuade Marcus that it would be disloyal of him, and some kind of curse on his own desire, not to act as Will's son for an afternoon. So Will made the call, heart thumping, and wangled a Saturday lunch invitation for the pair of them. Marcus came round just after midday, in the hairy jumper Fiona had given him for Christmas and a disastrous pair of canary-yellow cords that might have looked cute on a four-year-old. Will was wearing his favourite Paul Smith shirt and a black leather jacket that he liked to think made him look a little like Matt Dillon in *Drugstore Cowboy*. What was going on here, Will reckoned, was that Marcus was showing a refreshingly rebellious disregard for his dad's dandyism, so he tried to inculcate a feeling of pride, and to ignore the urge to take him out shopping.

'What did you tell your mum?' Will asked him in the car on the way over to Rachel's place.

'I told her you wanted me to meet your new girlfriend.'

'And she was all right about that?'

'No. She thinks you're mad.'

'I'm not surprised. Why would I take you to meet my new girlfriend?'

'Why would you tell your new girlfriend I was your son? You can think up your own explanations next time, if mine are no good. Listen, I've got some questions. How much did I weigh at birth?'

'I dunno. It was your birth.'

'Yeah, but you should know, shouldn't you? If you're my dad, I mean.'

'Surely at this stage in our relationship we're a bit beyond birth weights, aren't we? If you were twelve weeks old it might come up, but twelve years old …'

▷ **5** *blast away at sth.:* attack sth. **6** *profundity:* deep idea **14** *piss:* damn **25** *be glued to sth.* (infml): look at sth. with all your attention **30** *strike a deal:* come to an agreement **36** *mutuality:* Gegenseitigkeit **42** *Siouxsie* ['su:zi]: lead singer of the punk group the Banshees **43** *Roadrunner:* cartoon figure **46** *curse* [kɜ:s]: Fluch **47** *wangle sth.:* get sth. with difficulty **50** *cords* (pl): Kordsamthosen **51** *Paul Smith:* British fashion designer **53** *Matt Dillon:* American actor **55** *disregard for sth.:* rejection of sth. · *dandyism:* extravagant manner of dressing **55** *inculcate sth.:* fix sth. in a person's mind

'OK, so when's my birthday?'

'Marcus, she doesn't suspect we're not father and son. She's not going to be trying to catch us out.'

'But suppose it came up. Suppose I said, you know, Dad's promised me a new Nintendo for my birthday, and she said to you, when's his birthday?'

'Why is she asking me? Why isn't she asking you?'

'Just suppose.'

'OK, when's your birthday?'

'August the nineteenth.'

'I'll remember, I promise. August the nineteenth.'

'And what's my favourite food?'

'Tell me,' Will said wearily.

'Pasta with the mushroom and tomato sauce my mum makes.'

'Right.'

'And where did I go the first time I went abroad?'

'I don't know. Grenoble.'

'Doh,' said Marcus scornfully. 'Why would I want to go there? Barcelona.'

'OK. Got it. Barcelona.'

'And who's my mum?'

'Sorry?'

The question was so basic and yet so pertinent that for a moment Will was completely thrown.

'Your mum's your mum.'

'So you were married to my mum and you've split up.'

'Yeah. Whatever.'

'And does that bother you? Or me?'

Suddenly the absurdity of the questions got to both of them. Marcus began to giggle, a peculiar high-pitched miaow that sounded nothing like himself or any other human but proved to be extraordinarily infectious. Will launched into his own version of a giggling fit.

'It doesn't bother me. Does it bother you?' he said eventually.

But Marcus was unable to reply. He was still miaowing.

One sentence, the first sentence she said, was all it took to bring the whole thing, the elaborate past, present and future he had created for the two of them, crashing to the floor.

'Hi. It's Will and … Mark, is that right?'

'Marcus,' said Marcus, and nudged Will meaningfully.

'Come in, both of you. Come and meet Ali.'

Will had remembered every single tiny detail that Rachel had offered him that first night. He knew the names of the books she had illustrated, although he wasn't absolutely sure whether the first one was called *The Way to the Woods* or *The Way Through the Woods* – he would have to check – and her ex's name, and where he lived, and what he did, and … It was unimaginable that he could have forgotten Ali's name. That was one of his principal facts. That would be like forgetting when England had won the World Cup, or the name of Luke Skywalker's real father – it just couldn't be done, no matter how hard you tried. But she had forgotten Marcus's name – Mark, Marcus, it was all the same to her – and it was thus perfectly clear that she hadn't spent the last ten days in a sleepless fever of imagining and remembering and wondering. He felt crushed. He might as well give up now. These feelings were exactly what he had been so afraid of, and this was why he had been so sure that falling in love was rubbish, and, surprise surprise, it was rubbish, and … and it was too late.

Rachel lived just up the road from Camden Lock, in a tall, thin house full of books and old furniture and sepia photographs of dramatic, romantic Eastern European relatives, and for a moment Will was grateful that his flat and her house would never get a chance to meet, current north London seismological conditions prevailing. Her house would be warm and welcoming, and his would be cocky and cool, and he'd be ashamed of it.

She shouted up the stair: 'Ali!' Nothing. 'ALI!' still nothing. She looked at Will and shrugged. 'He's got his headphones on. Shall we go up?'

'He won't mind?' Will would have minded, when he was twelve years old, for reasons he didn't necessarily want to remember.

▷ **3** *catch sb. out:* prove that sb. is lying **30** *high-pitched:* very high in sound **32** *infectious:* spreading quickly **33** *giggling fit:* uncontrolled laughter **37** *elaborate* (adj): very complicated and carefully prepared **40** *nudge sb.:* push sb. gently **49** *World Cup:* winner of the football world championship, which was won by England in 1966 **50** *Luke Skywalker:* character from the film trilogy *Star Wars*, whose father was the evil Darth Vader **54** *crushed:* destroyed **58** *lock:* Schleuse **59** *sepia:* of a reddish-brown colour **62** *seismological conditions:* weather conditions **63** *cocky* (infml): too showy

Ali's bedroom door was indistinguishable from all the other bedroom doors: no skull and crossbones, no 'Keep Out' signs, no hip-hop graffiti; once inside, however, there was no question but that the room belonged to a boy stuck between the equally wretched states of childhood and adolescence in early 1994. Everything was there – the Ryan Giggs poster and the Michael Jordan poster and the Pamela Anderson poster and the Super Mario stickers ... A social historian of the future would probably be able to date the room to within a twenty-four-hour period. Will glanced at Marcus, who was looking bewildered. Standing Marcus in front of posters of Ryan Giggs and Michael Jordan was like taking an average twelve-year-old to look at the Tudors in the National Portrait Gallery. Ali himself was slumped in front of his computer, headphones still on, oblivious to his guests. His mother went over and tapped him on the shoulder, and he jumped.

'Oh, hi. Sorry.' Ali stood up, and Will immediately saw that this wasn't going to work. Ali was cool – basketball boots, baggy skate-punk trousers, shaggy grunge hair, even an earring – and his face seemed to darken when he took in Marcus's yellow cords and hairy jumper.

'Marcus Ali, Ali Marcus,' said Rachel. Marcus offered his hand, and Ali took it almost satirically. 'Ali Will, Will Ali.' Will raised his eyebrows in Ali's direction. He thought Ali might appreciate the understatement.

'Do you guys want to hang out up here for a while?' Rachel asked them.

Marcus glanced at Will and Will nodded once, while Rachel's back was turned towards him.

'Yeah,' Marcus shrugged and for a moment Will loved him, really loved him.

'OK,' said Ali, with even less enthusiasm.

Rachel and Will went downstairs; ten minutes later – time enough for Will to have dreamed up a whole scenario whereby the four of them took a house in Spain for the summer – they heard a door slam. Rachel went to investigate and came flying back into the sitting room seconds afterwards.

'I'm afraid Marcus has gone home,' she said.

Twenty-seven

Marcus had meant to try. He knew the lunch with Rachel was a big thing for Will, and he knew too that if he did well today, acted out his part, then Will might feel that he had to help him out with Ellie somehow. But this Ali kid never gave him a chance. Will and Rachel went downstairs, Ali stared at him for a few seconds and then started on him.

'There's no fucking way,' was the first thing he said.

'No?' said Marcus, in an attempt to buy himself some time. He had obviously missed something already, although he wasn't quite sure what.

'I'll tell you, if your dad goes out with my mum you're fucking dead. Really. Dead.'

'Oh, he's all right,' said Marcus.

Ali looked at him as though he were mad.

'I don't care if he's all right. I don't want him going out with my mum. So I don't want to see him or you round here ever again, OK?'

'Well,' said Marcus. 'I'm not surc it's rcally up to me.'

'It better be. Or you're dead.'

▷ **2** *skull and crossbones:* Totenkopf **4** *wretched:* unhappy **6** *Ryan Giggs:* Manchester United footballer · *Michael Jordan:* American basketball player **6–7** *Pamela Anderson:* Canadian actress who became famous in the series *Baywatch* **7** *Super Mario:* figure in a computer game **10** *bewildered* [bɪ'wɪldəd]: confused, amazed **12** *Tudors:* royal family that ruled England from 1485–1603 **17–18** *skatepunk trousers:* baggy trousers worn by skateboarders **18** *shaggy:* long and untidy **35** *investigate:* find out what is happening or has happened **43** *start on sb.:* attack sb.verbally

'Can I have a go on the computer? What games have you got?' Marcus knew that a change of subject wouldn't necessarily work. It worked sometimes, but maybe not when someone was threatening to kill you.

'Are you listening to me?'

'Yes, but … I'm not sure there's very much I can do at the moment. We've come for lunch, and Will … that's my dad, I call him Will, because, anyway … he's talking to Rachel, that's your mum –'

'I fucking know it's my mum.'

'– downstairs, and to be honest he's really pretty keen, and who knows? She might be keen on him, so – '

'SHE'S NOT KEEN ON HIM!' Ali suddenly shouted. 'SHE'S ONLY KEEN ON ME!'

Marcus was beginning to realize that Ali was nuts, and he wasn't sure what to do about it. He wondered whether this had ever happened before and, if it had, whether the kid who had been in his position was still here somewhere – either in pieces under the carpet, or tied up in a cupboard, where he was fed once a day on leftover bits of Ali's supper. This kid probably weighed three stone and only talked his own language that nobody else could understand, not that anyone ever listened anyway, not even his mum and dad, who he would never see again.

Marcus considered his options carefully. The least attractive, he felt, and also the most unlikely, was to stay here and pass the time of day with Ali, chat about this and that, have a laugh and a couple of games on the computer; that simply wasn't going to happen. He could go downstairs and join in with Will and Rachel, but Will had as good as told him to stay upstairs, and if he went downstairs he'd have to explain that Ali was a psycho who was on the point of cutting off his arms and legs, and that would be really embarrassing. No, Marcus's choice would simply be to dash downstairs without anyone noticing, sneak out of the front door and get a bus home; after a very brief moment's thought, that is exactly what he did.

He was standing at a bus stop near the Lock when Will found him. His sense of direction wasn't brilliant and he was actually standing on the wrong side of the road, waiting for a bus that would have taken him to the West End, so it was probably just as well that Will drew up alongside him and told him to get into the car.

'What are you playing at?' Will asked him angrily.

'Have I messed it up?' And then, although he shouldn't have said it, even though, or probably because, it was the first thing he thought of: 'Will you still help me out with Ellie?'

'What happened upstairs?'

'He's off his head. He said he'd kill me if you went out with her. And I believed him, too. Anyone would have. He's really scary. Where are we going?' It was raining now, and Camden was choked with traffic and market shoppers. Everywhere Marcus looked there were men and women with long wet straggly hair who looked like they probably played in Nirvana or one of the other bands Ellie liked.

'Back to Rachel's.

'I don't want to go back there.'

'Tough.'

'She'll think I'm stupid.'

'She won't.'

'Why not?'

'Because she thought something like this might happen. She said Ali could be difficult sometimes.'

That made Marcus laugh, 'Ha!', the kind of laugh you did when there was nothing much to laugh at. 'Difficult? He was going to tie me up and lock me in a cupboard and only feed me once a day.'

'Is that what he said?'

'Not in so many words.'

'Anyway, he's crying his eyes out now.'

'Really?'

'Really. Blubbing like a three-year-old.'

This cheered Marcus up no end; he was perfectly happy to go back to Rachel's, he decided.

As it turned out, running away from the house was the best thing Marcus could possibly have done. If he'd known it was all going to end so well, he wouldn't have been so panicky when Will found him at the bus stop. He would have just winked at Will like a wise old owl, and said, 'Wait and see'. When they got back, everything had changed: it was like everyone knew why they were there, instead of

▷ **10** *be keen on sb.* (infml): like sb.very much **29** *psycho* ['saɪkeʊ]: psychopath **31** *dash* (v): run **32** *sneak out:* leave very quietly and unnoticed **44** *off your head:* crazy **46** *be choked with sth.:* be full of sth. **48** *straggly:* untidy **62** *not in so many words:* not directly **71** *wink at sb.:* close one of your eyes briefly as a signal to sb.

pretending that the whole lunch thing was a way of Ali and Marcus getting together to play computer games.

'Ali has got something to say to you, Marcus,' Rachel said, when they walked in.

'Sorry, Marcus,' Ali snivelled. 'I didn't mean to say those things.'

Marcus couldn't see how you could threaten to kill someone by mistake, but he didn't want to make a thing of it; the sight of Ali snivelling away made him feel generous.

'That's OK, Ali,' he said.

'OK, shake hands, guys,' said Rachel, and they did, although it was a rather peculiar and embarrassing handshake. They went up and down much too far three times, and Will and Rachel laughed, which annoyed Marcus. He knew how to shake hands. It was the other idiot who was doing all the up-and-down business.

'Ali finds this very difficult.'

'So does Marcus, Marcus feels just the same, don't you?'

'About what?' He had drifted off temporarily. He was wondering whether there was any connection between Ali's tears and his ability to hurt: did it follow that because he cried so easily he wasn't hard? Or could it be that he was a psycho, and he would pull your head off with his bare hands, blubbing all the time? Maybe the crying had been a bit of a red herring, and Marcus was in even more danger than he had feared.

'About ... you know ... this sort of thing.'

'Yes,' Marcus said. 'I do. Exactly the same.' He was sure he would find out soon enough what he felt exactly the same about.

'Because you get into a pattern, and then each new person who comes along seems to represent some kind of a threat.'

'Exactly. And the last guy I – ' Rachel broke off. 'I'm sorry, I'm not comparing you to him. And I'm not saying that, you know, we're –' She broke off hopelessly.

Will smiled. 'It's OK,' he said gently, and Rachel looked at him and smiled back. Suddenly Marcus could see why people like Rachel and Suzie – nice, attractive women who you thought wouldn't give someone like that the time of day – might like Will. He had gone into this way of looking that he never used on Marcus: there was something in his eyes, a kind of softness that Marcus could see would really work. While he was listening to the conversation, he practised with his own eyes – you had to sort of narrow them, and then make them focus exactly on the other person's face. Would Ellie like that? She'd probably thump him.

'Anyway,' Rachel went on. 'The last guy I went out with ... He wasn't one hundred per cent good news, and he certainly couldn't work out how Ali fitted in, and they ended up ... not on good terms.'

'He was a weirdo,' said Ali.

'Look, I'm sorry that everything's become quite so ... unsubtle,' Rachel said. 'I have no idea whether ... I mean, I don't know, I just got the impression that on New Year's Eve ...' She made a face. 'Oh, God, this is so embarrassing. And it's all your fault, Ali. We shouldn't have to talk about this now.'

'It's OK,' said Marcus brightly. 'He really fancies you. He told me.'

'Are you going cross-eyed?' Ellie said after school on Monday.

'I might be,' Marcus said, because it was easier than saying he was practising a trick he'd learnt from Will.

'Maybe you need new glasses.'

'Yeah.'

'Can you get glasses that are stronger than that?' Zoe asked. She wasn't being nasty, he didn't think, just curious.

The problem was that they were walking to the newsagent's between school and home, and they weren't talking about anything in particular. Will and Rachel had been sitting down, facing one another, and basically talking about how much they liked each other. Walking along the street meant that Marcus kept having to twist his neck to do the eye thing, and he could see that this would make him look a little peculiar, but the trouble was that he and Ellie never did any sitting down and facing each other. They hung out at the vending machine, and sometimes, like today, they met up after school and just mooched around for a while. So what was he supposed to do? How could you gaze into someone's eyes if all you ever saw was their ears?

The newsagent's was full of kids from school, and the guy who owned the place was shouting at some of them to go outside. He

▷ **5** *snivel:* cry in a childish way **17** *drift off:* be somewhere else in your mind **22** *red herring:* sth. that takes your attention away from sth. else **34–35** *not give sb. the time of the day:* not pay any attention to sb. **44** *on good terms:* friendly with one another **46** *unsubtle* [ʌn'sʌtl]: lacking discretion; obvious **52** *cross-eyed:* having your eyes look towards each other **68** *mooch:* walk slowly with no particular purpose wasn't like Mr Patel, who never shouted and never told kids to clear off.

'I'm not going,' said Ellie. 'I'm a customer, not a kid.' She carried on browsing over the sweet display, her hand poised to strike when she saw something she liked.

'You, then,' said the owner to Marcus. 'Outside, please.'

'Don't listen to him, Marcus,' said Ellie. 'It's a breach of human rights. Just because you're young he's calling you a thief. I might take him to court.'

'It's OK,' said Marcus. 'I don't want anything.'

He stepped outside and read the postcards in the window. 'YOUNG DISCIPLINARIAN – 'UNIFORMS AVAILABLE' ... 'PUMA STRIKER BOOTS; SIZE 5 STILL IN BOX':

'You're a pervert, Marcus.'

It was Lee Hartley and a couple of his mates; Marcus hadn't had much trouble from them so far this term, probably because he hung around with Ellie and Zoe.

'What?'

'I bet you don't even know what those cards are all about, do you?'

Marcus couldn't see how the first sentence and the second went together: if he was a pervert, then of course he would understand what the cards were all about, but he let it pass, as he let everything pass at times like this. One of Lee Hartley's mates reached out, removed Marcus's glasses and put them on.

'Fucking hell,' he said. 'No wonder he doesn't know what's going on.' He reeled around for a moment, his arms stretched out in front of him, making grunting noises meant to show that Marcus was in some way mentally deficient.

'Can I have those back now, please? I can't see much without them.'

'Fuck off,' said Lee Hartley's mate.

Ellie and Zoe suddenly emerged from the shop.

'You pathetic little shitbags,' said Ellie. 'Give him those back or you'll get such a slap.'

Lee Hartley's mate handed Marcus the glasses, but she hit him anyway, hard, somewhere between his nose and his eye.

'Tricked you,' she said, and Zoe laughed. 'Now run along, all of you, before I get really cross.'

'Slags,' said Lee Hartley, but he said it quietly as he was walking away.

'Now why does hitting someone make me a slag, I wonder?' said Ellie. 'Boys are peculiar creatures. Not you, though, Marcus. Well, you're peculiar, but in a different way.'

But Marcus wasn't really listening. He was too overcome by Ellie – by her style, and her beauty, and her ability to beat people up – to pay any attention to what she was saying.

▷ **1–2** *clear off* (infml): rudely tell sb. to go away **4** *poised:* still but ready to move **7** *breach* (n): action that breaks a law **26** *reel around:* move around **39** *slag* (sl): whore

Twenty-eight

Twenty-four hours later Marcus was still buzzing, and Will was finding it difficult to adopt the right tone. It would be a mistake, he felt, for the boy to regard Ellie's assault on Lee Somebody's mate as evidence of an uncontrollable passion: surely it proved something like the opposite – that while he relied on teenage girls to defend him in the street, he was unlikely to be much of a catch for anybody. But then, maybe Will was being too traditional in his thinking. Maybe that's how things worked now, and until a girl had smacked someone in the eye for you she wasn't worth a second look. Either way, Marcus was even more smitten than he had been before, and Will feared for him.

'You should have seen her,' Marcus enthused.

'I feel as though I did.'

'Wham!' said Marcus.

'Yes. Wham. You said.'

'She's fantastic.'

'Yes, but ...' Will knew he would have to outline his theory that Marcus's current status as victim did nothing for him sexually or romantically, even though it would be a rocky conversational road. 'What do you think she thinks about having to get you out of trouble?'

'How do you mean?'

'It just ... It's not what normally happens.'

'No. That's why it's so great.'

'I'm not so sure. See, I think it'll be hard for Ellie to think of you as a boyfriend if every time she buys a Mars Bar someone steals your glasses and she has to turn herself into Jean-Claude Van Damme.'

'Who's Jean-Claude Van Damme?'

'Never mind. D'you see what I'm getting at?'

'What am I supposed to do about it then? Take karate lessons or something?'

'All I'm saying is, it might not turn out to be the sort of relationship you want it to be. In my experience romances don't develop in this way. This looks more like pet and owner rather than boyfriend and girlfriend.'

'That's OK,' said Marcus cheerfully.

'You don't mind being treated like a … like a gerbil?'

'No. Course not. That'd do me. I just want to be with her.'

And he said it with such sincerity, and with such a complete absence of self-pity, that for the first time ever Will was tempted to hug him.

Will had no intention of adopting the Ellie/Marcus/gerbil model with Rachel, and though he could recognize the simplicity and decency of Marcus's desire, his own was neither simple nor, frankly, decent, and it was with this knowledge he intended to proceed. At least Ellie knew who and what Marcus was, though, not that Marcus had any choice in the matter: that weird little speccy guy being tormented outside the newsagent's, that was Marcus, and nobody was pretending any different. The guy who turned up for lunch with his twelve-year-old son, that wasn't really Will, and somebody – namely Will himself – was certainly pretending different. One day, he thought, he might learn the lesson that lying about one's very identity was a purely short-term strategy, useful only in relationships that had a limited life-span. You could tell a bus-conductor or a taxi driver all sorts of rubbish, provided the journey was brief, but if you intended to spend the rest of your life with somebody, then it was kind of inevitable that she would find out a few things sooner or later.

Will decided he would correct any erroneous impressions he might have given slowly and patiently, but halfway through their first time out alone together, he was reminded of the old April Fool's Day joke about Britain changing over to driving on the right, and making

▷ **1** *buzz* (v): be full of excitement **3** *assault* [ə'sɔːlt] (n): attack **5** *rely on sb.*: depend on sb. **10** *smitten:* in love **11** *enthuse:* say excitedly **17** *current:* present **36** *gerbil:* Wüstenspringmaus **57** *erroneous:* mistaken the changeover gradually. Either you lied or you told the truth, it appeared, and that in-between state was pretty tricky to achieve.

'Oh,' was all Rachel said at first, when he told her he wasn't Marcus's natural father. She was trying and failing to pick up a clump of seaweed with her chopsticks.

'It's not really seaweed, you know,' said Will in a misguided attempt to make out that what he was telling her wasn't any kind of big deal – not to him, anyway. 'It's lettuce or something. They shred it and fry it and put sugar and – '

'So who is his natural father?'

'Well,' said Will. Why hadn't it occurred to him that if he wasn't Marcus's father, then someone else would have to be? Why did these things never occur to him? 'It's a guy called Clive who lives in Cambridge.'

'Right. And you get on OK with him?'

'Yeah. We spent Christmas together, actually.'

'So – sorry, I'm being a bit thick here – if you're not Marcus's natural father, and you don't live with him, then, you know, how is he your son?'

'Yes. Ha ha. I see what you mean. It must look very confusing from the outside.'

'Tell me how it is on the inside.'

'It's just that sort of relationship. I'm old enough to be his father. He's young enough to be my son. So – '

'You're old enough to be the father of just about anyone under twenty. Why this particular boy?'

'I don't know. Just one of those things. Would you like to move on to wine now, or do you want to stick with the Chinese beer? Anyway, tell me about your relationship with Ali. Is it as complicated as mine and Marcus's?'

'No. I slept with his father and nine months later I gave birth, and that's about it. Pretty straightforward, but these things usually are.'

'Yes. I envy you.'

'I'm, sorry to harp on about this, but I still haven't got it all worked out. You're Marcus's stepfather, but you don't live with him or his mother.'

'I suppose you could look at it that way, yes.'

'How else could you look at it?'

'Ha. I see what you mean,' he said thoughtfully, as if he had just that second worked out that there was only one way of looking at it.

'Did you ever live with Marcus's mother?'

'Define "live with".'

'Did you ever have a spare pair of socks at her house? Or a toothbrush?'

Say that Fiona had given him a pair of socks for Christmas. And say that he had left them at her house, and hadn't got around to picking them up yet. Then he could point out, with a clear conscience, that not only had he once kept a spare pair of socks at Fiona's house, *but they were still there!* Unfortunately, however, she hadn't given him socks, she had given him that stupid book. And he hadn't even left the book there anyway. So the dream sock scenario was just that – a dream.

'No.'

'Just ... no?'

'Yes.'

He picked up the last little spring roll, dunked it in the chilli sauce, put it in his mouth, and behaved as though it were way too big, so he wouldn't be able to speak for several minutes. Rachel would have to do the talking, and she would probably want to talk about something else eventually. He wanted her to tell him about the book she was currently illustrating, or her ambition to exhibit her work, or how much she had been looking forward to seeing him. Those were the kinds of conversations he had envisaged; he was fed up with talking about imaginary children, and even more fed up with talking about why he had imagined them in the first place.

But Rachel simply sat there and waited for him to finish his mouthful, and however much he chewed and grimaced and swallowed and choked he couldn't make a mini spring roll last forever. So he told her the truth, as he knew he would, and she was appalled, as she had every right to be.

'I never actually said he was my son. The words "I have a son called Marcus" never passed my lips. That's what you chose to believe.'

▷ **4** *clump:* small bunch **5** *seaweed:* Seetang · *chopstick:* pair of thin sticks with which Chinese eat food **34** *harp on about sth.:* keep talking about sth. **56** *dunk sth. in sth. else:* put sth. into sth. else (esp. a liquid)

'Yeah, right. It's me who's the fantasist. I wanted to believe you had a son, so I let my imagination run riot.'

'You know, that's a very interesting theory. I read this thing in the paper once about this guy who'd taken all these middle-aged women for a ride, cleaned them out of their life savings because they were convinced he was rich. And, the thing was, he didn't even have to do anything to prove it. They just believed him.'

'So he told them he was rich. He lied. That's different.'

'Ah. Yes. I see what you mean. That's sort of where the comparison breaks down, doesn't it?'

'Because you didn't lie. I just made it up. I thought, Cute guy, if only he had a kid, a geeky son, pre-teenage if possible, and then you turned up at my house with Marcus, and bingo! I made this crazy link because of some deep psychological need in me.'

It wasn't turning out as badly as Will feared it might. She was definitely seeing some kind of funny side, even though she clearly thought he was a weirdo.

'You shouldn't beat yourself up about it. Could have happened to anyone.'

'Hey, don't push your luck. If I want to be amused and tolerant, that's my business. I'm not yet at a stage where you can make jokes too.'

'Sorry.'

'But where does Marcus come in? I mean, you obviously hadn't hired him for the afternoon. There's some kind of relationship there.'

She was right, of course, and he rescued a potentially disastrous evening by telling her everything there was to tell. Nearly everything, anyway: he didn't tell her the reason he had come across Marcus in the first place was because he had joined SPAT. He didn't tell her that because he thought it might sound bad coming on top of a similar revelation. He didn't want her to think he had a problem.

Rachel invited him back for coffee after the meal, but Will knew that sex wasn't in the air. Or rather, there was a little, the merest whiff, but it was emanating from him, so it didn't count. He found Rachel so attractive that there would always be sex in the air when he was with her. All that seemed to be coming from her was a quiet amusement and a sort of baffled tolerance, and though he was grateful for these small mercies, they were very rarely, he would imagine, precursors to any kind of physical intimacy beyond a quick hair-ruffle.

Rachel made coffee in great big blue designer cups and they sat opposite each other, Rachel spread out on the sofa, Will bolt upright in an old armchair covered with some kind of Asian throw.

'Why did you think Marcus would make you more interesting?' she asked him after they had poured and stirred and blown and done everything else they could think of doing to a cup of coffee.

'Was I more interesting?'

'Yes, I suppose you were.'

'Why?'

'Because ... You really want to know the truth?'

'Yes.'

'Because I thought you were a sort of blank – you didn't do anything, you weren't passionate about anything, you didn't seem to have much to say – and then when you said you had a kid –'

'I didn't actually say – '

'Yeah, whatever ... I thought, I've got this guy all wrong.'

'So there you are then. You've answered your own question.'

'But I *had* got you wrong.'

'How d'you work that out?'

'Because there is something there. You didn't make it all up about Marcus. You're involved, and you care, and you understand him, and you worry about him ... So you're not the guy I thought you were before you brought him up.'

Will knew this was supposed to make him feel better about everything, but it didn't. For a start, he'd only known Marcus for a few months, so Rachel had raised some interesting questions about the thirty-six years he had let slip through his fingers. And he didn't want to be defined by Marcus. He wanted his own life, and his own identity; he wanted to be interesting in his own right. Where had he heard that complaint before? At SPAT, that's where. He had somehow managed to turn himself into a single parent without even going to the trouble of fathering a child.

There was hardly any point in moaning though. It was too late for that; he had chosen to ignore his own advice, advice that had served

▷ **4–5** *take sb. for a ride* (infml): cheat or trick sb. **5** *clean sb.out of sth.:* take all of sb.'s sth. (esp. money) **18** *beat yourself up about sth.* (infml): blame yourself for sth. **33** *emanate from sb.:* come from sb. **37** *mercy:* kindness · *precursor:* forerunner **40** *bolt upright:* sitting with your back straight him well for his entire adult life. The way Will saw it, the reason that some of the people at SPAT were in a state wasn't because they had kids – their problems had started earlier than that, when they first fell for someone and made themselves vulnerable. Now Will had done the same and, as far as he was concerned, he deserved all he got. He'd be singing with his eyes closed soon, and there was nothing he could do about it.

Twenty-nine

For three or four weeks – it couldn't have been any longer than that, but later on, when Marcus looked back on that time, it seemed like months, or years – nothing happened. He saw Will, he saw Ellie (and Zoe) at school, Will bought him some new glasses and took him to have his hair cut, he discovered through Will a couple of singers he liked who weren't Joni Mitchell or Bob Marley, singers that Ellie had heard of and didn't hate. It felt as though he were changing, in his own body and in his head, and then his mum started the crying thing again.

Just like before, there didn't seem to be any reason for it. And just like before, it began slowly, with the odd snuffle after dinner, which one night turned into a long, frightening burst of sobbing, a burst that Marcus could do nothing about, no matter how many questions he asked or hugs he gave her; and then, finally, there was the breakfast crying again, and he knew for sure that things were serious and they were in trouble.

But one thing had changed. Back in the first breakfast crying time, hundreds of years ago, he was on his own; now, there were loads of people. He had Will, he had Ellie, he had ... Anyway, he had two people, two friends, and that was some kind of improvement on before. He could just go up to either of them and say, 'My mum's at it again,' and they'd know what he meant, and they'd be able to say something that might make some kind of sense.

▷ **18** *snuffle:* cry

'My mum's at it again,' he said to Will on the second breakfast crying day. (He hadn't said anything on day one, just in case it turned out to be merely a temporary depression, but when she started up again the next morning he could see he'd just been stupidly hopeful.)

'At what?'

Marcus was disappointed for a moment, but he hadn't really given Will very much to go on. She could have been at anything, which was weird if you thought about it: no one could say his mum was predictable. She could have been moaning about Marcus coming round to Will's flat again, or she could have been on about him taking up the piano, or she could have found a boyfriend that Marcus didn't like very much (Marcus had told Will about some of the peculiar men she'd been out with since his parents had split) ... It was nice, in a way, contemplating all the things he could have meant when he'd said she was at it again. He thought it made his mum seem interesting and complicated, which of course she was.

'The crying.'

'Oh.' They were in Will's kitchen, toasting crumpets under the grill; it was a Thursday afternoon routine they'd got into. 'Are you worried about her?'

'Course. She's just the same now as she was before. Worse.'

That wasn't true. Nothing could be worse than before, because before it had gone on for ages and it had all come to a head on the Dead Duck Day, but he wanted to make sure that Will knew it was serious.

'So what are you going to do?'

It hadn't occurred to Marcus that he would have to do anything – partly because he hadn't done anything before (but then, before hadn't worked out so brilliantly, so maybe he shouldn't use before as any kind of example), and partly because he thought Will might take over. That's what he wanted. That was the whole point of having friends, he thought. 'What am *I* going to do? What are *you* going to do?'

'What am *I* going to do?' Will laughed, and then remembered that what they were talking about wasn't supposed to be funny. 'Marcus, I can't do anything.'

'You could talk to her.'

'Why should she listen to me? Who am I? Nobody.'

'You're not nobody. You're –'

'Just because you come round here for a cup of tea after school doesn't mean I can cheer your mum up. In fact, I know I can't.'

'I thought we were friends.'

'Ow. Fuck. Sorry.' In attempting to remove a crumpet, Will had burnt his fingers. 'Is that what we are, d'you reckon? Friends?' He seemed to find this funny too; at any rate, he was smiling.

'Yeah. So what would you say we are?'

'Well. Friends is fine.'

'Why are you smiling?'

'It's a bit funny, isn't it? You and me?'

'I suppose so.' Marcus thought about it for a little while longer. 'Why?'

'Because we're such different heights.'

'Oh. I see.'

'Joke.'

'Ha ha.'

Will let Marcus butter the crumpets because he loved doing it. It was much better than buttering toast, because with toast you had that thing where if the butter was too cold and hard all you could do was scrape off the brown that made toast what it was, and he hated that. With crumpets it was effortless: you just put a lump of butter on top, waited for a few seconds, then messed it about until it started to disappear into the holes. It was one of the few occasions in life where things seemed to go right every time.

'D'you want anything on it?'

'Yeah.' He reached for the honey, put his knife in the jar and began twirling it about.

'Listen,' Will said. 'That's right. We're friends. That's why I can't do anything about your mum.'

'How d'you work that out?'

'I said it was a joke that we're different heights, but maybe it's not. Maybe that's how you should look at it. I'm your mate and I'm about a foot taller than you, and that's it.'

'I'm sorry,' Marcus said. 'I'm not getting you.'

'I had a mate at school who was about a foot taller than me. He was enormous. He was six foot one when we were in the second year.'

▷ **9** *predictable:* behaving in a way that you expect **18** *crumpet:* flat, breadlike cake with small holes on one side **23** *come to a head:* reach a state where sth. dramatic happens **66** *twirl sth. about:* move sth. around

'We don't have second years.'

'Year whatever it is. Year eight.'

'So what?'

'I'd never have asked him to help if my mum was depressed. We used to talk about football and *Mission Impossible* and that was it. Say we were talking about whether, I don't know, Peter Osgood should be playing for England, and then I said, "Oi, Phil, will you talk to my mum because she's in tears all the time," he'd have looked at me as if I were nuts. He was twelve. What's he going to say to my mum? "Hello, Mrs Freeman, have you thought of tranquillizers?" '

'I don't know who Peter Osgood is. I don't know about football.'

'Oh, Marcus, stop being so bloody obtuse. What I'm saying is, OK, I'm your friend. I'm not your uncle. I'm not your dad, I'm not your big brother. I can tell you who Kurt Cobain is and what trainers to get, and that's it. Understood?'

'Yes.'

'Good.'

But on the way home Marcus remembered the end of the conversation, the way Will had said 'Understood?' in a way that was supposed to tell him that the conversation was over, and he wondered whether friends did that. He didn't think they did. He knew teachers who said that, and parents who said that, but he didn't know any friends who said that, no matter how tall they were.

Marcus wasn't surprised about Will, not really. If he had been asked to say who his best friend was, he'd have gone for Ellie – not just because he loved her and wanted to go out with her, but because she was nice to him, and always had been, not counting the first time he'd met her, when she'd called him a squitty little shitty snotty bastard. She hadn't been all that nice then. It wouldn't be fair to say that Will hadn't ever been nice to him, what with the trainers and the crumpets and the two video games and so on, but it would be fair to say that sometimes Will didn't look thrilled to see him, especially if he called round four or five days in a row. Ellie, on the other hand, always threw her arms around him and made a fuss of him, and that, Marcus thought, had to mean something.

Today, however, she didn't seem terribly pleased to see him. She looked down and distracted, and she didn't say anything, let alone do anything, when he went to see her in her classroom at breaktime. Zoe was sitting next to her, looking at her and holding her hand.

'What's happened?'

'Haven't you heard?' said Zoe.

Marcus hated it when people said that to him, because he never had.

'I don't think so.'

'Kurt Cobain.'

'What about him?'

'He tried to kill himself. Took an overdose.'

'Is he all right?'

'We think so. They pumped his stomach.'

'Good.'

'Nothing's good,' said Ellie.

'No,' said Marcus. 'But – '

'He'll do it, you know,' said Ellie. 'In the end. They always do. He wants to die. It wasn't a cry for help. He hates this world.'

Marcus suddenly felt sick. The moment he'd walked out of Will's flat the previous evening he'd been imagining this conversation with Ellie, and how she would cheer him up in a way that Will never could, and it wasn't like that at all; instead, the room was beginning to turn round slowly, and all the colour was draining out of it.

'How do you know? How do you know he wasn't just messing about? I'll bet you he never does anything like it again.'

'You don't know him,' Ellie said.

'Neither do you,' Marcus shouted at her. 'He's not even a real person. He's just a singer. He's just someone on a sweat-shirt. It's not like he's anyone's mum.'

'No, he's someone's dad, you little prat,' said Ellie. 'He's Frances Bean's dad. He's got a beautiful little girl and he still wants to die. So, you know.'

Marcus did know, he thought. He turned around and ran out.

He decided to skip the next couple of lessons. If he went to the maths class, he would sit and dream and get picked on and laughed at when he attempted to answer a question that had been asked an hour or a month before, or that hadn't been asked at all; he wanted to

▷ **12** *obtuse* (fml): unwilling to understand **34** *make a fuss of sb.*: show a lot of affection for sb.

be on his own to think properly, without irrelevant interruptions, so he went to the boys' toilets near the gym and shut himself in the right-hand cubicle, because it had comforting hot pipes running along the wall which you could sort of squat down on. After a few minutes someone came in and started kicking on the door.

'Are you in there, Marcus? I'm sorry. I'd forgotten about your mum. It's OK. She's not like Kurt.'

He paused for a moment, then unbolted the door and peered round it.

'How do you know?'

'Because you're right. He's not a real person.'

'You're only saying that to make me feel better.'

'OK, he's a real person. But he's a different sort of real person.'

'In what way?'

'I don't know. He just is. He's like James Dean and Marilyn Monroe and Jimi Hendrix and all those people. You know that he's going to die, and it'll be OK.'

'OK for who? Not for ... what's her name?'

'Frances Bean?'

'Yeah. Why is it OK for her? It's not OK for her. It's just OK for you.'

A boy from Ellie's year came in to use the toilet. 'Go *away*,' said Ellie, as if she had said it a hundred times before, and as if the kid had no right to be wanting a pee in the first place. 'We're talking.' He opened his mouth to argue, realized who he was about to argue with, and went out again. 'Can I come in?' Ellie said when he'd gone.

'If there's room.'

They squashed up next to each other on the hot pipes, and Ellie pulled the door towards her and bolted it.

'You think I know things, but I don't,' said Ellie. 'Not really. I don't know anything about this stuff. I don't know why he feels like he does, or why your mum feels like she does. And I don't know what it feels like to be you. Pretty scary, I should think.'

'Yeah.' He started to cry, then. It wasn't noisy crying – his eyes just filled with tears and they started to stream down his cheeks – but it was still embarrassing. He'd never thought he'd cry in front of Ellie.

She put her arm around him. 'What I mean is, don't listen to me. You know more than I do. You should be telling me things about it.'

'I don't know what to say about it.'

'Let's talk about something else, then.'

But they didn't talk about anything for a while. They just sat on the pipes together, moving their bottoms when they got too hot, and waited until they felt like going back out into the world.

Thirty

Will had vertigo, so he didn't like looking down. But sometimes it couldn't be helped. Sometimes someone said something, and he did look down, and he was left with an irresistible urge to jump. He could remember the last time it had happened: it was when he had split up with Jessica, and she had phoned him late at night and told him he was useless, worthless, that he would never be or do anything, that he had had the chance with her to – there was some peculiar, incomprehensible phrase she had used – *sprinkle some salt on the ice*, that was it, by having a relationship that meant something, and maybe a family. And while she was saying it he had started to get panicky, clammy, dizzy, because he knew that some people might think she was right, but he also knew that there was nothing in the world he could do about it.

He'd had just the same feeling when Marcus was asking him to do something about Fiona. Of course he should do something about Fiona; all that stuff about being the same but taller was bollocks, obviously. He was older than Marcus, he knew more ... Every way you looked at it there was an argument that said, get involved, help the kid out, look after him.

He wanted to help him out, and he had done in some ways. But this depression thing, there was no way he wanted to get involved in that. He could write the whole conversation in his head, he could hear it like a radio play, and he didn't like what he heard. There were two words in particular that made him want to cover his ears with his hands; they always had done, and they always would, as long as his life revolved around *Countdown* and *Home and Away* and new

Marks and Spencer sandwich combinations, and he could see no way in which he could avoid them in any conversation with Fiona about her depression. Those two words were 'the point'. As in, 'What's the point?'; 'I don't see the point'; 'there's just no point' (a phrase which omits the 'the', but one that counts anyway, because the 'the' wasn't the point of 'the point', really) … You couldn't have a talk about life, and especially about the possibility of ending it, without bringing up the fucking point, and Will just couldn't see one. Sometimes that was OK; sometimes you could be bombed out of your head on magic mushrooms at two in the morning, and some arsehole lying on the floor with his head jammed up against the speakers would want to talk about the point, and you could simply say, 'There isn't one, so shut up.' But you couldn't say that to someone who was so unhappy and lost that they wanted to empty a whole bottle of pills down themselves and go to sleep for as long as it took. Telling someone like Fiona that there was no point was more or less the same as killing her off, and though Will hadn't always seen eye-to-eye with her, he could honestly say he had no desire to murder her.

People like Fiona really pissed him off. They ruined it for everyone. It wasn't easy, floating on the surface of everything: it took skill and nerve, and when people told you that they were thinking of taking their own life, you could feel yourself being dragged under with them. Keeping your head above water was what it was all about, Will reckoned. That was what it was all about for everyone, but those who had reasons for living, jobs and relationships and pets, their heads were a long way from the surface anyway. They were wading in the shallow end, and only a bizarre accident, a freak wave from the wave machine, was going to sink them. But Will was struggling. He was way out of his depth, and he had cramp, probably because he'd gone

▷ **1** *vertigo:* fear of looking down when you are in a high place **3** *irresistable:* very strong **11** *clammy:* wet in an unpleasant way · *dizzy:* losing your balance **16** *bollocks* (sl): nonsense **27** *Marks and Spencer's:* British chain of department stores selling clothes and food **35** *be bombed out of your head:* (here) be high on drugs **35–36** *magic mushroom:* type of mushroom that causes hallucinations **37** *jam up against sth:* lie against sth. · *speaker:* loudspeaker **43** *see eye-to-eye with sb.:* share the same views as sb. **48** *drag sb.:* pull sb. **52** *wade:* walk slowly in water that covers part of your legs **53** *freak* (adj): unexpected **55** *be out of your depth:* be in water where you can no longer touch the ground standing up · *cramp:* Krampf in too soon after his lunch, and there were all sorts of ways he could see himself being dragged up to the surface by some smoothy lifeguard with blond hair and a washboard stomach, long after his lungs had filled with chlorinated water. He needed someone buoyant to hang on to; he certainly didn't need a dead weight like Fiona. He was very sorry, but that was the way things were. And that was the thing about Rachel: she was buoyant. She could keep him afloat. He went to see Rachel.

His relationship with Rachel was weird, or what Will considered weird, which was, he supposed, very different from what David Cronenberg or that guy who wrote *The Wasp Factory* considered weird. The weird thing was that they still hadn't had sex, even though they'd been seeing each other for a few weeks. The subject just never came up. He was almost sure that she liked him, as in she seemed to enjoy seeing him and they never seemed to run out of things to talk about; he was more than sure that he liked her, as in he enjoyed seeing her, he wanted to be with her all the time for the rest of his life, and he couldn't look at her without being conscious of his pupils dilating to an enormous and possibly comical size. It was fair to say that they liked each other in different ways.

(On top of which he had developed an almost irresistible urge to kiss her when she was saying something interesting, which he regarded as a healthy sign – he had never before wanted to kiss someone simply because she was stimulating – but which she was beginning to view with some distrust, even though she didn't, as far as he knew, know what was going on. What happened was, she would be talking with humour and passion and a quirky, animated intelligence about Ali, or music, or her painting, and he would drift off into some kind of possibly sexual but certainly romantic reverie, and she would ask him whether he was listening, and he would feel embarrassed and protest too much in a way that suggested he hadn't been paying attention because she was boring him stupid. It was something of a double paradox, really: you were enjoying someone's conversation so much that a) you appeared to glaze over, and b) you wanted to stop her talking by covering her mouth with yours. It was no good and something had to be done about it, but he had no idea what: he had never been in this situation before.)

He didn't mind having a female friend; his realization during his drink with Fiona that he had never had any kind of relationship with someone he hadn't wanted to sleep with still unsettled him. The problem was that he did want to sleep with Rachel, very much, and he didn't know whether he could bear to sit there on her sofa with his eyes dilating wildly for the next ten or twenty years, or however long female friends lasted (how would he know?), listening to her being unintentionally sexy on the subject of drawing mice. He didn't know whether his pupils could bear it, more to the point. Wouldn't they start hurting after a while? He was almost sure it wouldn't do them much good, all that expanding and contracting, but he would only mention the pupil-pain to Rachel as a last resort; there was a remote possibility that she might want to sleep with him to save his eyesight, but he'd prefer to find another, more conventionally romantic route to her bed. Or his bed. He wasn't bothered about which bed they did it in. The point was that it just wasn't happening.

And then it happened, that evening, for no reason that he could fathom at the time – although later, when he thought about it, he came up with one or two ideas that made sense but the implications of which he found somewhat disturbing. One moment they were talking, the next moment they were kissing, and the moment after that she was leading him upstairs with one hand and unbuttoning her denim shirt with the other. And the weird thing was that sex hadn't been in the air, as far as he could tell; he'd simply come round to see a friend because he was feeling low. So here was the first of the disturbing implications: if he ended up having sex when he had been unable to detect sex in the air, he was obviously a pretty hopeless sex detective. If, in the immediate aftermath of an apparently sex-free conversation, a beautiful woman started to lead you to the bedroom while unbuttoning her shirt, you were clearly missing something somewhere.

It began with a stroke of luck that passed him by at the time: Ali was away for the night, sleeping over at a schoolfriend's house. If Rachel had told him at any other stage of their relationship that she

▷ **3** *washboard:* (here) lean and muscular **4** *buoyant* ['bɔɪənt]: cheerful and lively **10–11** *David Cronenberg:* Canadian film director **11** *The Wasp Factory:* novel by Iain Banks **18** *dilate:* become larger **27** *quirky:* strange, odd **29** *reverie:* kind of daydream **34** *glaze over:* (of your eyes) go blank **40** *unsettle sb.:* make sb. feel uneasy **48** *expand:* become wider · *contract* [- ˈ-] (v): become narrower **49** *as a last resort:* as a last chance after everything else has failed **62** *low* (infml): depressed **65** *aftermath:* situation that exists after a particular event was unencumbered by her psychotically Oedipal son, he would have taken it as a sign from Almighty God that he was about to get laid, but today it didn't even register. They went into the kitchen, she made them coffee and he found himself launching into the whole thing about Fiona and Marcus and the point even before the kettle had boiled.

'What's the *point*?' Rachel echoed. 'Jesus.'

'And don't say Ali. I haven't got an Ali.'

'You've got a Marcus.'

'It's hard to think of Marcus as the point of anything. I know that's a terrible thing to say, but it's true. You've met him.'

'He's just a bit messed up. But he adores you.'

It had never occurred to Will that Marcus actually had any real feelings towards him, especially feelings that were visible to a third party. He knew that Marcus liked hanging out at his place, and he knew that Marcus described him as a friend, but all this he had taken merely as evidence of the boy's eccentricity and loneliness. Rachel's observation that there were real feelings involved kind of changed things, just as they sometimes did when you found out that a woman you hadn't noticed was attracted to you, so that you ended up reassessing the situation and finding her much more interesting than you ever had done before.

'You reckon?'

'Of course he does.'

'He's still not the point, though. If I were about to stick my head in the gas oven, and then you told me Marcus adored me, I wouldn't necessarily take it out again.'

Rachel laughed.

'What's so funny?'

'I don't know. Just the idea that I'd be there in that situation. If you ended up sticking your head in a gas oven at the end of an evening, we'd have to come to the conclusion that the evening hadn't been a raging success.'

'I …' Will stopped, and started, and then ploughed on anyway, with as much sincerity as he could muster, and with much more sincerity than the line could bear. 'I would never stick my head in a gas oven at the end of an evening with you.'

He knew the moment he'd said it that it was a big mistake. He'd meant it, but that was precisely what provoked the hilarity. Rachel laughed and laughed until her eyes filled with tears. 'That,' she said in between great gulps of air, 'is ... the ... most ... romantic ... thing ... anyone's ever said to me.'

Will sat there helplessly, feeling like the most stupid man in the world, but when things calmed down again they seemed to be in a different place, somewhere where they were able to be warmer and less nervous with each other. Rachel made the coffee, found some stale custard creams and sat down with him at the kitchen table.

'You don't need a point.'

'Don't I? That's not what it feels like.'

'No. See, I was thinking about you. About how you have to be fairly tough in your head to do what you do.'

'What?' For a moment Will was completely bewildered.

'Tough in your head', 'Do what you do' ... These were not phrases that anyone used about him too often. What the fuck was it he'd told Rachel he did? Work in a coalmine? Teach young offenders? But then he remembered he'd never actually told Rachel any lies, and his bewilderment took a different shape. 'What do I do?'

'Nothing.'

That's what Will thought he did. 'So how come I have to be tough to do that?'

'Because ... most of us think that the point is something to do with work, or kids, or family, or whatever. But you don't have any of that. There's nothing between you and despair, and you don't seem a very desperate person.'

'Too stupid.'

'You're not stupid. So why don't you ever put your head in the oven?'

'I don't know. There's always a new Nirvana album to look forward to, or something happening in *NYPD Blue* to make you want to watch the next episode.'

'Exactly.'

▷ **1** *be unencumbered by sb.:* not be burdened by sb. · *psychotic:* mad · *Oedipal:* (here) clinging to your mother **2** *get laid* (sl): have sex **17** *eccentricity:* strangeness **33** *raging:* great **34** *plough on* [plaʊ]: continue doing sth. **39** *hilarity:* loud laughter **41** *gulp* (n): act of breathing in **47** *custard cream:* type of biscuit **55** *offender:* person who has committed a crime **69** *NYPD Blue:* TV police series

'That's the point? *NYPD Blue*? Jesus.' It was worse than he thought.

'No, no. The point is you keep going. You want to. So all the things that make you want to are the point. I don't know if you even realize it, but on the quiet you don't think life's too bad. You love things. Telly. Music. Food.' She looked at him. 'Women, probably. Which I guess means you like sex too.'

'Yeah.' He said it sort of grumpily, as if she had caught him out somehow, and she smiled.

'I don't mind. People who like sex are usually pretty good at it. Anyway. I'm the same. I mean, I love things, and they're mostly different things from you. Poetry. Paintings. My work. Men, and sex. My friends. Ali. I want to see what Ali gets up to tomorrow.' She started fiddling with the biscuit, breaking off the ends in an attempt to expose the cream, but the biscuit was too soft and it crumbled.

'See, a few years ago, I was really, really down, and I did think about … you know, what you imagine Fiona's thinking about. And I really felt guilty about it, because of Ali, and I knew I shouldn't be that way but I was, and … Anyway, it was always, you know, not today. Maybe tomorrow, but not today. And after a few weeks of that I knew I was never going to do it, and the reason I was never going to do it was because I didn't want to miss out. I don't mean that life was great and I didn't want not to participate. I just mean there were always one or two things that seemed unfinished, things I wanted to follow through. Like you want to see the next episode of *NYPD Blue*. If I'd just finished stuff for a book, I wanted to see it come out. If I was seeing a guy, I wanted one more date. If Ali had a parents' evening coming up, I wanted to talk to his form teacher. Little things like that, but there was always something. And in the end I realized there would always be something, and that those somethings would be enough.' She looked up from the remnants of her biscuit and laughed, embarrassed. 'That's what I think, anyway.'

'Fiona must have things like that.'

'Yeah, well. I don't know. It doesn't sound like Fiona's getting the breaks. You need them too.'

Was that really all there was to it? Probably not, Will thought, on balance. There were probably all sorts of things missing – stuff about how depression made you tired of everything, tired of everything no matter how much you loved it; and stuff about loneliness, and panic, and plain bewilderment. But Rachel's simple positivity was something to be going on with and, in any case, the conversation about the point created a point of its own, because there was this pause, and Rachel looked at him, and that was when they started kissing.

'Why don't I talk to her?' said Rachel. They were the first words spoken afterwards, although there had been a bit of talking during, and for a moment Will didn't understand what she meant at all: he was trying to trace it back to something that had taken place in the previous thirty minutes, a half-hour that had left him feeling a bit shaky and almost tearful, and had led him to question his previous conviction that sex was some sort of fantastic carnal alternative to drink, drugs and a great night out, but nothing much more than that.

'You? She doesn't know you.'

'I don't see why that would matter. Might even help. And maybe you'd get the hang of it, if I showed you how. It's not so bad.'

'OK.' There was something in Rachel's voice that Will couldn't quite isolate, but he didn't want to think about Fiona just at that moment, so he didn't try very hard. He couldn't ever remember feeling so happy.

▷ **8** *grumpy:* bad-tempered **22** *miss out:* not know what is happening or will happen **34–35** *get the breaks* (infml): get the chance to get away from difficulties **36–37** *on balance:* after considering everything **40** *positivity:* positive attitude towards things **51** *carnal:* sexual

Thirty-one

Marcus was finding it hard to get used to the idea that winter was over. Pretty much everything Marcus had experienced in London had taken place in the dark and the wet (there must have been a few light evenings right at the beginning of the school year, but so much had happened since that he no longer had any recollection of them), and now he was able to walk home from Will's place in the late afternoon sunshine. It was hard not to feel that everything was OK the first week after the clocks had gone forward; it was ridiculously easy to believe that his mum would get better, that he'd suddenly age three years and suddenly get cool so that Ellie would like him, that he'd score the winning goal for the school football team and become the most popular person in school.

But that was stupid, in the same way that star signs were stupid, in his opinion. The clocks had gone forward for everybody, not just him, and there was no way that every depressed mother was going to cheer up, there was no way that every kid in Britain was going to score the winning goal for the school football team – especially every kid in Britain who hated football and didn't know which end of a ball to kick – and there was certainly no way that every single twelve-year-old was going to become fifteen overnight. The chances of it happening to even one of them were pretty slim, and even if it did, it wouldn't be Marcus, knowing his luck. It would be some other twelve-year-old at some other school who wasn't in love with someone three years older than him, and who therefore wouldn't even care very much. The injustice of the scene that Marcus had just pictured made him angry, and he marked his return home by slamming the door in a temper.

'Have you been round to Will's?' his mum asked. She looked OK. Maybe one of the clocks-forward wishes had come true.

'Yeah. I wanted to ...' He still felt he should come up with reasons for why he went round, and he still couldn't think of anything to say.

'I don't care. Your dad's hurt himself. You've got to go up and see him. He fell off a window-ledge.'

'I'm not going while you're like this.'

'Like what?'

'Like crying all the time.'

'I'm OK. Well, I'm not OK, but I'm not going to do anything. Promise.'

'Is he really bad?'

'He's broken his collar bone. And he's a bit concussed.'

He fell off a window-ledge. No wonder his mum had cheered up.

'What was he doing on a window-ledge?'

'Some sort of DIY thing. Painting, or grouting, or one of those Scrabble words. For the first time ever. That'll teach him a lesson.'

'And why do I have to go up?'

'He was asking for you. I think he's a bit doolally at the moment.'

'Thanks.'

'Oh, Marcus, I'm sorry, that isn't why he's been asking for you. I just meant ... I think he's feeling a bit pathetic. Lindsey said he was quite lucky it wasn't worse, so maybe he's having this big think about his life.'

'He can piss off.'

'Marcus!'

But Marcus didn't want an argument about where and why he had learnt to swear; he wanted to sit in his room and sulk, and that's exactly what he did.

He's having this big think about his life ... That had made Marcus so angry, when his mum had told him, and now he was trying to work

▷ **27** *slam sth.:* shut sth. with a loud noise · *in a temper:* in a bad mood **33** *window-ledge:* narrow shelf below a window **40** *collar bone:* Schlüsselbein · *be concussed:* be temporarily hurt in your brain **43** *DIY* (infml) = *do it yourself:* home improvement which you do yourself · *grout:* fill up gaps between bricks, etc. with some substance **46** *doolally* (infml): confused **55** *sulk* (v): be silently angry and feel sorry for yourself out why. He was quite good at working things out when he wanted to: he had an old bean bag in his room, and he sat on it and stared at the wall where he had stuck up some interesting stories out of the newspaper. 'MAN FALLS FIVE THOUSAND FEET AND LIVES'; 'DINOSAURS MAY HAVE BEEN WIPED OUT BY METEOR.' Those were the sorts of things that made you have a big think about your life, not falling off a window-ledge while you were pretending to be a proper dad. Why had he never had a big think before, when he wasn't falling off a window-ledge? Over the last year or so it seemed like everyone had been having big thinks, apart from his father. His mum, for example, never did anything else other than have big thinks, which was probably why everyone had to worry about her all the time. And why did he only want to see his son when he'd broken his collar bone? Marcus couldn't remember ever having come home before and his mum telling him to get on the train to Cambridge because his dad was desperate. All those hundreds and hundreds of days when his collar bone was all right, Marcus had heard nothing.

He went downstairs to see his mother.

'I'm not going,' he said to her. 'He makes me sick.'

It wasn't until the next day, when he was talking to Ellie about the window-ledge, that he began to change his mind about going to see his dad. They were in an empty classroom during the morning break, although it hadn't been empty at first: when Marcus had told her he wanted a chat, she'd taken his hand, led him inside, and scared off the half-dozen kids messing about in there, kids she didn't know but who seemed perfectly prepared to believe that Ellie would follow through with the terrible threats she was making. (Why did that happen? He wondered. She wasn't much taller than him, so how did she get away with this stuff? Maybe if he started to wear that sort of eye make-up and cut his own hair he'd be able to make people scared of him, too, but there would still be something missing.)

'You should go and see him. Tell him what you think of him. I would. Jerk. I'll come with you, if you like. Give him what for.' She laughed, and though Marcus heard her he had already drifted off by then. He was thinking about how nice it would be to have a whole hour on a train with Ellie, just the two of them; and then he was thinking how great it would be if he let Ellie loose on his dad. Ellie was like a guided missile in school, and sometimes it felt as though she were his personal guided missile. Whenever he was with her he could point her at targets and she destroyed them, and he loved her for it. She had beaten up Lee Hartley's mate, and she stopped people laughing at him quite so much ... And if it worked so well in school, why wouldn't it work away from school? There was no reason he could think of. He was going to point Ellie at his dad and see what happened.

'Will you come with me really, Ellie?'

'Yeah, of course. If you want me to. It'd be a laugh.' Marcus knew she would say yes, if he asked her. Ellie would say yes to just about anything, apart from a dance at a party. 'Anyway, you don't want to go up there on your own, do you?

He always did things on his own, so he had never bothered even thinking about whether there was a choice. That was the trouble with Ellie: he was frightened that when and if he didn't see her any more, he'd still be aware that there were choices, but it wouldn't do him any good because he wouldn't be able to get at them, and his whole life would be ruined.

'Not really. Would Zoe come?'

'No. She wouldn't know what to say to him, and I will. Just us.'

'OK then. Brilliant.' Marcus didn't want to think about what Ellie might have to say. He'd worry about that later.

'Have you got any money? 'Cos I haven't got the train fare.'

'I can get it.' He didn't spend very much; he reckoned he had at least twenty pounds saved up, and his mum would give him what he needed for the trip anyway.

'So shall we go next week, then?' It was nearly Easter, and they were on holiday next week, so they could stay overnight if they wanted. And Marcus would have to ring Ellie at home to make arrangements – it would be like a proper date.

'Yeah. Cool. We'll have a great time.'

Marcus wondered for a moment whether his idea of a great time would be the same as Ellie's idea of a great time, and then he decided not to worry about that until later.

▷ **5** *wipe out sth.:* destroy sth. completely **24** *scare sb. off:* make sb. go away by frightening them **26–27** *follow through with sth.:* put sth. into action **28–29** *get away with sth.:* manage to do sth. successfully **33** *give sb. what for* (infml): punish sb. **37** *let sb. loose on sb. else:* allow sb. to do as they like with sb. else **39** *guided missile:* rocket which is set on a particular target

Fiona wanted to come to King's Cross with Marcus, but he managed to talk her out of it.

'It'd be too sad,' he told her.

'You're only going for a night.'

'But I'll miss you.'

'You'll still be missing me if we say goodbye at the underground station. In fact, you'll have to miss me for longer.'

'It'll seem more normal to say goodbye at the underground, though.'

He knew he was overdoing it, and he knew what he was saying didn't make much sense anyway, but he wasn't going to risk a meeting between Ellie and his mum at the station. She'd stop him from going if she knew he was taking Ellie along to Cambridge to blow up his dad.

The two of them walked from the flat to Holloway Road station, and said goodbye in the tube entrance.

'You'll be OK,' she said to him.

'Yeah.'

'And it'll be over before you know it.'

'It's only for a night,' he said. By the time they reached the underground he'd forgotten he'd told her how much he would miss her. 'It's only for a night, but it seems like forever.' He was hoping his mum wouldn't remember this when he came back. If she did, he probably wouldn't be allowed down to the shops on his own.

'I shouldn't be making you go. You've had such a rough time lately.'

'I'll be fine. Really.'

Because he was going to miss her so much, she gave him an enormous hug that went on forever, while everyone walking past watched.

The tube wasn't crowded. It was mid-afternoon – his dad had worked out the train times so that Lindsey could pick him up from Cambridge on her way home from work – and there was only one other person in his carriage, an old guy reading the evening paper. He was looking at the back page, so Marcus could see some of the stuff on the front; the first thing he noticed was the photo. It seemed so familiar that for a moment he thought it was a picture of someone he knew, a member of the family, and maybe they had it at home, in a frame on the piano, or pinned on to the cork board in the kitchen. But there was no family friend or relative who had bleached hair and half a beard and looked like a sort of modern Jesus …

He knew who it was now. He saw the same picture every single day of the week on Ellie's chest. He felt hot all over, he didn't even need to read the old guy's paper, but he did anyway. 'ROCK STAR COBAIN DEAD'; was the headline, and underneath, in smaller writing 'Nirvana singer, 27, shoots himself'. Marcus thought and felt a lot of things all at once: he wondered whether Ellie had seen the paper yet, and if she hadn't then how she'd be when she found out; and he wondered if his mum was OK, even though he knew there was no connection between his mum and Kurt Cobain because his mum was a real person and Kurt Cobain wasn't; and then he felt confused, because the newspaper headline had turned Kurt Cobain into a real person somehow; and then he just felt very sad – sad for Ellie, sad for Kurt Cobain's wife and little girl, sad for his mum, sad for himself. And then he was at King's Cross and he had to get off the train.

He found Ellie underneath the departure board, which was where they had arranged to meet. She seemed normal. 'Platform ten b,' she said. 'It's in another part of the station, I think.'

Everyone was carrying an evening paper, so Kurt Cobain was everywhere. And because the photo in the paper was exactly the same picture that Ellie had on her sweatshirt, it took Marcus a while to get used to the idea that all these people were holding something that he had always thought of was a part of her. Every time he saw it he wanted to nudge her and point at it, but he said nothing. He didn't know what to do.

'Right. Follow me.' Ellie shouted in a pretend-bossy voice that would have made Marcus giggle at any other time. Today, however, he could only manage a weak little smile, he was too worried to respond to her in the way he usually did, and he could only listen to what she was saying, not the way she was saying it. He didn't want to follow her, because if she was out in front she was bound to notice the army of Kurt Cobains marching towards her.

'Why should I follow you? Why don't you follow me for a change?'

'Ooh, Marcus. You're so masterful,' said Ellie. 'I love that in a man.'

▷ **10** *overdo sth.:* exaggerate sth. **13** *blow sb. up* (infml): tell sb. off for sth. **66** *pretend-bossy:* seeming to be in control and ordering others around **74** *masterful:* dominant

'Where are we going?'

Ellie laughed. 'Ten b. Over there.'

'Right.' He stood directly in front of her and began to walk very slowly towards the platform.

'What are you doing?'

'Leading you.'

She pushed him in the back. 'Don't be an idiot. Get a move on.'

He suddenly remembered something that he'd seen in one of the Open University programmes his mum used to have to watch for her course. He'd watched it with her because it was funny: there were all these people in a room, and half of them were wearing blindfolds, and the other half had to lead the blindfolded half around and not let them bump into each other. It was something to do with trust, his mum had said. If someone could guide you around safely when you were feeling vulnerable, then you learnt to trust them, and that was important. The best bit of the programme was when this woman walked an old man straight into a door and he smashed his head, and they started having a row.

'Ellie, do you trust me?'

'What are you on about?'

'Do you trust me, yes or no?'

'Yes. As far as I can throw you.'

'Ha, ha.'

'Of course I trust you.'

'OK, then. Close your eyes and hang on to my jacket.'

'Eh?'

'Close your eyes and hang on to my jacket. You're not allowed to peek.'

A young guy with long, straggly bleached hair looked at Ellie, at her sweatshirt and then her face. For a moment it looked as though he was going to say something to her, and Marcus began to panic, he stood in between her and the guy and grabbed her.

'Come on.'

'Marcus, have you gone mad?'

'I'm going to guide you through all these people and I'm going to get you on the train, and then you'll trust me forever.'

'If I trust you forever, it won't be because I spent five minutes wandering around King's Cross station with my eyes closed.'

'No. OK. But it'll help.'

'Oh, fucking hell. Come on, then.'

'Ready?'

'Ready.'

'Eyes closed, no peeking?'

'Marcus!'

They set off. To get to the Cambridge train you had to go out of the main part of the station and into another, smaller part tucked away at the side; most people were walking in their direction to get the train home from work, but there were enough people coming at them holding newspapers to make the game worthwhile.

'Are you OK?' he said over his shoulder.

'Yes. You'll tell me if we have to go upstairs or anything?'

'Course.'

Marcus was almost enjoying it all now. They were going through a narrow passageway, and you had to concentrate, because you couldn't just stop dead or sidestep, and you had to remember that you'd sort of doubled in size, so you had to think about what sort of spaces you could fit into. This must be what it was like if you started driving a coach when you were used to a Fiat Uno or something. The best thing about it was that he really did have to look after Ellie, and he liked the feeling that brought with it. He'd never looked after anything or anybody in his whole life – he'd never had a pet, because he wasn't bothered about animals, even though he and his mum had agreed not to eat them (why hadn't he just told her he wasn't bothered about animals, instead of getting into an argument about factory farming and so on?) – and as he loved Ellie more than he would ever have loved a goldfish or a hamster, it felt real.

'Are we nearly there?'

'Yeah.'

'The light's different.'

'We're out of the big station and now we're going into the little one. The train's there waiting for us.'

▷ **9** *Open University:* institution of higher education organized around distance learning and open to everybody **11** *blindfold:* piece of cloth covering a person's eyes **28** *peek:* look **46** *be tucked away:* be difficult to find because it is in an unusual place **55** *stop dead:* stop walking suddenly

'I know why you're doing this, Marcus,' she suddenly said in a small, quiet voice that didn't sound like her. He stopped, but she didn't let go of him. 'You think I haven't seen the paper, but I have.'

He turned round to look at her, but she wouldn't open her eyes.

'Are you OK?'

'Yeah. Well. Not really.' She rummaged around in her bag and produced a bottle of vodka. 'I'm going to get drunk.'

Suddenly Marcus could see a problem with his guided missile plan: the problem was that Ellie wasn't actually a guided missile. You couldn't guide her. That didn't matter so much in school, because school was full of walls and rules and she could just bounce off them; but out in the world, where there were no walls and rules, she was scary. She could just blow up in his face any time.

Thirty-two

There was absolutely nothing wrong with the idea – it wasn't even particularly risky. On the contrary, it was just a mundane social arrangement, the sort that people make all the time, all over the place. If these people were ever to realize the possible consequences. Will reflected later, all the tears and embarrassment and panic that could ensue in the event of these arrangements going just slightly wrong, they would never arrange to meet for a drink again.

The plan was for Rachel, Will and Fiona to go to a pub in Islington while Marcus was up in Cambridge visiting his father. They would have a drink and a chat, then Will would absent himself and Rachel and Fiona would have a drink and a chat, as a result of which Fiona would cheer up, feel better about things and lose the urge to top herself. What could possibly go wrong?

Will arrived at the pub first, got himself a drink, sat down, lit a cigarette. Fiona arrived shortly afterwards; she was distracted and slightly manic. She asked for a large gin and ice, no mixer, and sipped at it nervously and quickly. Will started to feel a little uncomfortable.

'Have you heard from the boy?'

'Which boy?'

'Marcus?'

'Oh, him!' She laughed. 'I'd forgotten all about him. No. He'll leave a message while I'm out, I should think. Who's your friend?'

▷ **6** *rummage around in sth.:* search for an object in sth. **11** *bounce off sth.:* von etwas abprallen **15** *mundane:* ordinary **19** *ensue:* happen **29** *manic:* over-excited · *mixer:* (here) non-alcoholic drink that is added to alcohol

Will looked round, just to check that the seat beside him was as empty as he remembered it to be, and then back at Fiona. Maybe she was imagining people; maybe that's why she got down and cried a lot. Maybe the people she imagined were horrible, or as depressed as she was.

'Which friend?'

'Rachel?'

'Who's my friend Rachel?' Now he didn't understand the question. If she knew his friend Rachel was Rachel, what exactly was the information she required?

'Who is she? Where does she come from? How does she fit in? Why do you want me to meet her?'

'Oh. I see. I just thought, you know.'

'No.'

'I just thought you might find her interesting.'

'Will this happen every time you meet somebody? I have to see them for a drink, even though I don't really know you, let alone them?'

'Oh, no. Not every time, anyway. I'll weed out the rubbish.'

'Thank you.'

And still no Rachel. She was now fifteen minutes late. After a peculiar and pointless conversation about John Major's shirts (Fiona's choice of conversational topic, not his), and several lengthy silences, Rachel was thirty minutes late.

'She does exist?'

'Oh, she definitely exists.'

'Right.'

'I'll go and phone her.' He went to the payphone, got the answerphone, waited for a human interruption that never came, and went back to his seat without leaving a message. The only excuse he would accept, he decided, would involve Ali and a large articulated vehicle ... Unless she had never intended to come. He suddenly realized with terrible clarity that he'd been set up, that when Rachel had said that he would get the hang of it if she showed him how, this is what she had meant. He wanted to hate her, but he couldn't: instead he felt a rising panic.

Another silence, and then Fiona started crying. Her eyes filled up and started to leak down her face and on to her pullover, and she just sat there quietly, like a kid oblivious to a runny nose. For a while Will thought he could just ignore it, and it would go away, but he knew deep down that ignoring her was simply not an option, not if he were worth anything at all.

'What's the matter?' He tried to say it as if he knew it were a big question, but it came out all wrong; the gravity sounded, to him at least, like tetchiness, as if there were a 'now' missing from the end.

'Nothing.'

'That's not true, is it?' It still wouldn't be too late. If Rachel arrived breathless and apologetic at this second, he could stand up, make the introductions, tell Rachel that Fiona was just about to explain the root cause of her misery, and then shove off. He looked towards the door hopefully and, as if by magic, it opened: two guys in Man United away shirts walked in.

'It is true. Nothing's the matter. No thing. I'm just like this.'

'Existential despair, right?'

'Yeah. Right.'

Again, he hadn't got the tone of it. He'd used the phrase to prove that he knew it (he wondered whether Fiona thought he was dim), but quickly realized that if you knew it, these were precisely the circumstances in which you would give it an enormous body-swerve; it sounded flip and pseud and shallow. He wasn't cut out for chats about existential despair. It just wasn't *him*. And what was wrong with that? There was no shame in it, surely? Leather trousers weren't him. (He'd tried some on once, just for a laugh, in a shop called Leather-Time in Covent Garden, and he'd looked like a … Anyway). The colour green wasn't him. Antique furniture wasn't him. And depressive hippy-liberal women weren't him. Big deal. It didn't make him a bad person.

'I don't know if there's a lot of point in talking about this with you,' she said.

▷ **19** *weed out the rubbish:* remove the uninteresting or stupid ones **22** *pointless:* meaningless **31–32** *articulated vehicle:* lorry **33** *be set up:* be tricked, deceived **44** *gravity:* extreme seriousness **45** *tetchiness:* bad-temper **50** *root cause:* origin · *shove off* (infml): leave **52** *away shirt:* (in football) shirt that is worn by a team when it is not on its homeground **59** *swerve:* suddenly changing movement **60** *flip* (infml): not serious · *pseud* [sju:d]: trying to show off · *be cut out for sth.* (infml): have the abilities needed for sth.

'No,' he said, more cheerfully than was appropriate. 'I know what you mean. Shall we finish this and go, then? I don't think Rachel's going to show up.'

Fiona smiled sadly and shook her head. 'You could try persuading me that I'm wrong.'

'Could I?'

'I think I probably need to talk to somebody, and you're the only one here.'

'I'm the only one here that you know. But I'd be useless. You could throw that slice of lemon across the pub and hit somebody who was better than me. As long as you aimed away from that guy who's singing on his own over there.'

She laughed. Maybe his lemon joke had done the trick. Maybe she'd look back on those few seconds as a turning point in her life. But then she shook her head, and said, 'Oh shit,' and began to cry again, and he could see that he had overrated the power of the throwaway one-liner.

'Do you want to go and get something to eat?' he said wearily. He was going to have to look a long way down now.

They went to Pizza Express on Upper Street. He hadn't been there since the last time he had had lunch with Jessica, the ex-girlfriend who was determined to make him as unhappy and sleepless and out of touch and burdened by parenthood as she had become. That was a long, long time ago, before SPAT and Marcus and Suzie and Fiona and Rachel and everything. He'd been an idiot then, but at least he'd been an idiot with an idea, some kind of belief system; now he was hundreds of years older, one or two IQ points wiser, and absolutely all over the place. He'd rather be an idiot again. He'd had his whole life set up so that nobody's problem was his problem, and now everybody's problem was his problem, and he had no solutions for any of them. So how, precisely, was he, or anybody else he was involved with, better off?

They looked at the menu in silence.

'I'm not really hungry,' said Fiona.

'Please eat,' said Will, too quickly and too desperately, and Fiona smiled.

'You think a pizza will help?' she said.

'Yes. Veneziana. 'Cos then you'll stop Venice sinking into the sea and you'll feel better.'

'OK. If I can have extra mushrooms on it.'

'Good call.'

The waitress came to take their order; Will asked for a beer, a bottle of house red, and a Four Seasons with extra everything he could think of, including pine nuts. If he was lucky, he would be able to induce a heart attack, or find that he was suddenly fatally allergic to something.

'I'm sorry,' said Fiona.

'What for?'

'Being like this. And being like this with you.'

'I'm used to women being like this with me. This is how I spend most evenings.' Fiona smiled politely, but suddenly Will felt sick of himself. He wanted to find a way into the conversation that they had to have, but there didn't seem to be one, and there never would be while he was stuck with his brain and his vocabulary and his personality. He kept feeling as though he were on the verge of saying something proper and serious and useful; but then he ended up thinking. Oh, fuck it, say something stupid instead.

'I'm the one who should apologize,' he said. 'I want to help, but I know I won't be able to. I haven't got the answers to anything.'

'That's what men think, isn't it?'

'What?'

'That unless you've got some answer, unless you can say, "Oh, I know this bloke in Essex Road who can fix that for you", then it's not worth bothering.'

Will shifted in his seat and didn't say anything. That was precisely what he thought in fact, he had spent half the evening trying to think of the name of the bloke in Essex Road, metaphorically speaking.

'That's not what I want. I know there's nothing you can do. I'm depressed. It's an illness. It just started. Well, that's not true, there were things happening that helped it along, but …'

And they were away. It was easier than he could possibly have anticipated: all he had to do was listen and nod and ask pertinent questions. He had done it before, loads of times, with Angie and Suzie and Rachel, but that was for a reason. There was no

▷ **16** *overrate sth.:* think sth. is more important than it really is **28** *all over the place* (infml): in a mess **41** *call* (n): order **44** *induce sth.:* cause sth. **72** *anticipate sth.:* expect sth. **73** *pertinent:* relevant ulterior motive here. He didn't want to sleep with Fiona, but he did want her to feel better, and he hadn't realized that in order to make her feel better he had to act in exactly the same way as if he did want to sleep with her. He didn't want to think about what that meant.

He learnt a lot of things about Fiona. He learnt that she hadn't really wanted to be a mother, and that sometimes she hated Marcus with a passion that worried her; he learnt that she worried about her inability to hold down a relationship (Will restrained a desire to leap in at this point and tell her that an inability to hold down a relationship was indicative of an undervalued kind of moral courage, that only cool people screwed up); he learnt that her last birthday had scared her to bits, because she hadn't been anywhere, done anything, all the usual malarkey. None of it amounted to anything enormous, but the sum of her depression was much greater than its parts, and now she had to live with something that tired her and made her see everything through a greeny-brown gauze. And he learnt that if someone were to ask her where this thing lived (Will found it hard to imagine a more unlikely question, but that was just one of the many differences between them), she would say that it was in her throat, because it stopped her from eating, and made her feel as though she were constantly on the verge of tears – when she wasn't actually crying.

And that was it, more or less. What Will had been most frightened of – apart from Fiona asking him about the point (a subject that never even came close to showing its face, probably because it was clear in *his* face and even in his life that he didn't have a clue) – was that there was going to be a cause of all this misery, some dark secret, or some terrible lack, and he was one of the only people in the world who could deal with it, and he wouldn't want to, even though he would have to anyway. But it wasn't like that at all; there was nothing – if life, with its attendant disappointments and compromises and bitter little defeats, counted as nothing. Which it probably didn't.

They got a taxi back to Fiona's place. The cabbie was listening to GLR, and the disc jockey was talking about Kurt Cobain; it took Will a while to understand the strange, muted tone in the DJ's voice.

'What's happened to him?' Will asked the cabbie.

'Who?'

'Kurt Cobain.'

'Is he the Nirvana geezer? He shot himself in the head. Boom.'

'Dead?'

'No. Just a headache. Yeah, course he's dead.'

Will wasn't surprised, particularly, and he was too old to be shocked. He hadn't been shocked by the death of a pop star since Marvin Gaye died. He had been … how old? He thought back. The first of April 1984 … Jesus, ten years ago, nearly to the day. So he had been twenty-six, and still of an age when things like that meant something: he probably sang Marvin Gaye songs with his eyes closed when he was twenty-six. Now he knew that pop stars committing suicide were all grist to the mill, and the only consequence of Kurt Cobain's death as far as he was concerned was that *Nevermind* would sound a lot cooler. Ellie and Marcus weren't old enough to understand that, though. They would think it all meant something, and that worried him.

'Isn't he the singer Marcus liked?' Fiona asked him.

'Yeah.'

'Oh, dear.'

Suddenly Will was fearful. He had never had any kind of intuition or empathy or connection in his life before, but he had it now. Typical, he thought, that it should be Marcus, rather than Rachel or someone who looked like Uma Thurman, who brought it on. 'I'm not being funny, but can I come in with you to listen to Marcus's answerphone message? I just want to hear that he's OK.'

But he wasn't, really. He was calling from a police station in a place called Royston, and he sounded little and frightened and lonely.

▷ **1** *ulterior motive:* hidden but real reason **8** *hold sth. down:* successfully keep sth. **8–9** *leap in:* take the opportunity **12** *scare sb. to bits:* totally frighten sb. **16** *gauze* [gɔːz]: thin fabric of textile **31** *attendant:* accompanying **39** *geezer* (sl): man **49** *grist to the mill:* thing that is useful for a particular purpose **58** *empathy:* ability to understand other people's feelings **61** *funny:* (here) strange

Thirty-three

They didn't talk on the train at first: every now and again Ellie would give a small sob, or threaten to press the emergency stop button, or threaten to do things to the people who looked at her when she swore or swigged from her bottle of vodka. Marcus felt exhausted. It was now perfectly clear to him that, even though he thought Ellie was great, and even though he was always pleased to see her at school, and even though she was funny and pretty and clever, he didn't want her to be his girlfriend. She just wasn't the right sort of person for him. He really needed to be with someone quieter, someone who liked reading and computer games, and Ellie needed to be with someone who liked drinking vodka and swearing in front of people and threatening to stop trains.

His mum had explained to him once (perhaps when she was going out with Roger, who wasn't like her at all) that sometimes people needed opposites, and Marcus could see how that might work: if you thought about it, right at this moment Ellie needed someone who was going to stop her from pressing the button more than she needed someone who loved pressing buttons, because if she was with someone who loved pressing buttons, they would have pressed it by now and they'd be on their way to prison. The trouble with this theory, though, was that actually it wasn't an awful lot of fun being the opposite of Ellie. It *had* been fun sometimes – at school, where Ellie's ... *Ellieness* could be contained. But out in the world it was no fun at all. It was frightening and embarrassing.

'Why does it matter so much?' he asked her quietly. 'I mean, I know you like his records and everything, and I know it's sad because of Frances Bean, but – '

'I loved him.'

'You didn't know him.

'Of course I knew him. I listened to him sing every single day. I wear him every single day. The things he sings about, that's him. I know him better than I know you. He understood me.'

'He *understood* you?' How did that work? How did someone you had never met understand you?

'He knew what I felt, and he sang, about it.'

Marcus tried to remember some of the words to the songs on the Nirvana record that Will had given him for Christmas. He had only ever been able to hear little bits: 'I feel stupid and contagious.' 'A mosquito.' 'I don't have a gun.' None of it meant anything to him.

'So what were you feeling?'

'Angry.'

'What about?'

'Nothing. Just ... life.'

'What about life?'

'It's shit.'

Marcus thought about that. He thought about whether life was shit, and whether Ellie's life in particular was shit, and then he realized that Ellie spent her whole time wanting life to be shit, and then making life shit by making things difficult for herself. School was shit because she wore her sweatshirt every day, which she wasn't allowed to do, and because she shouted at teachers and got into fights, which upset people. But what if she didn't wear her sweatshirt and stopped shouting at people? How shit would life be then? Not very, he thought. Life was really shit for him, what with his mum and the other kids at school and all that, and he'd give anything to be Ellie; but Ellie seemed determined to turn herself into him, and why would anyone want to do that?

Somehow it reminded him of Will and his pictures of dead drug-takers; maybe Ellie was like Will. If either of them had real trouble in their lives, they wouldn't want or need to invent it for themselves, or put pictures of it on the walls.

▷ **4** *swig* (infml): drink in large amounts **38** *contagious:* ansteckend

'Is that really true, Ellie? Do you really think life is shit?'

'Course.'

'Why?'

'Because ... because the world is sexist and racist and full of injustice.'

Marcus knew this was true – his mum and dad had told him so often enough – but he wasn't convinced that this was what made Ellie angry.

'And is that what Kurt Cobain thought?'

'I don't know. Probably.'

'So you're not sure that he felt the same way as you.'

'He sounded as though he did.'

'Do you feel like shooting yourself?'

'Of course. Sometimes, anyway.'

Marcus looked at her. 'That's not true, Ellie.'

'How do you know?'

'Because I know how my mum feels. And you don't feel like that. You'd like to think you do, but you don't. You have too good a time.'

'I have a shit time.'

'No. I have a shit time. Apart from the time I spend with you. And my mum has a shit time. But you ... I don't think so.'

'You don't know anything.'

'I know some things. I know about that. I'll tell you, Ellie, you don't feel anything like my mum, or Kurt Cobain. You shouldn't say that you feel like killing yourself when you don't. It's not right.'

Ellie shook her head and laughed her low nobody-understands-me laugh, a noise that Marcus hadn't heard since the day they met outside Mrs Morrison's office. She was right, he hadn't understood her then; he understood her much better now.

They sat in silence for a couple of stops. Marcus looked out of the window and tried to work out how to explain Ellie to his dad. He hardly noticed when the train pulled in at Royston station, and he wasn't even completely alert when Ellie suddenly stood up and jumped off the train. He hesitated for a moment, then, with a horrible sick feeling, he jumped off after her.

'What are you doing?'

'I don't want to go to Cambridge. I don't know your dad.'

'You didn't know him before, and you wanted to come then.'

'That was before. Everything's different now.'

He followed her; he wasn't going to let her out of his sight. They walked out of the station, up a side road and then on to the High Street. They walked past a chemist and a greengrocer's and a Tesco, and then they came to a record shop which had a big cardboard cut-out of Kurt Cobain in the window.

'Look at that,' said Ellie. 'Bastards. They're trying to make money out of him already.'

She took off one of her boots, and threw it at the glass as hard as she could. She cracked it first time, and Marcus found himself thinking about how shop windows in Royston were much weedier than shop windows in London before he realized what was going on.

'Shit, Ellie!'

She picked up the boot and used it as a hammer, carefully smashing a hole big enough to lean through without hurting herself, and rescued Kurt Cobain from his record-shop prison.

'There. He's out.' She sat down on the kerb outside the shop, holding Kurt to her as if he were a ventriloquist's dummy, and smiling this weird little smile to herself; meanwhile Marcus panicked. He charged up the road, intending to run all the way back to London or on to Cambridge, whichever direction he was heading. After a few yards, however, his legs went all shaky, and he stopped, took a few deep breaths, and went back to sit with her.

'What did you do that for?'

'I dunno. It just didn't seem right, him being in there on his own.'

'Oh, Ellie.' Once again, Marcus was left with the feeling that Ellie didn't have to do what she had just done, and that she had brought the trouble she was in upon herself. He was tired of it. It wasn't real, and there was enough real trouble in the world without having to invent things.

The street had been quiet when Ellie broke the window, but the noise of breaking glass had woken Royston up, and a couple of people closing up their shops had run down to see what was going on.

'Right, you two. Stay there,' said a guy with long hair and a suntan. Marcus reckoned he had to be a hairdresser or someone who worked in a boutique. He wouldn't have been able to work something like

▷ **32** *alert:* fully aware, ready **41** *Tesco:* chain of supermarkets **54** *kerb:* edge between a pavement and a road **55** *ventriloquist:* Bauchredner/in · *dummy:* model which looks like a human being **57** *charge:* run that out a while ago, but if you hung around with Will long enough you picked stuff up.

'We're not going anywhere, are we, Marcus?' said Ellie sweetly.

When they were sitting in the police car Marcus remembered the day he had walked out of school, and the future he had predicted for himself that afternoon. He'd been right, in a way. His whole life had changed, just as he thought it would, and he was almost certain now that he would become a tramp or a drug addict. He was already a criminal. And it was all his mum's fault! If his mum hadn't complained to Mrs Morrison about the shoes, then he would never have got cross with Mrs Morrison for suggesting that he should keep out of the way of the kids who were giving him a hard time. And then he wouldn't have walked out, and … and he would never have met Ellie that morning. Ellie had something to answer for here. It was Ellie, after all, who had just chucked a boot at a plate-glass window. The point was that once you had become a truant, you started hanging out with people like Ellie, and getting into trouble, and being arrested and taken to Royston police station. Now there was nothing he could do about it.

The policemen were nice, really. Ellie had explained to them that she wasn't a hooligan or on drugs; she was simply making a protest, which was her right as a citizen, about the commercial exploitation of Kurt Cobain's death. The policemen thought this was funny, which Marcus took as a good sign, although it made Ellie very angry indeed: she told them they were patronizing, and they looked at each other and laughed a bit more.

When they got to the station, they were shown into a little room, and a policewoman came in and started talking to them. She asked them their ages and addresses, and what they were doing in Royston. Marcus tried to explain about his dad and the window-ledge and the big think and Kurt Cobain and the vodka, but he could see that it was all a bit of a muddle, and that the policewoman couldn't understand what his dad's accident had to do with Ellie and the shop window, so he gave up.

'He didn't do anything,' Ellie suddenly said. She didn't say it in a nice way, either; she said it as if he should have done something but didn't. 'I got off the train and he followed me. I broke the window. Let him go.'

'Let him go where?' the policewoman asked her. It was a very good question, Marcus thought, and he was glad that she'd asked it. He didn't especially want to be let go in Royston. 'We've got to phone one of his parents. We've got to phone yours too.'

Ellie glared at her and the policewoman glared back. There didn't seem much else to say. They knew the crime and the identity of the criminal; the said criminal had been apprehended and was in the police station, so they sat and waited in silence.

His dad and Lindsey were the first to turn up. Lindsey had had to drive, because of the broken collar bone, and she hated driving, so they were both in a bit of a state: Lindsey was tired and nervy, and his dad was grumpy and in pain. He didn't look like a man who'd had a big think, and he certainly didn't look like a man who until very recently had been desperate to see his only son.

The policewoman left them alone. Clive slumped on a bench that ran along one side of the room, and Lindsey sat down next to him, looking at him with concern.

'That was just what I needed. Thank you, Marcus.'

Marcus looked at his dad unhappily.

'He didn't *do* anything,' said Ellie impatiently. 'He was trying to help me.'

'And who exactly are you?'

'*Who exactly?*' Ellie was taking the piss out of his dad. Marcus didn't think that was a particularly good idea, but he was tired of wrestling with Ellie. 'Who *exactly*? I'm Eleanor Toyah Gray, aged fifteen years seven months. I live at twenty-three …'

'What are you doing messing around with Marcus?'

'I'm not messing around with him. He's my friend.' This was news to Marcus. He hadn't felt Ellie was his friend since they got on the train. 'He asked me to come with him to Cambridge, because he wasn't looking forward to a heart-to-heart with a father he feels doesn't understand him and who has abandoned him at a time when

▷ **14** *have sth. to answer for:* have done sth. bad for which you must bear the consequences **22** *exploitation:* act of taking advantage of sb./sth. **25** *patronize:* treat sb. in a way that shows you consider them unintelligent **32** *muddle:* state of confusion **45** *apprehend sb.* (fml): arrest sb. **49** *in a state:* looking unhappy and tired **53** *slump on sth.:* sit down on sth. **69** *heart-to-heart:* intimate conversation he needed him most. Great, aren't they, men? You've got a mother who wants to top herself and they're not interested. But they fall off a fucking window-sill and suddenly you're summoned for a talk about the meaning of life.'

Marcus slumped on the table and put his head in his hands. He was suddenly very, very tired; he didn't want to be with any of these people. Life was hard enough without Ellie shooting her mouth off.

'Whose mum wants to top herself?' Clive asked.

'Ellie's,' said Marcus firmly.

Clive looked at Ellie with interest.

'Sorry to hear that,' he said, without sounding either sorry or even particularly interested.

'That's OK,' said Ellie. She took the hint and said nothing for a while.

'I suppose you blame me for all this,' said his father. 'I suppose you think that if I'd stayed with your mother you wouldn't have gone off the rails. And you're probably right.' He sighed, and Lindsey took his hand and stroked it sympathetically.

Marcus sat bolt upright. 'What are you talking about?'

'I've messed you up.'

'All I did was get off a train,' said Marcus. His tiredness had vanished now. It had been replaced by the kind of anger which he didn't feel very often, an anger that gave him the strength to argue with anyone of any age. He wished you could buy this stuff in bottles, so he could keep it in his desk at school and sip from it throughout the day. 'What's going off the rails about getting off a train? Ellie's off the rails. She's nuts. She just broke a window with her boot because it had a photo of a pop star in it. But I haven't done anything. And I don't care if you left home or not. It doesn't make any difference to me. I'd have got off the train if you were still with Mum because I wanted to try and look after my friend.'

That wasn't quite right, actually, because if his mum and dad were still together, he wouldn't have been on the train in the first place, unless he'd been going to Cambridge with Ellie for some other reason that he couldn't imagine. 'I suppose you are a useless father, and that doesn't help a kid very much, but you'd have been a useless father wherever you were living, so I don't see what difference it makes.'

Ellie laughed. 'Yay, Marcus! Cool speech!'

'Thank you. I rather enjoyed making it.'

'You poor kid,' said Lindsey.

'And you can shut up,' said Marcus. Ellie laughed even harder. It was the anger juice talking – poor Lindsey had never done anything wrong, particularly – but it still felt good.

'Can we go now?' Ellie asked.

'We have to wait for your mother,' said Clive. 'She's coming with Fiona. Will's driving them up.'

'Oh, no,' said Marcus.

'Fucking hell,' said Ellie, and Marcus groaned. The four of them sat there staring at each other, waiting for the next scene in what was beginning to feel like a never-ending play.

▷ **16–17** *go off the rails* (infml): start behaving in a bad way **20** *mess sb. up:* cause sb. to have problems **42** *anger juice* (infml): power coming from your strong emotional feelings

Thirty-four

Life was, after all, like air. Will could have no doubt about that any more. There seemed to be no way of keeping it out, or at a distance, and all he could do for the moment was live it and breathe it. How people managed to draw it down into their lungs without choking was a mystery to him: it was full of bits. This was air you could almost chew.

He rang Rachel from Fiona's flat while Fiona was in the bathroom, and this time she answered the phone.

'You were never going to come, were you?'

'Well – '

'Were you?'

'No. I thought … I thought it might do you some good. Did I do a terrible thing?'

'I guess not. I guess it did me some good.'

'So there you are.'

'But as a general rule – '

'As a general rule, I'll turn up when I say I'm going to.'

'Thank you.'

He told Rachel about Marcus and Ellie, and promised to keep her informed. The moment he'd put the phone down Ellie's mother Katrina called and spoke to Fiona, and then Fiona spoke to Clive, and then she called Katrina back to offer her a lift to Royston with them, and then Will went home to get his car, and they drove off to look for Ellie's house.

While Fiona was collecting Ellie's mum, Will sat in the car listening to Nirvana and thinking about the Dead Duck Day. Something about now was reminding him of then; there was that same sense of unpredictability and absorption and chaos. The main difference was that today wasn't as ... well, as enjoyable. It wasn't that Fiona's attempted suicide had been a riot of fun and laughter; it was just that he neither knew nor cared about any of them then, and it had been possible for him to observe, with a terrible but neutral fascination, the kind of mess that people can make if they are wilful or unlucky or both. But the neutrality had gone now, and he was more worried about poor Marcus sitting with some deranged teenager in a small-town police station, an experience that Marcus would probably have forgotten all about by the weekend, than about the same boy's mother attempting to take her own life, the memory of which he was almost certain to carry with him to his grave. It seemed that whether you felt something, or whether you felt nothing, it didn't matter: your responses were off either way.

Ellies's mum was an attractive woman in her early forties, youthful-looking enough to get away with the tatty, faded blue jeans and leather biker jacket she was wearing. She had a shock of curly hennaed hair and nice crinkles around her eyes and mouth, and she seemed to have given up on her daughter a long time ago.

'She's mad,' Katrina said with a shrug as soon as she got into the car. 'I don't know how or why, but she is. Not *mad* mad, but, you know. Out of control. Do you mind if I smoke, if I open the window?' She fiddled around in her bag, failed to find her lighter, and then forgot about smoking altogether. 'It's funny, because when Ellie was born I really hoped she'd turn out like this, feisty and rebellious and loud and bright. That's why I called her Eleanor Toyah.'

'Is that something classical?' Fiona asked.

'No, it's pop,' said Will. Fiona laughed, although Will couldn't see why.

'Toyah Wilcox.'

▷ **28** *unpredictability:* unexpectedness · *absorption:* fascination **33** *wilful:* determined to have one's own way, esp. if it might bring trouble **35** *deranged:* crazy **44** *shock* (n): very thick mass **50** *fiddle around:* move your fingers around because you are nervous **52** *feisty* ['faɪsti] (infml): strong and determined **57** *Toyah Wilcox:* punk rock musician popular esp. in the early 1980s

'And now it's happened and she *is* feisty and rebellious and what have you, I'd give anything for her to be mousy and home every night. She's killing me.'

Will winced at Katrina's turn of phrase, and glanced at Fiona alongside him, but she gave no indication of being aware that the expression had anything but a figurative meaning.

'This is the last straw, though,' Katrina said.

'Ditto,' said Fiona.

'Until the next last straw, anyway.'

They both laughed, but it was true, Will thought. There would always be one more last straw. Ellie was killing Katrina, and Marcus was killing Fiona, and they would go on killing them for years and years. They were the Undead. They couldn't live, not properly, and they couldn't die; all they could do was sit in a stranger's car and laugh about it. And people like Jessica had the nerve to tell him that he was missing out? He didn't think he'd ever understand what that was supposed to mean.

They stopped to get petrol, cans of drink, crisps and chocolate bars, and when they got back into the car the atmosphere between them had changed: somewhere among the popping cans and the rustling crisp packets they seemed to have become a trio. It was almost as if they had forgotten why they were travelling in the first place; the journey had become the point of the trip. Will remembered from school coach trips that it was something to do with getting out and getting back in again, although he wasn't sure exactly what. Perhaps you didn't notice that you had created a feeling until you left it and went back to it, but there was a feeling now – a heady mix of despair, shared concern, suppressed hysteria, and straightforward team spirit – and Will could feel that he was inside it, rather than looking at it through a window. This couldn't possibly be what he was missing out on, because he wasn't missing out, but it still involved kids. You had to hand it to Marcus, he thought: the boy was awkward and weird and the rest of it, but he had this knack of creating bridges wherever he went, and very few adults could do that. Will would never have imagined that he would have been able to walk across to Fiona, but he could now; his relationship with Rachel had been entirely underpinned by Marcus. And here was a third person, someone he had never met before tonight, and they were swapping fingers of Kit-Kat and swigs of Diet Lilt as if they had already exchanged bodily fluids. It was kind of ironic that this strange and lonely child could somehow make all these connections, and yet remain so unconnected himself.

'Why did that guy shoot himself?' Fiona suddenly asked.

'Kurt Cobain?' said Will and Katrina together.

'If that was his name.'

'He was unhappy, I suppose,' said Katrina.

'Well, I gathered that much. What about?'

'Oh, I can't remember now. Ellie did tell me, but I switched off after a while. Drugs? A bad childhood? Pressure? That sort of thing, anyway.'

'I'd never heard of him before Christmas,' said Fiona, 'but he was quite a big deal, wasn't he?'

'Did you see the news tonight? There were all these heartbroken young people hugging each other and crying. It was very sad to watch. None of them seemed to be trying to break shop windows, though. Only my daughter wanted to express her grief like that, apparently.'

Will wondered whether Marcus had ever sat in his room listening to *Nevermind* in the same way that Will had sat in his room listening to the first Clash album. He couldn't imagine that he had. Marcus couldn't possibly have understood that kind of rage and pain, even though he probably had his own version of those feelings swilling around in there somewhere. And yet here he was, banged up in jail – well, sitting in a police station waiting room – because he had been accomplice to a crime that was somehow meant to avenge Kurt Cobain's death. It was hard to imagine two less kindred spirits than Marcus and Kurt Cobain, and yet they had both managed to pull off the same trick: Marcus forced unlikely connections in cars and police stations and Kurt Cobain did the same thing on international television. It was proof that things weren't as bad as they thought they

▷ **2** *mousy:* shy and quiet **4** *wince:* make a face because you are uncomfortable **7** *the last straw:* the last in a series of bad events that makes sb. then change sth. **21** *rustle:* make soft sounds **27** *heady:* strong, exciting **32** *hand it to sb.* (infml): admire sb. for sth. **33** *knack:* talent **37** *underpin sth.:* help sth. to become stronger **61** *swill* (v): move around **62** *be banged up* (infml): be locked up **64** *accomplice:* person who helps another in an act of crime · *avenge sb./sth.:* punish a person in return for sth. bad this person has done (esp. to sb.) **65** *kindred* ['kɪndrəd]: similar were. Will wished he was able to show this proof to Marcus, and to anybody else who might be in need of it.

They were nearly there now. Katrina was still chatting away, apparently completely reconciled to the idea that her daughter was in trouble again (the only route open to you, Will presumed, if you had the misfortune to have Ellie as a daughter), but Fiona had gone terribly quiet.

'He'll be OK, you know,' he said to her.

'I know he will,' she said, but there was something in her voice that he didn't like.

Will was not surprised to find that the vibes in the police station were bad – like most habitual users of soft drugs he was no fan of the police – but he was surprised to find these vibes were coming not from the front desk, where they encountered only a slightly strained civility, but from the interview room, where there was a frosty silence and a lot of angry glares. Lindsey and Clive were glaring angrily at Marcus, who was glaring angrily at the wall. A furious teenage girl (who looked, Will was gratified to see, not unlike a cross between Siouxsie and Roadrunner, except with the haircut of someone who had recently been released into the community) was glaring angrily at anyone brave enough to catch her eye.

'You took your time,' said Ellie, when her mother walked in.

'I took as long as it takes to make a phone call and drive here,' said Katrina, 'so don't start.'

'Your daughter,' said Clive, with a pomposity that didn't really suit a man wearing a University of Life sweatshirt and a plaster cast, 'has been insulting and aggressive. And your son,' he went on, nodding at Fiona, 'has clearly been mixing with the wrong crowd.'

'*Your* son,' hooted Ellie, but Fiona was still grim and silent.

'He told me to shut up,' said Lindsey.

'Diddums,' said Ellie.

The policewoman who had shown them in was beginning to let her enjoyment of their disharmony show in her face. 'Are we allowed to go?' Will asked her.

'Not yet. We're waiting for the shop owner to come down.'

'Good,' said Ellie. 'I want to give him a piece of my mind.'

'It's a her, actually,' said the policewoman.

Ellie blushed. 'Him or her, doesn't matter. She's sick.'

'Why is she sick, Ellie?' asked Katrina, in a tone which managed brilliantly to combine sarcasm and world-weariness, and which had clearly taken a very long time and a lot of practice to perfect.

'Because she's exploiting a tragic event for her own gain,' said Ellie. 'She has no idea what today means. She just thinks there's a few quid in it.'

'Why is she coming, anyway?' Will asked the policewoman.

'It's something we're trying here. You know, criminals face-to-face with victims of crime, so they get to see the consequences of their actions.'

'Who's the criminal and who's the victim?' asked Ellie meaningfully.

'Oh, Ellie, do shut up,' said her mother.

A nervous-looking young woman in her late twenties was shown into the room. She was wearing a Kurt Cobain sweatshirt and lots of black eye make-up and if she wasn't Ellie's older sister, genetic scientists would want to know why not.

'This is Ruth, who owns the shop. This is the young lady who broke your window,' said the policewoman. Ellie looked at the shop owner, bewildered.

'Did they tell you to do that?'

'What?'

'Look like me.'

'Do I look like you?'

Everyone in the room, including the police officers, laughed.

'You put that picture in the window to exploit people,' said Ellie, with noticeably less confidence than she had been exhibiting previously.

'Which picture? The picture of Kurt? That's always been there. I'm his biggest fan. His biggest fan in Hertfordshire, anyway.'

'You didn't just stick it in today to make some money?'

▷ **11** *vibes* (pl) (infml): atmosphere **14** *civility* (fml): politeness **20** *release sb.:* let sb. out of a place where they have been kept **25** *pomposity:* exaggerated importance of yourself **26** *University of Life:* belief that you have learned all your important things from life and not from education · *plaster cast:* Gips **29** *hoot:* say in a loud voice **31** *diddums:* expression meaning 'poor you' **40** *world-weariness:* state in which you are no longer excited by life **42** *exploit sth.:* use sth. to your own advantage · *gain* (n): financial profit **65** *exhibit sth.:* display, show sth. **68** *Hertfordshire* ['hɑːtfədʃə]: county in southern England

'Make some money out of all the grieving Nirvana fans in Royston, you mean? That would only work if it was a picture of Julio Iglesias.'

Ellie looked embarrassed.

'Is that why you broke the window?' Ruth asked. 'Because you thought I was exploiting people?'

'Yeah.'

'Today has been the saddest day of my life. And then some little idiot comes up and breaks my window because she thinks I'm trying to rip people off. Just … grow up.'

Will doubted very much whether Ellie was lost for words too often, but it was clear that if you wished to reduce her to a gaping, red-faced mess, all you had to do was find a twenty-something *doppelgänger* whose commitment to Kurt Cobain was even more devout than her own.

'I'm sorry,' she whispered.

'Yeah, well,' said Ruth. 'Come here.' And while the assembled and for the most part unsympathetic occupants of the police interview room watched, Ruth opened her arms, and Ellie stood up, walked over to her and hugged her.

It seemed to have escaped Fiona's notice that this embrace should have marked the end of the whole sorry cardboard-cut-out affair, but then Will had been aware for some time that more or less everything had passed her by since they stopped for petrol. It soon became clear, however, that she had been steeling herself for action, rather than daydreaming, and for reasons best known to herself she had decided that the time for action was now. She stood up, walked around the table, put her arms around Marcus from behind and, with an embarrassingly emotional intensity, addressed the policewoman who had been looking after them.

'I haven't been a good mother to him,' she declared. 'I've let things slide, and I haven't been noticing properly, and … I'm not surprised things have come to this.'

'They haven't come to anything, Mum,' said Marcus. 'How many more times? I haven't done anything.' Fiona ignored him; she didn't seem even to have heard.

'I know I don't deserve a chance, but I'm asking for one now, and … I don't know whether you're a mother or not?'

'Me?' asked the policewoman. 'Yeah. I've got a little boy. Jack.'

'I'm appealing to you as a mother . If you give us another chance, you won't regret it.'

'We don't need a chance, Mum. I haven't done anything wrong. I only got off a train.'

Still no reaction. Will had to hand it to her: once she had decided to fight for her child she was unstoppable, however wrong-headed the decision, and however inappropriate the weapons. What she was saying was barmy – she might even have been aware that it was barmy – but at least it was coming from a part of her that knew she had to do something for her son. It was a turning point, of sorts. You could imagine this woman saying all kinds of inappropriate things at peculiar times; but it was getting much harder to imagine finding her sprawled off a sofa covered in sick, and Will was beginning to learn that sometimes good news came in unpromising shapes and sizes.

'We're willing to cut a deal,' said Fiona. Was Royston law the same as *LA Law*? Will wondered. It seemed unlikely, but one never knew. 'Marcus will testify against Ellie, if you let him go. I'm sorry, Katrina, but it's too late for her. Let Marcus start again with a clean sheet.' She buried her face in the back of Marcus's neck, but Marcus shook her off and moved away from her and towards Will. Katrina, who had spent much of Fiona's speech trying not to laugh, went over to comfort her.

'Shut up, Mum. You're mad. Bloody hell, I can't believe how crap my parents are,' said Marcus with real feeling.

Will looked at this strange little group, his gang for the day, and tried to make some sense of it. All these ripples and connections! He couldn't get his head round them. He was not a man given to mystical moments, even under the influence of narcotics, but he was very worried that he was having one now, for some reason: maybe it was something to do with Marcus walking away from his mother and over to him? Whatever the explanation, it was making him feel very peculiar. Some of these people he hadn't known until today; some of

▷ **1** *grieving* (adj): feeling great sorrow **2–3** *Julio Iglesias:* Spanish singer of romantic songs **10** *rip sb. off* (infml): cheat sb. **12** *gape:* stare with your mouth open **14** *devout* [dɪ'vaʊt]: strong in your belief **17** *assemble:* (of people) gather together in a place **25** *steel yourself for sth.:* prepare yourself for sth. unpleasant **55** *LA Law:* American TV series about a law firm **56** *testify:* make a statement in a law court **65** *ripple:* activity that has effects them he had only known for a little while, and even then he couldn't say that he knew them well. But here they were anyway, one of them clutching a cardboard cut-out Kurt Cobain, one of them in a plaster cast, one of them crying, all of them bound to each other in ways that it would be almost impossible to explain to anyone who had just wandered in. Will couldn't recall ever having been caught up in this sort of messy, sprawling, chaotic web before; it was almost as if he had been given a glimpse of what it was like to be human. It wasn't too bad, really; he wouldn't even mind being human on a full-time basis.

They all went to the nearest burger bar for supper. Ruth and Ellie sat apart and ate chips and smoked and whispered; Marcus and his relatives carried on the sniping they had embarked on with such enthusiasm in the police station. Clive wanted Marcus to complete his journey to Cambridge, but Fiona felt he should return to London, while Marcus seemed too confused by his afternoon to feel anything very much.

'Why was Ellie with you in the first place?' Will asked him.

'I can't remember now,' said Marcus. 'She just wanted to come.'

'Was she going to stay with us?' asked Clive.

'Dunno. S'pose so.'

'Thanks for asking us first.'

'Ellie's not right for me,' said Marcus firmly.

'You've worked that out, have you?' said Will.

'I'm not sure who she is right for,' said Katrina.

'I think we'll always be friends,' Marcus continued. 'But I don't know. I think I ought to look for someone less – '

'Less rude and mad? Less violent? Less bloody stupid? There are any number of lesses I can think of.' This contribution was from Ellie's mother.

'Less different from me,' said Marcus diplomatically.

'Well, good luck,' said Katrina. 'There are a lot of us who've spent half our lives looking for someone less different from us, and we haven't found them so far.'

'Is it that hard?' asked Marcus.

'It's the hardest thing in the world,' said Fiona, with more feeling than Will wanted to contemplate.

'Why do you think we're all single?' said Katrina.

Was that really it? Will wondered. Was that what they were all doing, looking for someone less different? Was that what he was doing? Rachel was dynamic and thoughtful and focused and caring and different in more ways than he could count, but the whole point of Rachel, as far as Will was concerned, was that she wasn't him. There was a flaw in Katrina's logic, then. This thing about looking for someone less different ... It only really worked, he realized, if you were convinced that being you wasn't so bad in the first place.

▷ **12** *snipe:* criticize in an unpleasant way **43** *flaw:* mistake

Thirty-five

Marcus did end up going to stay with his dad and Lindsey. He felt sorry for them, in a funny sort of way: at the police station they had seemed really out of it, as if they weren't able to cope. Marcus hadn't thought about it before, but that evening you could really tell who lived in London and who didn't, and the ones who didn't just seemed more scared of everything. Clive and Lindsey had been scared of Ellie, for a start, but they'd been scared of Ellie's mum, and the police, and they'd moaned a lot, and looked nervous ... Maybe it wasn't anything to do with London; maybe it was more to do with the kind of people he knew now, or maybe he'd just got a lot older in the last couple of months. But he couldn't really see what his dad could offer him any more, which was why he felt sorry for him, which was why he agreed to go back to Cambridge with him.

Clive carried on moaning in the car. Why did Marcus want to get involved with someone like that? Why hadn't he tried to stop her? Why had he been rude to Lindsey? What had she ever done to him? Marcus didn't answer. He just let his father go on and on until eventually he seemed to run out of moans like you run out of petrol: they started to slow up and get quieter, and then they just disappeared altogether. The thing was, he couldn't be that kind of dad any more. He'd missed his moment. It was like if God suddenly decided to be God again a zillion years after creating the world: He couldn't suddenly come down from heaven and say, oh, you shouldn't have put the Empire State Building there, and you shouldn't have organized it so that African people get less money, and you shouldn't have let them build nuclear weapons. Because you could say to Him, well, it's a bit late now, isn't it? Where were You when we were thinking about these things?

It wasn't as though he thought his dad should have been around, but he couldn't have it both ways. If he wanted to be up in Cambridge with Lindsey, smoking pot and falling off window-ledges, fine, but he couldn't then start picking up on the little things – and Ellie was a little thing now really, even though when they'd been sitting on the kerb waiting for the police car to come, she'd seemed like the biggest thing ever. He'd have to find another job for himself. Will could do the little things, and his mum, but his dad was out of it.

They arrived back at his dad's place around ten-thirty, which meant it had taken him six hours to get to Cambridge – not bad, really, seeing as he'd been arrested halfway there. (Arrested! He'd been arrested! Taken to a police station in a police car, at least. He'd already stopped thinking of the broken window as something that had come out of playing truant, and that would lead on to being a tramp and a drug addict. Now he was free he could see he had overreacted. Instead, he took the Royston incident as a measure of how far he'd come in the last few months. He'd never have been able to get arrested when he'd first arrived in London. He wouldn't have known the right sort of people.)

Lindsey made them a cup of tea and they sat around the kitchen table for a while. Then Clive sort of nodded at Lindsey, and she said she was tired and she was going to bed, leaving the two of them alone.

'Do you mind if I roll a joint?' his dad asked him.

'No,' said Marcus. 'You do what you want. I'm not smoking any, though.'

'Too right you're not. Would you mind getting my tin down for me? It hurts me to stretch.'

Marcus moved his chair over towards the shelves, climbed upon it and started fumbling around behind the cereal packets on the top shelf. It was funny how you could still know tiny little things about people, like where they kept their tin, even though you didn't know what they were thinking from one week to the next.

He got down, handed the tin over and moved his chair back to the table. His dad started to roll himself a joint, mumbling into his cigarette papers as he did so.

▷ **22** *zillion* (infml): a very large number

'I've had a big think since, you know. Since my accident.'

'Since you fell off the window-ledge?' Marcus loved saying that. It sounded so daft.

'Yeah. Since my accident.'

'Mum said you'd been having a big think.'

'And?'

'And what?'

'I dunno. What do you think?'

'What do I think of you having a think?'

'Well.' His dad looked up from his Rizlas. 'Yeah. I suppose.'

'It depends, really, doesn't it? On what you've been thinking about.'

'OK. What I was thinking about was ... It frightened me, my accident.'

'When you fell off the window-ledge?'

'Yeah. My accident. Why do you always have to say what it was? Anyway, it frightened me.'

'You didn't fall very far. You only broke your collar bone. I know loads of people who've done that.'

'It doesn't matter how far you fall if it makes you think, does it?'

'I suppose not.'

'Did you mean what you said in the police station? About me being a useless father?'

'Oh, I dunno. Not really.'

'Because I know I haven't been great.'

'No. Not great.'

'And ... you need a father, don't you? I can see that now. I couldn't see it before.'

'I don't know what I need.'

'Well, you know you need a father.'

'Why?'

'Because everyone does.'

Marcus thought about that. 'Everyone does, you know, to get them going. And after that, I'm not sure. Why do you think I need one now? I'm doing OK without.'

'It doesn't look like it.'

'What, because someone else broke a window? No, really, I am doing OK without. Maybe I'm doing better. I mean, it's hard with Mum, but this year at school ... I can't explain it, but I feel safer than before, because I know more people. I was really scared because I didn't think two was enough, and now there aren't two any more. There are loads. And you're better off that way.'

'Who are these loads? Ellie and Will and people like that?'

'Yeah, people like that.'

'They won't be around forever.'

'Some of them will, some of them won't, but, see, I didn't know before that anyone else could do that job, and they can. You can find people. It's like those acrobatic displays.'

'What acrobatic displays?'

'Those ones when you stand on top of loads of people in a pyramid. It doesn't really matter who they are, does it, as long as they're there and you don't let them go away without finding someone else.'

'You really think that? It doesn't matter who's underneath you?'

'I do now, yeah. I didn't, but now I do. Because you can't stand on top of your mum and dad if they're going to mess around and wander off and get depressed.'

His dad had finished rolling the joint. He lit it and took a big lungful of smoke. 'That's what my big think was about. I shouldn't have wandered off.'

'It doesn't matter, Dad. Really. I know where you are if things get bad.'

'Gee, thanks.'

'Sorry. But … I'm OK. Really. I can find people. I'll be all right.'

And he would be, he knew it. He didn't know whether Ellie would be, because she didn't think about things that hard, even though she was clever and knew about politics and so on; and he didn't know whether his mum would be, because she wasn't very strong a lot of the time. But he was sure that he would be able to cope in ways that they couldn't. He could cope at school, because he knew what to do, and he had worked out who you could trust and who you couldn't, and he had worked that out down there, in London, where people came at each other from all sorts of odd angles. You could create little patterns of people that wouldn't have been possible if his mum and dad hadn't split up and the three of them had stayed in Cambridge. It didn't work for everyone. It didn't work for mad people and people

▷ **63** *gee:* word used to show surprise, annoyance

who didn't know anybody, or for people who were sick, or who drank too much. But it was going to work for him, he'd make sure of that, and because it was going to work for him he had decided that this was a much better way of doing things than the way that his dad wanted him to try.

They talked a little bit longer, about Lindsey and how she wanted a baby, and how his dad couldn't decide, and whether Marcus would mind if they did have one; and Marcus said that he'd like it, that he liked babies. He didn't really, but he knew the value of extra people around him, and Lindsey's baby would grow up to be an extra person one day. And then he went to bed. His dad gave him a hug and got a bit teary, but he was stoned by then, so Marcus didn't take any notice.

In the morning his dad and Lindsey gave him a lift to the station, and enough money for a taxi from King's Cross to the flat. He sat on the train looking out of the window. He was sure he was right about the acrobatics display; but even if it was all rubbish he was still going to carry on believing it. If it helped get him through to the time when he was completely free to make the mistakes that they were all making, then what was the harm?

Thirty-six

Wanting Rachel so much still frightened Will. At any time, it seemed to him, she might decide that he was too much trouble, or worthless, or no good in bed. She might meet someone else; she might come to the conclusion that she didn't want a relationship with anybody at all. She might die, suddenly, without warning, in a car crash on the way back from dropping Ali off at school. He felt as if he were a chick whose egg had been cracked open, and he was outside in the world shivering and unsteady on his feet (if chicks were unsteady on their feet – maybe that was foals, or calves, or some other animal), without so much as a Paul Smith suit or a pair of Raybans to protect him. He wasn't even sure what all this fear was *for*. What good was it doing him? None whatsoever, as far as he could see, but it was much too late to ask that now. All he knew was that there was no going back; that part of his life was over.

Most Saturdays now, Will took Ali and Marcus out somewhere. It had begun because he wanted to give their mothers a break ... No, that wasn't true. It had begun because he wanted to wriggle his way into Rachel's life, and he wanted to make her believe that there was some kind of substance to him. And it wasn't as if it was the worst job in the world; the first couple of outings had been difficult, because for some reason he'd tried to do the education thing, and he'd taken them to the British Museum and the National Gallery, and all three of them had been bored and tetchy, but that was mostly because Will

▷ **12** *teary:* about to cry **28** *foal:* very young horse **36–37** *wriggle your way into sth.:* (here) become a part of sth.

hated doing those things himself. (Was there a more boring place in the world than the British Museum? If there was, Will wouldn't want to know about it. Pots. Coins. Jugs. Whole rooms full of plates. There had to be a point of exhibiting things, Will decided. Just because they were old, it didn't mean they were necessarily interesting. Just because they'd survived didn't mean you wanted to look at them.)

But right when he was on the verge of abandoning the whole idea he had taken them to the cinema, to one of those dumb summer movies that were pitched at kids, and all three of them had had a great time. So now it was a regular thing: lunch at McDonald's or Burger King, film, shake at Burger King or McDonald's, whichever they hadn't been in at lunchtime, home. He'd taken them to Arsenal a couple of times, too, and that was OK, but Ali would still snipe at Marcus, given half a chance, and there was more than half a chance in a long afternoon in the family enclosure at Highbury, so football was kept for those rare times when they had run out of films that would not only insult their intelligence but the rest of them as well.

Marcus was older than Ali now. The first time they had met, when Marcus had been Will's son for the afternoon, Ali had appeared to be Marcus's senior by many years, but his explosion that day had blown his cover a little bit, and in any case Marcus had moved on in the intervening months. He dressed better – he had won the argument with his mother over whether he should be allowed to go shopping with Will – and he had his hair cut regularly, and he tried very hard not to sing out loud, and his friendship with Ellie and Zoe (which, much to everyone's surprise, had endured and deepened) meant that he was more teenage in his attitude: even though the girls prized and cherished his occasional eccentricities, Marcus was beginning to tire of their whoops of delight every time he said something daft, and he had – sadly, in a way, but inevitably and healthily – become more circumspect when he spoke.

It was strange; Will missed him. Since the egg had cracked Will had found himself wanting to talk to Marcus about what it was like to wander about with nothing on, feeling scared of everything and everybody, because Marcus was the only person in the world who might be able to offer him advice; but Marcus – the old Marcus, anyway – was disappearing.

'Are you going to marry my mum?' Ali asked out of the blue, during one of their pre-cinema fast-food meals. Marcus looked up from his chips with interest.

'I dunno,' Will mumbled. He had thought about it a lot, but could never quite make himself believe that he was entitled to ask her; every time he stayed over at her house he felt impossibly blessed, and he didn't want to do anything that would endanger his sense of privilege. Sometimes he hardly even dared ask her when he could see her again; asking her whether she was willing to spend the rest of her life with him seemed to be pushing it.

'I used to want him to marry my mum,' Marcus said cheerfully. Will was suddenly seized with the desire to pour his boiling-point fast-food coffee down the front of Marcus's shirt.

'Did you?' said Ali.

'Yeah. For some reason I thought it would sort everything out. Your mum's different, though. She's more together than mine.'

'Do you still want him to marry your mum?'

'Don't I get a say in this?' Will asked.

'Naah,' said Marcus, ignoring Will's interruption. 'See, I don't think that's the right way.'

'Why not?'

'Because ... You know when they do those human pyramids? That's the sort of model for living I'm looking at now.'

'What *are* you talking about, Marcus?' Will asked him. It wasn't a rhetorical question.

'You're safer as a kid if everyone's friends. When people pair off ... I don't know. It's more insecure. Look at it now. Your mum and my mum get on OK.' It was true. Fiona and Rachel saw each other regularly now, to Will's agonizing discomfort. 'And Will sees her, and I see you, and Ellie and Zoe, and Lindsey and my dad. I've got it sorted now. If your mum and Will get together, you think you're safe, but you're not, because they'll split up, or Will will go mad or something.'

▷ **8** *dumb* [dʌm]: stupid **9** *be pitched at sb.:* be aimed at sb. **15** *enclosure:* piece of land surrounded by a wall or fence · *Highbury:* area in London where Arsenal football team stadium is **22** *intervening:* that followed **27** *prize sth.:* value and treasure sth. **29** *whoop* (n): exclamation **31** *circumspect:* cautious, careful **43** *blessed:* fortunate **47** *push it:* be taking a big risk **52** *sort sth. out:* solve sth. **53** *together* (infml): normal, organized **66** *agonizing:* painful

Ali nodded sagely. Will's urge to scald had been replaced by an urge to shoot Marcus and then turn the gun on himself.

'What if Rachel and I don't split up? What if we stay together forever?'

'Fine. Great. Prove it. I just don't think couples are the future.'

'Oh, well thank you ... Einstein.' Will had wanted his comeback to be sharper than that. He wanted to think of some sort of socio-cultural marriage expert whose name two twelve-year-olds would instantly recognize, but Einstein was all he could come up with. He knew it wasn't right.

'What's he got to do with it?'

'Nothing,' Will mumbled. Marcus looked at him pityingly. 'And don't patronize me.'

'What does patronize mean?' Marcus asked, in all seriousness. So there it was. Will was being patronized by someone who wasn't even old enough to understand what the word meant.

'It means, don't treat me like an idiot.'

Marcus looked at him as if to say, well, how else *can* I treat you? And Will had every sympathy. He was really struggling to maintain the age gap now: Marcus's air of authority, the been-there-done-that tone in his voice, was so convincing that Will didn't know how to argue with him. He didn't want to either. He hadn't lost all face yet; there was still a tiny patch left, about the size of a small scab, and he wanted to keep it.

'He just seems so much older,' Fiona said one afternoon, after Will had dropped him off, and he had disappeared into his bedroom with a cursory thank you and a brusque hello to his mother.

'Where did we go wrong, eh?' Will asked plaintively. 'We've given that boy everything, and this is how he repays us.'

'I feel as though I'm losing him,' said Fiona. Will still hadn't got the hang of joking with her. What left his mouth with the weight and substance of froth on a cappuccino seemed to enter her ear like suet pudding. 'It's all Smashing Pumpkins and Ellie and Zoe and ... I think he's been smoking.'

Will laughed.

'It's not funny.'

'It is, kind of. How much would you have given for Marcus to be caught smoking with his mates a few months ago?'

'Nothing, I abhor smoking.'

'Yes, but …' He gave up. Fiona was determined not to see the point he was trying to make. 'Does it bother you that you're losing him?'

'Why do you ask that? Of course it bothers me.'

'It's just that you've seemed … I don't want to be crude about it, but you've seemed better recently.'

'I think I am. I don't know what it is, but I just feel less worn down by everything.'

'That's great.'

'I think I'm just on top of things more. I don't know why.'

Will thought he knew one of the reasons why, but he also knew that it would be neither wise nor kind to elaborate. The truth was that this version of Marcus really wasn't so hard to cope with. He had friends, he could look after himself, he had developed a skin – the kind of skin Will had just shed. He had flattened out, and become as robust and as unremarkable as every other twelve-year-old kid. But all three of them had had to lose things in order to gain other things. Will had lost his shell and his cool and his distance, and he felt scared and vulnerable, but he got to be with Rachel; and Fiona had lost a big chunk of Marcus, and she got to stay away from the casualty ward; and Marcus had lost himself, and got to walk home from school with his shoes on.

Marcus came out of his room scowling.

'I'm bored. Can I go and get a video?'

Will couldn't resist it: he had a theory he wanted to test out. 'Hey, Fiona. Why don't you get your sheet music out, and we can murder "Both Sides Now"?'

'Would you like to?'

'Yeah. Sure.' But he was watching Marcus, whose expression was that of a boy who had been asked to dance naked before a mixed audience of supermodels and cousins.

▷ **1** *sagely:* wisely · *scald* [skɔːld]: burn with hot liquid **6** *comeback* (n) (infml): reply **23** *scab:* hard, dry covering that forms over a healing wound **27** *cursory:* brief **28** *plaintively:* sadly **32** *suet* ['suːɪt]: hard animal fat used in cooking **33** *Smashing Pumpkins:* pop group **39** *abhor sth.:* hate sth. very much **53** *shed sth.:* lose sth., get rid of sth. · *flatten out:* (here) become more normal **61** *scowl:* be angry **64** *murder sth.* (infml): enjoy sth. a lot, have a lot of fun with sth.

‘Please, Mum. Don’t.’

‘Don’t be silly. You love singing. You love Joni Mitchell.’

‘I don’t. Not any more. I bloody hate Joni Mitchell.’

Will knew then, beyond any shadow of a doubt, that Marcus would be OK.

Dpa – Fotoreport (Getty Harvey)

Nick Hornby was born in 1957. He is the author of four novels to date.

His first novel, *Fever Pitch*, is about football and its fan culture and won him instant success. His second, *High Fidelity*, deals with pop music and probes into the question whether music enables you to live life better or whether it simply offers a retreat from life.

About a Boy is his third novel, and was followed by *How to Be Good*, which looks at marriage and how one of the partners is affected by the spiritual conversion of the other person.

The first three novels have all been filmed. *About a Boy* was released in April 2002, with Hugh Grant starring as Will.

Besides writing, Nick Hornby also works as the pop music critic for *The New Yorker*.

He lives in Highbury, in north London. Once married, he has an autistic son.